cocksure

cocksure

erotic fiction by
BOB VICKERY

alyson books
los angeles | new york

Printed in Canada

THIS TRADE PAPERBACK ORIGINAL IS PUBLISHED BY ALYSON PUBLICATIONS,
P.O. BOX 4371, LOS ANGELES, CALIFORNIA 90078-4371.
DISTRIBUTION IN THE UNITED KINGDOM BY TURNAROUND PUBLISHER SERVICES LTD.,
UNIT 3, OLYMPIA TRADING ESTATE, COBURG ROAD, WOOD GREEN,
LONDON N22 6TZ ENGLAND.

FIRST EDITION: JUNE 2002

02 03 04 05 06 **a** 10 9 8 7 6 5 4 3 2 1

ISBN 1-55583-739-5

COVER DESIGN BY MATT SAMS.
COVER PHOTOGRAPHY BY NAUGHTY BOYS.

Contents

Introduction ix
Surfer Joe 1
Queer Punk 13
The Daddy Thing 25
Overboard 36
In the Fetish Room 47
Calming Down 57
Dads 67
When Angelo Comes 80
A Star Is Born 85
Porn Writer 98
Stavros's Place 110
Southern Boys 123
Immersion 135
Visiting Santa 145
In the Alley With Angelo 157
Family Values 169
Brain Fever 179
Vampire 189
Brother John's Traveling Salvation Show 211
Blind Date 224
Tony's Big Adventure 237
Giving Phone 248
Incubus 259
Calls From Mike 272
Firestorm 282
Physical Therapy 293
Unplanned Stop 305
Fantasies 317
Birds 329
Hitch Cock 341
Chimeras 353
Knowing Johnny 359

INTRODUCTION

Whenever I go through my fan mail (I get about a mailbag a week, and I'm not even counting the E-mail), I notice one question keeps popping up more than any other: *Bob, how does someone get to be a successful porn writer like you?* Normally, I just shitcan letters like that. I mean, it's hard enough getting published without encouraging the competition. However, now that I've got my own anthology out, I'm feeling magnanimous. So I'll answer the question. It takes a special kind of man to be a successful porn writer. If you want to make it big-time in this biz, you have to have certain *qualities*.

First, you have to be *hot*. I'm not talking "kind of good-looking if the light is right," but dick-throbbin', ball-churnin' *hot*. This is something of a no-brainer. I mean, a good writer can only write what he knows about, right? If you're writing about home repair, you have to know how to swing a fuckin' hammer, right? In the same way, if you're writing about hot gay sex, then you have to have hot gay sex. Lots of it. And the only way a man gets lots of hot gay sex is by being hot. I mean, is that fuckin' obvious or what? So if you're not hot, I suggest you limit your creative literary efforts to sensitive poetry about social injustice—the stuff that gets read in the back rooms of coffeehouses.

Oops, excuse me a second, I gotta get the door.

Hello? What, you've come here to repair my phone? It's about fuckin' time, the fucker's been out of service for almost a week. Yeah, it's right over there.

OK, where was I? Oh, yeah, second, you have to do the research. If you want your stories to have that special ring of authenticity, you have to go out and have as much sex as possible—with anybody willing to give you a tumble. You cannot afford to pass up any chance you get to have sex, no matter how much you feel like doing something else instead. This is what separates the dedicated porn writer from the dilettante. A dilettante will spend his spare time stretched out on the couch, popping a beer and watching the latest *Survivor* episode on the tube. A dedicated porn writer, on the other hand, uses every spare moment he has cruising parks, johns, docks, alleys, movie theaters, Bible study classes, you name it, in search of new material. Do you know how many hours of deep-sea fishing Ernest Hemingway logged before he wrote *The Old Man and The Sea*? Think about it.

Hey, you over there, how much longer you gonna fuck around with that phone? What's that? It's awfully hot in here? Is it all right if you take off your shirt? Yeah, sure, I don't care. In fact, I think I'll take mine off too. Yeah, I work out. Yeah, I know it shows.

What was I talking about? Oh, yeah, third, take notes. All the time. Don't rely just on your memory. It's too easy to get distracted in the heat of the moment and forget that choice turn of phrase you may have heard that would have added the perfect touch to your story. So when someone murmurs to you, "Yeah, fuckface, that's right, uh-huh, slobber on my slimy, throbbing fuck pole," *take a moment to write that down.* I mean, that could be the line that turns your whole story around. Yeah, I know, this kind of takes some of the spontaneity out of the moment, but that's the price you pay for writing good porn. I get some of my best material this way.

What, you're still hot? You want to take off the rest of your clothes? Sure, I don't care... Holy shit! Do you lob softballs with that thing? Hey, what're you doin'? Easy, easy, you'll jam my zipper if you tug down too hard.

Hey, look, I gotta go now. Anyway, just do what I told you and you'll be cranking out quality porn in no time.

Oh, yeah, baby, yeah, uh-huh, that's right.

So later, dudes. Hope you like the stories.

Yeah, fucker, take it all. Breathe through your nose. Uh-huh.

Bob Vickery
www.bobvickery.com

SURFER JOE

Man, the swells were coming in today...one, two, three, you could set your watch by them, smooth and glassy, rearing up high, the lips ruffled by a steady offshore breeze, and then those suckers would arc into the most beautiful fucking tubes, almond-shaped crystal caves I could shoot through like a bullet down a shotgun barrel. It was *righteous*! Even after I was done for the day and was strapping my board down to my car roof, I watched as the waves kept marching in, one after another, 15-footers. It broke my heart to leave them behind, but Scooter told me if I'm late for work one more time, my ass is grass, there are plenty of other surf bums he can find to take my place. I whip down Kuhio Highway, cruising past Princeville; KSRF, Kauai's golden oldies station, is on the radio, and I'm *stoked*! What a bitchin' day! I pull a joint out of the glove compartment and fire up, sucking in the smoke as music blasts over me. When I swing past Donkey Beach, Iron Butterfly's "In-A-Gadda-Da-Vida" comes on the radio, and that awesome organ music threads through my sun-fried brain like a red-hot needle. Fuck it, job or no job, I pull over to a bluff, crank up the volume to full high, and let the music pound over me, like an orgasm, like some swell from a New Zealand typhoon crashing on top of me as the fat red sun slowly slips over the lip of the Pacific. Out-fucking-rageous!

I peel into the parking lot of the Windrigger like some demented fool, tourists scattering. Scooter gives me the evil eye as I charge in through the kitchen door, but I just point to the clock on the wall, which says 6 o'clock on...the...nose. Scooter shakes his head. "One of these days, Joe," he mutters. "One of these days..." But he lets me go to the locker room, where I put on my waiter's monkey suit. In a couple of minutes I'm out on the floor taking orders, delivering food like waiting is my *life*. It's a busy night, the height of the tourist season; the surrounding hotels are all booked and the Bermuda shorts crowd is ready for bear. I wink and smile, throw out a few jokes, add a little local color. The customers eat it up; the tips are good, even better than good—these folks seem to be looking for excuses to get rid of their money tonight. Who am I to get in their way?

He's sitting over by the window that looks out on the bay, alone, dressed better than the rest: slacks, a button-down Pierre Cardin shirt, tie. It's around 11 now, things have started slowing down. His eyes track me as I cross the room, locking onto me like a friggin' missile guidance system. I sneak glances at him whenever I pass by. Not bad looking in a mature kind of way, pushing 40, some gray around the temples, but lean and fit, the neck muscular, the eyes level and gray. Chances are he's been on Kauai for at least a few days; he doesn't have the mainlander's fish-belly look. In fact, he's got a nice sun-glow about him. He looks well-heeled; I noticed that first, before anything else.

I stop by at his table and give him my friendliest grin. "Everything OK?" I ask. "Do you want some coffee or something? Dessert maybe?"

The man doesn't say anything for a couple of seconds. "Sure," he finally says. "Coffee would be nice. You got any Kona?"

I shoot him a look to see if he's goofing me. He catches my glance and laughs.

"I guess that was pretty stupid. This is Hawaii. Of course you have Kona."

"That's OK," I say, grinning. "I'll bring you a cup."

I return a few minutes later and lay the cup in front of him. He looks up at me. "Have you lived on Kauai long?" he asks.

I shake my head. "I'm only here for the winter, while the surf's good. It dies down around March, and then I'll push on west. Bali, maybe."

"Ah," he says. "A surfer." He has a nice smile. "I see you guys out there on the waves from my hotel window. It looks like a great life."

I shrug. "Yeah, it's OK." I shoot him a significant look. "Only sometimes it's hard to come up with the bread to live on."

We look at each other in silence for a couple of seconds. He runs his tongue over the edge of his teeth and swallows. "Yes," he says slowly. "It always boils down to that, doesn't it?"

I don't take my eyes off him. "I'll say. There's a surfing tournament in Oahu next week that I'd love to go to. But I just don't have the cash." I put an edge to my voice. "A hundred and fifty bucks would just about cover my expenses."

The man takes a long, careful sip from his cup. He raises his eyes to me again. Beneath their calm, I see a certain sadness. No, not sadness, *resignation*. "I would think even a hundred would be helpful," he says slowly.

I consider this and then nod my head. "You're right," I say. "A hundred dollars would do the trick." I smile again. "Well, it was nice talking to you, mister. But it's quitting time for me." I nod toward the window. "I think I'll just stand under those palm trees over there and look at the moon for a while."

The man smiles back, playing along. "All right." He holds out his hand. "My name's Steve."

I take his hand and shake it. I hold on to it a little longer than necessary and give it an extra squeeze. "I'm Joe," I say. I let go. "See you around, Steve."

Steve nods. "I'm sure you will."

I return to the locker room, change back into my Ripfly board shorts and T-shirt, and step outside. It's cooler now, but the air still has a soft, warm feel to it. I walk across the sand to where the clump of palms is. The moon is full tonight and hangs over the Pacific like some yellow beach ball. The wind has shifted around, blowing in from the ocean, and I can smell the salt in it. The bay is sheltered, and the waves hiss against the sand. When I reach the first tree, I lean against it and look out over the water.

Steve joins me a few minutes later. "Hello, Joe," he says.

"Hi, Steve," I answer. We stand there looking at each other. In the light of the moon, I can see that Steve is nervous, his eyes have difficulty meeting mine. I pull him over and kiss him, pressing my body against his. Steve loosens up right away. He wraps his arms around me in a bear hug as his tongue pushes into my mouth.

I'm the first to break the kiss. "If you don't mind," I say. "I like to take care of business first."

There's a pause. Steve clears his throat. "OK," he says. He pulls out his wallet and I watch as he counts out five twenties. I fold them and put them in my shirt pocket. I reach up and run my hand through Steve's hair. After a beat, he pulls me to him and we kiss again. Steve's hands slide under my T-shirt, and I feel his fingers explore my torso, playing lightly over the skin, tugging at the muscle. I cup Steve's ass with my hands and pull him toward me, grinding my hips against his. His stiff dick pushes up against my own, and he starts dry-humping me in hard, slow thrusts. He slides his hand down the front of my board shorts, squeezing the bulge that's pushing up against the fabric. "You got something in there for me?" he croons. "Something I can swing on?"

"Yeah," I say. "You wanna see?" I open the Velcro flap of my shorts. Steve slides his hand down inside and cups my balls. He gives them a slight tug. "That's quite a handful, Joe," he says. "They're going to fill my mouth nicely." I start pulling down my shorts, but Steve stops me. "No," he says softly. "Let me do it." He drops down to his knees and presses his mouth against the front of my shorts, gently biting the outline of my hard dick, then works his mouth up the length of the bulge, dampening the cloth with his spit. Hooking his hands inside my shorts, Steve pulls them down slowly, teasingly, inch by inch. My dick sways heavily, and a light breeze blows in from the ocean, playing against my naked skin, tickling the hairs on my balls.

Steve looks up at me, his face pure in the moonlight. "Take everything off," he says, his voice tight with excitement. "I want to see you naked."

"OK," I say. I pull off my T-shirt, kick off my shoes, and step out of my shorts. When I'm naked, I stand in front of Steve with my legs apart, my arms hanging down by my side. The cool sand squishes between my toes, and moonlight pours over my body like liquid silver. Steve sits back on his heels and lets his eyes sweep up my body. "Holy Jesus," he says softly. He raises his arm and lays his hand on my chest, his fingers uncertain. He squeezes my right nipple between his thumb and forefinger, super gently, like he's afraid I'll give him hell if he does it any harder.

"You can get rougher, man," I say. "I won't break." Steve increases the pressure of his fingers, raises his other hand and grabs my left nipple as well. His hands start wandering down my torso, tugging at my skin, pulling at the muscle, his eyes hard and bright. "Fucking beautiful," he says, his voice rougher. He wraps his palm around my dick and pulls the foreskin up and down the shaft. It only takes a few strokes to get me fully hard. Steve bends my stiff dick down and lets go suddenly. It springs up and slaps against my belly. He does it again, and then leans forward and buries his face in my balls. I feel his hot breath on my nut sac and then his wet tongue. He opens his mouth and sucks my balls in, rolling them around inside his mouth as his hand keeps on stroking my dick.

I run my fingers through his hair, then close my hands around it in tight fists. I tug his head from side to side. "Yeah," I growl. "Suck on those balls. Juice them up." His tongue plays on them faster, saliva dripping from his mouth.

He pulls back, grinning. "You taste salty," he says.

I look down at him. "I've been in the ocean surfing all day. I didn't have time to shower." I smile slowly. "What's the matter? Don't you like salted nuts?"

Steve laughs. He drags his tongue against my balls again and then slides it up the shaft, rolling it around my cock head, pushing into my piss slit. My dick has gotten as hard as dicks get, and I'm ready to crank this up to another level.

I push Steve back onto the sand and straddle his chest. Propping his head up with my hand, I slide my dick full down his throat, my pubes mashing against his nose, my balls pressed tight against his chin. Steve gags, but when I try to pull out, his hands grab my ass and keeps me pressed tight against his face. I feel his tongue go fucking crazy as it wraps around my dick. He finally lets me go, and I start pumping my hips, plowing his face with deep, long strokes. Steve feeds hungrily on my fat dick, slobbering over it, as he pulls his pants down around his knees. I spit in my hand and then reach back and start jacking him off. Steve groans loudly. His hand plays against my ass, squeezing the cheeks, prying them apart, probing into my ass crack. I feel his finger press against my asshole and then push on inside. Knuckle by knuckle, he worms his finger up my chute, twisting it, pushing in deeper. Now it's my turn to groan. I lift my head into the cool night and let the sound roll up my throat and out my mouth.

I close my eyes and let the sensations wash over me: Steve's probing finger, his hot, wet mouth, the hiss of the waves, the breeze rustling through the palm leaves, the broad, shiny path of the moon hanging over the Pacific. Steve bobs his head back and forth, pulling the sensations out of me, the little electric jolts that tingle through my body getting stronger and stronger. I can feel his mouth pulling my load out of my balls, coaxing it, and I help him along, sliding my dick in and out the tight circle of his lips. One more plunge into his mouth brings me right to the brink. I pull out so that the tip of my dick rests against the tip of his tongue, and then I just slide my dick hard in. That does the trick. The first wave of the orgasm sweeps over me as I whip my dick out of Steve's mouth, and then my load slams hard into his face, splattering against his cheeks, his eyes, into his hair. I surf the orgasm as I did the ocean swells this morning, letting it curl over me, lift me up high, my body light and free. I cry out as my muscles spasm and my jizz rains down on Steve's face. Steve groans too, and his load squirts up between his fingers, spewing out across his chest. "Far fuckin' out!" I laugh, as I milk the last of my load out of my dick. I collapse down on top of him, his come hot and wet against my skin, and after a couple of beats I roll off him onto the sand. We don't say anything, just listen to the surf whisper against the beach. The moon is rising high in the sky; it's like a searchlight, casting shadows against the ripples of the sand. Even after Steve gets up and dresses, kisses me, and leaves I just lie there naked on the beach, in the moonlight, the low surf whispering in my ears. I hear the breeze through the palm leaves blowing offshore, stronger now. A good sign. The surf should be high tomorrow.

I close my eyes and drift off to sleep.

I tell my buddy, Andy, about my experience the next day as we ride the waves in a cove 2½ miles beyond where the Kuhio Highway ends. We're out beyond the reef, bobbing up and down on the swells, waiting for a good one to roll in that we can ride. Since the only way to the cove is by hiking over two miles of broken lava, we've got the place to ourselves.

Andy smiles as I describe the scene last night under the palm trees. "Was that the first time you ever sold your ass?" he asks.

I shoot a glance at Andy, unsure of his reaction. But his expression is good-natured, his blue eyes calm and curious. "No," I say. "I've done it a few times before. These tourists I meet in the restaurant are out here trying to live out all these vacation fantasies." I laugh. "Sometimes the fantasy includes scoring with, oh, my God, a *surfer*!" I wiggle my eyebrows. "It's such an easy way to make a little cash. And everybody leaves happy."

Andy grins, his teeth flashing in his dark face. He's a surfer's poster boy all right: sun-streaked hair, steady blue eyes, his tanned body nicely muscled from years of paddling hard against surf and rip tides. "Hell," he says, "Whatever gets you through the day." He looks behind him and then pushes up onto his knees. "I'm going to ride this one in," he says.

I check out where he's looking. Andy's right. The swell coming in is big and righteously formed. Even out beyond the reef it's rearing up about eight feet high. I crouch down on my board too, both of us paddling madly to catch the crest. The swell picks us up just as it hits the reef and curls beautifully, Andy and me poised on the lip like we've been pulled up by invisible strings. Andy's full on his feet now, hunched over, pausing for the briefest eye-blink of time before plunging down into the belly of the beast. I join him, giving out a kamikaze cry. Andy looks over his shoulder at me, just for the briefest instance, and the thrill of this wild ride crackles between us like a bolt of lightning. We both laugh as the blue-green glassy cave rears over and above us and we shoot through it at a crazed, breakneck speed. Andy's right before me, if he wipes out, I'm dog-meat, there'd be no way I could maneuver around him. But he rides up and down the flank of the giant wave like a bullet, slicing, arcing, piercing and pivoting in and around its falling lip. I watch his muscle-packed body, poised and tensed and yet impossibly relaxed, effortlessly working the power of the water crashing all around him and it's *just...fuckin'... beautiful*! We plummet down the crystal hole at an insane speed, the opening just before us, but always pulling back whenever we seem to gain on it. We never do make it out; the tunnel pinches shut at the last moment and the wave slams hard on top of us. What feels like a ton of water crashes down on me, and I go spinning in the foamy soup, clawing my way to the surface. I stagger out of the water, my board shorts pulled down around my knees.

Andy's standing on the beach, watching me, laughing. I look at him and laugh back. "That was fuckin' fantastic!" I yell. I start to tug my shorts back up.

"You don't have to do that," Andy says, grinning. He rips open the Velcro snap of his shorts and pulls them off. Naked, he grabs his board and dives back into the surf. When he's beyond the surf line, Andy hoists himself up on his board and starts paddling out, his smooth, white ass gleaming in the sun. What the hell, I think. I tug off my shorts and run into the surf buck-naked as well.

We ride in the next wave standing side by side on our boards, the wind and spray whipping over our naked bodies. I keep stealing glances over at Andy. He stands easily on his board, his feet planted wide apart, a half smile on his face, though with his eyebrows pulled down in concentration. The muscles of his body ripple as he steers his board up and down the face of the wave, maneuvering it along with the onrushing momentum of the water. He is so goddamn beautiful! The wave we ride is smooth and clean and green and long, and I feel the water rumble like a freight train as we both get caught up again in the ride home. I reach out and touch the glassy wall beside me, and my hand skims along the surface in a trail of foam as I shoot past it. As before, Andy rides ahead of me, and my eyes feed on his naked flesh: the powerful shoulders, the sharp V of his back, that perfect, pale ass. This is his element, more than land will ever be. He owns the waves as much as any dolphin or shark, and I fucking love him for it.

We ride the wave out to the end, until it deposits us with motherly gentleness right at the lip of the beach. My board glides in beside Andy's, no more than a foot apart. Andy's eyes gleam with the buzz from the ride, and his mouth is open in silent laughter. Without thinking, I hook my hand around his neck and pull his face against mine. My tongue pushes hard into his mouth, and I french him for all that I'm worth. Andy freezes with surprise, and then responds eagerly, his tongue playing with mine, thrusting between my lips and into the back of my mouth. I pull him into a tight embrace and feel the length of his naked skin, his muscular body pressed hard against mine. The next wave comes crashing in, swirling up around our thighs, pushing us off balance, and we fall over laughing. Andy rolls over on top of me, grinning, as the foaming surf washes over us and recedes. He reaches down and wraps his hand around my dick. "Let's go back to the beach towels," he says. "And do this proper."

We stagger to our feet and race across the hot sand to the shade of the palm trees that fringe the beach. Our towels lie stretched out side by side, and we collapse onto them. Andy pulls me to him and kisses me again. I feel his dick harden against me as he dry-humps my belly. He pulls back, grinning. "You're not going to charge me for this, are you?" he laughs.

I laugh too. "No, Andy. This one's on the house." I spit in my hand and wrap it around our two dicks. They both slide up and down inside the circle of my fingers, cock flesh to cock flesh—Andy's dick fat, pink, and cut, mine darker and uncut. Andy bends down and flicks his tongue against my nipple, then nips it gently. I close my eyes for a moment and sigh. Andy nips a little harder and then drags his tongue down my torso, digging it into my belly button. I let go of our dicks and run my fingers through his hair, shaking his head gently from side to side. Andy continues his descent and it isn't long before I feel his wet tongue slide down my boner, and then back up again, slicking it with his saliva. He opens his mouth and nibbles his lips down my cock shaft. I groan and push my hips up, thrusting my dick deep down Andy's throat. Andy starts bobbing his head up and down, his tongue wrapped around my dick, and I fall back on the beach towel and groan as the sensations sweep over me. Off in the distance, the surf gives a steady, muffled roar, and the wind rustles the palm leaves overhead. The sun winks in and out between the moving leaves, splashing across my face. I crane my neck and watch as Andy sucks enthusiastically on my dick. It is such a sexy sight: my cock shoving in and out of this hot man's mouth. Andy looks up, and our eyes lock; I slowly thrust up until my dick is full in his mouth, watching Andy watching me, getting more and more excited at seeing him take my meat all the way in. "Shift around," I growl. "I want a little sixty-nine action going with you."

Andy's only too happy to do this. He pivots until his dick thrusts out right above my face. I raise my head and drag my tongue against his shaft, then take it full in. Andy begins pumping his hips, and we settle down to a steady rhythm of fucking each other's face, nice and slow. I love Andy's dick in my mouth, and I give it a good going-over, slobbering over it, licking it, making it real familiar with the inside layout of my mouth and tongue. I run my hands up and down Andy's body, feel the hard muscle, the smooth skin. I reach up and squeeze his ass cheeks, massaging them with my fingers, pushing his crack apart, playing with his asshole, before I go back and continue to explore the rest of his body. Andy returns the favor, stroking and kneading my flesh, tweaking my nipples, getting to know my body with the same intimacy that he works a wave he's surfing. I don't know how long we play with each other like this. I could do it for-fucking-ever. I wouldn't mind if time stopped and I had to spend the rest of eternity on this beach, Andy sucking my dick while he fucks my mouth in long, lazy strokes. He finally takes my dick out of his mouth and looks up at me. "You know, Joe," he says. "I would really love you to fuck my ass right now."

There's an awkward moment. "Well, you see, Andy," I say. "I don't have the right...precautions with me."

Andy rolls over and unzips his knapsack. He pulls out a tube of lube and a small foil packet. "Trojan Express!" he says. "Don't leave home without it!"

I laugh. "You do a lousy Karl Malden."

I take the tube and squirt a dollop on my palm. I reach over and pry apart Andy's ass crack. Andy pushes his hips up to give me better access. I massage my greasy fingers against the pink rosebud of his asshole, and then slip a finger inside and push on up to the third knuckle.

Andy gives off a loud sigh, a hairbreadth shy of a groan. "Jeez, that feels good, Joe," he says. I start finger-fucking him, sliding my finger in and out the warm, tight velvet of his chute. This time Andy does groan. He thrusts his hips up and spreads his legs farther apart. I slip a second finger in, and Andy goes apeshit, riding up and down my fingers like some kind of wild man. His dick is hard and throbbing, and as I push my fingers up harder, I notice a little, clear pearl of precome ooze out of his piss slit.

"You enjoying yourself, Andy?" I grunt.

Andy raises his head and pins me with his stare. "I'd enjoy myself a hell of a lot more if you cram your dick up my ass," he growls.

I grin. "Well, if that's what you want..." I lean back and roll the condom down my hard dick. Andy is flat on his back, watching me with burning eyes. I lean forward, propped up by an arm on either side of him, and poke my dick between his legs. I find his asshole and proceed to burrow on in. Andy gasps as I skewer him inch by inch until my balls are pressed tight against him. I just lie on top of him for a moment, motionless, savoring the sensation of my dick flesh squeezed tight by warm velvet.

I start pumping my hips. After a few strokes, Andy and I fall into rhythm again, with him pushing up his hips with each thrust of my dick inside him. I lean forward and kiss him, gently this time, my mouth working over his hungrily. I quicken my pace, fucking his ass in quick, short thrusts, my balls bouncing against his thighs. I wrap my palm, still smeared with lube, around Andy's dick and start jacking him off, timing my hand strokes to meet each thrust of my dick up his ass. Andy looks up, his mouth open, his eyes wide and startled, as if he can't quite believe all this is happening to him. He pulls me down, and we kiss again, harder this time, his mouth fused to mine, his tongue deep down my throat. I wrap my arms around him in a bear hug, feeling his muscular body, now slippery with sweat, squirm against mine, separating with and joining my body in wet, slapping sounds. We roll over, and now Andy's on top, his sweat dripping from his face onto me as I continue my thrusts. I can feel my body respond to his, match its movements, and we slide into the great cosmic fuck-dance.

The more we fuck, the more I get swept up into it. It's like surfing again, losing myself in the rush of a wave, propelling across the glassy green water. I gauge my thrusts carefully, pulling up to the lip of the orgasm and then backing down at the last second. Andy and I ride this wave together, teasing each other's flesh, drawing us to the brink and pulling back, taking desperate risks that pay off as the sensations ratchet up to higher and higher levels.

Finally I groan out to Andy, "I'm just going to have to shoot this load. I can't wait any longer."

"OK," Andy pants. "Go for it. I'm right behind you."

I pull out until the head of my dick is just inside Andy's asshole. Then I thrust full in, to the whole length of my shaft. That does the trick. The orgasm sweeps over me and I let it carry me off, groaning loudly as my dick spasms my load into the condom up Andy's ass.

I slide my greasy hand up and down Andy's dick and feel his body shudder. He cries out as his load gushes out, splattering against my face, coating my cheeks, my lips, my forehead. One spasm after another wracks his body until the orgasm finally plays itself out. With a groan, Andy rolls over and collapses on the towel beside me.

We lie still for a few minutes, listening to the roar of the surf. Sweat mingles with Andy's load, and the thick drops start trickling down my face. Andy bends over and licks my face clean. We sit up, arms around each other's shoulders, and watch the ocean stretched out before us. The swells are still rolling in, high and true.

"The waves are still mighty righteous," Andy says. "I'm going to surf some more."

"I'm going to hang out here for a few minutes," I say. "I'll join you later."

Andy jumps to his feet and grabs his board. I watch him as he runs naked into the surf. The whole picture—Andy's surf-muscled body, the green-blue Pacific, the dazzling sky and white sands—is so *beautiful* it doesn't seem it could be real. A few minutes later, Andy's riding a wave in, his arms out, his legs apart. From where I sit, I can't see his board, just Andy, skimming effortlessly across the water like some naked sea god. I sit there, dazzled. *Just fucking beautiful,* I think. I grab my board and run out into the surf to join him.

QUEER PUNK

I'm still half-asleep, staring up at the ceiling and wondering whether I should get up. Part of me just wants to roll over and catch a few more Z's, but I don't think my body can take the lumps in the couch anymore. (Darlene told me she found the couch in front of some apartment building a couple of blocks away during a trash pickup day). I can hear Darlene and her dickhead boyfriend, Buck, in the bedroom; it sounds like they're having a fight. I guess that's better than the times when I have to listen to them fuck, hearing Buck groan like he's got a bad case of the trots. I can't make out most of what they're saying, but every now and then I hear my name. Ol' Buck is probably ragging on Darlene again about how much longer her deadbeat little brother is going to be hangin' around. If it weren't for me, I don't think they'd have anything to talk about.

The bedroom door opens and Buck walks in, wearing nothing but his Jockeys. He glances at me once, giving me the evil eye as he makes his way to the kitchen. I give him back my best "fuck you too" look. A few seconds later he's back with a carton of orange juice in his hand. He takes a swig from it. "So, Jamie," he says. "How's the job hunt going?"

I shrug. "No luck yet, Buck," I say. I catch myself checking out his body again. It really pisses me off when I do that. Buck works out regularly with his weight set, and his body is tight and cut, but he's such an asshole. I'd cut off my dick before I had anything to do with him. Still, I can't help copping a look at him every now and then.

Buck takes another gulp of orange juice. "You know, they're looking for a busboy over at that Italian restaurant on Haight."

I turn my head and stare at the ceiling again. "Thanks. I'll check it out." *When monkeys fly out my ass,* I think.

I can feel Buck's eyes on me. "Another thing, Jamie," he says. "I don't want you using my weight set anymore. You never put the weights back right."

I ignore him, and he goes back into the bedroom. A little later he comes back out again, dressed for work. (He runs a forklift at some Kmart in Daly City.) We don't look at each other, and when he leaves he slams the front door. What a douche bag.

A few minutes later, Darlene walks in wearing a bathrobe. "Good morning, Jamie," she says.

"Hi," I grunt.

Darlene scratches her head and yawns. "You want some breakfast?"

I shake my head. "Naw. Maybe a cup of coffee."

Sitting at the kitchen table with her, I can see that Darlene is trying to work herself up to say something. I decide to make it easy for her. "I *am* going to look for work today," I say.

She looks apologetic. "I'm sorry about Buck."

I laugh. "So am I." I shake a cigarette out of the pack and light it. "What do you see in him? He's such a loser."

"Yeah," Darlene snorts. "Unlike the parade of winners you've called boyfriends." She bums a cigarette from me and lights it, even though I know she's trying to quit. She breathes out a cloud of smoke. "Listen, Jamie," she says. "I got to go to work soon. How about you doing the laundry? Buck's been grousing about running out of clean shirts, and I just don't have time to do it myself today." I make a face, and Darlene's eyes shoot daggers at me. "Don't give me a hard time about this, Jamie," she says in a pissed tone of voice. "I've already had to deal with Buck's bullshit this morning, and I don't want any attitude from you."

I don't say anything.

"OK, fine," Darlene snaps. "I'll do the goddamn laundry myself when I get home from work."

I push my chair out and get up. "Oh, chill out, Darlene. I'll do the fuckin' laundry."

Darlene still looks pissed; I guess I didn't agree *nicely* enough.

She gets up and piles the dishes in the sink. When she leaves, the "goodbye" she throws over her shoulder at me is like a fuckin' icicle.

As soon as she's gone, I go to the bedroom and work out with Buck's weight set. I check myself out in the mirror as I do my curls. I look fuckin' *good*, my biceps pumped up nicely, my pecs hard and defined. I put the dumbbells down and pose, flexing my arms, checking out my definition. Hot stuff. I drop my shorts and stare at my reflection. My dick flops against my thigh, half-hard, but under my gaze it stirs and stiffens, the head flaring out. I fuckin' love my cock, the *meatiness* of it, its redness and thickness, how the veins snake up the shaft. I wrap my hand around it and begin stroking, first slow and easy, then picking up the tempo till my balls are a bouncing blur. I pull my dick down and let it slap against my belly, and then shake it at my reflection. "You want to suck on it?" I croon at the hot naked stud looking back at me. "You want me to fuck your face, ram this dick down your throat?" A sexy punk with too much attitude stares back, sneering, shaking *his* dick at me as well. I walk up to the mirror and start humping my reflection, my body pressed tight to the glass, my hands grabbing the corners of the closet door. The mirror feels smooth and cool on my skin as I thrust my cock up and down against it. It doesn't take long before I'm ready to shoot. Groaning, I squirt my load on the mirror and watch as it drips down over my reflection. I wipe my hand across the splattered jizz and lick my fingers clean. Then I clean off the rest of the load with my jockeys and get dressed.

I gather all the dirty laundry and take it to the Laundromat down the block. The place is empty, and as the clothes are washing, I sit out on the front step, soaking up rays and smoking the last cigarette in my pack. I think about my living situation. I've got to line up some kind of gig, get some money so I can get my own place. I've been in San Francisco about three weeks now, and it's pretty clear that I've just about milked dry the setup I've got going with Darlene.

When the laundry's done, I toss it into one of the dryers and walk down to Haight Street for more cigarettes. I pass the winos lined up by the supermarket, the panhandlers, runaways, and dopers on the street corners, and buy some Marlboros at the mom-and-pop over by the park. On my way back, I check out the neighborhood piercing studio. It would be bitching to get my nose pierced, or an eyebrow, but that shit costs more money than I can afford. I push the idea out of my head.

The first thing I see back at the Laundromat is the open dryer door. *Oh, shit!* I think. A quick check shows that everything's been cleaned out of the dryer, not just Darlene's and Buck's stuff, but most of the clothes I own as well. The fucker didn't even leave any of my old ratty underwear behind. "Fuck!" I shout, kicking the dryer door as hard as I can. It slams against the dryer and bounces open again, and I kick it again, hard enough to put a crack in the window. I storm outside and cross the street without looking. A car screeches to a stop and the driver gives me a 20-second blast on his horn. I spin around and kick one of his headlights out. The dude gets out of his car, and I just wait with clenched fists. He has second thoughts, calls me an asshole, and drives off. I laugh, but I still feel like ripping someone's head off.

Darlene is the first to come home. Even before I open my mouth, I can see she's had a bad day and is not in the mood for any bullshit. When I tell her what happened, she freaks out.

"What a goddamn stupid thing to do, Jamie!" she shouts at me. "I can't believe you just left that stuff by itself for anybody to rip off!"

She goes on like this for a few more minutes. I smoke a cigarette, slouched in a chair, and pretend like I don't hear her. After a while she storms off to the bedroom, but when she reaches the doorway, she turns around again and glares at me. "When Buck gets home, you can go ahead and tell him what happened," she snarls. "You tell him you lost his favorite shirt, the one he always goes bowling in." She slams the door. *Jesus Fuckin' Christ,* I think.

I'm not about to hang around to hear Buck piss and moan at me. I change into my one last T-shirt, the one that says QUEER PUNK, and head out to Haight Street. A few guys are jamming on one of the street corners, playing guitars and congas, and I hang loose there for a while, toking up whenever the joint they're circulating comes to me. Later, I grab a burrito somewhere and wash it down with a couple of beers, then wander up to Club DV8 to see what's happening. Some group called Hog Maw is playing tonight;

even out here on the street their music is loud enough to pop an eardrum. The gate man sits on his stool by the door, cracking his knuckles and staring at the world with his fat, biker's face. I wait till a group of people show up, pushing through the door, and I crowd in with them, slipping by without paying. By the time the gate man sees me, I'm already in. "Hey, you," he yells, but I dive into all the bodies crammed together on the dance floor and lose the fucker.

The band sucks, but I like the way the noise just sweeps over me, pushing everything else out of my head. I grab a beer at the bar and watch the dance floor, checking out the guys. There's some hot meat out there tonight, bodies pumping to the music, slick with sweat, ripe, smelly, pierced, tattooed. My eye suddenly snags on one of them, not because of his tight, muscular body (which *is* hot) but because of the T-shirt he's wearing, with THE BOOGERS written across it in black and red. I bought that shirt in a Chicago punk club last year; any doubt I might have that it's the same shirt goes out the window when I see the grease stain in the back that I got from changing the oil in my car. That's the fucker who ripped me off.

It looks like he's dancing by himself. I push through the crowd toward him, sometimes losing him in the crush of squirming bodies, but then catching sight of him again, closer each time. I finally squeeze through right behind him. His shaved head, muscles, and the ring in his left ear make him look like a punk Mr. Clean. Just then, the band stops playing. I put my hand on his shoulder and he turns to face me, his eyes narrowed. Along with a pierced ear, he's got a ring through his nose, and another piercing in his left eyebrow. I smile at him. "Hey, man," I say. "I like your shirt." Then I slug him as hard as I can.

The dude falls against the stage but then comes back at me like a hound from hell. We start slugging it out on the dance floor. He gets a good one to my right eye but I connect flat on his nose; blood streams down over his nose ring and splatters my Boogers shirt. He tries a head butt on me, but I jerk away in time and hit him with a body tackle. We're down on the floor now, sometimes me on top, sometimes him. The crowd around us is cheering us on. When I'm on top again, I pull my fist back to give him a pounding so hard his parents will die. Somebody grabs my arm before I get a chance and yanks me to my feet. It's the gate man. "OK, you little shithead," he growls, "you've caused enough trouble for the night." He pins my arm behind my back and shoves me forward through the crowd. People are hooting and jeering on both sides of us. My upper lip is cut, and I can taste my blood as it flows into my mouth.

When we reach the door, the gate man gives me a final hard shove, and I go crashing into a parked car. A couple of seconds later, the other guy goes flying through the door as well. The gate man stands at the doorway, glowering at us with a face like raw ground chuck. "If I see you guys here again," he snarls, "I'll rip your fuckin' heads off." He points a fat finger at me. "That goes especially for you, asshole." He goes back inside the club.

I climb to my feet and spit the blood out of my mouth. The other guy has pulled off his (or rather *my*) T-shirt and is dabbing his bloody nose with it. His body is lean and muscular; his abs are cut like a six-pack and his pecs are hard and ripped. Both his nipples are pierced. His arms are covered with tattoos; I can't make them out in this light, just a few scattered images—tits, skulls, knives with blood, that kind of shit.

"You want to give me my shirt back?" I growl.

He looks at me and then at the shirt in his hand. "Oh, is this yours?" he asks, his eyes wide. He blows his nose into it. "Here," he says, tossing it to me. I let it fall to my feet. We glare at each other.

His eyes flick down to my Queer Punk T-shirt and then back to my face again. "You queer?" he asks.

OK, I think. *Here comes the bullshit.* It looks like we really *are* going to have to take up where we left off in the club. "Yeah," I say, squinting my eyes. "What of it?"

"Nothing," he shrugs. "Except I'm queer too."

I didn't see that one coming. "So?" I finally say, after a couple of beats.

He grins, and for once it's not a "fuck you" grin. "So do you want to fuck?"

"Are you for real?" I laugh. But I start wondering what he looks like naked.

The dude shrugs. "Hey, it was just a thought." A few seconds go by. "We could keep on fighting if you want to do that instead," he adds. It's like we're on a date, trying to figure what movie to see.

I take in the muscles, the tattoos, the piercings. In the streetlight, his body shines with sweat, and I can see the meaty bulge in the crotch of his torn jeans. His lip is puffed up where I hit it, pushing his mouth into a permanent sneer. His dark eyes sneer too, looking hard at me, challenging me. I feel my dick growing hard. I haven't been laid since I moved to this city, and I'm getting real tired of fucking my fist. "OK," I say slowly. "If I get to choose, then I choose fucking."

The dude laughs. "All right!" he says. He sticks out his hand. "I'm Crow."

I take his hand and shake it. "Jamie," I say.

Crow lives in a shotgun apartment on Fell Street, one long hallway with a whole bunch of rooms branching off it. He tells me he shares it with four other guys, but it feels as if half of fuckin' Haight Street is crammed into this place. A tape deck blasts from one of the rooms in the back, playing something from Smashing Pumpkins, and I hear laughter and loud voices. People wander in and out of the kitchen, mostly guys, but a few chicks too. The place smells of grass, incense, and ripe garbage. It makes Darlene's and Buck's apartment look like Graceland.

Crow's room is nothing more than a storage closet with a mattress on the floor. There's no other furniture in it; no other furniture could *fit* in it, but there are piles of clothes stacked along the walls. I recognize some of my stuff, and damned if I don't see Buck's bowling shirt, a neon-blue polyester piece of shit that should be taken out somewhere and burned.

Crow sees me staring at the clothes. "You can have them back if you want," he says, grinning.

I don't say anything, I just pull him to me and pry open his mouth with my tongue. Crow wraps his powerful arms around me and starts grinding his crotch against mine; I can feel the bulge of his dick rub against mine, a slow, circular massage of cocks separated by blue denim. With a sudden jerk, he topples us both onto his mattress. He grabs my wrists and pins my arms down as he continues to dry-hump me nice and slow. His tongue pushes into my mouth and down my throat, almost deep enough to taste the burrito I had for dinner.

I bury my face in his armpit and lick the sweat from it, breathing in deep. Crow's body squirms on top of mine, and he bends his neck so that he can stick his tongue in my ear. I trace my own tongue across his firm pecs to his left nipple. It's huge, sticking out sharp and erect like a little toy soldier, with the ring in it gleaming in the light from the bulb overhead. I place the metal hoop between my teeth and tug at it. Crow reaches up to yank the string that turns out the light, but I pull his arm away. "I want to see your body," I tell him.

Crow's mouth curves up into a slow smile. "OK, man," he says, "if you want a show, I'll give you one." He stands up at the foot of the mattress and kicks his boots off. I lie back with my hands behind my head and watch. He unzips his jeans and drops them, revealing a pair of bright red bikini briefs. He looks fuckin' hotter than hell in them.

"Nice briefs," I say. "You've been hitting some high-class Laundromats."

Crow just laughs. He slowly, teasingly pulls them down, first showing his pubes, then the base of his dick shaft, thick and promising. He stops there. "You want to see more?" he asks, eyebrows arched.

I don't answer, but just reach over and yank his briefs down; his half-hard dick swings heavily between his legs. It's a beautiful dick, fat and meaty, with a dark red head that flares out from the shaft. His foreskin is pierced with a thin steel ring. I just about shoot a load looking at it.

"Christ," I whisper. I never saw anything like it before.

Crow looks proud. "I had it done a couple of months ago." Under my eyes his dick slowly stiffens and gets harder. "Check it out," Crow urges. "It won't bite."

I get up on my knees, but Crow holds me back at arm's length for a second. "Get naked first," he orders. Only after I strip does Crow let me take his dick in my hand. I work the foreskin back and forth over the head, watching as the ring winks in and out of sight. Crow's fat dick is fully stiff now, and the feel of his warm, hard meat inside my hand gets my own cock all stiff and juiced up. I squeeze his dick, and a drop of precome oozes out of the piss slit. I lick it up, whirling my tongue around the head, tasting the saltiness of the spermy pearl. I look up at Crow and grin. "My favorite flavor," I say.

"Yeah," Crow grins. "Mine too." We both laugh.

I work my lips down the length of Crow's shaft in small nibbles until my nose is buried deep in his pubes. I inhale deeply, breathing in the musky, pungent odor of Crow's cock and balls. Crow begins pumping his hips, and his dick slides easily in and out of my mouth; I feel the ring scrape inside my cheek, and I run my tongue over it. I wrap my hand around Crow's balls; they have a solid heft to them that feels like they were made for my palm. I squeeze them as I twist my head from side to side, giving his dick the full treatment with my tongue. Crow groans loudly. He seizes my head with both hands and thrusts his dick deep down my throat, mashing his pubes into my face. Then he pulls back and continues fucking my face in long, steady strokes. My other hand plays over his body, kneading the muscles of his torso, feeling his hard ass, tugging his tit rings. With his dick still in my mouth, I look up past the cut abs, the muscle-packed torso, the bull shoulders, to his face staring down at me from what seems like miles. Crow grins. "You're a real pig for dick, aren't you?" he croons. "You just can't fuckin' get enough of it." And he's right. I'm a dick pig for sure, and I've got my face buried in the trough tonight.

I take his cock out of my mouth and start flicking his balls with my tongue. They hang loose and heavy above my face, furred lightly, the left nut lower than the right. I suck them both into my mouth and slobber my tongue over them, drool running down my chin. Crow starts beating my face with his dick, slapping my cheeks, my nose, and eyes with it.

My tongue blazes a wet trail down the hairy path to Crow's asshole. His ass cheeks are fleshy and muscular; I bury my face between them and then burrow in deep, probing his bunghole with my tongue. Crow goes apeshit, writhing around, grinding his ass into my face. I replace my tongue with my finger, working it slowly up his chute and then corkscrewing it around.

Crow groans loud and deep. "How do you feel about fucking my ass?" he rasps.

"I feel just fine about it," I tell him.

He rummages under a pile of clothes and comes up with a jar of lube and a rubber. "Lie down on your back," he growls. He straddles my hips and wraps his greased hand around both our dicks, squeezing them together. I look down at the sight of it: our two cocks being stroked together, slipping and sliding against each other inside Crow's big, callused hand. Crow bends over and we kiss again.

I take the lube from him and grease up my hand as well. Reaching behind, I pry apart Crow's ass crack and slide my grease-slimed finger inside his bunghole again. Crow squeezes his asshole tight, and I feel the muscles clamp down around my finger. I slowly pull it out, wiggling it all the way, and then shove it hard back in. Crow's body squirms against mine, and I push a second finger in. Crow groans loudly.

I hold my condomed dick up straight as Crow lowers himself onto it. It slides into his ass smoothly, and Crow eases onto it like he's sinking into a hot bath; he closes his eyes and sighs loudly, and the look of pleasure on his face is so intense I almost laugh. He begins riding my dick, pushing off my body and then sliding down again, and I pump my hips to meet him stroke for stroke. It's such a fuckin' hot sight, his pierced, tattooed, muscle-packed body sliding up and down my cock. I wrap my still-greasy hand around his dick and stroke it long and slow. With my other hand I tug on his nipple rings, first the right one, then the left, then back to the right again. Crow's eyes glaze with pleasure, and something close to a whimper comes out of his open mouth.

I pull his head down and kiss him hard, pushing my tongue deep down his throat as I pound his ass. Crow turns into a fuckin' maniac. He wraps his arms around me, and we roll around on the mattress, him snarling and howling like some goddamn animal. I feel like I'm in a segment from *Wild Kingdom*. I hear footsteps down the hallway outside and then a laugh. "Go, Crow!" someone yells out.

Crow's on his back now, and I shift to overdrive, roaring down his ass like he's just so many miles of bad road. Each pounding I give him seems to shove Crow deeper into the mattress. One hard thrust gets my dick in full to the balls; I grind my hips and slowly tear up his ass. Our eyes lock onto each other; Crow's are bright and sharp, not missing a thing. I see the challenge in them. He wraps his legs around me and clamps his ass muscles tight; my dick feels like it's gripped in soft velvet, and as I pull out and then thrust back in it, I feel like my whole fuckin' body is about to implode. Crow's lips are pulled back and his eyes laughing. The message in them is clear enough: *Don't even* think *you're running this show.* I pump my hips a few more times and Crow matches me thrust for thrust, drawing me to the edge with a skill that blows my mind. The things I could learn from this guy! I groan loudly, and Crow reaches down and pushes hard against my nuts. Sweet Jesus, I just explode in that boy's ass, my dick squirting what feels like a couple of quarts' worth of jizz into the condom.

Before the last spasm is over, Crow flips me on my back and sits on my chest. As he fucks his hand, I reach up and pull down hard on his tit rings. He gives a whimper that trails into a long groan. His balls are pulled up tight now, and his dick is as stiff as dicks get. He's going to blow any second now. He begins to spasm, and then the first load of jizz squirts out of his dick, full in my face. Crow cries out as his wad rains down on me, sliming my face, dribbling down my chin and into my open mouth.

Crow collapses on top of me. Through the closed door I can hear Pearl Jam on the tape deck down the hall. After a few seconds, Crow raises his head and starts licking his own pearl jam off my face. When he gets to my mouth, we kiss again, not like before, just nice and tender. I close my eyes and drift off to sleep, with Crow's naked body sprawled on top of mine.

The next morning Crow gives me back all the clothes he swiped. I catch him looking at Buck's butt-ugly bowling shirt. I hand it over to him. "Here," I say, "Do you want it?"

Crow's happy to take it. He tells me that one of the guys is moving out in a couple of days, and if I'm looking for a place to crash, the room is mine. I say yes without looking at it.

The sun is just rising when I finally step out onto Haight Street. The winos and other homeless are just beginning to stir in the shop doorways. As I walk by, one of them sleepily asks if I have any spare change. I give him another one of Buck's shirts and then just head on toward home, grinning.

THE DADDY THING

He's leaning against the strip of brick wall dividing a porno video arcade and a Korean mom-and-pop, his pose not pathetic (if it were pathetic, I'd just drive on), but awkward, self-conscious. He's young, but not young enough to be a runaway, somewhere in his early 20s maybe. Unlike so many of the others hustling the street, he doesn't look wasted or strung out. Or schizophrenic and dangerous. In fact, I'm not even sure he *is* hustling. *Is he a police decoy?* I wonder. *Or maybe just waiting for a bus?* But he seems too ill at ease to be a decoy, and the nearest bus stop is two blocks down the street. I'm interested, but I'm also feeling very wary.

I circle the block and then slowly cruise by him again. Our eyes lock, and he doesn't turn away. I keep on driving. The third time around the block, I pull over alongside the curb. I've got Vivaldi's *The Four Seasons* playing on the tape deck, and as "Winter" pours out of the speakers I let him have it with my heaviest eye fuck. After a couple of minutes of glancing at me, then away, then back to me again, he ambles over to the car. I turn down the music and lower the passenger window.

"Howdy," he says.

"Hi," I answer. I like his face. He's got an expressive mouth and dark eyes that are large and set wide apart, giving an impression, however spurious, of innocence. He's wearing a loose flannel shirt and those stupid baggy shorts slung down low on his hips, so it's hard to get a clear impression of his body. The hang of the shirt suggests leanness. I'm grateful to see that he's got nothing pierced— at least nothing I can see. The last time I did this, the guy I picked up had a Prince Albert. I had to call the whole thing off, paying him $50 for his trouble. Kids.

I scrutinize him closely, looking for anything, a glance, a tone, that might hint at possible violence. I detect nothing, and I unlock the passenger door. "Get in." I'm feeling very conspicuous, a middle-aged man in a late-model BMW in this neighborhood. He slides in and I pull away.

"What's your name?" he asks as I swing onto Van Ness Avenue.

"Sam," I say. I glance over toward him. "What's yours?"

"Coyote," he says.

Jesus. I'm sure there's some colorful story behind the name, but I'm not interested in pursuing it. "Look," I say. "I'm not good with nicknames. Do you have a real name I can call you?"

He gives me a sharp glance. "Chris," he finally says. We ride on in silence. I keep waiting for him to ask me what I'm "into" and to start naming prices, but he just sits there quietly, looking out the window. He's got his elbow bent and his arm draped over the back of the seat. His hand is surprisingly large and strong. I notice that he bites his nails.

"How long have you been doing this?" I ask. It's a square thing to ask, but I'm curious.

He shoots me another sharp look. "Doing what?" he asks, all innocence.

"Hustling."

He doesn't say anything for a long moment. "Two months," he finally replies. "How long have you been paying for sex?"

I've pissed him off. I decide not to rise to the bait. "Longer than two months," I answer pleasantly.

I wonder if he's telling the truth about the two months. Still, it might be true. He certainly seems raw. "I just moved to San Francisco four months ago," he says, as if reading my mind. "Nobody told me how fucking expensive this city is. And how hard it is to find a job."

"Look," I say. "Just so there are no misunderstandings, I'll pay you $100, which I believe is the going rate."

"Yeah, fine," Chris says. We don't talk for the rest of the ride back to my place.

He takes off his clothes in my bedroom, like he's alone in the room, going to bed. I'm already naked, lying on top of the bedspread, watching him. He's lean all right, the muscles in his torso as cleanly defined as the girders of an unfinished building. His arms are powerful, the biceps rounding nicely, the forearms popped with veins. His nipples poke through a light dusting of chest hair that fans out across his pecs and descends down his flat belly. I take in the tone of his muscles, the clear smoothness of his skin. Sweet Jesus, but I love the bodies of young men!

When he pulls down his briefs (which are ratty and torn), his dick springs up, half-hard, and sways heavily between his thighs. *I got lucky tonight*, I think.

He looks at me from the foot of the bed, slowly stroking his dick, his face blank. "So what do you want me to do?" he asks.

"Sit on my chest," I say.

Chris climbs onto the bed and straddles me, his knees pressing against my sides. His strokes have gotten him fully hard now, and his dick points at the ceiling, gently twitching. My eyes trace the veins that snake up the shaft. I lightly run my hands over his torso, my fingers barely touching him. Chris puts his hands behind his head and poses for me. My caresses are more urgent now; I tug at his skin, squeezing his muscles, feeling their hard smoothness beneath the silkiness of his skin. I reach up with both hands and squeeze his nipples, not gently. Chris closes his eyes.

"Scoot up," I say. "Drop your balls in my mouth."

Chris's balls hang loose in their fleshy sac, filling my mouth. I roll my tongue over them, sucking on them gently, as I continue squeezing Chris's nipples. Chris slaps my face with his dick. My eyes travel up the muscled expanse of his body to his face. His dark eyes return my stare, giving nothing away. I inhale deeply, breathing in the sharp, musky scent of his dick and balls.

Chris rubs his dick across my mouth, smearing my lips with his precome. I open my mouth and he slides his dick in full, until his balls press against my chin. He stays there motionless for a moment, his cock head pushing against the back of my throat. "Yeah," he croons. "You got a hot man's dick in your mouth, uh-huh, fucker. That's what you wanted, right? To suck on a hot stud's thick cock?"

Yeah. That's right. Talk dirty to me.

He begins pumping his hips, sliding his cock in and out of my mouth. His large hands grasp my head on either side, not forcefully, just to keep my mouth a steady target as he fucks my face. One of my hands moves over his body, squeezing the hard muscles of his torso, twisting his nipples, as my other hand furiously strokes my dick. Our eyes lock together, and his lips curl up into a slight smile. "You like having the dick of a hot stud in your mouth, fucker?" he growls. "You like feeling the stud's balls slap against your chin while he fucks your face?"

It's a little hard to answer with my mouth full of dick, so I just grunt my agreement.

He pulls out of my mouth and scoots back a few inches, posing for me again. His cock bobs in front of my face. I raise my head to suck it, but he pulls away. "Just worship it for a while, fucker," he says.

It's a dick that deserves worship. My eyes feed on it hungrily as he strokes it slowly, teasingly. He makes me beg for it before I get to suck it again.

When he finally shoots, his load pulses out and splatters onto my face, one squirt after another. I shoot when he does. In fact, I've been holding back, waiting for him, and I cry out as my body spasms with my orgasm. After the last of my load oozes out between my fingers, I collapse back onto the bed, panting.

I look up at Chris. "Damn!" I say. Chris laughs. I let him use my shower, and 15 minutes later he's out the door, my $100 in his back pocket. I make sure to get his phone number before he leaves.

Alex looks at me across the table at the Café Flore. "So how many times have you seen this guy?" he asks.

I take a sip from my wine cooler. "I don't know," I say. "Four or five times, maybe." Actually, I've seen Chris nine times, but I feel embarrassed admitting this. "Lately we've been talking a little, after sex." I shake my head. "You wouldn't believe this guy's life. He's got no job skills. He doesn't even have a high school diploma. He lives in some slum residential hotel with a bunch of crackheads and speed freaks. The only way he can support himself is through hustling."

"So?" Alex asks. "You're happy with the arrangement, aren't you?"

I don't say anything for a while. I say, "I keep wondering where he's going to end up 10 years from now. It won't be pretty."

Alex shoots me a hard glance. "Christ, you're not falling for this guy, are you?"

I take a long sip from my drink. "No," I finally say. "I'm not." I look away. Across the room two men sit at a table by the window: one is middle-aged, the other much younger, early 20s maybe. They're smiling, and the older man has his hand resting on top of the other's.

I shake my head and look back at Alex. "You know, I never did get 'the daddy thing' before—why an older man would want to hang out with someone much younger. I could see the sex part, but afterward? What the hell interests do they have in common, with all those years between them? What do they talk about after they've finished fucking?"

Alex shrugs. "Maybe they don't talk."

I give a small laugh. "Yeah, right." We sit in silence for a while. I watch a fly buzzing against the window, beating its head against the glass. "I've been thinking about how cushy my life is," I finally say.

"Are we on a new subject now?" Alex asks.

"No," I say. "Not really." I look at him. "I make good money, I've got a nice place, things are all right." I lean forward. "But you know, Alex, there are all these things I *know,* things I've *learned.* And no one to pass this knowledge on to. This kid is making so many goddamn stupid mistakes, and there are so many things I could teach him."

Alex groans and rubs his hand across his face. He looks at me. "Just what do you have in mind, Sam?" he asks. "*Reforming* him?"

I take a sip of wine. "A straight man has sons to pass on what he knows. A gay man's only option is to go out and find his sons."

Alex laughs. "You're showing your paternal instincts in some mighty strange ways." I don't say anything. Alex leans back in his chair, his eyes trained on me. He shakes his head. "Holy shit, are you ever setting yourself up for a major fall."

I glance back at the couple across the room. "You think so?" I ask absently.

I dream that I'm at the opera, watching *La Traviata,* and someone's cellular phone is ringing. I keep waiting for the moron to switch it off, but it just rings and rings. After a while I realize that the phone really *is* ringing. I groggily pull myself out of my sleep and glance at the clock. It's almost 2:30.

I fumble for the receiver. "Hello?" I mumble.

"Sam?"

I recognize Chris's voice right away. I pull myself up, rubbing my eyes. "Do you know what fucking time it is?"

"Sam, I'm at the police station."

That wakes me up quickly enough. "What happened?" I say. I can hear voices in the background. Some woman is shouting, loud and drunkenly. Chris says something, but I can't make out his words. "Will you speak louder?" I ask impatiently.

"I got busted for robbery," Chris shouts in the phone.

I let a beat go by. "Jesus Christ, " I say.

"They're going to throw me in jail, Sam." There's a brief pause. "They gave me one phone call and you're the only person I could think of to call." I can hear the desperation in his voice now. There's another pause, not so brief. "I was hoping you'd post bail for me."

"Oh, yeah? And just how much *is* bail?"

I hear Chris talking to someone in the background. "Five hundred dollars," he finally says.

I run my fingers through my hair. *This is just fucking perfect,* I think. I don't say anything.

"Sam, you'll get it back after I appear in court." Chris's voice is strained tight. I still don't say anything. "*Please,* Sam," he pleads. "If you don't do this, I'll go to jail!"

"What station are you at?"

"The Mission Station. Over by 19th Street."

I sigh. "OK, just give me time to get dressed. I'll be there in an hour."

A long pause. "I really fuckin' appreciate this, man." Chris's voice trembles with relief.

"Yeah, right," I say. I hang up.

We don't leave the station until it's after 5 o'clock. Chris is slumped in the front seat, wedged against the door. He stares sullenly ahead.

"You want to tell me what happened?" I ask.

Chris shrugs but says nothing.

"Look," I say. "You dragged me out of bed at 2:30 in the morning. I've just shelled out $500 to bail your sorry ass out of jail. The duty officer told me you mugged some guy and robbed $100 from him. The least you can do is tell me your version." I notice I'm using the same tone my father used on me during my more serious juvenile fuck-ups. This is not a happy revelation.

Chris pulls a cigarette out of his jacket pocket. I'm about to tell him that he can't smoke in my car but decide to let it ride. Chris lights up, inhales deeply and exhales a long cloud of smoke. "I didn't rob anybody," he says. "The old fuck owed me the money."

"Christ," I mutter.

"He did!" Chris snaps. "He picked me up on Polk Street, drove to an alley, and said he'd pay me $100 if I went down on him." Chris glares at me, as if I were the guy. "I don't usually do that, but I needed the money. Rent's due. And I so sucked his stubby little dick. After the old shit came, he told me to get the fuck out of the car, that he wasn't going to pay me anything. So I hit him a few times and took $100 out of his wallet." Chris's voice is getting louder. "He had more—I could have taken it all, but I just took what the motherfucker owed me. I got out of the car, and a couple of blocks later the cops pulled me over. That bastard had waved them down and told them I'd mugged him."

I don't say anything for a long time. The streets are turning gray from the early morning light, and cars are beginning to switch off their headlights. I glance toward Chris. "Do you have any idea how fucked up your life is?" I say. "You need to take a long, hard look at yourself. You are one sorry bastard."

"Yeah, well, fuck you!" Chris says.

I slam on my brakes. The car behind me honks loudly. "Get out!" I snap. Chris doesn't move. I shove his shoulder. "I said get the fuck out!"

Chris turns to me. There are tears in his eyes. "OK, I'm sorry," he says.

I look ahead, gripping and releasing the steering wheel. More cars are honking. "I don't fucking believe this," I finally say. I start driving again.

"Can we go to your place?" Chris asks meekly.

I glance at him. He looks like he's on the verge of losing it big time. I don't say anything for a while. Finally I sigh, "All right." I turn the steering wheel and head toward home.

The first thing I do when I get back is call in and tell my secretary I'm taking the morning off. Chris stands in the middle of the living room, watching me as I talk to her. After I hang up, I look at him. "I'm going back to bed," I say. "And try to get a little of the sleep I lost last night." I start taking off my clothes. Chris stands there, still watching me cautiously. "You look like you could use some sleep yourself," I say less harshly.

We strip and climb under the covers. I close my eyes, feeling Chris's body press against mine briefly, before he rolls over and faces the wall. We've never actually slept together, and it feels strange having him in bed with me for reasons other than sex. After a couple of minutes, I drift off to sleep.

When I wake up, the clock says it's almost 11:30. I stir and glance over toward Chris. His eyes are trained on me, and I get the disquieting feeling he's been watching me all the time I was sleeping. "Did you get any sleep?" I ask him.

He shrugs. "A little." He still looks subdued.

I'm feeling more charitable now. I reach over and squeeze the back of his neck. "That guy's not going to press any charges," I say. "He's not going to risk the embarrassment."

We lie in bed together without speaking. I keep on massaging the back of his neck, my fingers gently kneading his flesh. Chris closes his eyes. I pull him to me and kiss him gently, my lips just barely pressing against his. I'm still not fully awake, and my kisses are sleepy and distracted. We kiss again, harder this time. Chris shifts his body and wraps his arm around me, pulling me against him. I reach down and squeeze my hand around both our dicks, feeling his cock swell and harden against my own. I start stroking them both, dick flesh against dick flesh, balls pressed against balls.

Chris rolls over on top of me. He takes hold of my wrists and pins my arms above my head, his mouth still fused to mine. He begins dry-humping my belly, his now-stiff dick pushing against me. He bends down and buries his face into my armpit, licking it, bathing it with his tongue. "Yeah," I murmur. "That's right, lick it good." His face burrows deeper into my pit and then travels down across my torso. I close my eyes, feeling his mouth on my left nipple, flicking it with his tongue, nipping it. His mouth continues its trip down my body, across my belly. He runs his tongue up the length of my dick and then swallows it whole, sliding his mouth up and down my shaft. Chris has never sucked me off before; until now it has been an unwritten rule that cock sucking falls outside the services he's willing to offer me.

"Turn around," I say. He pivots his body, and soon we're both eating dick, both having our dicks slobbered over. Chris worms a finger up my asshole, working it in knuckle by knuckle, as he sucks me off. I groan, my voice muffled by my own mouth full of dick. Chris's lean body writhes on top of mine, flesh pressing against flesh. He's got another finger up my ass, and he jabs both of them in and out in quick, short strokes. All these things he's doing are new; he's pulling sensations out of me that I've never had in bed with him before. I start sucking on his balls as my hand slides up and down his spit-slicked shaft.

"Why don't you fuck my ass?" I ask him.

"OK," Chris says. All his confidence is back now; it's like the scene in the car never happened. He breaks free and fishes the condom and lube out of the drawer in the nightstand next to the bed. I lie back, hands behind my head, watching as he rolls the condom down his dick, admiring once again the muscularity of his body, the smoothness of his skin. My lust is quickly melting away all my previous aggravation. I arch my back as he slowly impales my ass.

Chris lies on top of me, his cock full up my ass, and grinds his hips. I groan, and he smiles slyly. He may be hopeless outside of bed, but he's in his element now, and we both know it. He starts pumping my ass, his strokes deep and sure, and I wrap my legs around him, pushing up every time he slams into me. He bends down and kisses me again, thrusting his tongue into my mouth. I slide my hands down his smooth back, squeezing the hard flesh of his ass, feeling the bunched muscles of his thighs. Chris's torso presses against mine, I can feel his muscles flex against my body.

We roll over, and now I'm on top. I sit erect so that I can look down at Chris. I run my hands over his torso, flicking his nipples, pinching them. I squeeze my ass muscles tightly, just as Chris thrusts his dick hard up my ass. Chris gasps. I do it again at his next thrust, and Chris gives a full groan this time. *Yeah, sucker,* I think. *The old guy is good for a few tricks himself.*

I reach behind and massage Chris's balls with my hand, squeezing them gently, imagining the creamy load inside them. They've pulled up tight against his body, and I know it won't be long now before he shoots. Chris's lube-slicked hand is wrapped around my dick, stroking it in sync with each thrust of his hips. He pulls his dick almost completely out, holds the position for a second, and then plunges in hard. I feel his body shudder, and he cries out sharply. The orgasm sweeps over him one spasm after another, and I ride it out on top of his thrashing body, feeling his load pump into the condom up my ass.

Chris continues stroking my dick, and I feel myself getting close. "Slide down," he says. "And let me suck on your balls."

I move down his chest and drop my balls in Chris's mouth. He tongues them as he strokes my dick. I lean back, eyes closed, feeling Chris draw me to the brink. When I do come, I groan loudly, my load squirting out, splattering against Chris's face. I collapse onto the bed beside Chris and then kiss him, tasting my come on his lips. I roll over, and we lie there silently, our bodies pressed together.

I glance at the clock. It's a little after 12. "I got to go," I say. "There's stuff I have to do in the office."

"All right," Chris says. As I climb out of bed and head toward the bathroom, I glance back. Chris is lying on the bed on display, his hands behind his head, his legs spread open, his half-hard dick pressed against his thigh. He's wearing a small, self-satisfied smile, and I know he's convinced he's running the show again, that our having sex has swung the balance of power back to his side. Along with the inevitable arousal, I feel a flash of irritation.

I think about this as I shower. When I come out of the bathroom, Chris is sitting on the edge of the bed, slipping on his boots. I dress in silence. I glance at Chris in the mirror as I knot my tie. He's propped up on his arms, watching me, his eyes shrewd. I pull my wallet out of my pocket, fish out a handful of bills. "Here," I say.

He looks at the money, startled. "You don't have to pay me, man," he says. "Not this time." But he keeps his eyes trained on the money.

"Yeah, I do," I say. "I want to keep things between us on these terms." I hold the money out to him. "I included an extra $50 for the oral sex."

Chris looks at me, and some of the cockiness drains out of his face. Neither of us moves for a couple of beats. Finally, Chris reaches over and takes the money. "Thanks," he says quietly. I feel the power shift back to me again, but I get precious little enjoyment from it. "I'll give you a call," he says, "when I find out when my court date is."

"All right," I say. He leaves a couple of minutes later.

I look out the living room window as Chris walks out the front door of the building and onto the street. His hands are jammed into his pants pockets, and his shoulders are slumped down. I just stand there, watching him, my eyes following his back until he turns a corner and is out of sight. The son of a bitch is such a lost soul. "Christ," I mutter.

Even as I negotiate the city traffic a few minutes later, I can't get that last image of him out of my mind. I turn on the radio and listen to Otis Redding sing "Sittin' On the Dock of the Bay." Downtown, there are ragged men on nearly every street corner, holding out signs, begging for money, styrofoam cups clutched in their hands. *Chris in 20 years,* I think. Otis sings about how his loneliness won't leave him alone, and I can feel the tears well up in my eyes. *Maybe I will go along with him when he goes to court,* I think. A car behind me honks, and I see that the light has turned green. I put the car in gear and head toward work.

OVERBOARD

Ridley came across Hanson by accident, reading a letter by the narrow beam of the trouble lamp hanging from a Tom Cat undercarriage. The moon was out tonight, nearly full, and it hung over the Arabian Sea like the eye of God. If it weren't for the moon, Ridley might have made his escape, but he was caught fully exposed in the pale light that washed over the deck. Hanson glanced up and smiled at him in a way that could only mean trouble. Ridley was alarmed by the jolt of excitement he felt; if he wasn't careful, he would suffer tonight, badly.

"Hey, Tom," Hanson said. "Where you been hiding yourself? I haven't seen you in days."

Ridley shrugged but said nothing. He pulled a cigarette out of the pack in his shirt pocket and stuck it in his mouth.

"Let me have one," Hanson said, and Ridley pulled one out for him too. Ridley struck a match, and Hanson leaned over and lit his cigarette, his hands cupping Ridley's. Ridley's throat tightened and his mouth went dry. *This is such bullshit,* he thought. Hanson looked at him full in the face above the flame of the match, his eyes full of shrewd assessment.

Ridley glanced at the letter in Hanson's hand. "A letter from home?" he asked, even though he recognized the purple ink and large looping letters and knew damn well who it was from.

"It's from Elaine," Hanson said. His grin widened. "She tells me she misses my bod."

"Poor bitch," Ridley said.

Hanson laughed. "Really," he said, "where've you been? You're not avoiding me, are you?"

"I've been busy," Ridley said irritably. He took a long drag from

36

his cigarette and looked out over the ocean. The moon was huge tonight; he felt he could reach up and pull it from the sky.

"I've missed you," Hanson said.

Oh, shit! Ridley thought. *Here it comes. Thinking about Elaine has got him all hot and bothered.* "Tough shit," he said. But his hand shook, and he knew that the glowing tip of his cigarette was betraying this to Hanson. He dropped the cigarette angrily and stubbed it out with his toe. "I gotta go." He took a step back toward the flight deck.

Hanson reached out and wrapped his hand around Ridley's biceps. "Just stay a moment," Hanson said, his voice low and urgent. Ridley stood still, his body rigid. He kept his head turned away, but he didn't shake off Hanson's hand. "Why are you acting like this?" Hanson asked. "I thought we were friends." In spite of himself, Ridley was impressed. When he wanted to, Hanson could do "injured" beautifully.

Ridley turned his head. Moonlight washed over the planes and angles of Hanson's face, making him look like he was carved in marble. He stared miserably into Hanson's eyes, his mind in turmoil. "Eddy," he said slowly. "Stop fucking with me."

Hanson gave him a boyish grin, full of charm. He took Ridley's hand in his own and laid it on his crotch. "Feel how hard it is, Tom," he said. "See what you do to me."

Ridley jerked his hand away. "Yeah, right, asshole. You got your hard-on from thinking about Elaine."

Hanson shook his head and laughed. "Does it matter?" He unzipped his fly and pulled out his cock. It stuck straight out, slightly twitching, pale in the light of the moon. "Come on, Tom," he crooned. "Give me a little relief. You know you want it."

Ridley shook his head. "Forget it." But he couldn't take his eyes off Hanson's dick; the memory of how it felt in his mouth flooded his brain.

Hanson unbuckled his belt and pulled his trousers down to mid thigh. His cock bobbed, and his balls, made heavy by the warm tropical night, swung low between his thighs. "I love the way you suck my dick, Tom." Hanson said. "Just one more time, for old times' sake, OK?"

Fuck! Ridley thought. He took a few steps forward and dropped to his knees, burying his face in Hanson's balls. They smelled of musk and fresh sweat, and he inhaled deeply as he pulled his own cock out and started stroking. He could spend the whole night just doing this, nuzzling Hanson's nut sac, the hairs tickling his face, the loose folds of flesh bunching around his nose and spilling into his open mouth. He looked Hanson full in the face as he bathed his balls with his tongue. Hanson's mouth curled up into an easy smile, and he slapped Ridley's face with his dick.

Ridley slowly licked the length of Hanson's shaft, ending with a swirl of his tongue around the fleshy knob. He opened his mouth and nibbled down the cock until his nose was buried in the thatch of dark-blond pubes. Hanson started pumping his hips, fucking Ridley's face, slow at first and then with increasing tempo. He grasped Ridley's head with both hands and shoved his dick full in, the head slamming against the back of Ridley's throat. Ridley gagged, but Hanson held on tight. "Take it all in, baby," he crooned. "Don't fight it." He let go, and Ridley twisted his head from side to side, rolling his tongue around the shaft as his hands wandered over Hanson's lean torso, pulling on the flesh, tweaking the nipples, squeezing the smooth ass muscles that clenched and unclenched with each thrust of Hanson's hips.

They settled into a natural rhythm, Ridley's mouth sliding down with each thrust of Hanson's hips. Ridley wrapped his hand around Hanson's balls and tugged on them, not gently. "Yeah," Hanson groaned, "pull on my nuts. Make me feel it." He shoved his cock deep down Ridley's throat and kept it there, grinding his hips, his hands forcing Ridley's head to keep still. Ridley grew dizzy from lack of oxygen, and when Hanson finally pulled out, Ridley gasped for air.

"You bastard," he growled, but his dick was iron solid and his heart raced with excitement. He reached up and twisted Hanson's nipples viciously, but Hanson just laughed and continued fucking his mouth.

Soon Hanson was breathing heavily, his forehead beaded with sweat. Ridley cradled Hanson's balls in his palm, feeling how much they had tightened up, swollen now with the load his mouth was pulling out of them. Hanson could shoot at any moment. Ridley slid his mouth up to the very tip of Hanson's cock and then swallowed it whole, his lips swooping down the shaft. He pressed hard between Hanson's balls, and Hanson groaned loudly, his dick sharply throbbing. He pulled out of Ridley's mouth just as the first of his load pulsed out, splattering against Ridley's face in thick, sluggish drops. Ridley stroked his own dick furiously, triggering his orgasm as the last of Hanson's come rained down on him. Ridley closed his eyes and groaned, feeling his dick squirt in his hand, his load oozing out between his fingers. When he opened them again, Hanson had already pulled up his trousers and was buckling his belt.

Ridley watched him, his softening cock still held in his hand. Hanson looked down at him, frowning. "You better clean yourself up," he said curtly. Ridley wiped his sleeve across his face and climbed to his feet, his gaze never leaving Hanson. Hanson's eyes avoided Ridley's as he tucked his shirt into his trousers. Elaine's letter lay on the deck, and he bent down, picked it up, and stuffed it in his back pocket. He glanced briefly at Ridley. "See you around," he said, and walked off onto the flight deck.

Ridley's eyes followed him across the moon-bathed deck. He kept his mind blank, pulling his trousers up and tucking in his shirt with movements that were crisp and methodical. He walked to the edge of the deck, shook another cigarette out of the pack in his pocket, and smoked it. The ocean hissed as the ship's hull cut through it, and the path of moonlight dancing on the water looked solid enough to walk on. Ridley continued puffing on his cigarette, strangling every thought that tried to rise up in his mind. After a while, he flicked the butt into the ocean and turned away.

By the time he made it to the hatchway, his hands were shaking with anger. He held onto the metal edge of the hatch, hard enough for it to hurt, as the rage slammed into him like a gale-force wind. *"That motherfucker!"* he snarled. He slammed the hatch shut as hard as he could. It clanged against the bulkhead and bounced open again, hitting him full across the length of his body just as the ship did a sharp pitch sideways. Ridley staggered back a few feet, stumbled over the gunwale, and suddenly he was falling in empty space. He plunged into water, struggled upward, and broke the surface coughing and sputtering. The shock of it was so startling that it took a full half-minute before he realized he had fallen overboard.

The ship glided by him, the muffled roar of its engines throbbing through the hull. Ridley was paralyzed by disbelief. *Holy fuck!* he thought. He started shouting as loud as he could, shouting until his throat was raw and his lungs burned. There were no answering calls, no one peered over the gunwale. "Help me, you motherfuckers!" he screamed. He kept shouting even after the ship had pulled away and begun to shrink into the distance, its lights floating above the ocean like a flying city. He kept shouting even when the only noise that came out of his mouth was a hoarse croak. He treaded water and watched, incredulous, as the lights of the ship got smaller, came together, and finally blinked out below the horizon.

They'll come back, Ridley thought. *When they find I'm missing, they'll figure out I must have fallen overboard, and they'll put out a search for me.* Because he could think of nothing better to do, he started swimming out toward where the ship had disappeared, down the bright path of moonlight that stretched before him. The sea had a faint phosphorescence, something he had never noticed before, and every time he dipped his hand into it, the water gave off a pale, green glow.

Slowly, stroke by stroke, the fear began to seep in. Ridley pushed it out at first, concentrating on his swimming form, but it kept coming back, stronger each time. It didn't take long before panic pushed everything else out of his mind. *Oh, fuck, I'm going to die!* he thought.

It still didn't seem real. Less than an hour ago he had been on the flight deck with Hanson. *How could this be happening to me?* he wondered, amazed. The panic came roaring over him. *The ship will come back. They'll miss me at reveille, figure out I fell overboard, and come back to find me.* But he knew that it would be hours before anyone realized he was missing, and hours more before they decided he was probably overboard. By then, the ship would be hundreds of miles away, too far to ever find him. Because he could think of nothing better to do, Ridley kept swimming down the path of moonlight.

By late morning the next day, he was too exhausted to swim anymore. He had slipped off his trousers, tied the end of the legs together, and made a float out of them, like he had been taught in basic training. The sky above was cloudless, the wind had died down, and the ocean had flattened out into a metallic smoothness. It was like floating on a pond. The tropical sun beat down on Ridley, he could feel its heat on the top of his head, and his ears and neck prickled with sunburn. His eyes stung from the salt water, and his throat was dry and swollen.

That night Ridley watched the stars wheel slowly around overhead, dimmed by the full moon's brighter light. He tried to track the path of the Southern Cross, the only constellation he recognized, but he kept slipping in and out of sleep. The ocean was still calm, but there was a change to it, the phosphorescence was brighter than the night before. Ridley rolled over on his makeshift life preserver, his face just above the water. He cut his arm through the waves, watching the vivid green glow that trailed behind it. It was getting harder for him to collect his thoughts, to tell what was real and what wasn't. He kept getting the feeling that someone was floating next to him, Hanson maybe, or another shipmate, or one of his buddies from high school, and he would turn to say something, only to realize with a shock that he was alone. He closed his eyes. Hanson was murmuring in his ears; he couldn't make out the words, just the tone: joking, angry, tender, the murmuring never stopped.

By noon the next day, Ridley had pretty much lost any awareness that he was floating in the middle of the Arabian Sea. He had conversations with many people, but Hanson was the one he talked to most often. Ridley's eyes were almost swollen shut by sunburn and the sting of salt water, blinded by the sun's reflection, but sometimes he could still make out Hanson drifting in the water beside him.

"You better get up, Tom," Hanson said, grinning. "The chief's going to chew your ass good if he catches you in your bunk."

"I don't feel so good, Eddy," Ridley said thickly.

"The chief doesn't like goof-offs, Tom," Hanson said. He looked angry now. "You better get your ass in gear."

"I'm not goofing off," Ridley protested. He tried to lift his head higher but gave it up after a brief struggle. "Something's wrong."

"I don't know why I put up with you," Hanson said. "I don't know why I let you suck my dick."

"You bastard!" Ridley snarled. He swung out at Hanson but his hand only slapped feebly against the water's surface. "You bastard," he repeated, more softly. He squinted up at the sky and then at the water around him. "Where am I?" he asked, but Hanson was gone.

For a brief instant his mind was lucid, and he remembered everything. *I'm not going to make it through the day,* he thought. This saddened him, but only remotely, like it was the death of someone else he was contemplating. Still holding on to his inflated trousers, he drifted back out of consciousness.

He awoke in shade, and the escape from the sun was so unexpected and such a blessed relief, it drove everything else out of his mind, even curiosity. Hands were pulling at him, tugging his arms out of the water. "Eddy?" he mumbled, dazed. There was no response, just the incessant pulling, the hands hoisting him out of the warm water and onto a surface that was solid and flat. *Is this really happening?* he wondered. He tried to move, to open his eyes, but all he could do was shake. Hands held up his head, fresh water trickled into his mouth, and he drank thirstily. He could make out movement through the slits of his sunburnt eyelids, but nothing more than that. He closed his eyes and when he opened them again, it was night, and the moon shone palely over him. There was another body next to his, curled up against him on the small deck and sleeping. *Is this really happening?* he wondered again. He reached over and laid his hand on the hip of his neighbor. *Eddy?* he wondered. The man stirred and nestled closer to him, throwing his arm across Ridley's chest.

Ridley spent the next day in the boat's well under a tarp strung up against the mast. There were fish everywhere, piles of silvery bodies all around him, some still flopping about, and their stench made his belly cramp with nausea. He felt like he was in some twilight state, not asleep but not fully awake either. Everything vibrated with unreality. Every now and then a pair of hands would lift his head and offer him water, which Ridley drank meekly. He had not realized before that Hanson's hands were so brown.

He woke up that night like he had the night before, the boat rocking gently, and with the sleeping form nestled up against him. He had been dreaming of Hanson—it was a dream this time, not a hallucination, and because he could tell the difference he knew he was getting better. He stirred, and the body next to him stirred too. Moonlight streamed into the boat's well, but the two of them were still within the shadow of the tarp. A soft fluid stream of words issued out of the darkness.

"I don't understand," Ridley said. "I don't speak your language."

The flow of words continued, urgent, coaxing. Ridley lay still. He could make out nothing of the man's features, whether he was young or old, handsome or not. Ridley felt a hand on his chest, its fingers gently stroking his skin. Ripley remained motionless, lulled by the rocking of the boat, the balmy, tropical night, and the play of fingers on his body. The stream of words continued, barely more than a whisper, as the hand moved up and stroked Ripley's face. Ripley turned his head and pressed his lips against the palm. There was a stir of movement next to him, and the warmth of breath on his face. Lips kissed his mouth, gently at first, and then with greater intensity as the hand slid down Ridley's body and wrapped around his dick. Ridley felt the pressure of a body against his, and he reached out and stroked the warm flesh, the smooth skin with the hardness of muscle beneath it. There was a touch of lips against Ridley's chest, the feel of a tongue flicking against his nipple as the hand continued stroking his dick. Ridley sighed, and there was the sound of soft laughter.

The mouth made its way down Ridley's body, the lips soft and damp, and Ridley reached down and ran his fingers through the thick, coarse hair. He felt the tongue drag across the length of his cock and then the warm, wetness of the mouth, of lips sliding up and down his shaft, and he sighed again, louder. He began pumping his hips, with slow, measured thrusts, fucking the mouth as a hand gently squeezed his balls and then slid down and pushed against his asshole. There was the probe of a finger, and then it entered him, knuckle by knuckle. Ridley widened his legs and pushed up, opening himself up to the thrust of the finger.

Ridley reached over and gently pulled at the body next to him. There was a rustle of movement as the body pivoted around, and soon Ridley was sucking on a hardened dick, thick and uncircumcised, while his own dick was swallowed by the eager, wet mouth. Ridley squirmed in the darkness, pushing hard against the lithe body next to him, feeding on the dick as the warm mouth fed on his. The boat rocked gently in the night, and he could hear the murmur of the waves against its side. The mouth working his dick was skillful and eager; Ridley could feel his load being pulled from him, and he knew that if this continued his orgasm would be triggered in a matter of seconds.

The mouth stopped. A stillness lay heavy and potent in the darkness. The body next to Ridley repositioned itself once more. Hands pushed Ridley's knees apart, there was a sound of spitting, and Ridley felt the cock push up between the crack in his ass. Ridley reached down and guided it in, and the cock entered him inch by slow inch. The soft voice began murmuring again, low and unceasing, as Ridley felt the weight of a body on top of his. The cock thrust into his ass, and Ridley pushed up to meet it, squeezing his ass muscles tight. There was the sound of a trailing groan, and then the hot, wet mouth on his again, the tongue pushing against his own. The cock slid in and out of his ass, slowly at first, almost tentatively, and then with increasing tempo. Ridley reached up and pulled the head down, biting the lips, wrapping his arms around the torso and squeezing tightly. The moon had progressed enough in the night sky so that its light now angled in beneath the tarp, shining on a pair of brown legs entwined around Ridley's own.

The cock was pumping Ridley's ass furiously now, the heavy balls slamming against him with each thrust. Drops of sweat dripped down on him from above; Ridley could feel the hot breath across his face. The murmuring had stopped, giving way instead to little gasps, groans, and whimpers. A spit-slicked hand was stroking Ridley's hard dick, sliding up and down the shaft in time with each thrust of the dick in his ass. Gradually, stroke by stroke, Ridley could feel his load being pulled from him. From the increasing volume of the groans above him, Ridley guessed that the other was not far from shooting either. There was a final deep thrust of the dick and then a sharp cry. The body in Ridley's arms shuddered, the dick pulled out of his ass, and Ridley felt the hot rain of come splatter across his belly and chest. The hand slid across his torso, smearing the come, and then wrapped around Ridley's dick again. It slid up and down Ridley's shaft, now slippery with spit and come, and Ridley let loose with a long trailing groan as his load pulsed out, one spasm after another, mingling with the smear of come that already caked his belly. One final spasm rippled through his body, and then he sunk back onto the hardness of the boat's deck. The body above him collapsed on top of him, the arms wrapping around his torso, the mouth on his again. The two of them lay like that, flesh pressed against flesh, both of them now fully bathed in the light of the setting moon. Ridley heard the other's breathing become slower and more regular. After a while, he drifted off to sleep as well, lulled by the rocking of the boat.

The reporter from *Stars and Stripes* sat in the chair next to Ridley's hospital bed, his voice low and deferential. It was the first time Ridley had ever been given celebrity treatment, and it made him uncomfortable. The street sounds of New Delhi floated through the ward window, providing a constant background of noise. After three days Ridley hardly noticed them anymore. "So what were you thinking of while you were adrift?" the reporter asked.

Ridley was quiet for a long time. "I don't know," he said. He licked his lips and swallowed. "I got kind of confused after a while."

Ridley could tell that the reporter was disappointed with his answer. He felt a flash of irritation. "Look," he said. "What difference does it make what I was thinking?"

The reporter leaned back in his chair and fixed Ridley with a level look. "You're hot news, buddy," he said. "A Pakistani fisherman plucking you out of the ocean after you were adrift for almost two days: Do you have any idea how *miraculous* that was?"

"Yeah," Ridley said. "I do."

There was a brief silence. "Maybe you were thinking about Jesus," the reporter prompted.

Ridley didn't say anything for a while. Outside, a taxi was honking its horn nonstop. Ridley closed his eyes and then opened them again. He felt drained of energy. "Yeah," he said. "I was thinking of Jesus."

"And maybe your mother?" the reporter continued, his tone warming up.

"That's right," Ridley said. "Her too."

The reporter scribbled furiously in his notepad. He asked a few more questions, and, to get rid of him, Ridley gave him whatever answers he thought would most please him. When he was finally alone again, Ridley settled back into his bed and closed his eyes. The heat poured in through the open window, thick and sluggish, like a river of mud. Images floated through Ridley's mind, not of the ocean but of the dark well of the boat, of invisible hands and a mouth exploring his body to the sound of lapping water. After a couple of minutes, he drifted into sleep.

IN THE FETISH ROOM

I meet Nancy down on the hotel terrace that overlooks El Plaza de la Democracia. She's idly stirring her coffee, staring with bored eyes at the flock of pigeons that circle the fountain. I slip into the chair across from her.

"*Buenos días,*" I say.

"Go to hell," she replies.

"Oh," I say. "It's going to be one of those days, huh?" She shrugs and says nothing, keeping her eyes trained on the plaza. It's barely 9, but we're already getting a faceful of diesel fumes from San José's downtown traffic. I hate to think what my lungs must look like after three days in Costa Rica. Nancy finally turns her head toward me. "It looks like it's going to rain." She pauses. "Again."

"Nancy, would it make you feel better if I slit my throat?"

Nancy picks up the butter knife and runs her thumb over its edge. "I don't think it's sharp enough," she says. "Maybe I can get the waiter to bring a steak knife."

The waiter comes over, and I order eggs and toast. He smiles at me, and I smile back. I glance over at Nancy and catch the look she's giving me. The waiter heads back to the kitchen. "I'm not cruising him, Nancy," I say, trying to keep the testiness out of my voice.

Nancy gives a little laugh. "Brian, do you think I care?"

"I don't know what you're thinking. I beginning to feel like we're an old married couple."

Nancy says nothing. I can tell by the slow, deliberate way she sips from her cup that I've really pissed her off with that last remark. *I shouldn't have asked her to come here with me,* I think, not for the first time. She puts her cup down and glares at me. "It just

47

would have been nice," she says, enunciating each word slowly, "if you'd done a little *research* before convincing me to come down here with you. All this talk about beaches and rain forests. And now we're here at the height of the goddamn rainy season. The hotel clerk told me that the hotel is practically empty, that it'll probably rain every day for the next month."

"I had other things on my mind," I say. Nancy knows I'm talking about my breakup with Doug, that the only reason I took this vacation and asked her to come along was that I was going crazy in San Francisco. A silence lies between us like a dead flounder. "I bought a guidebook," I finally say. "Maybe we can find something to do indoors." Nancy rolls her eyes. I page through it. "Look," I say. "There's a museum of pre-Columbian art. Ceramics and jade work. They even have a collection of fertility fetishes. That could be interesting."

"Why don't you just club me over the head?" Nancy says. "That would be more merciful than boring me to death."

"I don't have a club on me," I say. "What if I push you in front of a truck instead?" *Two death threats in the past five minutes,* I think. *We're approaching emotional meltdown here.*

I take a taxi to the museum, leaving Nancy to stew on the terrace. *Six more days of this,* I think glumly, as the cab threads through San José's morning rush hour traffic. The museum's located on top of a hill, next to a small park of banana trees and bougainvillea. There are office buildings nearby, and the street is filled with people leaning into the wind, scurrying to work before the storm breaks. I pay the driver and run to the museum entrance, feeling the first drops of rain splatter against my face.

From the museum lobby I can see thunderclouds racing toward the building from the western mountains. Raindrops begin pelting the windows, making the glass panes shimmy. I buy a ticket from the guard in the lobby and walk through the door. The museum is deserted. I walk among the displays like a millionaire among his private collection.

Except I'm not entirely alone. There's another guard leaning against the wall, much younger than the one in the lobby, with a bushy mustache and dark eyes that follow me around the room as

48

I move from display to display. He fills his uniform well; I glance at him, taking in the lean, athletic build, the wide shoulders. He regards me with half-lidded eyes, his arms folded across his chest. His broad face and high cheekbones suggest Indian blood.

I look at the ceramic vessels molded into jaguars and frogs, the green jade pectorals shaped like solar disks, the death masks. The rain continues to drum against the windows, coming down in sheets so heavy that I can't see anything beyond the smear of water running down the glass panes. I move into one of the museum's interior rooms; there are displays of gold and silver jewelry, shaped like birds and small animals. There are no windows here, and the sound of the rain is only a muffled throb in the background. The guard follows me, leaning against the doorjamb, watching me, his face expressionless. My eyes meet his, and I smile at him, but he just regards me with his dark, sleepy eyes. "Is this museum always so empty?" I ask him in Spanish.

The guard shrugs. "The rain keeps people away. And there are few tourists this time of year."

"It must get boring for you," I say.

The guard shrugs again at the obviousness of my remark, saying nothing. He shifts his weight to his other foot and looks away, frowning. I go back to looking at the displays. I'm having trouble concentrating, feeling his eyes on me. *Is he afraid I'm going to smash the glass and steal something?* I wonder. I drift toward the room I just left. The guard blocks my way.

"Once you leave a room," he says, "you can't go back to it."

I think he's joking, and I give a short laugh. "What kind of rule is that? I want to look at some of the jades again."

"You can't go back," the guard repeats, his voice louder. He's taller than me by a good four or five inches. He stands in front of me like a linebacker.

"That's crazy," I say, my gaze locked with his. He returns my stare impassively. After a few beats, I give it up and return to the displays of old jewelry, feeling the blood rush to my face.

"Are you a tourist?" he asks a moment later.

I'm staring at a gold pendant of a two-headed vulture. I look up. "Yeah," I say, keeping an edge to my voice.

"Why would a tourist come to Costa Rica during the rainy season?"

"Because I'm also a fucking idiot." I'm not sure how well I've translated this into Spanish, but his mouth curves up into a faint smile. It's a generous mouth, wide and sensual. A small scar creases his upper lip, and I find myself wondering how he got it.

"And you're here in San José alone?" he asks.

He's bored, I think. *He just wants to talk with someone.* "Yeah," I say. I don't feel like explaining Nancy to him.

I go back to the displays, but I'm barely looking at the objects inside anymore.

"There are other displays in the next room you might like," he suddenly says.

"Oh, yeah?" I reply. "What of?"

The guard pushes his hat back and leans against the wall, his eyes trained on me. "Just go and look," he finally says.

"Later," I say, just to be difficult. I go back to looking at the display in front of me. I hear the sound of a match striking. I look up and see the guard lighting a cigarette, still staring at me. There's a sign immediately above him, saying PROHIBIDO FUMAR. The puffs he takes off the cigarette are jerky and irritable. "You should go see the other room," he finally says, "before any other visitors come."

I look at him for a few beats. "All right," I say. "I'll go look at the damn room." I walk through the door indicated by the guard.

It's the smallest of all the rooms, in the heart of the museum, accessible only by the one door that I've just walked through. The lighting is muted, except for a single display case in the middle of the room. A spot mounted directly overhead shines down on it, bathing it in a pool of light. I walk over to it.

Inside the case is a series of erect cocks. They're positioned neatly in a row, all of them arcing up toward the ceiling, like fledglings waiting to be fed. I stare at them for a long time. They're really beautifully done, each one distinct from the other. One cock is stylized and sleek, a thick, obsidian shaft that rises straight up in a smooth column, its balls two smooth ovals at its base. Another cock is wonderfully realistic, curving upward, veined, the head flaring out, the balls plump and fertile. There are ceramic cocks, jade cocks, stone cocks, even a small gold pendant cock. Unlike with the meticulously catalogued displays in the other rooms, there's no text giving any explanation to the contents inside the case: how old these cocks are, where they were found, what purpose they were supposed to serve. They seem almost hidden in this small room, an embarrassment to the museum, and yet the loving way they're displayed makes the room feel something like a shrine as well.

"Do you like them?" the guard's voice asks.

I turn around. He's right behind me, his eyes trained on me. I can smell the tobacco on his breath. "Yeah," I say slowly. "I do."

The guard grins again. His teeth flash white against his dark skin. "I thought you would." He leans forward conspiratorially, a pointless gesture since we're the only ones in the room. "When the museum is empty I spend my time here, looking at them." He points to the curving ceramic cock with the veined shaft. "That's my favorite one."

"Why?" I ask. The room is completely dead to sound. I have no idea whether there's still a storm pounding outside. I can feel the heat from the guard's body. My dick begins to stiffen.

"Because it looks so much like my own dick," the guard says, laughing. "I could have been the model for it."

I look at the ceramic dick again. "Really?" I say, because I can't think of a better reply. I'm visualizing the guard naked, and my dick stirs again.

"You don't believe me?" the guard asks, smiling slyly, one eyebrow raised.

He looks like such a parody of "the Latin lover" that, in spite of my arousal, I have to stifle an impulse to laugh. I give him the answer he wants to hear. "No," I say. "Not for a second."

"Oh, yeah?" the guard growls. "You think I'm lying?" His mouth is pulled down in an angry scowl, but his eyes crinkle with pleasure.

"You're damn right," I growl back. I stand up tall and push my chest out. "Either you prove it, or I'm going to think you're a lying sack of shit."

The guard gives a theatrical sneer, pure Clint Eastwood. "All right, gringo," he spits out. "You asked for it." He unbuckles his belt with a dramatic flourish and pulls his trousers down below his knees. He's wearing striped boxers, which he pulls down too. His dick springs up, fully hard, and bobs between his thighs. "There," he says triumphantly. "See what I mean?"

I stare at the guard's dick as he stands next to the display case of pre-Columbian erect cocks. I never would have imagined this scene even 15 minutes ago, and my mind buzzes from the surreal turn reality has taken. I say a silent prayer of thanks that Nancy didn't come along after all.

"Turn left," I say. "Give me a profile view."

The guard obeys me, standing, hands on hips, so that his erect cock is inches from those in the case. My eyes shift between the two dicks: one flesh, the other ceramic. "You're right," I say. "They do look alike." I reach over and lightly run my fingers along the length of his shaft. "Your dick curves up slightly more," I say. "And it's not as tapered." I wrap my hand full around the shaft and skin the foreskin back. "Your cock head is fleshier, rounder, almost dome-like." The guard squeezes his abdominals, and I can feel his cock throb in my hand. "And the ridge that runs along the underside of your cock is more pronounced." With my other hand, I squeeze his balls. "And, of course, your balls hang much lower." I look up at him, my hand sliding up and down his shaft. "But all in all, the resemblance is striking."

The guard looks pleased. "See, I told you so."

I give his dick a few more strokes, rolling his balls around in the palm of my other hand; they spill over in their fleshy sac like two meaty little eggs. I look at the guard, and he returns my stare, calmly, his mouth curved into a lazy smile. "So where do we go from here?" I ask.

"Well," the guard laughs, "you could start by sucking my dick."

I laugh with him. "Sounds like a plan." I drop to my knees and bury my face into his balls, feeling the hairs tickle my face, breathing in their faint musky smell. I hold them in my hand again and kiss them tenderly. His balls hang heavy in their fleshy sac, dark, almost black, plump with his load. As I roll my tongue over them, I feel the guard's dick press against my cheek. I look up into his face as I suck on his scrotum and see him returning my stare, his guard's cap pushed back, black curls spilling over his forehead.

Grinning, he takes his dick and rubs it over my face, precome smearing my cheeks and mouth.

I open my mouth, and he shoves his dick in, all the way, until the head pushes against the back of my throat. I seal my lips around the shaft and start sucking. It throbs in my mouth, and slowly, lovingly, I slide my lips up the column of flesh. When I have only the cock head left in my mouth, I swirl my tongue around it and push my tongue tip into the piss slit. The guard grasps my head with both hands and starts pumping his hips, sliding his dick in and out of my mouth with quick, short thrusts.

I unzip my pants and start tugging on my own cock. The guard reaches down and wraps his hand around it. "Nice," he says. He unbuckles my belt. "Why don't we get naked?"

I glance at the door behind us. "What if someone walks in?" I ask.

"No one comes in the mornings," he says. "Especially during a storm." He runs his fingers through my hair and tugs on it. "Except a stray crazy gringo, now and then."

What the hell, I think. I stand and let my pants drop. The guard reaches up to remove his hat. "No," I say. "Everything but the hat." He looks at me. "I have this thing about uniforms," I explain.

The guard grins and leaves the hat on his head. He quickly strips off the rest of his uniform, and I follow suit. The guard's body is smooth, the flesh the color of lager ale, the nipples wide and very dark. He turns to toss his clothes aside, and my eyes take in the play of the muscles in his torso, how they tighten and ripple under the mocha skin. When we're both naked, the guard pulls me to him and plants his mouth against mine, snaking his tongue deep into my mouth. I slide my hands down his back and cup his ass cheeks; they're smooth and tightly bunched with muscle. I pull his hips against mine, dry-humping his hard belly with my stiff dick as we continue to kiss. The guard reaches down and cups my balls in his hand, gently tugging them. He lowers me onto the floor at the foot of the display case, pinning my hands above my head as his mouth moves down my neck and across each nipple. He nips the tender flesh and then rolls his tongue over it, sucking on each nipple gently, bringing them both to hardness. He releases my arms and gives me a series of butterfly kisses down my belly, his lips light and papery. I stare up at the black obsidian cock that towers above me by the edge of the case as the guard's lips finally slide down the shaft of my dick.

I can tell that he likes dick. He eats mine greedily, his mouth swooping up and down the shaft, his tongue swirling around it, his teeth nipping the head. He pulls it out of his mouth and stares at it. "What a handsome dick you have," he says, laughing. "What a wonderful fetish it would make!"

"Pivot around," I say. He needs no persuading. He shifts his body around, his arms straddling my body, his long legs splayed out above my head, his thick, dark dick hanging above my face. I crane my head up as he pumps his hips down, and soon we're feeding on each other's dick, fucking each other's mouth. The silence of the small, interior room is nearly total, punctuated only by the slurping of our mouths and our sighs and groans. The guard moves his body like a dancer, grinding his hips in slow, circular motions, swaying his torso rhythmically above me, twisting his head back and forth as his mouth slides up and down my dick shaft. His hat has long since fallen off and lies upside down on the floor beside us.

The guard pulls my dick out of his mouth and reaches over for his trousers, crumpled on the floor a short distance away. He pulls out a condom package from the back pocket and looks at me. "How about I fuck that pretty ass of yours," he says.

"All right," I answer.

He straddles my torso as he rolls the condom down his dick. I reach up and twist his nipples, my eyes sliding down his body, caressing it with their gaze. I'm a sucker for Latin men, their smooth brown skin, their dark eyes and crisp black hair, their easy smiles, and the thought of this man plowing my ass sets my dick twitching like it has a life of its own.

The guard slides down, grabs both my ankles, and hoists my legs around his torso. He spits in his hand and slicks up his dick. I feel it poke against my asshole and then slowly slide in. Spit is a lousy substitute for lube, and I grit my teeth, my eyes focused on the guard's face, which hovers above me. He watches me intently with narrowed eyes, pausing each time I grimace and then pushing on. When he's completely in, he waits patiently, and then begins to pump his hips, slowly, the thrusts at first short and tentative. I breathe in with each thrust, focusing my eyes on his, arching my back, pushing up to receive each downward plunge of his dick. My asshole tingles with the sensations the guard draws out. He picks up his pace, and soon his dick is slamming into my ass in fast, deep thrusts. I wrap my legs around him and meet him stroke for stroke, squeezing my ass tight. The guard groans and then grins down at me. He plunges all the way in my ass and grinds his hips. His cock roots into me like he's digging for gold, and my own groans bounce off the ceiling of the small, enclosed room. I wrap my hand around my cock and start stroking like there's hell to pay.

The guard's eyes are no longer sleepy; their lids are pulled back, fully exposing the whites around the dark irises, giving his gaze a fierce intensity. Sweat beads his forehead and drips onto my face with each hard thrust of his body. The guard bends his head down and kisses me, his mouth wet and hungry, and once again I feel his probing, snaking tongue.

The little whimpers he's been giving off every time his cock plunges up my ass are getting longer now, increasing in volume. His balls have pulled up tight against his body, and his arms, supporting his weight, are beginning to tremble. He plunges full in and keeps his cock there, grinding his hips in a slow, lazy dance. I squeeze my ass muscles tightly as he pulls out, and this elicits another, trailing groan. With his next plunge, I reach up and give his right nipple a savage twist. The guard cries out, and his body spasms violently. "Yeah," I growl, as his body thrashes in my arms and his dick pumps out his load into the condom up my ass. I squeeze his body tightly with my legs, trying to bring as much of his skin against mine as possible as his orgasm sweeps over him. He collapses on top of me with a final sigh and lies there heavily. I can feel his heart beat against my chest.

After a few beats, he lifts his head and looks into my eyes. "I want to see you shoot your load," he says. "On my face."

"No problem," I say.

The guard lies on his back, his hands behind his head, and watches me with bright eyes as I sit on his chest and stroke my dick. He grunts his encouragement with each little groan I give, and when it's obvious I'm getting close, he wraps his hand around my balls and gives them a good tug. He laughs when my load shoots out, splattering against his face, dripping down his cheeks and chin. I lean forward and lick it off, dragging my tongue over his face before thrusting it into his mouth for a final, lingering kiss. We lie like that for what seems like a long time before we separate and start getting dressed.

"Do you do this a lot?" I ask as we pull our clothes back on.

The guard shrugs as he knots his tie. "From time to time. On quiet days with few visitors."

"I wouldn't think that many gay men would come by."

The guard flashes me a sly smile. "Men, women, I'm quite happy fucking them both."

The rain is still coming down when I leave the museum, though the storm seems to have lost some of its intensity. From the taxi returning to the hotel, I absently watch the rain pounding on the pavement outside. I think about the guard. Then I think about Nancy.

That night Nancy and I eat dinner at Tin Ho's on Calle 11. The rain beats down on the leaves of the baby palm trees in the inner courtyard as we share bowls of Thai noodles and curry chicken boiled in coconut milk. I'm feeling mellow and content, and Nancy, to her credit, is trying to be a good sport. But I can see the creases in the space between her eyebrows and the restlessness in her eyes. In my new expansiveness, I feel a wave of sympathy toward her. I look at her across the table. She looks good; the candlelight bathing her face makes her look like a young girl and gives her blond hair a soft glow. "I really liked that museum I went to this morning," I say. "Maybe you should pay it a visit tomorrow. By yourself." Nancy looks at me suspiciously. "You should go there early, to beat the crowd," I add. *Leave it at that,* I think. *Let whatever happens, happen.* A couple walks in and a wet gust of wind blows into the restaurant. I hold my hand against the candle flame to keep it from flickering out.

CALMING DOWN

Tonight I almost tear out somebody's windpipe on my way to my nightly meditation meeting. All over a parking space. I just found a space and am backing into it, when some jerk in an MG zips in from behind and grabs it. I honk my horn, he flips me off, I call him an asshole, he calls me a motherfucker, and I'm out my car and heading toward him with both fists clenched before I get a grip. *Is this worth going back to jail?* I ask myself. I take two deep breaths and return to my car. When the guy sees I'm not going to fight, he starts jeering at me, calling me a pussy, a faggot. Since he doesn't know me, I guess the last is just a generic insult. Even in the car, with my hands gripped so tight around the wheel that my knuckles are white, I seriously consider that maybe it *is* worth three more months in the slammer to back into that little yuppie shit-mobile of his at full acceleration. I don't. I drive off and find a space two blocks away. My stomach is in knots and my throat's so constricted that I can hardly breathe. There's murder in my heart. I go to meditation.

The guy with the beard and beads, whose name I can never remember, is already in the guided part of the meditation. Still steaming, I shuck my shoes off next to the door and park my butt on the nearest empty pillow. Everyone else's eyes are closed. I take a few deep breaths and close my eyes as well. My thoughts are chaos. After a while I give it up and look around the room. I check out the blond guy with all the muscles, whom I've had a hard-on for since I joined this group three weeks ago. Tonight he's sitting right across from me. I let my mind drift to images of what he must look like naked.

Every time I look at this guy, I'm reminded of one of those

angels on the Christmas cards I used to see as a kid. It isn't just the blond hair or the mild blue eyes, it's this air of *calmness* about him. It hangs over him like a shield of light. I feel I could lob a cherry bomb at him and he wouldn't flinch; he'd just turn his steady blue gaze on me and ask me what was on my mind. *What must it feel like to be so calm?*

With his eyes closed, I can ogle him openly. He's just wearing a tank top for a shirt, with a yin-yang symbol embroidered on it and the inscription FREE TIBET written underneath. He really does have a fine, fine body: shoulders like a bull's, biceps pumped up and nicely rounded, a tight waist, muscular pecs. The hands that lie on his knees, palms up, are huge; he could crush a casaba with them. His feet are big too. Next to all the other shoes by the door, his Birkenstocks look like a couple of small rafts. I keep thinking of the line "big hands, big feet, big dick" and wonder if it's true. I do a creative visualization of him ramming his thick dick hard down my throat, and for the first time since the incident over the parking space I begin to relax.

He opens his eyes, and suddenly we're looking at each other eyeball to eyeball. I glance away, but when I sneak another look at him his eyes are still trained on me. *What the hell,* I think. I give him my best barroom eye-fuck, throwing in a little leer to make it interesting. His expression never changes, and after a couple of seconds, he closes his eyes again and sinks back into meditation. But after the session's over, he comes up to me and asks if I'd like to catch a cup of something hot with him. I say, "Yeah, sure."

We go to some café nearby. I order a bowl of split pea soup with crackers; he orders red zinger herbal tea. He asks me my name.

"Bill," I say. I ask him his.

"Star," he says.

How precious, I think. New Age pretentiousness really gets on my nerves.

As if reading my mind, he gives a small smile. "It's a '60s thing. My folks were a couple of Haight-Ashbury hippies. They wanted something cosmic-sounding for their kids. I've got a sister named Moon and another named Earth."

I grin. "What was your dog's name? Pluto?"

Star smiles. "No, Benny. *I* got to name him."

I laugh and Star laughs too. Things start to loosen up between us. "Have you been meditating long?" Star asks.

I shake my head. "Just since I joined this group three weeks ago." Star nods. "You looked pretty new at it."

I give a sour smile. "Is it that obvious?" I pick up a pack of crackers and try to open it. For some reason the cellophane won't tear. I struggle with it for a few seconds without making any headway. A small sunburst of rage explodes inside my head. I throw the crackers down and bare my teeth at Star with something I hope can pass as a smile. "How long have you been meditating?" I ask, my voice thin with anger.

Star reaches over and takes one of the cracker packages. "You got to tear it right here," he says. "Right where the red line is." He tears the cellophane easily and hands it to me.

His expression is bland, but there's humor in his eyes. The rage wells up inside of me again. *The son of a bitch is laughing at me.*

"Thank you," I say tightly.

"You're welcome," he replies. There's a moment of tense silence, tense at least on my part. Star seems completely at ease. We look at each other. Star wiggles his eyebrows. Suddenly I laugh, and the rage passes off like steam.

Star smiles. "Welcome back," he says.

"Thanks," I say, this time meaning it. I take a deep breath. "You handle tantrums well." I give a wry smile.

Star shrugs. There's another pause. "Nine years," Star says. I look at him blankly. "You asked me how long I've been meditating. It's been nine years."

I let this sink in. "No wonder you're so goddamn serene," I finally say.

Star grins. "I have my bad days too, you know." The thought flashes through my mind that his worst days are probably better than my best. Star takes a sip of tea. Even the way he raises his cup to his mouth is calm, the movement of his hands measured and simple

"Why do you meditate?" I ask, with genuine curiosity.

"It's part of my practice." Star catches my uncomprehending stare. "I'm a Buddhist. Meditation is one of Buddhism's cornerstones."

I turn this over in my mind. "A Buddhist? I thought all you guys were bald, wore orange robes, and sold carnations at airports."

Star smiles. "Those are Hare Krishnas. Different religion altogether"

We sit in silence for a few seconds. "Stairway to Heaven" is playing over the sound system. "So what prompted you to join the meditation group?" Star finally asks.

I swallow a spoonful of soup and give him a level stare. *Well, here goes.* "It's one of the terms of my probation. To join some kind of stress-reduction program." I keep my voice matter-of-fact. "I just got out after three months in jail. For assault." Star looks at me with his calm gaze and says nothing. After a while the silence is more uncomfortable than speaking, so I continue on. "I was shit-faced and got sucked into some stupid fight outside of a bar, where I beat some guy to a pulp. He wound up in the hospital. This wasn't the first time I got in trouble with the law over something like this, so they threw the book at me." I shrug. "I'm a mean drunk. Another condition of my probation is that I join a 12-step program. I meet with them every morning before work."

"How's it been going for you?" Star asks. Part of me is grateful he's listening to this with no sign of disapproval. Another part is getting a little tired of all this relentless *calmness.*

I shrug again. "I take it from day to day." I give a laugh with precious little humor in it. "The hard part is my temper. I'm such a bad-ass son of a bitch. It doesn't take much to get me started."

Star doesn't say anything. I look around the room and then back at him. I give a thin smile. "You didn't realize when you asked me to join you that you were dealing with a psycho from hell, did you?"

Star's expression is thoughtful. "No, I didn't," he says slowly. "It certainly makes things more interesting."

We slip into another silence. I'm beginning to feel more than a little ill at ease. Finally I shake my head and laugh. "I keep expecting you to try to convert me now."

Star looks genuinely surprised. "Convert you? To what?"

I shrug uncomfortably. "You know, Buddhism."

Star laughs. "I don't give a rat's ass whether you become a Buddhist or not." He gives me a curious look. "Why did you think I did?"

"I don't know," I say. "I shared a cell with a Jesus freak for a few weeks." I laugh, remembering it. "The son of a bitch knocked off a 7-Eleven, and he kept trying to save my soul." I pick up my spoon, turning it over in my hand. "It got on my nerves after a while."

Star leans back in his seat and hitches his thumbs under his belt. "I'm not looking for any converts," he says. He drains his cup and places it back in the saucer. He grabs his jacket. "Let's take a walk."

I look at him, startled. "OK."

We walk around the neighborhood, going no place in particular. It's a typical San Francisco summer evening, which means I'm freezing my ass off. But I like the bite in the air; it keeps my mind alert. Star and I don't say much, but it's nice having him walk beside me. We climb Telegraph Hill and look down at Alcatraz, its red signal light muffled behind the banks of fog rolling in. We pass a dark doorway. I pull Star in and suddenly we're all over each other, kissing, rubbing our bodies together, breathing hot and heavy. Star cups my ass with those giant hands of his and pulls my crotch against his; his dick is hard and urgent under his cotton pants. He dry-humps me for a couple of minutes with his mouth fused over mine, his tongue pushing deep enough down my throat to taste what I had for breakfast.

"Let's go back to my place," he whispers.

"No problem," I say.

Star's apartment suits what little I know of his personality: simple, uncluttered. There are a few pieces of furniture, not much: a futon, a bean bag chair, a small table and set of chairs, a potted ficus in the corner. In an alcove there's a bench press and set of weights. A single picture hangs on the wall: a series of circles within circles, filled with animals, demons, meditating figures, flowers.

"It's a Tibetan mandala," Star says, noticing the direction of my gaze. "It represents the universe." He inserts a CD in his player. Indian sitar music fills the room.

"Nice," I say.

Star comes over and we pick up where we had last left off. I slip my hands under his T-shirt. "This feels very nice," I murmur.

Star grins. "It's all part of my plan to convert you."

I laugh. I plant my mouth over his, and we kiss hard. My hands begin kneading the flesh of his torso. It's firm under my fingertips, and the muscles underneath have the feel of hard rubber. I run my thumbs back and forth across his nipples. Star closes his eyes. I can trace each abdominal ridge, the cut of each pectoral. I can't wait to see this guy naked. I tug at his shirt; Star lifts his arms, and I pull it over his head. His torso is as beautiful to look at as it is to feel. The skin is the color of pale honey and has a silky resiliency and smoothness under my fingers. I lift his arm and bury my face into his left pit. The musky smell of fresh sweat fills my nose, its sharp taste flavors the saliva in my mouth. I move down to his left nipple and run my tongue around it. Star sighs audibly. I suck on it and give it a playful nip with my teeth. The nipple swells to hardness in my mouth. I trace a wet trail across Star's chest with my tongue and give his right nipple equal time.

I am not by nature a gentle lover. I like my sex rough, I like to wrestle in bed, snarl and spit, spank, plow ass hard and fast, or fuck throat mercilessly. But tonight all bets are off. I feel this irresistible need to be *tender*. The feeling's so new to me, it almost seems kinky. I decide to just kick back and let it happen. I slide my tongue down the ridges of Star's abdominals and across the rough fabric of his pants. His dick swells against the white cotton. I kiss it gently, running my tongue against the cloth, darkening it with my spit.

I reach up and untie the drawstring. I glance up at Star's face. He's looking down at me, his blue eyes bright, his lips parted. There's a lamp on the wall behind him, and the blond hair lit from behind frames his head like a halo. I slowly pull down his pants.

His dick lives up to the promise of his hands and feet; it flops heavily and half erect against his thigh: red, thick, fleshy, traced with blue veins, the head swollen and blood engorged. I give a sharp exhalation of breath, just shy of a whistle. "Jeez, Star, do you fuck with that or play baseball with it?"

Star laughs. I love this man's laugh; it's open and easy, with a sense of adventure in it. "I just do the usual things with it," he says.

"Well, do them to me, man," I growl. I take his dick in my mouth and move my lips up the shaft until my nose is buried in his dark-blond pubes. Star sighs, and his dick swells to full hardness in my mouth. I start working it, sliding my lips up and down the shaft, rolling my tongue over it. Star lays his hands on my head, not roughly, just as a guide as he pumps his hips and fucks my mouth with deep slow strokes. I close my eyes and feel his cock move in and out of my mouth, filling it with dick flesh. I open my throat wide and, with an effort, manage to take it all in each time he shoves his hips forward.

I run my hands across the hard flesh of his ass cheeks, prying them apart, burrowing my fingers into the crack. I find his asshole and massage it, then let one finger push up inside. Star squirms and grinds his hips hard against my face. Pulling away from Star's cock, I slide down and press my lips against his ball sac, kissing it softly. Scrotal hairs tickle my mouth. I stick my tongue out and give his balls a good washing. They hang heavy in their fleshy pouch, plump and swollen. I open my mouth wide, taking them both in, rolling my tongue over them.

Star reaches down and pulls me to my feet. He kisses me on the mouth, my eyes, all over my face. He unbuckles my belt and pulls my jeans and boxers down around my ankles.

"You have a beautiful cock," he murmurs, stroking it slowly with his hand.

"It's not as big as yours," I reply. I can't bleed all of the regret from my voice.

Star shrugs and smiles. "I'm used to that. Bigger isn't always better, you know." And damn if he doesn't say that with enough sincerity that I actually believe he means it.

He leads me to his futon, and in a matter of seconds we're sprawled on top of it, kissing. Star wraps his legs around mine and spreads himself full-length on top of me. My body feels like every nerve ending in it is wired to the sensation of his skin against mine. He sits up and wraps his hand around both our cocks; we fuck his huge fist in unison, cock flesh against cock flesh, his balls pressed against mine. I reach up and squeeze his nipples, not gently. Star closes his eyes briefly but then looks down at me and smiles.

He pivots around and takes my dick in his mouth, deep-throating me in a slow, long tempo. From this position, all I can see is his ball sac swinging heavily above my face, and the crack of his ass. From the CD player Ravi Shankar is doing hot licks on his sitar.

I do the same on Star's balls, lifting my head and sucking eagerly on his meaty scrotum. My tongue moves higher up, and I bury my face between Star's ass cheeks, probing into his asshole. From the way Star's body writhes against mine, I can tell the sensations are driving him wild. I wrap my hand around Star's dick and begin to stroke it. We ease into a smooth rhythm, each stroke and lick of mine in sync with Star's slow, steady sucks. The old horizontal dance I love to do so well.

Star comes up for air. He turns his head and looks at me. "I would really love to fuck your ass right now, Bill," he says. "Would that be all right with you?"

I laugh because he sounds so *polite*. "Star," I say, "As far as I'm concerned, you can fuck me blind."

Star grins. "What if I just fuck you until you need glasses?" Old joke, maybe, but it's still funny. I laugh again. He reaches into the drawer of a bed stand next to the futon and pulls out a condom and jar of lube.

In no time at all I have my legs over his shoulders, and Star is readying himself for the initial plunge. He places his hands on my hips, and his cock head probes against my asshole. With excruciating slowness, he enters me. I shut my eyes and grimace from the size of him. "I know, buddy, I know," he murmurs. "I'll go easy." He begins fucking me with a gentle, slow tempo, whispering reassurances, his hands caressing my torso. I open my eyes and see his face right above mine, his eyes watching me carefully. I move my body in pace with his, and everything's all right again; the feeling of him filling me excites me into new hardness. Star smiles. He quickens his pace, thrusting deep, grinding his pelvis against me. I reach down and cup his balls in my hand, squeezing them gently. Star smears a dollop of lube onto his hand and starts jacking me off. He bends down and we kiss, thrusting our tongues deep into each other's mouths.

Star pulls away to an upright position. He starts breathing deeply and steadily, exhaling in a loud sigh with each thrust of his hips. After a while it dawns on me that this is fucking as meditation, that he's using the same breath techniques that I've seen him use during the evening classes. I try to match my breath with his, and eventually I get something of the hang of it: withdraw, inhale; thrust, exhale. Star notices my attempts right away. "Yeah, Bill, that's right," he pants. "Let's see where we can go with this."

Sensations sweep over my body, starting from my asshole and radiating out. I have never felt so intensely the act of being fucked. I groan and close my eyes, letting Star's dick and lube-smeared hand work their wonders on me. "Open your eyes, Bill," Star says urgently. "Don't drift away." I open my eyes and see Star looking down at me, sweat along his forehead, his eyebrows knitted in concentration. I hold his gaze, and we fuck like this, eyes locked, breathing synchronized, bodies thrusting and pulling away in a rhythm that comes more smoothly together with each stroke. I reach up and run my hands over his torso, now slippery with sweat. I seem to be aware of everything around me with a sharpness of detail I've never experienced before: the softness of the futon under my back, the patterns on the leaves of the ficus plant behind Star, each note played on the sitar from the CD. But mostly I'm aware of Star; I feel myself drawn up out of my body and pulled into those blue, blue eyes of his. It no longer requires any effort to match breaths or thrusts with him; we seem to be moving as one body now.

Star's breathing becomes faster, more ragged. His face is drenched with perspiration, and his lips are pulled back into a soundless snarl. But his gaze never wavers from mine. I know he's ready to come any moment now, and I can feel the load being pulled up from my balls as well. It would be easy for me to shoot, but I manage to hold on, to wait for Star; it feels like I have more control over my body than I've ever had before. Star groans. I reach up and twist his nipple, and that seems to be what it takes to push him over the edge. He thrusts deep and hard one final time and then cries out. He bends down and kisses me, his torso squirming against mine, and then I feel his dick pulse inside me as his load squirts into the condom up my ass. At the same time I feel my own load rise up from my balls, and I cry out, my voice muffled by his mouth. My spunk shoots out onto my belly, one spermy gob after another. Star embraces me in a bear hug, pressing his body tight against mine, as I shudder out the last of my load. We lie together in silence, me wrapped in Star's strong arms, feeling his heartbeat against my chest. I want this feeling of flesh on flesh to last forever, to just freeze time right here in the afterglow of a good cosmic fuck, maybe my first. But inevitably Star pulls his dick out of my ass and rolls over on his back.

I lie there on the futon, staring up at the ceiling. "Jesus, Star," I say. "That was fuckin' incredible!"

He smiles. "Yeah, it's nice when it goes right, isn't it?" He kisses me again, and we lie together on his futon, his arm wrapped around me, my head nestled against his shoulder. I feel myself drifting off to sleep. Reluctantly, I force myself to get up.

"You know you can spend the night here," Star says.

But I have to go to work in the morning, and I turn down his offer with some real regret. Star takes this, like everything else, with equanimity. A thought flashes through my head, a snake in Eden: It would have been nice if he had shown at least *some* disappointment at my refusal. "Maybe we can do this again?" I say, trying to sound casual. I scan his face carefully for his reaction.

Star smiles. "Yeah, I'd love to." He seems to mean it. *Leave it at that,* I think. *Don't push it.* I get up and start putting my clothes on. I look down at him on the futon as I button my shirt. He looks like a jungle cat relaxing. He looks beautiful. I hold that picture of him in my mind as I walk out the door.

As I drive home, a car suddenly switches into my lane, cutting me off. I have to slam on my brakes to avoid hitting it. It's half a mile later before I realize that I didn't felt the slightest bit of anger at the driver. I move through the traffic of the city streets toward home like a rock falling toward the center of the earth.

DADS

I glance at my watch and make a mental calculation of how much time I have before I have to make my appearance at Jason's school. It's early evening now, and the park is getting dark; there are only a couple of streetlamps off in the distance that provide any kind of illumination, that plus a half moon rising over in the east. *A mugger's paradise,* I think, and then push the thought out of my head. When my dick is doing all the thinking I try not to let practicalities like that get in the way. Every now and then a break in the shrubbery gives me a glimpse of the city: the streets fanning out below, ending in the greater darkness of the bay. Solitary figures lean against trees or emerge from the shadows and saunter by—the sharp, cruisy look in their eyes giving lie to the casualness of their stride. Over and over the ritual repeats itself—our gazes locking together, the quick scan of each other's body, then the eye lock again, this time with a question in it: *Interested in a little action?* Or else the turn of the head, with the unspoken message: *Move on.* I don't think it's excessive vanity on my part to note that I get a hell of a lot more of the first reaction than the latter. I'm wearing a T-shirt tight enough to feel like a second skin, showing off the cut of my muscles, the pumped-up biceps and pecs. (I've gone straight to the park from my daily workout at the gym; my hair's still slicked down from the shower.) I've busted my ass to look good, and I have no qualms about strutting my stuff. Alice tells me I've become quite a peacock since our divorce, but she doesn't understand the courtship rituals of the gay community that demand this kind of behavior.

I see him perched on the back of a park bench, his knees wide apart, his feet planted on the seat. A cigarette hangs loosely between his index and middle fingers, smoke lazily curling up. I get the impression that he's young, maybe more from the posture of his body—half self-conscious, half bored—than from anything I can discern from his face, which is hidden in shadow. His body is lean and well-defined; like me, he's wearing a T-shirt that shows off his physique. But I don't get the impression that he's on display, as I am; he sits slouched over his knees in an attitude that seems without pose. I begin to wonder if he might be some straight dude who's wandered into this gay feeding ground, clueless to what's going on around him. I find myself *very* interested.

I sit on the bench, next to his feet, and lean back, my arms resting along the back. There's not the slightest shift in his posture or attitude to give any acknowledgment of my presence. I look up at him. "It's a nice night, isn't it?" I say. OK, as an opening line it doesn't exactly sparkle. But success in park cruising rarely results from verbal wit. He turns his head and looks straight at me, a gesture that pulls his face out of shadow for a moment. His features are regular and smooth: a strong jaw, deep-set eyes, high cheekbones. I can see that my first impression was right. He *is* young, early 20s maybe, a good eight or nine years my junior.

He takes a puff from his cigarette and exhales out of the corner of his mouth. "I guess so," he says. A silence lies between us like roadkill.

I make another stab. "What's your name?" I ask.

He looks at me again for a few seconds. "Terry," he finally says. He doesn't ask me mine.

After a few more seconds, I stand. "See you around, Terry," I say.

"Do you want to fuck?" he asks my back.

I turn around and face him. His face looks pale and chaste in the faint light from the streetlamp. I try to imagine what he would look like naked. The image I come up with is very nice. "Yeah," I say. "As a matter of fact, I do."

Terry swings his legs around and stands up. He drops his cigarette and grinds it out with the toe of his boot. "Let's go," he says.

Terry's dick thickens out nicely as I suck on it, twisting my head from side to side for maximum effect. His hands lightly grasp my head and he fucks my face with long, slow thrusts, like a runner pacing himself. My hands slide under his T-shirt, kneading the hard flesh, tweaking the nipples. I give them a good twist and Terry grunts his appreciation. I work my hands down his back and over his smooth ass, squeezing the cheeks. Terry slams his dick hard down my throat and then leaves it there, grinding his hips, his balls pressed against my chin. When he pulls out again with killing slowness, I nibble at the meaty shaft, my tongue working on it feverishly. Terry gives a long, drawn-out sigh. "Yeah," he says gruffly. "That's good."

He pulls me to my feet and kisses me, ramming his tongue into my mouth with the same force that he rammed in his dick a few seconds ago. I wrap my arms around him and press my body hard against him. My pants and shorts are down around my ankles, and my hard dick stabs against his belly. He reaches down, wraps his palm around both our dicks, and begins stroking. Both our dicks are leaking precome, and they slide against each other with a slipperiness that makes my body tingle.

Terry drops to his knees and I feel the warmth of his mouth around my cock. I start pumping my hips to maximize the sensation. He's a good cocksucker, energetic and skillful, and the shivers of pleasure that ride over my body come quicker and harder. He takes me to the brink, and just when I'm ready to shoot, he pulls back. His mouth drops down to my balls and sucks on them as the threat of shooting recedes. We're surrounded on all sides by high bushes, and the darkness is near total; my only contact with him is the feel of his invisible wet tongue sliding over my balls and dick. Terry's lips move up my cock, kissing the shaft wetly, and then he swoops down and starts sucking me off again. Once more the sexual tension rises inside, building to climax, and once more, when my dick is on the point of spasming out its load, Terry pulls back. I groan my frustration.

"Yeah," Terry growls. "You're just dying to shoot, aren't you, fucker?" Before I can answer, he's sucking me off again, pulling my load up from my balls once more. I thrust hard and deep down his throat, a spasm shoots through my body, and this time I go over the edge, squirting my load into the warm, wet confines of Terry's mouth. He sucks greedily, squeezing out every last drop. He finally stands and starts beating off. I reach down and squeeze his balls, and with a loud groan, he shoots, splattering his jizz against my shirt. When he's done, he leans forward and kisses me, pressing his naked body against mine.

A couple of minutes go by. I gently disentangle myself. "Listen," I say, "I have to go."

The moon has risen above the tops of the bushes, lighting up his face with a dim glow.

"What, you got a date or something?" he asks. I can't tell whether he's being flippant or genuinely resentful.

"No," I say. "A PTA meeting."

I wander all over the damn school building before I finally find Jason's classroom. I'm half an hour late, and I've missed the orientation. The parents are milling around, waiting for a chance to talk with the teacher about their children. Alice spots me and fixes me with a murderous glare. I go up to her, adopting a contrite expression.

"Listen, I'm sorry I'm late," I say. "Things just got piled up."

"The least you could have done is wear something a little dressier," she whispers vehemently. She looks down at my T-shirt. "What's that spilled down your front?"

Oh, jeez, I think. *Terry's load.* "Nothing," I say, crossing my arms in front of me. "Just some coffee. I was in such a damn hurry I wound up spilling half of it." I put a slightly aggrieved tone in my voice, like somehow the accident was her fault for making me hurry. Alice just rolls her eyes and walks away.

When I finally meet Jason's teacher, she tells me that Jason is doing fine. "He tends to daydream, though," she says. "It's not a serious problem, but sometimes he seems a little distracted."

Like father, like son, I think.

The next day Jason and I are in my car crossing the Bay Bridge; one of the lanes is closed for bridge maintenance, and the traffic is bumper-to-bumper. Jason has recently picked up an interest in Greek mythology, sparked by some project in school, and every time we ride together lately it's been my job to tell one of the stories. (I bought a copy of *Bullfinch's Mythology* a couple of weeks ago just to bone up on this stuff.) We've already covered the Trojan War and Ulysses' long, problematic sail back to Ithaca. Now I'm telling Jason the myth about the Golden Fleece. Jason is particularly caught up in the story because he shares his name with the hero. I get to the part where Jason is trying to steal the fleece from the king only to find that it's guarded by a dragon.

"If a dragon is guarding the fleece, then how could the king get to it?" Jason asks. He's always looking for ways to trap me in an inconsistency, as if I wrote the damn myth.

"He couldn't," I answer. "Nobody could get to it."

"Well, then, what good was it?" Jason asks. "Why did the king care if Jason took it or not?" He gives me a look like "Explain that, sucker!"

"It was a tourist attraction," I reply. "People would come from all around to look at it from a distance. The locals made money selling souvenirs: ashtrays, key chains, T-shirts that said MOM AND DAD SAW THE GOLDEN FLEECE AND ALL I GOT WAS THIS LOUSY T-SHIRT. That kind of thing."

Jason is 11 and too old to let on that he thinks any of my jokes are funny. He rolls his eyes in a way that is pure Alice, but I can tell he's amused. I decide that now is a good time to bring up another subject. "I saw your teacher last night," I say. "She's worried about you being too easily distracted."

Jason shrugs and looks out the window, searching for a distraction. I switch back to the Golden Fleece and capture Jason's attention again. I'll leave the edifying lectures to Alice.

Later, after I fix dinner for Jason and me, the two of us go to a Jackie Chan movie. Jason loves these action flicks, which Alice won't take him to because she thinks they're too violent. Tonight Jason gets to watch the bad guys get the pummeling they deserve while I sit in my seat lusting after Jackie Chan. God help me, I've always had a special weakness for athletic clowns. The movie is longer than anticipated, and I don't get Jason home till after 10. "Tell your mom I'm sorry I kept you out so late," I say as I give him a goodbye hug. I watch him as he runs up the sidewalk; I don't pull away until he's safely inside.

Whether it was the movie or something else, I'm really feeling an adrenaline pump. I turn on the radio and find a good rock and roll station. Mick Jagger comes on, singing about how he can't get no satisfaction, and I join in, my fingers tapping time against the steering wheel. I feel completely uninspired by the thought of returning home and going to bed. At least alone. What I really want, I decide, is to get laid. Barring that, then at least a little social mixing.

I tick off my options and finally decide on one of the bars on Castro. I am not by nature a bar person; I don't normally deal well with crowds and noise. But I decide *What the hell, it's been a while, maybe it'll be fun this time*. I make my way through the city streets, turn on Castro Street, and grab the first available parking space.

I pick the Detour for no other reason than that it's the first bar I stumble across. It's after 11 and Friday night; the place is packed. I push my way through the crowd until I can belly up to the bar. After a couple of minutes I catch the bartender's eye and order a Michelob. I pull out my wallet and drop a couple of bills on the bar, which the barkeep scoops up.

"Is that your kid?" a voice next to me asks.

I turn and see a man to my right, about my age, maybe a couple of years older. He's smiling at me and indicates, by a nod of his head, the picture of Jason I keep in my wallet.

I smile back. "Yeah," I say. "His name's Jason.

"How old is he?" the man asks. He has an easy smile that is very engaging. His eyes are brown and friendly, and his face gives off a comfortable masculinity.

"Eleven," I say. "Going on 30."

The man laughs. He reaches back, pulls out his wallet, and flips it open like a cop showing ID. Inside is the picture of a young boy wearing a baseball cap, a bat slung over his shoulder. "This is my boy, Matthew. He's 9."

I take in the boy's brown eyes and wide grin. "He looks like you," I say.

The man's smile broadens, like I just paid him a compliment. I like the way *he* likes being compared to his kid. I bet the guy's a good father. I quickly take in the broad shoulders, the chest hairs poking above the shirt button, the muscular forearms beneath his rolled-up sleeves.

I hold out my hand. "My name's Joe," I say.

"I'm Pete," he says. We shake hands. He raises his bottle of beer. "To fatherhood." We clink bottles and each take a sip. Pete looks at me. "So is Jason a turkey baster baby?"

I blink. "I beg your pardon?"

"You know," Pete says. "Artificial insemination. Matthew's mom is a lesbian. We were friends for years before we decided to coparent. It was a hell of a job getting her pregnant. I'd go to her bathroom and jerk off into a pimento jar, give it to her and she'd go to her bedroom with a turkey baster. It took months before she conceived."

I grin. "Maybe you should have taken the pimentos out of the jar first." Pete laughs. I take another sip of my beer. "Actually, Jason got conceived the old-fashioned way. By good old traditional screwing. I was married to his mom. For five years."

Pete raises his eyebrows. "Kinky."

I shrug. "Yeah, well, that was my experiment with normalcy. I've pretty much worked it out of my system."

It doesn't take long before we start comparing notes about our kids. Pete's boy is a pitcher in Little League, loves soccer, and is a huge fan of Michael Jordan. "He gets all this jock stuff from his mom," he says laughing. "He sure as hell doesn't get it from me. I have to read the sports section every morning so I can talk to him about Barry Bonds and who the Giants are going to trade for next, all that stuff. It's fuckin' murder."

I tell Pete about Jason's drawing and story writing skills, about how at 11 he can kick my ass in chess, and about the huge battles Alice and I have over his joining the Boy Scouts. "She tells me the Boy Scouts will give Jason a chance to meet new friends and learn important values. I tell her the only value he'll learn is gay bashing." I look at Pete with wide eyes. "She's totally clueless about this. She thinks I'm just being PC." Pete shakes his head sympathetically.

We order more beers and keep talking about our kids. I have never done this before, actually compared notes with another gay man on raising a son, and I surprise myself with what a good time

73

I'm having. After a couple of hours my voice is getting hoarse from shouting over the noise in the bar. "Listen," I say to Pete. "You want to come over to my place and continue this conversation?" Pete agrees instantly.

Back at my apartment, I fish a couple of beers out of the refrigerator and join Pete in the living room. He's picked up a photo album from a bookshelf and is going through the pictures. He looks at a shot of me and Jason on the Sausalito ferry. "Jason looks like a nice kid," he says.

"He is," I say. I sit next to him, going over the photos with Pete. Our knees brush together and I make no effort to break the contact. After a while, I put my arm around Pete's shoulder and pull him toward me. We give each other a long, wet kiss, our tongues finding their way into each other's mouth like foxes coming home to their burrows. The photo album slides off my lap and onto the floor as I push Pete back onto the couch, wrapping my arms tightly around him. We grapple each other in wrestlers' clenches; Pete thrusts up and we roll off the couch and onto the shag carpet, our mouths never separating. I slide my hand down the front of Pete's jeans and cup his crotch; the bulge I feel under the frayed denim is a promising handful.

"You got something there for me, buddy?" I croon. "Something meaty I can swing on?"

"Yeah," Pete says, his eyes bright. "Just come and get it."

We begin a feverish undoing of buttons and zippers. I pull Pete's jeans down, revealing a pair of boxer shorts with rocket ships on them. I give a small laugh. "Who the hell are you? Buck Rogers?"

Pete gives a sheepish smile. "Matthew gave them to me for my birthday last month."

"Well, I'm sorry," I say, grinning. "But they have to go." I yank them down below his knees. Pete's hard cock flops against his belly. This is one of my favorite moments in life, getting acquainted for the first time with the dick of a hot man. It's like Christmas, unwrapping the main gift; sometimes you find you're stuck with a box of underwear, sometimes you get a full Lionel train set. Pete's dick definitely falls within the train set category: fat and long, the cock head flaring into a wide red knob. I tug his T-shirt up and straddle his legs, looking down at his body, taking in the solid torso, the cut of his pecs, the hard belly. "You are one hot fucker," I say, wrapping my hand around his dick. I begin stroking it, and then bend down and press my lips against the meaty shaft, kissing it softly. I let my tongue trail along its length, swirling around the cock head, probing into the piss slit. This is the dick he stroked in his lesbian friend's bathroom, a pimento jar clutched in his free hand as he thought the sexy thoughts needed to coax out the load that would later become his son. For some reason, I find the image incredibly erotic. I slide my tongue down to the base of the shaft and then onto the hairy scrotal sac. I pull down my own pants and begin stroking my dick as I bury my nose into Pete's balls, inhaling deeply. The musky, ripe smell of a male in rut fills my lungs. I open my mouth wider and suck in his balls, rolling them around with my tongue, savoring their taste and texture. My own cock is hard and urgent in my hand. I look up and my eyes meet Pete's; his pupils are wide and dark, and his gaze bores into me as I tongue his ball sac. I reach up and squeeze his nipples, and he closes his eyes and groans.

I pull my head back. "Let's go back to the bedroom."

Pete nods. "I thought you'd never ask."

We pull up our pants high enough to stumble down the hallway to the bedroom. Pete walks ahead of me, affording me a sight both comical and very sexy: his rocket ship boxers pulled up as far as his thighs, with his ass exposed to my lecherous gaze. It's a beautiful ass, smooth and tight, creamy white beneath a mocha tan line. I quickly play in my mind all the things I intend to do with that ass in the next few minutes. My dick gives a throb of anticipation.

It just takes us a minute to throw off what clothes we're still wearing, and we fall onto my bed, naked. I spread out on top of Pete, my mouth fused to his, feeling his bare flesh against mine. The guy is beautiful, and I want to taste every inch of his body. I cover his face with kisses and then work down, along his neck, his shoulder, finally nuzzling under his armpit, drinking in the sweet/acrid taste of his sweat. I swing my head around and suck on his nipple, nibbling it gently between my teeth, rolling my tongue around it. Pete sighs deeply, and I repeat this with his other nipple. My tongue pushes through the forest of his chest hairs, tracing their path as they descend down his hard belly and into the thicket of his pubes. I hold his dick in my hand again and gaze at it for a couple of seconds, enjoying how its warmth spreads into my palm, how it pulses with every beat of Pete's heart. I bend down and take it in my mouth again, working my lips down the shaft, rolling my tongue around it. Pete pumps his hips, and I match his movements, bobbing my head with each thrust of his hips. I close my eyes, concentrating on the sensation of having a mouth full of *dick*.

"Holy shit!" Pete exclaims.

I quickly open my eyes and look up. "Did I nip you too hard," I ask, all concern. But Pete is staring over toward a box on top of my dresser. "Are those the shoes that flash red lights when you walk?" he asks.

I give Pete an exasperated look. "Yeah," I say. "I bought them for Jason. What about them?"

"Matthew's been bugging me for weeks to buy him a pair, but I can't find a store that sells them." Pete is all excitement. "Where the hell did you *find* them?"

"Look," I say, trying to keep the testiness out of my voice. "Could we squirt our loads first before we get into a discussion of comparison shopping?"

That shuts Pete up for a moment. He flashes me an apologetic look. "Sorry about that," he says. His mouth curves up into a slow smile. "Why don't you sit on my chest and fuck my face?"

Somewhat mollified, I straddle him, swinging my dick above his face. I shake it at him. "You sure you don't have any more questions about shoes?" I ask him. "It might be a while before you have your mouth free again." Pete grimaces and then just lifts his head, swallowing my dick. He works his tongue around it as I start pumping my hips. The mood returns to me as I watch my dick slide in and out of the mouth of this handsome man. I lean back and let the sensations ripple over me, stroking Pete's cock behind me.

But I find I'm still hungry for dick in my mouth. I pivot around and in the space of two heartbeats we're both just slurping away like two pigs in the trough, both of us sucking cock like there's hell to pay. I run my hand over Pete's firm ass and then burrow it into his crack, rubbing my fingers lightly against his bunghole. Pete quickly shifts so that I get better access. I push my finger inside, up to the first knuckle, and then worm it in deeper. Pete's ass clamps around it in a tight, velvet grip, and as I move on up to the third knuckle, Pete groans loudly. I push hard against his prostate, and he goes wild, thrashing his hips, kicking his legs. I finger-fuck him energetically, his groans bouncing off the ceiling and out the window. *Well*, I think, *I guess I'm giving David Letterman a little competition with the neighbors.*

I pull my finger out. "I think it's time that I give you a good fucking," I say.

Pete grins and spreads his legs wide. "Go for it, man."

I reach over to my bedside table, yank open the drawer, and pull out a packet of condoms and my jar of lube. Pete watches intently as I grease up and sheathe down. I sling his legs over my shoulders and, carefully, with excruciating slowness, I impale his sweet asshole. Pete starts groaning again. I can tell this boy likes to make noise in bed. I settle into a rhythm of quick, sharp thrusts. "Tell me, Pete," I grunt, between strokes. "Where'd you buy those neat Dockers your kid was wearing in that photo of yours?"

Pete looks at me startled, then laughs. "OK, are we even now?" he asks.

I shove my dick all the way up his ass and leave it there, grinding my hips against him. Pete gasps. "No," I grunt. "Not till I fuck you silly." I bend down and plant my mouth over Pete's. We play dueling tongues as I pummel his ass good.

Pete twists around and we switch to doggy-style, my hands anchoring his hips, his body pushing hard against mine. I slide my hands up his torso, kneading the hard muscle, my thumbs rubbing against the tough little nubs of his nipples. I twist them roughly, and Pete cries out. I wrap my arms around him and he pulls his body tight against mine, my chest sliding over his sweat-slicked back. I reached down and wrap my hand around his dick, stroking him in time to the thrusts of my hips. He shudders, and leans his head back, and I seize the opportunity to thrust my tongue deep in his ear. "Sweet Jesus, can you ever fuck!" he groans.

We settle into a steady rhythm, me plowing Pete's ass, Pete fucking my hand, our bodies pressed together, front to back, the sweat shining on our skin. My breath rasps in and out of my lungs, I can feel the sweat trickle down my face, and each thrust of my dick sends a thrill of sensation through my body. Pete gives a low whimper, and as I skewer him, the whimper turns into a long trailing groan. I reach down and cup his balls in my hand; they're tight against his body, ready to drop a load. I give them a squeeze and Pete's body spasms in my arms. He cries out loudly as his load squirts into my hand, coating my fingers with his thick, creamy jizz. I hold on to his body as it bucks in my arms, until he falls forward, spent. I continue pumping his ass, feeling my load being pulled out from my balls. I give a loud groan.

Pete turns his head toward me. "If you're going to shoot," he growls, "I want to see it."

"OK, fucker," I pant. "Here goes."

I pull out of his ass and rip off the condom. Pete turns in the bed so that he's facing me, his eyes watching intently. A few, quick strokes of my hand is enough to push me over the edge. I groan again and push my hips forward. My jizz splatters against Pete's face in ropy wads. "Yeah," Pete growls. "Shoot that load." He reaches up and twists my nipples as the last of my jizz spews out. I bend down and lick it off, my tongue trailing along his cheeks and eyes, kissing his lips.

We lie in bed together for a long time, my head on Pete's chest. I can feel his heart beat against my cheek. After a few minutes I drift off into sleep.

The next morning is a repeat of last night, only this time, Pete gets to fuck me instead. By the time we finally crawl out of bed, it's almost 11 o'clock. I fix Pete a cup of coffee and pour one for myself as well.

We sip in silence, feeling the morning-after shyness of strangers who have fucked the night before. "Does Jason like miniature golf?" he finally asks.

"Yeah," I answer. "He loves it."

"There's a good course right across from the Oakland Coliseum," he says. "Maybe the four of us can take in a round some time."

We make a date for golf for Tuesday night. As I kiss Pete good-bye, I press up against his body. "The Mervyn's over on Geary Boulevard," I whisper in his ear. Pete gives me a quizzical look. "That's where I bought the shoes."

Pete grins. "Thanks. Maybe I can pick Matthew up a pair this weekend." He kisses me again and leaves.

I close the door, return to the bedroom, and slip off my robe. As I shower, I call up the sensation of Pete's naked flesh pressed tonight against mine. My dick begins to stiffen thinking about next Tuesday. After miniature golf is over and the kids have been dropped off at their respective moms' places, then it'll be the dads' turn for fun and games. I can hardly fuckin' wait.

WHEN ANGELO COMES

It's the first sunny day after a week of rain, and I have Lionel wheel me out to the grassy area by the duck pond. The ground is still soggy, and the wheels sink into the soft mud. "I'm going to have to take you back to the terrace, Mr. Green," Lionel says, and he starts to tug the chair out of the twin ruts we've created.

"No, wait," I say. "Just let me stay for a little while, OK?" I like it here by the pond, watching the sunlight play on the water and the mallards paddling around. It's the first time I've been out in days, and the thought of just sitting here, feeling the sun on my face, is very appealing.

Lionel looks hesitant. "I can't stay here with you," he says. "I got to look after the others too."

"I'll be fine, really," I say. I can hear the edge to my voice. "Angelo's coming by in a little while," I add, making my tone friendlier. "He'll wheel me back to my room. Just tell him I'm out here when he shows up, OK?"

Lionel stands there, gauging the situation. "All right," he finally says. I can tell he's still uneasy about this arrangement. I feel a flash of irritation, but then, I guess it'd be his ass on the line if I rolled into the pond and drowned among the ducks. Or some other, equally senile thing.

He turns to go. "One last thing, Lionel," I say. Lionel stops and turns toward me again. "You got a cigarette you can spare?"

Lionel shakes his head as he fishes one out of his shirt pocket. "You're hell-bent on getting my ass fired, aren't you, Mr. Green?" he says, as he hands one to me.

"It'll be our little secret," I say. I stick it in my mouth, and Lionel lights it for me. He leaves me there, puffing away, staring out at the pond. This is my first cigarette in weeks. I inhale deeply, feeling the smoke make the heady trip down into my lungs. I look down at the cigarette dangling between my fore and middle fingers. *What an old man's hand,* I think. *All those wrinkles and veins. What a crock of shit old age is.* I take another drag and look out over the pond.

Mike and I are standing on the edge of Stowe Lake in Golden Gate Park, watching the ducks bobbing on the water's surface. There's a light rain falling and we've taken shelter in the Japanese pagoda, perched on the lake's shore and deserted now, except for us. Mike pulls me to him and kisses me, snaking his tongue into my mouth. He reaches down and cups my hard dick, straining against the rough denim of my jeans. "Sweet Jesus, Jack, you are so goddamn beautiful," he murmurs. He tugs the zipper of my jeans down and slips his hand inside.

"Mike..." I say, glancing around.

But Mike will not be put off. He pulls my dick out and starts stroking it. After a few seconds he drops to his knees and slides his lips down the shaft. I sigh and push my hips forward. Mike makes serious, hungry love to my dick, dragging his tongue up its length, twisting his head from side to side. I close my eyes and let the sensations sweep over me as the rain beats out a tattoo on the pagoda's roof.

"Enjoying this nice day, Jack?" I hear a voice say. I turn, and there's Angelo, smiling, in a blue checked cotton shirt and khaki slacks, the sun gleaming off his crisp black hair.

I give a snort of laughter. "Actually, I was reminiscing," I say. "Or something to that effect." I hold out my hand, and he shakes it. Angelo's grasp is firm and dry. I can feel the ridge of calluses in his palm from the weights he works out with. "You're looking good," I say. "Whatever you're doing, keep doing it."

Angelo's smile widens, and his teeth gleam in his dark face. He glances out toward the mallards quacking at each other contentedly. "I like ducks," he finally says. He looks toward me again. "When I was a kid, my dad used to take me and my kid brother, Joey, to the park to feed the ducks." He laughs. "Once, Joey tried to feed one by hand and he fell in. Dad and I had to fish him out."

I laugh along with him. I try to picture Angelo as a young boy on a family outing. It's an attractive image. A breeze comes in from across the water, ruffling Angelo's hair, and he closes his eyes to receive it. Angelo is by nature a sensualist. I take in the handsome head with its strong chin and finely molded nose, the muscular neck. "Maybe we should head back inside, now," I say gently. "That sun is getting hot."

Angelo's eyes are friendly. "Sure thing, Jack."

He wheels me back to my room, locking the door behind him. I turn on the CD player. The room fills with Louis Armstrong singing "Satin Doll." Angelo turns to me, eyebrows raised. "The usual, Jack? Or do you want something different?"

"Naw, Angelo," I smile. "The usual will be just fine."

Angelo starts pacing up and down the room, swaying to the beat of the music. He pulls off his shirt and lets it drop to the floor, as Louie's gravelly voice growls out the lyrics.

Angelo steps into the pool of light created by the late morning sun slanting through the blinds. Bands of light and shadow play along his torso, highlighting every cut of muscle. Angelo has a smooth, tight body, not overly developed but still nicely chiseled. He slides his hands across his pectorals and down the ridged bands of his abdominals. He kicks off his loafers and pulls his socks off. I sit there in my wheelchair, hardly breathing, my eyes fixed on him. Angelo unzips his fly, slowly, teasingly. He's not wearing any underwear, and his pubes peek out from the open flaps of his pants.

Slowly, lovingly, Angelo slips his pants down past his hips and lets them fall around his ankles. He steps out of them, kicking them aside. My heart is racing. If I were hooked to a monitor, like some of the old coots are in this place, I'm sure the nurses would be breaking down the door now. "Just stand there," I croak. "In the sunlight."

Angelo's lips curl up into a slow, lazy smile. He lets the sun play over his mocha skin, swaying gently, his half-hard cock swinging heavily between his thighs. I can see why a man's dick is some- times called a root. That's what Angelo's looks like: a thick, fleshy, tree root, roped with veins. The red tip of his cock head pushes out of the surrounding folds of foreskin like a bud coming to bloom in one of those stop-frame photo sequences. Angelo's balls are low-hanging and swollen, resting like two eggs in the fleshy sac.

Angelo wraps his hand around his dick and starts stroking it, his face dreamy, detached, his eyes shut.

"Open your eyes," I say roughly. "Look at me while you're beating off."

Angelo opens his eyes and pins me with his gaze. His irises are dark brown, almost black, blending in with the pupils, giving his stare a heightened intensity in the dim room. He thrusts his hips toward me and quickens the pace of his strokes. I just sit there, unmoving, breathing hard, as I watch the coltish head and neck, the muscular young body gleaming with a sheen of sweat. *Sweet Jesus,* I think. *It's visions like this that make me believe there is a God.*

"Turn around," I order. "Slowly."

Angelo obeys. I stare at the muscular back, the broad shoulders that taper down to the narrow hips, the sweet, perfect ass, its flesh so tender and smooth. Angelo keeps turning until he's facing me again. A crisp lock of hair falls across his forehead, and his eyes have a glazed cast to them. The song on the CD ends, and there's a brief silence filled only with Angelo's quick grunts and the slapping sound of his hand sliding up and down his dick. Then the next song comes on, "Sophisticated Lady."

Angelo is breathing heavily now. "I could shoot anytime now, Jack," he pants.

"Go ahead," I growl. "On my face."

Angelo steps forward until he's standing right in front of me. He arches his back and groans loudly, and suddenly a volley of sperm blasts from his dick and splatters against my face, followed by another and then another. I receive this spermy blessing gratefully, with closed eyes and open mouth. Angelo's body convulses with each pulse of his dick until, with a final shudder, he's done.

I open my eyes again and look at Angelo, standing naked in front of me. He smiles, rueful and amused, and his beauty, once more, cuts through me like a surgeon's scalpel. I feel his come drip down my face sluggishly, and I scoop up a dollop of it with two fingers. I lick the fingers thoughtfully. "Rum raisin," I say. "My favorite flavor."

Angelo laughs. He gets a washcloth and towel for me from the bathroom, and as I clean up, he pulls on his clothes. When he's done, I open the drawer to the nightstand and pull out a wad of twenties. I peel off five of them and place them in Angelo's hand.

"Thanks, Jack," he says. He raises his eyebrows. "Same time next week?"

"You got it," I say.

We shake hands, a rather silly formality given the intimacy of just a few minutes ago, but I like this ritual of closure. "On your way out, would you tell Lionel to come here?" I ask. I feel exhausted. I need to have Lionel put me to bed so I can take a nap.

"Sure thing," Angelo says. He closes the door behind him, and I close my eyes.

What I excites me most about Mike when I have sex with him is his face. Or rather the expression on his face. Every time we fuck, he has this look of wonder. With every stroke, his eyes grow wide, his lips part as if he's never experienced any of these pleasures before and never even knew they existed. I plunge into his ass with sure, swift strokes, and when I'm full in, I grind my hips slowly.

"Oh, Jesus, Jack," Mike groans. His dick is fully hard, twitching, and he reaches down and starts beating off, the strokes of his hand in sync with each thrust of my hips. My face is inches above his, our eyes are locked together, our gaze unwavering. Beads of sweat trickle down my face and splash onto him. "You are so goddamn beautiful," Mike pants. "So goddamn, fuckin' beautiful." One final thrust sends me over the edge and I groan loudly, my body spasming. "Yeah, baby," Mike croons. "Shoot your load. Let me feel it." It's decades before AIDS; we have nothing but contempt for rubbers, and my dick pulses its spermy load deep up the farther reaches of Mike's asshole.

Lionel comes in and lifts me out of my wheelchair and into the bed. I sink into the mattress and think about Angelo, about how quickly time passes, about the time when Angelo himself will finally have to pay some young man who isn't even born yet to come to his room and jerk off for him. I close my eyes and let sleep come embrace me like a lover.

A STAR IS BORN

Mom walked into the living room, her arms full of groceries, Buzz following right behind her with the rest of the bags. I was sitting on the couch, watching *Cop Jizz,* one of my favorite Butch O'Horrigan porn videos. I was at the part where Officer Butch had two burglars "assume the position," palms against the wall, legs spread out, as he fucked one and then the other while reading them their Miranda rights. "Good heavens!" Mom exclaimed. "Are you still watching that trash? You were glued to t2he screen when I left the house this morning!"

"That's all Jude does," Buzz smirked. "Watch porn videos and read about the lives of porn stars in his smut magazines." His voice became singsong. "Jude wants to be a porn star too. Just like his idol, Butch O'Horrigan." Lucky for Buzz Mom was there, or I'd have jumped up and slugged his ugly face.

"Oh, stop it, Buzz," Mom said impatiently. She turned toward me. Both burglars were on their knees now, eyes closed and mouths open as Butch squirted his thick, hot load onto their faces. "Turn that fool thing off, Jude," she said, "and help me unload these groceries."

In the kitchen, Buzz and I took the cans out of the paper sacks and started placing them in the cupboard. I glanced over and saw that Mom's back was turned to us. I leaned over toward Buzz. "The minute Mom leaves the room, I'm going to pound your butt good," I whispered.

"The only thing you can pound is your pud," Buzz whispered back.

That night over dinner Buzz wouldn't stop needling me about how I wanted to go to Hollywood and be a porn star. It didn't take long before I was holding my fork and knife tight enough to make

BOB VICKERY

my knuckles white. I slammed my fist on the table. "Shut up!" I snarled. "You don't know anything, you big jerk. Why couldn't I be a porn star?"

Dad snorted, and Mom threw me an exasperated look. "Oh, Jude, you can't possibly be serious," she said.

"Why not?" I said turning to her, feeling the blood rush to my face. "I work out at the Y every day! I've got a good, tight body! And my dick's as big as any of those guys' in the videos!"

"It's not as big as Butch's," Buzz taunted. I gave him a murderous look. I glanced at Uncle Jack, but he just watched calmly, saying nothing.

"Jude, will you stop being such a dreamer," Mom said, her voice taking on an edge. "Thousands of young boys across the country want to be porn stars. Just like you. It's just a phase they go through. Quit being such a silly boy."

"*I'm not a boy!*" I shouted. Everyone at the table stared at me, shocked by my tone.

"Don't you talk to your mother like that," Dad growled, his eyes burning holes in me.

I jumped to my feet and glowered at them all, even Uncle Jack. "I'm a man, not a boy. I'm 18 years old," I said, feeling tears sting my eyes. "I'm grown up. And I know, deep down, that if given half a chance, I could be as big a porn star as anyone."

Buzz laughed raucously.

I raced up to my room and slammed the door behind me, flinging myself on my bed.

A few minutes later I heard the bedroom door open and shut, but I didn't look up. I felt the bed sink as someone sat beside me. "It's tough when no one shares your dream, isn't it?" I heard Uncle Jack's voice say.

I turned my tear-streaked face to him. "Oh, Uncle Jack, I know I could be a porn star. I just know it! And all they do is laugh at me."

"I know, Jude," Uncle Jack sighed. Neither one of us said anything for a long while. Uncle Jack laid his hand on my shoulder. "Would it make you feel any better if I told you I think you'd make one helluva porn star?" He chuckled. "If you pardon my French."

"Oh, Uncle Jack," I sobbed. I gave him a big hug.

Uncle Jack broke away. "This is for you," he said, stuffing something into my hand. I opened my fingers and saw a crumpled wad of bills. I counted out $400.

"Uncle Jack!" I gasped.

"It's yours, Jude," Uncle Jack grinned. "Go to Hollywood. Follow your dream. Take a stab at being a porn star. If it doesn't work out, at least you can't say you never tried."

"Uncle Jack, I can't take your money!" I said, my head swimming.

Uncle Jack chuckled. "It's mine to give, Jude. I've been hustling my ass down at the piers ever since I first moved to this podunk town seven years ago. I've earned it fair and square." He winked. "Just don't tell your Mom. She's such a tightass."

The next day Uncle Jack drove me to the train station. It was just the two of us; Mom and Dad refused to ride along to see me off on "this fool's chase" as Mom called it. I stood on the empty train platform with Uncle Jack.

"I better get on board," I said. My heart was beating harder than a piston.

"You scared, kid?" Uncle Jack asked, his eyes regarding me shrewdly.

I smiled weakly. "My knees are knocking together, if you want to know the truth."

Uncle Jack thrust a package in my hands. "Here," he said gruffly. "This might help."

Surprised, I tore open the wrapping. "Uncle Jack!" I gasped. "It's your Jeff Stryker dildo!"

"It's yours now, kid," Uncle Jack said grinning. "I thought it might bring you luck."

I felt a lump rise in my throat. "But Uncle Jack, you take this wherever you go! You're never without it!"

Uncle Jack shrugged. "It's time to pass it on to the next generation." He smiled. "You'll need it more than me, anyway. You're going to have to really practice your ass work if you want to be a porn star."

I couldn't speak for a few seconds. "I'll think of you every time I use this, Uncle Jack," I finally said, my voice quivering with emotion.

Uncle Jack took out his handkerchief and blew his nose. "Go on," he said gruffly. "Get out of here before I start bawling like some old woman."

The train started pulling away. I gave Uncle Jack a quick hug, tears in my eyes, and jumped onto the moving stairs. I stuck my head out the car's window and waved. Uncle Jack waved back at me from the platform. He stayed there, still waving. "Don't forget to write!" he called out after me. A few seconds later, the train rounded a bend and he was out of sight.

Things were hopping back at the quarter booth section in Frenchy's Adult Bookstore, with me on my feet (and knees) all day, servicing the customers. There was a brief lull between the lunch-time crowd and the first wave of the after-work rush hour. I stole a moment to step outside and get a breath of fresh air. Spike and Cowboy were already there, leaning against the plate-glass window, talking and laughing. They were all right guys, I guess, but sometimes I got a little miffed at how often they goofed off, leaving me with all the customers impatiently waiting for their blow jobs. I didn't want to get Spike and Cowboy in Dutch with the boss, so I never said anything to Frenchy. But it wasn't fair.

"Hey, squirt," Spike said, grinning. "How's it hanging?"

"OK, I guess," I said. I wiped my brow with the back of my hand. "I'm beat."

"You work too hard," Cowboy said, sticking a piece of gum in his mouth. "You don't have to be such a damn perfectionist every time you suck some customer's dick."

He shouldn't chew gum, I thought. *It makes him look cheap.* "I believe in giving the customer his money's worth," I said. "Besides, it gives me a chance to work on my oral technique for when I finally get a role in a porn movie."

Spike snickered in a way unpleasantly reminiscent of Buzz. "You still chasing that rainbow, kid? I thought four months in this soulless town would have beaten that out of you."

"I never thought stardom'd drop in my lap," I said, a trifle defensively. "All I need is one lucky break, a chance to show what I've got."

"Kid," said Cowboy, shaking his head, "we all come to this town with dreams of making it as porn stars." He grinned, but his eyes looked wistful. "But let's face it. The closest any of us is going to get to a porn video is on our knees in one of the booths back there. The sooner you realize that, the better." He spit his gum out onto the street. "Time to get back to work." He turned and walked back inside Frenchy's. Spike followed, and with a sigh, I joined them.

There was already a good crowd gathered by the video booths. I noticed Mr. Werner, a regular, heading the line, dressed nattily in an Armani sports coat and blue silk tie. The guy was a bantam cock, short and wiry, his dark red hair (just beginning to gray at the temples) clipped short. Spike sidled up to him, smiling, but Mr. Werner directed his sharp, blue gaze in my direction. He lifted his eyebrows, and I nodded. I walked into one of the booths, slipped some tokens in, and waited. Mr. Werner joined me a few seconds later.

"Hey, Jude," he said, smiling, as he unbuckled his belt. "Life treating you OK?"

"Sure, Mr. Werner," I said, dropping to my knees. "I can't complain." I tugged his slacks and Calvins down to his ankles. His thick, red cock bobbed in front of me, half-hard, twitching in the light that flickered from the video that was playing. "Nice," I murmured, wrapping my hand around it, stroking it to full hardness. I always made sure to give Mr. Werner special attention. Both Spike and Cowboy suspected he was a video producer of some sort. Since they usually thought that of any client who wore a necktie and didn't pick his nose in public, I took this claim with a certain grain of salt. Still, you never could tell.

I skinned back Mr. Werner's foreskin, gently kissed the fat cock head, and then slid my lips slowly down his shaft. Mr. Werner sighed. "That's a good boy," he murmured. He started pumping his hips, and I twisted my head back and forth to give his dick maximum exposure to my tongue. I cradled his balls in my hand and then tugged on them gently while I slid my other hand under his shirt, kneading his torso, tweaking each nipple. "Yeah," Mr. Werner sighed. "That's right." He slid his dick in and out of my mouth in an easy, dreamy rhythm.

I heard two short beeps. "Damn," he muttered, fishing a cell phone out of his jacket pocket. "Yeah?" he snapped. I went back to sucking him off. "This isn't a good time to talk, Brian," he growled. I heard the drone of a voice from the other end of the phone. "He did what?" Mr. Werner barked. More drone. "That little bastard!" He shut the phone, scowling, and put it back in his pocket. He shook his head, pulling his dick out of my mouth. "Sorry, kid," he said. "I don't think I'll be shooting a load after all. I got to tend to business problems."

There goes my tip, I thought. "Nothing serious, I hope?

Mr. Werner pulled up his trousers. "Serious enough! We're shooting a video, and the star's personal fluffer took a powder. The star's throwing a major sulk in his dressing room."

I'll be darned! I thought. *Spike and Cowboy were right about Mr. Werner after all!* Mr. Werner slapped his forehead. "Hey, wait a second!" He grabbed me by the shoulders and looked me in the eye. "Kid, how would you like a job as a fluffer?"

I stared at him, my mouth open. "You mean I'd actually get to work on the set of a porn video?"

Mr. Werner smiled. "Get the stars out of your eyes, son. There's nothing glamorous about being a fluffer. It's just grunt work." He looked around the booth. "Still, it's got your current gig beat, hands down." He smoothed back his hair. "Well, what do you say? You want the job?"

"Heck, yes, Mr. Werner!" I exclaimed, my heart pounding.

Sound technicians, cameramen, gofers, and assistants swarmed around us as Mr. Werner and I walked onto the set. It looked like they were filming some kind of cowboy fantasy: Spotlights were trained on bales of hay stacked in a mock-up of a stable. Mr. Werner led me to a chubby, pink-faced man in a green and aqua aloha shirt. "Sam," he said. "Meet the new fluffer." Mr. Werner turned to me. "This is Sam Kincaid, the director."

Kincaid wore the expression of a water buffalo being savaged by a pack of hyenas. His eyes quickly scanned me. "You ready to go to work?" he snapped. "That is," he added, his voice thick with sarcasm, "if we can convince our *star* that you're a suitable replacement for *Eduardo*."

"Sure thing, Mr. Kincaid!" I exclaimed.

"Then start fluffing," Kincaid said. He nodded curtly toward a nearby dressing room door. "He's in there. Good luck. You're going to need it." He turned away and started talking to one of the lighting guys.

I walked up to the door and knocked timidly. "Yeah?" a baritone voice said from inside. I opened the door. Inside, a man sat at a dressing table with his back to me, wearing a cowboy hat and a pair of scuffed-up boots. And nothing else. I quickly took in the muscular back and broad shoulders tapering down to a narrow waist. The man pivoted around on his chair and faced me.

"Oh, my God," I gasped. "You're Butch O'Horrigan!"

Butch gave me a deadpan glance. "No shit," he said. His eyes flicked down my body and back to my face. "And who the fuck are you?"

"I—I'm the new fluffer."

"The hell you are!" Butch sneered. His blue eyes narrowed. "You get your ass out of here and tell Kincaid that either Eduardo fluffs me or I walk."

All I was aware of was how completely and utterly *suckable* Butch's meaty cock looked, nestled between his muscular thighs, the head peeking coyly from the uncut foreskin. I swallowed and licked my lips. "Mr. O'Horrigan," I said, my voice quivering with emotion. "I am your biggest fan *ever*. I own every one of your videos, from *Come-Soaked Cocksuckers* to *Cop Jizz*. I thought that scene in *Dick Pig Chow Down* when you squirted seven loads in 30 minutes was...inspirational. It changed my life." I meekly took a step forward. "I realize that you're used to fluffers more...sophisticated than someone like me." I took another step forward and knelt down in front of him. I hesitantly put my hands on Butch's knees and slowly spread them apart. "But if you do me the incredible *honor* of letting me suck your dick, not as a fluffer but as your most ardent admirer, I will die a happy man."

Butch looked down at my face, still scowling. But he didn't shake my hands off. "How did you like my performance in *Cop Jizz*?"

he finally asked. His eyes flashed angrily. "The fuckin' critics said it was too *mannered*."

"They're ignorant clods," I said passionately. "You were...transcendent in *Cop Jizz*. I swear, I cried at the end when you fucked your partner one last time after he'd been shot by that street punk."

"That *was* my best scene," Butch agreed thoughtfully. His eyes darted down to me again. After a second, his mouth twitched up into a smile. "What the hell. Let's give it a try." He spread his knees farther apart. "OK, kid, get to work and chow down."

With my heart hammering, I cradled his dong, still massive even when limp, gently in the palm of my hand, the head flaring out magnificently like a dark, fleshy plum. I stared at the meaty tube in awe. I knew Butch's dick as well as I knew my own, I'd seen it hundreds of times in dozens of videos, lusted and slavered over it, shot copious loads in honor of it. And now it was resting in my hand, waiting for me to suck it. The air hummed with unreality.

I bent forward and pressed my lips gently against Butch's cock head, then opened my mouth wider and slid my lips down the shaft until my nose was pushed tightly against Butch's honey-blond and neatly clipped pubes. *Oh, my God!* I marveled. *I actually have Butch O'Horrigan's dick in my mouth!* I twisted my head from side to side as my lips slid back up the fleshy shaft. Butch gave a soft sigh, and I felt his dick slowly harden in my mouth. I increased the tempo of my cock sucking, sliding my lips up and down the increasingly tumescent shaft, cradling Butch's bull nuts in my hand. I proceeded to make serious love to Butch's dick, showering it with all the pent-up devotion I'd been feeling for it all these long years, kissing it, sucking on it, rolling my tongue over it, swallowing it deep down my throat and then pulling my lips up the shaft again with agonizing, sucking slowness. Butch breathed heavily, thrusting his hips up to meet each downward slide of my mouth. My hands slid up the smoothly shaven torso, kneading the hard muscle, tweaking each nipple. I slid a hand down between Butch's legs, under his low-hanging nut sac to the pucker of his ass. I worked a finger up the tight hole, knuckle by slow knuckle, slowly corkscrewing it. Butch gave a groan that was loud and heartfelt. He clamped his hands tightly around my head and fucked my mouth in deep, sure strokes. His eyes were closed and he was panting heavily. His body suddenly trembled.

Butch quickly pushed me away. "Whoa!" he gasped. "That was close!" He rolled his eyes. "Kincaid would shit a brick if I shot a load here instead of out on the set." He glanced down at me. "I owe you an apology, kid. You're good. Damn good." Butch climbed to his feet and stretched. "It's show time!" he said, winking at me. He walked out of the room, his now stiff cock bobbing between his muscular thighs.

I slowly climbed to my feet, still tasting Butch's dick in my mouth. When I finally returned to the set it looked like I'd walked into a funeral. Kincaid sat on his canvas chair, his face buried in his hands. Butch stood next to him, his expression glum and his hard-on at three-quarters mast and sinking fast.

"What's wrong?" I asked.

Kincaid didn't say anything. After a couple of beats, Butch looked over at me. "They just found Buck Hardon, my costar, passed out drunk on his dressing room floor."

Kincaid moaned. "I swear to God, I'm going to go back to filming hemorrhoid commercials. I can't take porno anymore." He looked around the set with bleary eyes. "It cost me $4,000 to set up today's shoot and that son of a bitch pulls a stunt like this. I'm going to kill the motherfucker. I'm going to put Ben-Gay in his lube."

"Wait a second," Butch said, looking at me. "I've got an idea."

"Oh, Jesus," Kincaid groaned. "Aren't things bad enough?"

Butch nodded toward me. "Why don't you put the kid in the scene? He's not bad-looking. And he gives great head. I can personally swear to that."

Kincaid regarded him blankly. "Let me get this straight," he finally said in a low, quiet voice. "You're suggesting that we put the *fluffer* in the costarring role of this video?"

"What have you got to lose?" Butch asked. "You're going to have to pay the crew anyway. And me," he added pointedly. "You might as well put us to work."

Kincaid just sat there with his face in his hands. After a couple of minutes he raised his head and looked dully at me. "What do you say to this?" he asked, his tone flat and hopeless.

"Mr. Kincaid," I said slowly, my heart pounding hard enough to crack a rib, "my only reason for living is to be a porn star. If you put me in this video, I swear by all I hold sacred that I won't disappoint you."

"The kid's got spunk," Butch said. "You have to give him that."

"The only spunk I'm interested in is what he squirts during the money shot." Kincaid snapped. He rubbed his eyes tiredly. "What the hell. If I'm going to go down the tubes, I might as well pull all the stops out." He turned to the makeup guy. "Get this guy ready. We shoot in 10 minutes." He looked at me. "What's your name, kid?"

"Jude," I said excitedly. "Jude Garland."

"Of course," Kincaid laughed mirthlessly. "What else would it be?

Butch glared at me. "You've been riding my ass for the whole damn cattle drive, Jeb," he growled. "It's time you got taken down a notch or two."

"Oh, yeah? I snarled. "You think you're *man* enough for the job?"

"I know I am," Butch snarled back. "The question is, Are you man enough to *take* it?" He grabbed me by my flannel shirt and threw me onto the bales of hay. With a couple of quick tugs he ripped my shirt off, followed shortly by my boots and jeans. I snarled and cursed, but it didn't take long before I was stripped naked and on my back, Butch towering over me, scowling, his thick, red dick as stiff as dicks get and bobbing heavily between his thighs. My own dick was just as stiff and just as ready for action. Butch bent down and planted is mouth on mine. We kissed hard and furiously, and I snaked my tongue into his mouth.

"Cut!" Kincaid said. He turned to an assistant. "Lube Jude up and get a condom on Butch." There was a flurry of activity, assistants powdering me dry, combing back my hair, greasing up my asshole, as others slid the condom down Butch's massive dong. "Get a shot of Butch from down and behind," Kincaid ordered a cameraman. "Right when he slides his dick in." He stepped back, and all the assistants raced off the set.

I lay flat on my back on the bales of hay, Butch bending down over me, the cameraman squatting behind him. Another cameraman perched in the scaffolding above us, and a third one knelt alongside of us. "OK, baby," Butch whispered to me. "Let's make this good!"

"Action!" Kincaid called out.

I felt the tip of Butch's dick poke against the pucker of my asshole. I raised my hips up to give him better access, and Butch slid in, inch by slow inch, his face right above mine. I locked my gaze with his as he skewered me, and for an instant I forgot that this was a film set, all I was aware of was that right now, at this moment, Butch O'Horrigan's huge dick was pushing up into my ass. "Oh, yeah," I groaned. Butch started right off pumping his hips, thrusting his thick dick in and out of my ass with long, skillful strokes, his heavy balls slamming against me. He paused for a moment, his dick full up my ass, and ground his hips. I groaned loudly and pulled his head down, frenching him hard. When Butch resumed pounding my ass, I thrust my hips up, meeting him stroke for stroke, my legs wrapped tightly around him. Butch sat up, straddling me, giving the cameraman a chance to shoot the length of his muscular torso. I reached up and twisted Butch's nipples, *hard,* at the same time that I squeezed my ass muscles tight. Butch looked down at me, startled, and the groan that escaped his lips seems to have nothing to do with acting. All those hours of working out with Uncle Jack's Jeff Stryker dildo were paying off.

Kincaid stood in our line of sight, making a frantic, rolling gesture with his hands. I had no clue what he meant, but Butch immediately wrapped his arms around us and rolled us off the bales onto the floor of the set. I was on top now, astride Butch, and I squirmed my body against him, leaning forward, giving the cameraman a clear shot of Butch's dick sliding in and out of my asshole. I was amazed how light and in control I felt! I rode Butch's dick like a race car, effortlessly, smoothly, hugging the curves, each downward slide of mine in perfect sync with Butch's upward thrusts. I could *feel* Butch being carried along, and I let my instincts take over, coaxing him to the brink of shooting, gauging by the stiffness of his dick and the volume of his groans how close he was getting, then slowing down at the last second, pulling back, only to whip him up to a frenzy again. I'd got my right hand wrapped around my own dick, stroking it with each thrust of Butch's, feeling the orgasm beginning to pull from my balls, getting closer and closer to its own release. The lights were baking both of us, and sweat streamed down our bodies, stinging my eyes, slicking our torsos, making our skin *gleam*. Butch's eyes were wide and startled, and either he was giving the performance of his life or else he really was losing himself in the moment, oblivious to the cameras and crews around us. Kincaid gave me the "wrap it up" signal, but I didn't think Butch was even aware of Kincaid anymore. *It's up to me now,* I thought. Butch pulled out, with only the tip of his dick still inside my ass. As he slid back in, I squeezed my ass muscles *tight* while I twisted his nipples. Butch cried out loudly, pulled out and whipped his condom off. I couldn't see his spurting cock, but I could feel his hot load splatter against my back, one volley after another, his jizz sliding down across my skin in a thick, sluggish trail.

Kincaid nodded to me, and it just took me a few quick strokes to push me over the edge. My dick throbbed in my hand as my load spurted out, slamming against Butch's chin, his cheeks, into his open mouth. "Oh, yeah," Butch groaned, "soak me good." I cried out loudly, projecting for dramatic effect, my body spasming with each pump of my dick. By the time I was done, Butch's face was coated in a thick mask of spunk. I bent down and dragged my tongue across his face, lapping up the creamy drops, and ended with giving Butch a lingering kiss.

"Cut!" Kincaid shouted. There was a moment of silence, and then the entire crew burst into applause. Kincaid rushed up, his eyes shining. "Sweet Jesus, that was fuckin' amazing!"

Butch looked up at me, grinning, one drop of come which I missed still dangling from his chin. "Kid," he said, "you got what it takes! You're going to be a *star*!"

I'd never worn a tuxedo before, and I found it all a strange experience: the stiffness of the collar, the tight fit of the cummerbund. Mom was sitting next to me, all decked out in blue taffeta, with a gardenia corsage on her left shoulder. Buzz was sitting one seat beyond her, his wrists and ankles sticking out of his rental tux, and Dad and Uncle Jack sat on my other side. Butch was at the podium onstage, in front of the banner proclaiming "Gay Adult Video Awards." Because he'd won Best Actor last year, it was his duty to announce this year's winner. He read off the names of the nominees, and when he got to mine, he gave me a quick glance and winked. He fumbled with the envelope, and there was a collective hush as we all waited. He pulled the card from the envelope, glanced at it, and beamed: "And the winner is...Jude Garland!"

There was a thunderous crash of applause. I climbed to my feet, dazed, and stumbled up the stage steps to the podium. "Way to go, kid," Butch whispered in my ear as he handed me the statuette, his hand lightly patting my ass.

I stood at the podium, clutching the award, my chest so tight that I could hardly breathe as I looked out at the sea of faces before me. Mom was sobbing, and Buzz was on his feet whooping and pumping the air with his fist. Dad was clapping wildly, and Uncle Jack beamed. I just stood there, feeling the waves of applause that crashed down on me, one right after the other, the cheers and wolf whistles. *They love me!* I marveled. *They all love me! I'm a* star! Tears streamed down my face as the applause continued to roll over me undiminished.

PORN WRITER

I run into my neighbor Mark in the apartment house lobby on my way out. "Yo, Bob," he says, smiling. "Where you off to so early?" We walk out the front entrance together.

"I'm having breakfast with a friend," I say. "It's kind of a Saturday morning ritual. Gives us a chance to catch up and talk about people who aren't there to defend themselves."

There's a moving van pulled up to the entrance, and the movers are currently in the process of hoisting a grand piano up to a fourth-story window. We watch their progress for a minute. Mark turns to me again. "How's the porn-writing business? Still cranking out the smut?"

"Yeah," I say. "I'm trying something new. I'm writing a story where I'm the hero."

Mark laughs. "Are you serious?"

"Yeah," I say. "Why? You think it's a bad idea?"

Mark shakes his head. "Jeez, Bob. What an exercise in vanity that would be!" His eyes sweep up and down my body. "And besides," he says, grinning, "you're a nice guy but hardly jack-off material. You'd have to do some *major* embellishing."

I smile. "Really?" I say. There's a sharp, snapping sound of a rope breaking, the whistling of air, and a sudden shadow on the sidewalk growing rapidly bigger. Mark looks up. "Holy shit!" he screams. He flings himself to the left, just as the piano comes crashing down on the sidewalk. Splinters of wood and ivory shower over the both of us.

Mark climbs unsteadily to his feet, shaken but unharmed. He looks at me with wide eyes. I smile back. "Gee," I say. "That was close."

Mark stares down at the pile of kindling that was once a piano. He looks at me. He looks at the smashed piano. Then back at me. "You know, Bob," he says slowly, his voice trembling. "I don't think it's such a bad idea after all, you writing a stroke story where you're the hero." He attempts a smile that comes out very sickly. "A hot stud like you...hell, it would be criminal if you *didn't* put yourself into one of your stories. Maybe a whole anthology." He's talking faster now, his words coming out in a jumble. "Hell, I'd give anything to read about you having sex, Bob. It would be so...fuckin'...*hot*!" Perspiration is pouring down his face.

"Stop, Mark," I say, smiling. "You're too kind."

Mark leaves me shortly afterward. When he's half a block away, he breaks out into a fast run. He must have a pressing engagement somewhere.

I get into my car and drive out to my breakfast date with Eddie. Because he lives in the East Bay and I live in San Francisco, we compromise by meeting at a diner in Berkeley. When I get there, I see Eddie with someone I don't know, sitting in a booth by the plate-glass window that overlooks the street. Eddie sees me at the door and waves me over.

"Hey, Bob," he says, grinning. "How ya doing?"

"I'm doing all right," I say. I look over at the guy sitting next to Eddie. Eddie catches my glance. "This is my friend Jack," Eddie says. "I ran into him outside and asked him to join us." Jack's face is well-scrubbed and smooth, with cheeks that are pink and cherubic and a mouth that reminds me of a moist keyhole. "Jack just got a novel published," Eddie goes on. "I thought you two might hit it off." Eddie's eyes shift over to Jack. "Jack, this is Bob Vickery. He's a writer too."

I shake Jack's hand. "Congratulations," I say. "Your first book?"

Jack gives a polite smile. "Actually, my fourth."

There's a pause. I notice that Jack doesn't ask me about my writing. Eddie seems to notice this too.

"Bob's been published a lot too," he says.

Jack peers at me over his wire-rimmed glasses. "Oh, really?" he asks. "What's your genre?"

I give him back his polite smile. "Short stories. Mostly erotica."

"Oh," Jack says. "Porn."

"Yeah," I say pleasantly. "I guess you could call it porn."

Jack picks up a knife and uses it to clean under a fingernail. He looks bored. "That's nice," he says.

Eddie sits up. He glances at me and then back at Jack. "Hey," he says, "A lot of talented writers are writing porn nowadays."

Jack gives him a tolerant smile. "Look, I'm not trying to be rude to your friend here, Eddie, but give me a break. There's writing, and then there's hack work." He looks toward me. "No offense, but I think we all know which category porn fits in."

"Wait a second," Eddie says, his voice rising in volume.

I cut him off with a gesture. "Let it drop, Eddie," I say pleasantly. "The man's entitled to his opinion."

Jack glances at his watch. "Oh, jeez, it's late. I have to run." He finishes his coffee and climbs out of the booth. "See you around, Eddie." He turns toward me. "Nice meeting you, Bob. I hope I didn't hurt your feelings."

I give a self-deprecatory wave of my hand. "Not at all," I say. I hold out my hand. "Good luck with your book."

Jack shakes my hand and leaves. Eddie gives me a long, level stare. "You took that very graciously."

I shrug. "It's no big deal. He's probably right about porn writers. I never claimed to be Dostoyevsky."

Jack is outside, standing on the curb, waiting for a break in the traffic. There's a lull in our conversation, and Eddie and I watch him from our booth. Jack steps off the curb and starts a mad dash across the street. He miscalculates. A diesel truck comes tearing down the road and hits him square in the grill. Jack's body flies 20 or so feet into the air and lands in the other lane with a sickening splat that can be heard even 30 feet away and through a quarter inch of plate glass. A cement mixer coming the other way runs over his body and then roars off. What's left in the road is gruesome and stomach wrenching. Suddenly, a pack of dogs come racing around a corner and descend on the bloody pulp, snapping and snarling. They run off, carrying in their slavering jaws various bloody bones with tatters of carrion attached.

Eddie slowly turns and looks at me. I smile. "It seems that Jack has had an accident," I say.

Eddie doesn't say anything for a long time. He swallows and tries to speak. Nothing comes out. He swallows again. "You know, Bob," he finally says. "Have I told you how talented a writer I think you are?"

"No," I say thoughtfully. "I don't think you have. It's nice to hear you finally say it."

Eddie swallows again. "I—I'm sorry. I really love your stories. I think you're a wonderful writer. One of the best."

I raise an eyebrow. "*One* of the best?"

"Th—the best," Eddie says hurriedly.

"Eddie, please," I say, smiling indulgently. "You go too far."

Eddie glances at his watch. "I—I have to go now, Bob." He looks at me, his eyes pleading. Off in the distance, we can faintly hear dogs howling. "That is, if it's all right with you."

I laugh. "Of course it's all right. You don't need my *permission*, Eddie, you big jerk. It's not like you're my slave or anything." I smile. "You're just a character I created." Eddie climbs out of the booth. "Oh, and Eddie," I say. "I'm tired of crossing the Bay Bridge for breakfast. Next Saturday, let's eat somewhere in San Francisco, OK?"

"Sure, sure, Bob," Eddie says. He beats a hasty retreat. I look back at the red stain on the road that is all that's left of Jack. "Poor Jack," I say, shaking my head.

That night I go to the Stud for a drink and a little relaxation. Because it's Saturday, there's a lively crowd and the mood is high. I lean against the wall, sipping my beer, watching the men dancing.

"Can I buy you a drink?"

I turn and see some guy standing to my left, his eyes trained on me. My eyes sweep down his body, taking in the broad shoulders, the chest muscles straining against the tight T-shirt, the pumped-up biceps, the narrow hips, the conspicuous bulge in the too-tight jeans. I look back at his face, noting the flawless set of his features. I stifle a yawn and smile politely, holding up my beer. "Thanks," I say. "But I'm not done with the one I have."

He looks crestfallen. I turn and go back to watching the men on the dance floor. I can see him out of the corner of my eye, shifting his weight from one foot to the other. The song comes to an end, and there's a brief period of silence. I glance at my watch.

The guy lightly puts his hand on my shoulder. I look at him, frowning. His eyes are wide and a startling, clear blue. His mouth is finely molded, and his jawline strong. Of course, there's a cleft in his chin. "Look," he says, "I'm not trying to be pushy, but when I saw you across the room, I had to speak to you. You have this sort of *aura,* I can't put it into words..."

Here we go again, I think. "A sort of brooding masculinity?" I ask.

"Yeah!" he says, excited, "that's it!"

"A quiet, steady calm that hints of smoldering sexual fires?" I ask.

"Yeah," he says, his voice rising, "you got it exactly!" He smiles, flashing teeth that are even and dazzling white.

I look at him more closely. "You look familiar."

He coughs modestly in his hand. "Perhaps you know me through my work. I'm in porn. Gay porn." He grins boyishly and sticks out his hand. "The name's Butch. Butch O'Horrigan."

"Yeah, I recognize you now," I say. "I've seen a bunch of your videos." I shake his hand. "I'm Bob." His grip is firm and dry. He looks at me expectantly. *Oh, well,* I think. *It won't hurt to at least talk with the guy.* "Do you live here in San Francisco?" I ask.

Butch shakes his head. "Naw, I live in L.A. I'm just up here to shoot a flick." He takes a drink from his Evian. "I've spent the entire day today having sex in front of a camera with some of the hottest guys in gay porn. Men that look like fuckin' *gods,* gods with big dicks, that is. But when I saw you just a few minutes ago, I realized that next to you, they were dreck. I could tell by your expression, by the way you hold yourself that you're something special, a man of character. I don't give a shit that your hairline is receding or that you've got a slight paunch or that you're on the rainy side of 40, or that..."

"I think you've made your point," I say.

"I've got to ask you," Butch goes on, "what do you do for a living? Are you a fighter pilot? A race-car driver? A Hollywood stuntman?

I smile indulgently. "Well, actually, since you ask, I'm in the porn business myself. I write it. My name's Bob Vickery."

Butch stares at me, his mouth open, his eyes about to pop out of his head. "Oh, my God!" he whispers.

I raise my eyebrows. "You've heard of me?"

Butch nods his head slowly. "Sweet Jesus," he says softly. "Are you really Bob Vickery?"

I smile and shrug my shoulders modestly. "In the flesh."

"I can't believe it," Butch says, his voice choked. He takes my hand in both of his. "You're an *idol* to me!" He shakes his head in amazement. "This is fuckin' incredible, I'm actually talking to Bob Vickery!"

"Please, stop," I say, laughing modestly.

"Hold on," Butch says. He pulls a beat-up magazine out of his back pocket. "This has your latest story in it. I always carry it around with me." His eyes take on a pleading look. "Do you think you could autograph it for me?"

"Sure," I say, good-naturedly. I take the magazine from him and page through it. I look at him, surprised. "You've ripped out all the pictures of the naked guys!" I say.

Butch gives a gesture of dismissal. "Aw, they got just in the way," he says. "I just buy the magazines to read your stories."

I pull out a pen from my shirt pocket and sign my autograph across the front page of my story "Subway Studs." "Here you go," I say pleasantly, handing the magazine back to Butch.

Butch takes it, his eyes brimming. "I will keep this with me forever. The only way anybody will take this from me is if they pry it from my cold, dead fingers."

"Butch, please," I say.

Butch gives me a searching look. "Look, Bob, I know I'm just a porn star and that all I have to offer you is my muscles, my face, and my nine-inch dick, but could you possibly consider having sex with me tonight?"

I clear my throat. "Butch," I say, "you seem like a nice guy..."

"Please," Butch begs, his expression desperate.

I sigh. "All right. If it means so much to you, I'm willing to go along."

"All right!" Butch says. His eyes are bright with excitement. "I've heard about how good porn writers are in bed. This should be a night to remember for the rest of my life!"

I give a self-deprecating smile. "I'll try my best."

Another man approaches us. "Hi," he says to me, ignoring Butch. "I don't know if you recognize me, but I'm a Calvin Klein underwear model. I just happened to see you from across the room and thought you might want a little company..."

"Fuck off," Butch snarls.

I try to hide my smile.

I lead Butch over to my Porsche, parked just down the block. Butch gives a low whistle. "Nice wheels," he says. "Is it new?"

"I just bought it last week," I say. I laugh. "You wouldn't believe how much money I make writing porn. It comes in faster than I can spend it."

"Whatever they pay you, I'm sure it's not enough," Butch says, his eyes glistening with hero worship.

I reach over and squeeze his thigh. It feels like granite. "You're a sweet guy," I say. "But you really have got to stop giving me all this praise. I'm very modest by nature." We're silent the rest of the ride home.

We don't take three steps inside my apartment before Butch pins me to the wall, his body pressed against mine, his tongue deep down my throat, his bulging crotch rubbing against mine in slow, grinding circles. I reach back and cup his ass with my hands, pushing his hips even harder against me. "I want you so bad, baby," Butch gasps. He begins pulling off my clothes.

"Easy, baby, easy," I murmur, laughing. I gently push him away. "We've got all night."

Butch is panting, and his eyes have a wild, almost crazed look to them. We just barely make it to the bedroom before he's on me again. He pushes me onto the bed and fumbles with my belt. He's so excited, he can't get the buckle undone. He gives a frustrated whimper. I push his hands away and unbuckle my belt for him. I slowly pull down my zipper. "Yeah, that's right," Butch growls. "Get naked." He yanks my jeans down past my hips, hooks his thumbs under the elastic waistband of my boxers and pulls them down too.

His jaw drops down in amazement. "Holy shit!" he says. He looks up at me, his eyes wide. "Are all porn writers so well-hung?"

I smile. "Only when they get to write the story."

Butch quickly strips and jumps into bed with me. He straddles my hips, wrapping his hand around both our dicks, squeezing them together. He slowly strokes them, sliding his hand up and down the twin, meaty shafts. Butch's dick is thick and long and red, the head poking out of the foreskin like some animal climbing out of its burrow. My dick, however, is even thicker and longer. I slide my hands up his torso, feeling the play of muscles, like hard rubber under velvet. I flick both his nipples lightly with my thumbs, then pinch them. Butch groans. "Oh, baby, that feels so good," he moans. I slide my hands over his biceps. They feel like cannonballs.

Butch slides down and buries his face in my balls. I feel his tongue lap over my sac, tasting it, teasing it, sucking on it. I lean my head against the pillow and let myself sink into the sensations. Butch's hot, wet tongue slides up my dick shaft, slowly, lovingly, until it reaches the head. Butch squeezes my dick, first gently, and then with increasing pressure. My cock head deepens in color, from pink to angry red to purple. Butch loosens his grip and presses his lips against it, taking the head into his mouth. He slides his mouth down my fuck pole, his lips nibbling gently, his tongue writhing against it. He's forced to come to a stop before he's even halfway down, but damn if Butch doesn't shift the angle of his head and forge on down. He makes it three quarters of the way down but has to stop again, his mouth pulled back wide by the thickness of my dick shaft. He's breathing heavily through his nose, the air whistling in and out. Butch shifts again, and, impossibly, he continues on down until his nose is mashed against my pubes. No one has ever been able to do that before, though many have certainly tried. I am truly amazed. As Butch's hot mouth slides back up the fleshy pole again, the shaft of my dick reappears, inch by slow inch, like a rabbit Butch is pulling out of a hat. Butch finally pulls away, panting.

"Incredible," I murmur, impressed.

Butch grins. "I once spent the weekend with a sword swallower from a traveling circus. He taught me all sorts of tricks." Butch wraps his hand around my dick again and starts stroking. After a couple of beats, he resumes sucking on it.

"Turn around," I growl. "Let's get a little sixty-nine action going."

Butch pivots his massively muscular body around, and in no time we're chowing down on each other's dick like a couple of sex-crazed cannibals. I look across at Butch and pull his cock out of my mouth. "You having a good time?" I ask.

Butch is sucking on my scrotum. "I'm having a ball," he says, his mouth full. He slides his tongue up the shaft of my giant schlong and starts sucking on it again. His technique is truly masterful, and it only takes a couple of minutes of his skillful mouth before I have to pull out.

"Easy," I pant. "I don't want to come just yet." I look over at Butch. "I'd love to fuck your ass right now. That is, if you think you can handle my throbbing gargantuan fuck muscle."

Butch shakes his head and grins. "I just love the way you porn writers talk!" he says. He looks dubiously at my dick. "Well...I'm willing to give it a try. But you have to go slow."

"I promise," I promise.

I open the drawer to the bedside night table and pull out a condom package and jar of lube. Butch watches with wide eyes. "I never saw a condom so big!" he says, as I pull it out of the package.

"I have to have them made especially for me," I shrug as I roll it down my dick shaft. "The fuckers cost me a bundle, but no commercial brand will fit me."

I sling Butch's legs over my shoulders and guide my sheathed cock into the crack of his ass. With infinite patience, I slowly, lovingly push into his bunghole. Butch grimaces, and a sheen of sweat breaks out on his forehead, but he takes it like a trooper. I pause when I'm halfway in. "Are you OK?" I ask, concerned, but he just nods his head without saying anything, his eyebrows knitted together. I push a couple of more inches in. Butch groans, and I count to 10 before the next long thrust. When I'm finally all the way in, I lie on the bed, next to Butch, not moving, just letting him get used to the feeling of my monstrous dong up his ass. After a couple of minutes of this, I start pumping my hips, slowly at first, but then with a faster tempo. My eyes are locked on Butch's face, ready to quit any time he gives me the signal, but he says nothing. After a while he starts moving his hips in sync with mine, pushing forward to meet each one of my thrusts inside him. He rolls over on top of me, and it doesn't take long before we're enthusiastically boinking, our bouncing bodies making the bedsprings creak in protest.

I wrap a lube-smeared hand around Butch's dick and start stroking him, timing my strokes with each thrust of my hips. Butch groans piteously. "Oh, that feels so good!" he moans. He bends down and kisses me, thrusting his tongue deep down my throat. His body squirms against mine, slick with sweat, and I can feel the muscles of his torso ripple against my flesh.

Butch pins my arms down, his teeth bared, his eyes burning with a fierce light. He wiggles his hips and squeezes his ass muscles tight. I groan loudly. "Damn, that's nice!" I exclaim.

Butch just grins. I wrap my legs around him, and with a quick upward thrust, twist our bodies around, pivoting him onto his back. "OK, baby," I snarl. "Get ready for the plowing of your life!" I push my hips forward, sliding my dick full up Butch's ass. Butch's eyes turn up in their sockets and he whimpers piteously. For a moment I'm afraid I've ruptured the poor guy, and I start to pull out.

"Oh, God," Butch cries out. "Don't stop! Please!"

That's all the encouragement I need. I plant a hand on each of his shoulders and start giving this boy a truly serious fucking, thrusting my Brobdingnagian wand of love repeatedly in and out of his tight, tight ass. Butch groans loud enough to wake the dead or at least the neighbors, pushing his hips up to meet me, tightening his velvet ass-muscles around my meaty schlong, squeezing hard. My body shudders from the sudden stab of pleasure, and soon my groans are mingled with Butch's. We wrestle and tussle in bed, snarling and spitting, me plowing ass, my lube-greased hand wrapped around Butch's cock, each thrust of my hips and stroke of my hand ratcheting the two of us up to another level of pleasure.

One final, long, hard push is all I need to topple me over the edge. I cry out as my body begins to spasm.

"Pull out, quick!" Butch gasps. "I want to watch you squirt your load!"

I pull my dick out of his ass and rip the condom off. The first volley of spunk arcs across space and slams *hard* onto Butch's face. His head snaps back and cracks against the wall behind the bed. "More, more..." he groans. He doesn't have to beg; my one-eyed Komodo dragon is spitting out a steady torrent of jizz. Soon, Butch's face looks like something crawling with banana slugs. Butch slides his hand across his face and makes a feeble effort to wipe off the mask of spunk that thickly drips over his cheeks and chin. He wraps his come-slimed hand around his dick and starts beating off with short, quick strokes. It only takes a few seconds before he gives a long trailing groan, his back arches and his own load splatters out from his dick head onto his chest and chin, the higher drops mingling with my own joy juice. He collapses back onto the bed, gasping, his eyes closed. After a while I begin to feel uneasy. The last guy I fucked had an orgasm so intense he passed out and had to be carted off to the emergency room of the local hospital. (The next day he was on my doorstep, begging for more. I had to call the cops.)

I put my hand on Butch's shoulder and gently shake it. "You OK?" I ask.

Butch slowly opens his eyes. He looks stunned. "I...I had no idea sex could be that good!" he whispers.

I relax. He's OK. "Yeah," I say. "I hear that a lot."

Butch wants to spend the night so that I can fuck him again first thing tomorrow. I have to gently but firmly get him dressed and escort him to the door. I have a busy day tomorrow, and I don't want my sleep disrupted by a sex-crazed porn star begging for more.

As I start getting ready for bed, I notice that I'm out of dental floss. *How annoying,* I think. Fortunately, there's an all-night drugstore on the corner of my block. I get dressed again and walk out of my apartment. On the street, I pass the neighborhood sidewalk café. The evening is warm, and there are people sitting at the outside tables. Four men are seated at the table closest to the sidewalk. I can't help noticing the bulge of muscles under their tight T-shirts.

As I walk past, one of them reaches out and lightly touches me on the arm.

"Excuse me," he says. "Me and my buddies are members of the U.S. Olympic gymnastics team. We were just talking about Gore Vidal's line that everyone is essentially bisexual. Although none of us have ever had sex with a man before, we decided that we would like to put that statement to the test. Could we please go up to your apartment and have sex with you like crazed weasels?"

I glance at my watch. "Gee, guys, it's pretty late," I say. I sigh. "Well, what the hell."

"All right!" the guy says, grinning. The four young gods get up from their seats and join me on the sidewalk.

Damn! I think, as we walk into my bedroom and start to strip. *The life of a porn writer can sure be exhausting!*

STAVROS'S PLACE

The alley is shabby, but the door at the end of it isn't. It can't be seen from the street, the alley takes two twists before finally ending in a crumbling stucco wall in which the door is set. But now, standing in front of it, I notice its darkly gleaming wood, the heavy brass knocker, recently polished, set below a peephole. Next to it, screwed into the wall, is an equally well-polished brass plate with the single word STAVROS. I grasp the knocker and rap loudly.

For a long time nothing happens. I wonder if the place is empty. Off in the distance I hear a baby crying, and I think of young Dimitri. The peephole suddenly slides open, and a bloodshot blue eye peers out at me. "What do you want?" a gruff voice asks.

I take my cap off and hold it in both my hands. "Please, I would like to see Mr. Stavros."

The eye rolls down, taking in my patched shirt, my trousers stained with dried fish blood. "What for?"

I keep my gaze level with the eye peering at me. "I am looking for work," I say.

There's a bark of laughter from the other side of the door. "Go away," the voice says. The peephole slams shut.

I stand there for a minute, staring at the door. Then I turn around slowly and start walking down the alley. I hear the door suddenly open behind me. "Hey, you!" the voice calls after me. I turn to see an old man with the face of a hyena standing in the doorway. "Come in," he says. "Mr. Stavros might be interested in seeing you after all."

I follow the old man into a small hallway with whitewashed walls. There's a fountain at the end of it, and a straight-backed wooden chair. The old man nods at it. "Sit there." He disappears behind another door. I wait a long time, staring at the fountain. In the middle of it stands a statue of a young girl holding a tipped vase. A steady stream of water pours out of the vase into the pool below. I close my eyes, the music of the tinkling water filling my ears.

The old man opens the door again. "Mr. Stavros will give you five minutes," he says. He walks away, not bothering to see if I'm following. I jump to my feet and run after him. We go down a dark hallway lit by narrow windows that run just beneath the ceiling. It is late afternoon, and the sun's rays slant in, laced with dust motes. The old man takes me to a closed door. He knocks and opens it, walking away without a word.

I stand in the open doorway and look in. The room is small but has the feel of luxury. A Turkish rug, pale blue and rose, lies on the floor before a wide desk, as polished and richly grained as the door outside. A ceiling fan whirs softly overhead. A man, Stavros presumably, sits behind the desk in a leather-upholstered chair. He is the fattest man I have ever seen. He regards me with half-lidded eyes, set like raisins in the thick pudding of his face. "Petros tells me that you are looking for work," he says, his voice soft and tired.

"Yes, sir," I say.

"Do you know what kind of establishment this is?" Stavros's eyes are sleepy, bored.

"Yes." I pause. "This is a place where men...pleasure other men."

Stavros regards me silently for a very long time. Fat spills out from under his shirt collar, giving the impression that his head is melting in thick, uneven lumps. I shift my weight to my other foot. "What is your name?" he finally asks.

"Nikos Kazanzakis."

"How old are you, Nikos?"

"Twenty, sir."

Stavros sighs. "Have you ever pleasured a man before? Do you even understand what such a term means?"

"I am a quick learner," I say, choosing my words carefully. "And I'm good with my hands." This was not meant as a joke, but Stavros's mouth curves up into a thin smile.

He leans forward. "Why do you want to work here?"

"I'm a fisherman," I say. "From the island of Hydros. I have a wife and an infant son, who depend on me for their survival." I try to keep my voice even, but the mention of Kyria and Dimitri is like a knife in my heart. "The fishing season has been very poor this year. The waters are all fished out, empty of life. I've come here to Athens, looking for work." I wipe my hand across my forehead. In spite of the fan, the air in the room hangs heavy with heat. "But I have not been able to find any. In a park in the Plaka district I heard about this place. Some men were talking about it." I look Stavros full in the face. "And so I thought I would look for work here."

Stavros gives a low, rumbling laugh that makes his jowls tremble. "This is a well-appointed establishment," he says. "My clients include many rich and powerful men. Do you think I would hire any bumpkin, out-of-work fisherman than knocks on my door?"

I feel the blood rush to my face. I wait until I can trust myself to answer without insult. "No, sir," I say. "Forgive me, I was foolish to come here." I turn to go.

"Stand still!" Stavros barks. I stop. His eyes scan up and down my body. "Come back tomorrow at 11 o'clock."

I feel a surge of hope. "Does this mean..."

"This interview is over." Stavros dismisses me with a wave of his hand. "Good day."

This time, when I knock, Petros lets me in right away. "Follow me," he says. His tone is curt, but at least he no longer talks to me as if I were some stray mongrel dog. He leads me down a different hall than the one we walked through yesterday. One side opens up into a courtyard, the walls dazzling white in the late-morning sun. Potted flowers ring another fountain, this one a trio of stone dolphins with water spouting out of their mouths. A breeze bends the arc of the water, and I feel a light mist against my face. Petros knocks on a door and barks, "He's here."

The door opens. A young man stands in the doorway, dressed in a thin silk robe. His skin is dark and his hair is very black, which makes the blue of his eyes all the more startling. I have never seen eyes that shade of blue, like the turquoise of the sea in shallow water. His robe is the same color as his eyes and moves across his body like a cascading stream. He smiles at me, and his teeth gleam in his dark face. "Come in, Nikos," he says. "I apologize for Petros. He has the manners of a goat."

I walk into a dim room, the blinds of the window drawn so that only thin beams of sunlight stream in. There's a bed at the far end, a couple of chairs, a side table with a pitcher and basin, a small rug, nothing more. "I thought I was going to see Mr. Stavros," I say.

The young man shakes his head. "I am Mr. Stavros's...agent. He has asked me to conduct this interview." He smiles his brilliant smile again. "My name is Gregor." His eyes scan down my body and then back to my face. "Mr. Stavros was right. You're very handsome."

"Mr. Stavros said that?"

"No, not in so many words. But you wouldn't have been called back for a second interview if he didn't think that." Gregor settles himself into a chair. "Please remove your clothes."

"Wh-what?"

Gregor smiles. "Nikos, forgive me, but in this establishment, modesty is *not* a virtue. Your coin of entrance here is your beauty. I must determine the value of that coin before we can consider your employment." He gestures toward me. "Please."

I hesitate and then pull off my shirt and my shoes. I undo the top three buttons of my trousers and then stop. "If you don't wish to do this, Nikos," Gregor says softly, "we can always end the interview now."

"No," I say quickly. "I'm fine." I pull down my trousers and kick them aside. I stand naked in front of Gregor.

Gregor's gaze slowly slides down my body and then back up to my face. "Turn around, please," he says.

I turn around. Even with my back to Gregor, I can feel the warmth of his gaze. I stop when I'm facing him again. Gregor's eyes gleam. "You really are quite beautiful, Nikos," he says softly. He reaches over and traces his fingers down the side of my face. "I love your eyes—they're so dark and liquid. There's a shyness in them, but underneath the shyness, a fierceness. I can see that you could be a dangerous man if aroused to anger." His fingers rest lightly on my lips. "Your mouth is beautifully formed, the lips very

full and sensual. It would be a great pleasure to kiss such a mouth."
His hand slides down my torso. "And your body..." Gregor shakes his
head. "Nikos, your body is magnificent. Fishing must be hard work
for you to have such powerful muscles. And yet there's a grace to
your body that I find heartbreaking." His hand slides behind me,
running down my back. He squeezes my ass cheeks. "I have not
seen such an ass as yours except in museums, carved in marble on
statues of gods, Apollo maybe, or Dionysius." He takes his other
hand and wraps it around my cock. "And your prick! Nikos, your
prick is a work of art: thick, fleshy, veined." He starts stroking it. "It
must take one's breath away when hard." Gregor smiles and steps
back. "Nikos, you are blushing."

My face feels hot. "No man has ever said such things to me
before. Or touched me in that way."

Gregor leans back in his chair, his smile still on his lips. "Does it
displease you?"

"No, " I say carefully. "I don't find your behavior displeasing."
I pause. "Just...strange."

Gregor laughs. "Well, get used to it, Nikos. Because if you work
here, you will get this from the clients regularly." Gregor stands up
and undoes the sash of his robe. With a shrug of his shoulders, the
robe falls to his feet. He stands in front of me, naked. "All right,
Nikos," he says, "Now I must see how skilled you are in pleasuring
a man. I want you to suck my cock." His voice is calm and level, as
if this conversation between us is perfectly ordinary. Gregor's cock
is already half erect; it presses against his thigh, brown and meaty,
the head like a dark, round pebble.

My head swims with confusion. "Gregor," I protest. "You go
too fast."

Gregor's expression is sympathetic. "Forgive me, Nikos. But I
must see how deep your commitment is. If you find this kind of
work...distasteful, then it is better that *I* notice this rather than
some client." He looks at me expectantly.

I drop to my knees in front of him. His dick is fully hard now,
throbbing, inches from my face. I grasp it with my hand and
squeeze it. I have never touched another man's prick before, and
the air hums with unreality. I lean forward and slide my mouth

down the shaft. I start bobbing my head back and forth, my eyes squeezed shut.

After a minute of this, Gregor pulls back, freeing his dick from my mouth. "Nikos," he says gently. "You are very clumsy at this." I feel the blood rush to my face again, but I say nothing. "Do you even know what a good blow job feels like?"

I don't answer immediately. "My wife," I say slowly, "is a virtuous and modest woman."

"Ah," Gregor says, nodding. "I understand." He laughs. "Fortunately I am neither virtuous nor modest. So perhaps I can give you some useful instruction. Stand up."

I climb to my feet, and Gregor drops to his knees before me. He cradles my dick in the palm of his hand and looks up at me. "Sucking dick is a very subtle art," he says. "You must lead up to it slowly, tease the client." He squeezes my dick. "Pay close attention, Nikos. First, I will start with your balls." He buries his nose in my balls and breathes deeply, shaking his head. I feel his tongue flicking across the sac, first lightly and then with increasing force. He opens his mouth and my balls spill inside. Gregor sucks on them, rolling them around with his tongue, his eyes never leaving mine. Tingles of pleasure shoot through my body. Still sucking on my nut sac, Gregor slides his hands up my torso and grips my nipples. He squeezes them hard. I groan, and my dick swells to full stiffness, lying heavily against his cheek.

Gregor slowly slides his tongue up the shaft of my dick. When he gets to the head, he swirls his tongue around it, probing into my piss slit. He presses his lips against the head and leaves them there for a moment. I'm breathing heavily now. He looks up at me, his eyes playful. "Notice how that makes you hungry for more, Nikos," he says. "How much you wish me to suck on your dick now. Sometimes it's good to torment the client, make him wait. It makes the moment of gratification all the sweeter." Without warning, he slides his lips full down my shaft. His mouth moves up and down my dick, drawing out sensations that flood over me like warm seawater. He stops and again looks up at me. "Are you paying attention, Nikos?" he asks. "You mustn't lose yourself in the sensations. You have to learn these techniques I'm showing you."

I open my eyes and look at him. "Yes, Gregor," I say. "I'm paying attention."

Gregor continues sucking my cock. Once more, pleasure washes over me, and it is only with the greatest difficulty that I keep from sinking into it. Gregor removes my cock from his mouth and looks at me. "Did you see how I twisted my head from side to side as I sucked? This increases the sensations along the shaft. And how I rolled my tongue around your dick? And yes, I *do* suck, it's not just a figure of speech. I seal my lips tight around your dick and create a partial vacuum in my mouth. This creates sensations of great pleasure for a man."

"I understand," I say. I feel a thin band of sweat trickle down my forehead, and I wipe it away with the back of my arm.

Gregor reaches down beside the chair and picks up a small green bottle. He pours several drops of thick, white liquid into his hand. He rubs the cream over his fingers. "Spread your legs farther apart," he says.

I obey. Gregor reaches under my legs, and I feel his hand pry apart my ass cheeks. His fingers burrow inside the crack, and then begin massaging my asshole. One finger pushes inside me. I instinctively clamp my ass muscles tight. Gregor looks up into my face. "Relax, Nikos," he says. "Accept what I'm doing to you."

I try to obey, willing my ass muscles to relax. Gregor's finger pushes deeper in. At the same time he begins sucking my cock again. This time his other hand is wrapped around my dick, following his lips as they slide up and down the shaft, his finger fucking my ass in long, slow thrusts. I groan loudly, and my knees tremble. Gregor pulls away, and looks at me, amused. "I think you are beginning to learn how much pleasure a man's body is capable of, Nikos," he says. "The asshole is a treasure chest with many precious secrets locked inside. What I'm showing you is just a mere taste, a few of my simplest tricks. Look at how hard your dick is now and how your balls are pulled up tight. These are some of the signals a man's body gives that he is about to shoot his load. It is important that you be aware of this so that you can stop in time. A truly skilled cocksucker can draw a man to the brink of shooting many times before finally triggering his orgasm." Gregor smiles. "But because time is limited, I must bring the first part of your lesson to a close. Observe me closely."

Gregor puts my dick back in his mouth and continues with his cock sucking. He teases the shaft with his tongue as his finger slides in and out of my asshole. Another finger joins the first, and he bends his knuckles. The jolt of pleasure is sharp and unexpected, and I give a long, trailing groan. Gregor increases the pace of his cock sucking; my dick glistens with his saliva, and I can feel my load being pulled from my balls with each descent of his mouth. Without warning, he presses a finger hard between my balls as the fingers of his other hand push all the way up into my asshole. I cry out, and my body shudders violently. Gregor jacks me off as I shoot, pulse after pulse of my thick load splattering against his face. When the last drop has squirted out, I sink into a chair. I look at Gregor with dazed, astonished eyes. Gregor regards me calmly, my load dripping down his cheek.

The room is silent except for the sound of the fountain in the courtyard outside. Gregor wipes his face with a towel. "Well, Nikos," he says, "Did you learn anything?"

"I...I had no idea..." I swallow. "You are most skillful, Gregor."

Gregor laughs. "These are skills I can teach you, Nikos. If you're willing to learn."

"Does that mean that I can work here?" My heart beats hard inside my chest.

Gregor nods. "Yes, I think so. In fact, I want you to start tonight." He kisses me on the mouth. "But we have much work to do until then." He leans back, his hard dick lying against his belly. "I want you to suck my cock again, Nikos. Using the techniques that I've just shown you. And when you've mastered those, there are others you'll need to learn."

I lean forward and run my tongue up Gregor's dick. Outside, the fountain splashes softly.

The room where the clients meet us is large and sparsely furnished: a bar on one end, a few couches and chairs positioned along the walls and in alcoves. The windows are open to let in the night air, and a slight breeze stirs through, scented faintly with jasmine. Other young men, my fellow "escorts," sit by the bar or casually lean against the wall. There is something very polished and confident in the poses of their bodies, and I feel clumsy beside them. The clients sit at the bar or on the sofas, some talking to escorts, some alone. Gregor has dressed me simply, in tight black slacks and a white cotton shirt with an open collar. "You don't need any embellishments, Nikos," he said when he gave me the clothes. "Your looks can speak for themselves."

I have a soft drink in my hand (none of the escorts are allowed to drink alcohol), and I stand next to the fireplace, my eyes trained on the flagstone floor. I glance up and see Gregor talking to a man who came in alone a few minutes ago. Gregor is smiling and nodding. They both look in my direction, and Gregor motions for me to join them.

"Nikos," he says. "I'd like you to meet Mr. Waverly. Mr. Waverly is an American visiting Athens for a few days."

I look at him with curiosity. I have never been this close to an American before, much less spoken to one. Mr. Waverly is tall, at least half a head taller than me, with dark blond hair and the beefy body of an ex-football player. He looks like he's in his late 30s. "Hello, Mr. Waverly," I say, my lips stumbling over the foreign name.

He holds out his hand to me. "Call me Jack," he says. I shake his hand, looking directly into his face. His eyes are gray and very bold. They scan down my body and back to my face. "I've heard about your place. From friends." He winks. "I thought it would be an exciting experience to come here." His Greek, though heavily accented, is surprisingly good.

Gregor smiles politely. "Nikos is new to us, Mr. Waverly. He would be most happy to attend to your pleasure." He pauses discreetly. "However, if you wish for someone more experienced..." He leaves the rest of the sentence hanging in the air.

Jack shakes his head. "No," he says, smiling at me. "That won't be necessary." I can see the excitement in his eyes. And the hunger. "I think Nikos and I will get along just fine." He turns to Gregor. "I'm ready now." I feel a slight shock at how abruptly all of this is transacted.

Gregor leads us upstairs. On the stairway, Jack throws an arm around my shoulders, like we've just finished a football game and are off to the showers. *Do all Americans behave like this?* I wonder. Gregor escorts us to a room and closes the door behind us. Jack and I look at each other. He grins. "Nervous?"

"Yes," I say. "Does it show?"

Jack laughs. "A little. Around the eyes. You look like you might bolt."

"I'm sorry," I say. "Please forgive my inexperience."

Jack laughs. "Don't apologize. It's the ultimate fantasy. To fuck a virgin in a whorehouse." He walks over and kisses me on the mouth, his tongue pushing through between my lips. It is so strange to feel whiskers against my face. "Let's get naked," he says.

We quickly strip. Jack's body is solid and massive, the chest hairless, the skin of his torso as red as his face. His cock is red too, and it lies half-hard against his thigh, leaking precome. I stare at it.

"Do you like it?" Jack asks.

I look up into Jack's face. Jack is grinning, and his eyes gleam. "I have never seen a circumcised cock before," I say. "Why do you Americans do it?"

Jack shrugs. "Beats the hell out of me." His eyes scan my body slowly. "Christ, you're beautiful," he says softly. He reaches over and squeezes my dick, stroking the foreskin up and down the shaft. His hand is large and callused, the knuckles sprouting blond hairs, the fingernails broad and square. I have still not gotten used to seeing this *man's* hand wrapped around my dick. Even Kyria hardly touches it. I find it very exciting, and my dick stirs and stiffens to full hardness in his grasp. Jack's eyes meet mine, and the hunger in them is naked and urgent. I have seen that look on men's faces in Hydros when a particularly beautiful woman walks by. How strange that I should inspire the same look.

Jack runs his tongue over his lips. "Nikos, I don't know what is allowed here and what isn't. Sweet Jesus, I would love to fuck your ass! Can I?"

Gregor has spent the afternoon introducing me to his collection of dildos to prepare me for such a question. I walk over to the night-stand, open the drawer, and pull out a condom package and jar of grease. I hand them to Jack, smiling, saying nothing. Jack laughs, wraps his arms around me, and we topple onto the bed.

I start to roll over, but Jack stops me. "I want to look at your face when I fuck you," he says. "I want to see your expression every time I shove my dick up your ass." He bends down and we kiss again, our mouths working hard against each other. I feel his fingers, slippery with grease, burrow into my ass crack and push against my bunghole. Two fingers slide in, moving up and down, and I tremble with the sensations. I spread my legs wider and push my hips up. Jack pulls his fingers out and slowly, inch by inch, slides his dick up my ass. His eyes peer deeply into mine. "Yeah, Nikos," he murmurs, "Relax, let it happen, that's it, baby, accept it." I stare back at him, my mouth open, my eyes wide, my breath coming out in shallow pants. Gregor's dildos were nothing like this, nothing like a living cock. I groan softly. Jack pulls out slowly until I can feel the head of his cock just barely inside my asshole. He suddenly thrusts in, all the way, burying his cock deep inside me. I cry out and pull his head down, kissing him fiercely, biting his lips. Jack pumps his hips, his dick sliding in and out of my ass, his balls slamming against me, his broad chest squirming against mine. For one instant he keeps his dick full up my ass and grinds his hips against mine. I groan again, louder than before. Jack wraps his hand around my hard dick and starts beating me off, his strokes in time to the plowing he's giving me.

We roll over, Jack on his back now, me straddling him above. My hands slide up and down his torso, kneading the flesh, grabbing it, feeling the hardness of a man's body, so different than a woman's, so exciting in this difference. Jack varies his strokes, sometimes making them long and deep, sometimes fucking me with quick, sharp thrusts. His eyes burn into mine, his lips are pulled back into a snarl. He reaches up and strikes my chest with his fist, his fingers opening up into a long caress that slides down my torso. His other, grease-smeared hand works up and down my dick, each stroke pulling me closer to the point of final release. I run my fingers through his hair and then close them into fists, shaking his head from side to side. When I was younger, before I married Kyria, I would sometimes get drunk and fight men in the local tavern.

Sex with Jack feels like one of those brawls, the same excitement, the pitting of one man's strength against another, only this time, instead of pain, we try to weaken each other with the pleasure we can inflict on the other's body.

Jack gives a low whimper. He pulls out and then thrusts again, deep up my ass. His body trembles beneath me, and he cries out. I feel his muscles convulse under my hands, he arches his back, and his dick throbs inside me as he squirts his load into the condom up my ass. His body thrashes violently, and I clamp my thighs together, holding on until he collapses onto the bed, still panting.

He looks at me with dazed eyes. His hand is still stroking my cock, sliding up and down the shaft. "How close are you to coming, Nikos?" he asks.

"Just keep doing what you're doing," I gasp. "I'm almost there." And indeed, it takes just a few more strokes of Jack's hand before my own orgasm is triggered. I groan as my load arcs out into the air, splattering against Jack's face, coating it with thick, creamy ooze. Jack accepts it with closed eyes and open mouth. I collapse beside him, and he slides his arm under me, pulling me toward him. We lie next to each other in silence until we hear Gregor's discreet knock on the door, telling Jack he has five more minutes.

Jack sighs. Then he laughs lightly. He gets up and starts dressing. "I come into Athens regularly for business, Nikos. Maybe I can see you again next time I'm here."

I smile. "All right."

On his way out, Jack kisses me lightly and slips a tip into my hand. I glance down and see that it's more than I would make at a week of fishing. I put the money in the pocket of my slacks, still lying crumpled on the floor. Gregor comes in shortly afterward.

"Well?" he asks, his eyebrows raised.

"Gregor, I would be happy to continue working for you. Or rather for Stavros. Just as long as I can visit my family on Hydros regularly."

Gregor grins. "Mr. Waverly left very satisfied. I think we can work something out, Nikos." He raises his eyebrows. "Do you think you can take on another client tonight? Things are very busy downstairs."

I nod. "Yes, I think so. Just give me a few minutes alone first, all right?"

Gregor winks and leaves the room, closing the door behind him. I lie on the bed, staring up at the ceiling. *How strange life is,* I think. After a few minutes I sit up and start getting dressed to join the party down below.

SOUTHERN BOYS

I walk into the Birmingham bar with one of two objectives: to get drunk or get laid, whichever comes first. Maybe both. My mood is as bleak as a toxic waste dump, and I need a quick distraction over the shit-ass turn my life has taken. The bar is small and generic; the only thing that gives it away as gay (besides the conspicuous lack of women) is the Tom of Finland poster on the wall: a sailor groping a marine on a park bench, the bulges of their dicks as big as basketballs.

The bartender greets me with a nod and I order a Seagram's and 7UP, my bad mood drink. I knock it off in a couple of gulps and order another. It's only after I knock that one off as well that I bother to look around. It's about 11 o'clock, and I guess the place is as crowded as it's going to get; there are a couple of dozen guys around, plus an additional five or six shooting pool in the back room. A few men are looking me over, seeing if I'm worth a tumble. I turn my back on them and order another 7 and 7. "Hadn't you better ease up a bit?" the bartender asks.

I glower at him and he returns my stare calmly. I force myself to smile. "All right," I say. "Pour me another and I'll nurse this one along." After a pause, the bartender pours me another drink and walks away to the other end of the bar. I take a sip and look around again.

He's standing by the cigarette machine, his eyes trained on me. As soon as our eyes meet, he looks away. I scrutinize him carefully: mid-to-late 20s, neatly clipped blond hair, the body of a college jock (track maybe, or swimming), awkward posture. Good-looking in a squeaky-clean sort of way. He looks at me again, and I train my eyes on him with an unwavering stare. He maintains eye contact, but it's obvious it's killing him to do so. I don't smile or nod or even give him a cruisy look. But I don't turn away either. After a minute of this, he walks over.

"Hi," he says. I nod. Silence. "What's your name?" he asks.

"Steve." Another silence. "What's yours?" I ask, because it seems to be required of me.

"Joe," he answers, after a brief hesitation. By his tone, I'm almost sure he's lying. God save me from closet cases. He takes a swig from a bottle of Calistoga. "Do you live in these parts, Steve?" he asks.

I take another sip from my drink. "I'm just passing through." Another silence. These silences don't bother me, but I can tell he finds them awkward as hell.

"What kind of work do you do?" he finally asks.

"Look," I say. "Do you want to fuck?"

Joe blinks and then laughs nervously. His face turns a bright pink. "You get right to the point, don't you?"

"I'm sorry, I'm just not in a bullshit mood tonight."

We stand side by side, backs against the bar. Some god-awful country-western ballad is twanging over the jukebox, all about cheating women and breaking hearts. "I don't live in this city," Joe says. "I don't have a place to..."

"That's all right," I say. "I have a motel room about a mile away."

Joe's eyes flicker uncertainly. It's clear he's excited. It's also clear he's scared shitless. I sip my drink, staring into space, waiting. "Look," he says, "why don't we just talk for a while."

"Joe," I say, turning my head toward him. "I'm not trying to be rude, but I don't want to fuckin' talk. With you or anybody else. I came to this bar to get laid. If you want to go back to the motel with me, fine. If not, then don't waste my time."

Joe doesn't say anything. I start to walk away. "OK, I'll go with you," he says.

"Fine," I say. I knock off the rest of my drink. "Let's go."

He follows me in his car to the motel. I notice that he parks in a corner of the lot farthest from the lighted sign. As he walks toward me, he looks around nervously. This is all so tedious. When we walk into my room, he checks to make sure that the curtains are tightly drawn. Only then does he start to relax.

I start pulling off my clothes. He stands there in the middle of the room, watching me. I give him a hard stare, and he starts undressing as well. My original impression of Joe as a jock seems accurate; his body is smooth and nicely toned, the muscles of his torso sharply defined. I can tell his skin is usually pale, but right now it's a bright pink. He pulls down his briefs, and his dick springs up, fully hard, thick, cut, and very red. *Do dicks blush?* I wonder. His balls hang low, furred by a light blond fuzz.

I cross the room and wrap my arms around him. We kiss, Joe at first tentatively, then with growing excitement. He presses his body tightly next to mine and thrusts his dick hard against me. I run my hands down his back and squeeze his ass; the cheeks feel smooth and firm under my fingertips. He reaches down and wraps his hand around my dick, stroking it slowly. "So beautiful," he murmurs.

We tumble onto the bed. I reach over to turn off the lamp, but he catches my wrist and stops me. "No," he says, "I want to look at your body. I want to watch you as you fuck me."

He says "fuck" energetically, like a small boy using a swearword he's been taught is bad.

"All right," I say. I fall back on the bed, with my hands behind my head. "But first, how about sucking my dick?"

Joe blushes again. "Sure," he says. He bends down and runs his tongue around my right nipple, hardening the nub. He does the same for the left nipple, this time gently biting it. I feel my cock stir. Joe slides his tongue down my belly into the forest of my pubes. He wraps his hand around my dick and squeezes it. A drop of precome leaks out, and he laps it up, then rolls his tongue around the head of my dick. His eyes sweep over my body and the ache in his face is so keen it feels like a slap. Suddenly I feel a twinge of sympathy for the guy. I reach over and brush the hair from his forehead and then leave my hand resting on his temple. Joe seems startled by this gesture.

He takes my cock in his mouth, nibbles down the shaft and then freezes for a moment, my dick crammed deep down his throat, his nose mashed against my pubes. With killing slowness his lips slide up the shaft as his tongue plays around it. Joe proceeds to make serious love to my dick, sucking on it, licking it, flicking his tongue across it, stroking it. It's clear this boy hasn't had a good dick to play with for a long time. I'm beginning to imagine what his life is like: stuck in some podunk town somewhere, maybe even married with kids, driving up to Birmingham whenever the hunger for dick becomes too strong to push down, and then tearing loose with any stray guy he can pick up. Joe is now sucking on my balls, rolling them around with his tongue, burrowing his face in them. He looks up at me, my nut sac in his mouth, and I can see the excitement in his eyes, and the fact that I'm the cause of it makes me feel it too.

My open suitcase is lying beside the bed. I reach into it and pull out a tube of lube and pack of rubbers. "OK, Joe," I say. "What do you say I plow your ass now?"

Fucking Joe is a little disconcerting. His eyes never leave my face, and he wears this expression of...*wonder,* like he can't quite believe this is happening, like he's having some kind of religious revelation. I know I'm pretty good, but I'm not *that* good; whatever he's experiencing now goes beyond me and my technique. I plunge into his ass with deep, sure strokes, and Joe cries out with each thrust. He doesn't say "hallelujah," but the noise he makes is close enough. I wrap my hand around Joe's dick and stroke it in time with each thrust of my hips, and Joe shudders with pleasure. When I finally feel the orgasm sweep over me, I groan loudly. Joe wraps his legs around me and squeezes tight, pulling my face against his. My body spasms its load of jizz into the rubber up Joe's ass, and Joe shoots right at the final throb of my dick. He cries out so loudly that I start worrying about people in neighboring rooms complaining to the manager. I kiss him again just to shut him up.

Afterward we lie side by side in the bed, my leg thrown over Joe's, my arm under his neck. He gives a long sigh. "Sweet Jesus," he says. "A-fuckin'-men" I reply. We lie like that for what seems like a long time. Somebody is out in the parking lot with his car radio turned on full blast. More shit-eating country and western.

"Christ," I mutter. I shake my head. "I can't tell you how much I hate the music here."

Joe gives a slight smile. "Oh, yeah? Where you from?"

I get out of bed and reach down for my briefs. "San Francisco."

Joe's eyes sweep over my body. They still look hungry. "You're a long way from home."

I pull my briefs up, and then my jeans. "Yeah," I finally say, "well, it's a long story." Joe doesn't say anything, just stays there in bed looking at me. I sit down on the edge of the bed. "My old man lives not far from Birmingham, some hick town about 40 miles away. He had a heart attack a couple of weeks ago. He's got no one to look after him, so I'm drafted to do the job. As soon as he's on his feet..." I clap my hands loudly. "I'm outta here."

Joe reaches over and runs his hand down my back. "Are you close to your father?"

I have to laugh at that. "Hell, no! I haven't seen him in three years, when he kicked me out. He writes sometimes, mainly to explain to me how I'm going to burn in hell." I turn my head and look at Joe. "He doesn't exactly approve of my 'lifestyle choices.' " I laugh again, with precious little humor. "I bet it damn near killed him to ask me to help him out." I look around the room. "And so now I'm back in shit-ass Alabama."

"You're doing a decent thing," Joe says. "It shows you got a good heart."

"Yeah," I grunt. "That's me all over."

At the door, we kiss again. "Christ be with you," Joe says, just before walking out.

"Whatever," I say.

The first few days at my father's house are like walking in a minefield. For both of us. I watch my father a number of times start some poisonous remark and choke it off; he at least has enough native wit to realize how little it would take to make me to pack my bags and leave. There's still the same old evil gleam in his eyes, but it's tamer now, more subdued. *He should have had a heart attack years ago*, I think. *It would have done him a world of good.* I feel a twinge of guilt for that thought, but only a small one.

Some woman from his church, Sarah, comes around from time to time, bringing groceries or an occasional casserole. Other than that, I'm his only link with the world. Sarah is fat and motherly and relentlessly cheerful. When, in answer to her question, I tell her I'm from San Francisco, she gives a little worried cluck. "You be careful, Steve," she says. "San Francisco is Satan's playground." After that, I go upstairs to my room and shut the door whenever she visits.

When Sunday comes around my father seems unusually edgy. I'm in the kitchen reading the paper and drinking a cup of coffee when I hear his cane knocking against the floorboards down the hall. He pushes open the kitchen swing door but doesn't come in. He just stands there staring at me.

I raise my head. "Yeah?"

"I want to go to church this morning," he says. "Service starts at 11 o'clock."

"All right," I say. "Just let me know when you want me to drive you." I go back to my paper.

He still stands in the doorway, not moving. I raise my head again. "I want you to go to the service with me," he finally says.

I stare at him. "You've got to be kidding."

I can see his head shake in agitation and his face turn red. "Everyone knows you're here. Sarah had to blab it to anyone who'd listen. How do you think it looks for me if my own son doesn't go to church?"

"Sorry, Dad," I say. "I don't do church anymore." I return to my paper.

He still doesn't move. "Maybe if you did," he said, his voice quivering with anger, "you wouldn't be a—"

"If I were you," I say quietly, "I'd think carefully before finishing that sentence." We glare at each other. "The first time I hear the word 'pervert' or 'sodomite' or any word like that," I continue in the same even tone, "I'll pack my bags and be out of here within the hour."

Dad spins around and disappears down the hall, his cane clattering in agitation. A few minutes later I walk by his room and glance in through the open door. He's sitting by the window, staring out. I notice how frail and puny he looks. "Oh, all right," I say irritably. "I'll go to church with you."

The church is pretty much as I remember it, a shabby little brick building next to a Taco Bell. People inside greet me with a hearty enthusiasm, and I listen and reply with a tight smile, being as polite as I can manage. My father doesn't look like he just sucked a lemon, the closest expression to 'happy' that I've ever seen him wear. The organ music starts up and we sit in one of the pews. The two ministers walk in and take a seat by the altar. I remember the older man, Brother Thomas, from before I left town the last time. But it's the younger minister that grabs my attention. He's Joe, the guy I picked up in the Birmingham bar last week. *Well, I'll be damned,* I think. I stifle an impulse to laugh.

I nudge my father's side. "Who's the new minister?" I ask.

"That's Brother Richard," he replies. "He's been here for about a year."

I watch Richard during the entire service: the hymn singing, the benediction, the offering, the sermon (given by Brother Thomas). When Brother Thomas starts whaling away, talking about all the sinners, and reaches the part about the sodomites, I look for a reaction from Richard. But he just sits there calmly, his eyes closed as if in prayer. *You fucking hypocrite!* I think.

Afterward, as we file out, Richard is out front, greeting the congregation. My father shakes his hand. "I want you to meet my son, Steve," he says.

Richard's eyes swing toward me, a greeting on his lips. His mouth drops open.

"Hello, Brother Joe," I say.

"It's *Richard*," my father hisses.

"I'm sorry," I say. "I never was good at names." Richard's face is beet red. He just nods, saying nothing.

The next Sunday, I refuse to enter the church. I drop my father off, grab breakfast at a downtown diner, and swing by a couple of hours later to pick him up. As my father hobbles toward the car, I see Richard in the church doorway, staring at me. My father is stiff with anger that I didn't go with him, and we ride home in silence.

A couple of days later, I'm in the kitchen washing dishes. My father is upstairs, taking his postlunch nap. Heat pours into the room like thick molasses, and I can feel beads of sweat trickle from my armpits down the sides of my body. The doorbell rings, a rarity, since the only visitor Dad ever gets is good, righteous Sarah. I walk over to the front hallway and yank open the door. Richard stands framed in the doorway.

"Well," I laugh. "This is a surprise."

"I came to check up on your father," Richard says, his mouth drawn in a grim line. "To see how he's doing." His cotton shirt is wet with sweat and plastered against his torso.

"He's sleeping," I say. I open the door wider. "Do you want to come in?"

Richard follows me into the kitchen. I pull open the refrigerator and hold up a beer. "Thirsty?" I ask.

After a pause, Richard nods, and I toss it to him. I take another. I hold up my bottle to him in toast. "To chance encounters," I say.

Richard's blush gets even redder. "I guess you think this is pretty funny," he says.

"No," I say. "I think it's pretty sad."

Richard takes a deep pull from his beer. "Well, fuck you."

I laugh. "My, you're feisty today."

Richard shrugs and takes another long pull. "I just get tired of being judged by other gay men for being a Christian. They come across so damn self-righteous."

I stare at him. "Haven't you got that reversed?"

Richard sighs. "Yeah, well, you're right. It works both ways." He takes another sip from his beer. "People are such assholes."

I laugh. "You're not talking at all like a minister." I'm finding Richard's frankness surprisingly sexy. I take in the swell of his tight, compact torso against his damp shirt and feel my dick stir.

Richard glares at me. "How do you know what a minister talks like?" He wipes the back of his hand against his brow. "You're just as bad as *them*. All you do is think in stereotypes."

"You know," I say, "you're very sexy when you're pissed."

Richard gives me a long, hard stare. His shoulders sag. "I've been thinking about that time in Birmingham. A lot. Even before I saw you later in church."

I nod. "It *was* hot, wasn't it?" My dick has stiffened to full hardness now. We sit silently in the crushingly hot room, the only sound being the ticking of the kitchen clock. I reach over and wrap my hand around the back of Richard's neck, and pull him across the table. We kiss long and hard, our tongues pushing deep into each other's mouth. I pull away. "Wait a second," I say.

I push open the kitchen door and look up the stairs. Dad's bedroom door is closed. Even from down here I can hear him snoring. I return to the kitchen, pull Richard out of his chair, and push him against the refrigerator. I kiss him again, grinding my hips against his. My dick strains against my jeans, hollering to be let out.

"Your father..." Richard says.

"Sleeping the sleep of the righteous," I answer. I reach down and unzip Richard's fly.

"This is crazy," Richard murmurs. But he makes no effort to stop me. I tug his jeans down below his knees. His white jockeys are spotted with drops of prejizz. I slip my hand inside them and give his hard dick a squeeze.

"It feels like you're happy to see me," I say. I drop to my knees, hook my thumbs under the elastic waistband, and pull his briefs down. His dick springs out, as thick and red as ever, and his balls hang heavily in the heat, like swollen fruit. I squeeze his dick again, and another clear drop of prejizz oozes out. I lap it up and then slide my mouth down the meaty shaft. Richard groans. He places his hands on either side of my head and starts pumping his hips, sliding his dick in and out of my mouth. I tug on his balls, feeling their heft in the palm of my hand as I feed on his hard, fat cock.

I stand up and swing Richard around, pushing him on top of the kitchen table. A plastic plate goes clattering to the floor. I hike his sweat-drenched shirt up over his chest and twist his nipples hard. Richard groans. I replace my fingers with my mouth, sucking on his nipples, rolling my tongue around them, biting them. Richard's flesh squirms under my mouth. I slide my tongue down his torso, tasting the salty slick of his sweat, feeling the smooth hardness of his jock's body, not stopping until my face is buried in his balls. I sniff in their rich, musky smell and then open my mouth and let his ball meat fall in. Richard digs his fingers into my hair and twists my head from side to side as I roll his nuts around with my tongue. "Yeah," he growls, "suck on those balls. Lick them good."

My tongue slides down the dark, sweaty path to his asshole, and I burrow into his crack, licking the sweet rose of his bunghole. Richard groans again, louder. He pulls me up and unbuckles my belt. I pull down my zipper and drop my jeans. My dick springs up, and Richard wraps his hand around both our cocks, squeezing the dick flesh together. I look down at the sight, Richard's fat, red dick pressed against my dark, thick uncut one, both cock heads weeping prejizz. Richard starts stroking them with his encircling fingers, pulling the two foreskins up and down the twin shafts of flesh as I reach down and roll his heavy ball sac in my hand. I lean forward and we kiss, our tongues thrusting into each other's mouth. The old wooden table creaks and groans under our weight, threatening to break apart into pieces. I've been eating meals on this table since I was a toddler; I never thought I'd be putting it to this use.

Richard bends down and takes my dick in his mouth, and I push my hips up hard, thrusting my cock deep down his throat. He takes it like a trooper, sucking on it, massaging it with his tongue, making love to it. I close my eyes and let the sensations sweep over me—Richard's warm, wet mouth on my dick and the feel of his hands as they explore my body. Richard pries apart my ass crack and massages my asshole with his finger. I groan. Slowly, knuckle by knuckle, he worms his finger up my chute. I raise my head and look up at the ceiling, the heavy, hot air pressing down on me, my face and torso dripping with sweat. I can feel my load being pulled up from my balls; each downward slide of Richard's lips brings me closer to the brink. My knees start to tremble, and then the orgasm is triggered. I groan loudly, and whip my dick out of Richard's mouth, my jizz spewing out, splattering against his face. As the last drops spurt out, the kitchen door swings open and I see my dad standing in the doorway.

"Jesus Christ!" I mutter. I grab my jeans and yank them up, even as my load continues to pump out. Richard scrambles off the table and stands transfixed, my jizz dripping down his face. My father stares at us, bug-eyed. Blood rushes to his face, and a strangled noise escapes from his mouth. He clutches his chest. *Oh, my God!* I think. *I've killed him for sure!* I rush toward him.

"Get away from me!" he hollers. He stumbles out of the kitchen into the hallway.

I look at Richard. He's wiping his face with his sleeve and pulling his clothes on. "You better get out of here," I tell him, nodding toward the back door. Richard doesn't need to be told twice. He hightails it out, tucking his shirt in his unzipped pants, as I hurry into the hallway. My father lies on the floor clutching his chest. I kneel beside him, and he swings at me with his free fist, hitting me along the side of the head. "I told you to stay away from me, you goddamn faggot," he yells. A blood vessel is throbbing on his forehead, and I can see the whites all around his irises. I rush back to the kitchen and dial 911. Ten minutes later an ambulance comes and carts him away.

Richard calls late at night. "I heard your father's in the hospital. How's he doing?"

"The doctor says he'll be OK," I reply. "It wasn't a heart attack, just some kind of spasm. They're keeping him in the hospital overnight for observation." I pause. "He refuses to see me."

Nothing from the other end of the line. "So what are you going to do now?" Richard finally asks.

I give a short, humorless laugh. "I'm already packed. I'm leaving first thing tomorrow."

"Who will look after your father?"

"I don't know," I say. "It won't be me, even if I wanted to. If he sees me again, it probably *would* trigger a heart attack." I sigh. "Maybe he can work out something with Sarah." I suddenly realize something. "How did you know he was in the hospital?"

"He called Brother Thomas," Richard says. "I was fired this afternoon."

"Christ," I mutter. Neither one of us says anything for a while. I can hear Richard's labored breathing over the phone. "So what are *you* going to do?"

Richard sighs. "I don't know. Get out of town, at least for a while. I can't stay here."

An inspiration seizes me. "Why don't you ride back with me to San Francisco? Spend some time in Satan's playground."

Silence on the other end of the line. "Why the hell not?" Richard finally says.

When I pull up to Richard's place the next morning, he's waiting for me on his front doorstep, two suitcases beside him. He jumps into the car, smiling broadly.

"What are you so goddamn happy about?" I ask.

Richard shrugs, still wearing his idiot grin. "I'm not sure." He slouches down in his seat, his back against the door, facing me. "I don't understand it, but right now I'm feeling...not bad."

"I understand it," I say. "It's how I felt three years ago when I left this shit hole."

Richard laughs. "So now we're just a couple of outcasts riding across the country." He wiggles his eyebrows. "Like Butch Cassidy and the Sundance Kid."

"Or Thelma and Louise," I say. I glance at him. "That was an example of camp humor. If you're going to be queer now, you're going to have to cultivate a talent for it."

Richard shakes his head. "So many things I have to learn."

I turn on the ignition, and we peel out.

IMMERSION

Nick's sister called him that afternoon, crying so hard that Nick could hardly understand the words she gulped out. He didn't have to. He'd been expecting this call for some time now, and he comforted her absently, letting himself be distracted by the various street scenes outside his window: a couple laughing, teenagers skateboarding by, two drivers arguing over a parking space. He ended the conversation promising to fly back to New Jersey the next day, on the earliest flight he could get. After he hung up, he remained sitting in the chair, staring blankly at the telephone. *I should call the airlines and make a reservation,* he thought. But he didn't move. After a while, he picked up a pack of cigarettes, shook one out, and lit it. He smoked the cigarette calmly, flicking the ashes out the window because he didn't feel like walking across the room and fetching the ashtray. Late afternoon turned into evening, the streetlights blinked on, and he still remained in the chair. The phone rang on two different occasions, but he ignored it each time. He had long since finished the pack, which he had crumpled and thrown out the window, so he just remained in the chair, in the dark, his mind blank.

The only thing he could see in the darkness was the green glow of the VCR's clock. He didn't stir until it said it was almost midnight. When he finally did climb out of his chair and walk across to the kitchen's light switch, it felt like he was wading through water. He flicked on the switch, wincing at the sudden burst of light, and looked around the room. The kitchen sink was full of dirty dishes, there were open cartons of Chinese takeout on the counter, and the garbage can was full to overflowing. *I should clean this place up,* he thought. *It looks like a dump.* He went over instead to the kitchen table and picked up the gay newspaper he had left there earlier. He turned the pages slowly, his eyes scanning up and down each one, until he finally stopped near the back of the paper. He tore out an ad and stuffed it in his back pocket.

He walked into his bedroom, flicking on the light. The expression on his face was calm, except for his eyes, which seemed to focus on the objects around him with a heightened intensity. He unbuttoned and took off his shirt, opened his dresser drawer, and pulled on a T-shirt that hugged his muscular torso like a second skin. He grabbed his car keys and walked out the door.

He had never actually been to this particular sex club before; in fact, he hadn't been to any sex club or bath in years, and the address in the ad in the gay newspaper was for a street unfamiliar to him. He drove down the city streets with the car's overhead light on and his gaze shifting rapidly from the street map to the road ahead and then back to the map again. He finally found the right street, then the right block, then the right building, and parked his car. Other men were streaming down the dark street and into the inconspicuous entrance lit by a single bulb overhead. Nick walked in, paid the requested fee, and climbed the flight of linoleum stairs that led into the club.

The place was dim, with pools of light that washed down the walls and spilled onto the corridor floors at irregular intervals. Some kind of digital electronic music pumped out of the speakers, the chords limited, the beat pulsing and intense. Men walked silently down the twisting hallways, their eyes hungry or hooded. Or both. Because Nick was a handsome man, Greek-American, with crisp, black curls, dark eyes, and a wide, sensual mouth, many of the men he passed stared into his face in open invitation. Nick returned every stare, his expression unreadable, but at least not set in the hard lines of rejection. A few of the men turned and followed, their eyes trained on Nick's wide shoulders and tight haunches. Nick wandered down the corridors, into the mazes and out the other end into the dimly lit orgy room. He leaned against the far wall and waited.

One of the men slipped into the room and stood a few feet from Nick. Others joined him until Nick was surrounded by an irregular ring of bodies. Someone approached him and tentatively laid his hand on Nick's chest. Nick stared at him, not moving. Emboldened, the man slipped his hand underneath Nick's T-shirt, the fingertips sliding against the smooth, hard muscles. He grasped Nick's left nipple and squeezed. Nick's eyes never left the man's face, and he nodded his head slightly. The man's other hand rubbed up and down Nick's crotch, pressing through the thick denim against the bulge underneath. Nick stirred, pushing his hips away from the wall, and the man undid Nick's belt, pulled down his fly, and with two quick jerks pulled Nick's jeans and shorts down around his thighs. Nick hooked his thumbs under his T-shirt and pulled it off, letting it drop to the floor.

The circle of men closed around him, half predatory, half worshipful. Nick was standing directly beneath one of the covered bulbs, and light spilled down on his naked flesh, shadows catching in the curves and contours of his muscles, the hollows of his eye sockets, the underside of his chin. To the men who surrounded him, he looked like an apparition. Another one approached, then a third, then all of them, crowding around him, jockeying for space, for some access, however limited, to Nick's hard flesh. Their hands were all over Nick, tugging at his skin, stroking it. The mouths followed soon afterward: moist, hungry, the tongues sliding across Nick's skin, leaving long, wet trails behind. Nick accepted them all, shifting his gaze from face to face, even letting his mouth curl up in an encouraging smile whenever a given stroke seemed hesitant and nervous. He rejected no one, regardless of age or body type or degree of beauty. One of the mouths found its way to his dick, and Nick sighed. Another man crawled down between Nick's legs and, craning his neck, bathed the loose folds of Nick's ball sac with his tongue.

Nick pushed away from the wall and into the center of the dark room. Now the men had access to every inch of his flesh. Tongues licked him everywhere, over his nipples, into his armpits, into the crack of his ass, licking his asshole as if it were a puckered ice-cream cone. Lips moved up his neck and finally planted themselves on Nick's mouth. Nick felt a tongue snake into his mouth, and he frenched the kisser back enthusiastically. He kissed one mouth and then another, and then others after that. Some of the men were skillful kissers, some were clumsy, but Nick paid them all equal attention.

The tongue up his asshole was replaced by a finger that massaged the pucker of flesh without penetrating inside. Nick exhaled slowly, relaxing his muscles, opening himself to the sensations that tingled through his body. He spread his legs farther apart and bent over slightly. The finger pushed inside him, tentatively at first, then with greater assurance, knuckle by slow knuckle, corkscrewing up until it pressed against Nick's prostate. Nick groaned. He closed his eyes, feeling the finger up his ass while another mouth worked his dick. His dick was stiff and urgent, but the orgasm eluded him, and his mind still buzzed with thoughts, no matter how much the mouths and hands worked him over. *This isn't working,* he thought. *I can't drown myself in this.*

He pulled his dick out of the latest cocksucker's mouth. "Let me fuck you," he said.

The man looked up at him, his face a pale oval in the dim light. He cleared his throat uncertainly. "There's no fucking allowed in this club," he said, his voice apologetic. "If you try, the monitors will kick us both out."

Nick didn't say anything, and after a while the man went back to sucking him off. Nick pulled out again. "I really need to fuck some ass," he said, his voice taking on an edge. The man looked up at him again but said nothing. "Look," Nick said. "Is there someplace around here where I can fuck ass?"

The man rose to his feet. Now Nick could see that he was young, late 20s maybe, short and wiry with a square, blunt face. He didn't speak for a long time. "Yeah," he finally said. "I could take you to a place."

Nick gently shook off the hands and mouths that were still feeling and tasting his body. He bent down and pulled up his jeans, then slid his T-shirt back on. "Let's go," he said.

The two of them stopped outside the club's entrance. "Do we need to drive?" Nick asked.

The man shook his head. "No," he said. "This place is only a couple of blocks away. We can walk." He was at least a head shorter

than Nick, but his body was solid and compact. He looked up at
Nick, his eyes hard and curious. "What's your name?" he asked.

"Nick."

The man still stood in front of Nick, as if waiting for something.
After a few beats, he cleared his throat. "I'm Tim," he said finally.
"In case you're interested."

"OK," Nick said.

Tim still didn't move. "We could go back to my place," he said.
"You could fuck me there." He ran his hand through his shaggy hair
and looked up into Nick's face. His voice was hard, even belligerent.
"In fact, I'd love it if you did."

Nick seemed to consider this. "Are we talking about all night?"
he asked.

Tim laughed uncertainly. "Well, eventually I'd like to get some
sleep."

Nick shook his head. "I'm not going to be sleeping tonight."

Tim stared at him. *Fucking tweaker,* he thought, not saying
anything.

Nick zipped up his jacket. "It's cold. Why don't you take me
to this place you know about?"

After a couple of beats, Tim nodded. "OK," he said.

It was a beat-up leather bar over on Harrison Street, the door a
black leather curtain tacked onto the frame with corroded chrome
studs. The space inside seemed to suck up light, and Nick could
just dimly make out the forms of men lined against the wall or
bellied up to the bar. The only illumination came from a monitor
mounted over the bar showing a fisting video.

Tim turned to Nick. "Do you want a drink first?" he asked. "Or
should we get right to the action?"

"I don't need a drink," Nick said.

Tim gave a snort of laughter and shook his head. "OK, man," he
said, "then follow me."

They threaded their way through the length of the bar. The air
vibrated with hip-hop and the buzz of conversation and occasional
laughter. Nick's eyes slowly adjusted to the dim light, and the features of the men around him came into some kind of shadowy
focus. It was a rough crowd, with weather-beaten faces and hard

eyes like black glass marbles. The crowd thickened the farther back they went, until they were surrounded by a crush of bodies. By the light of a few shaded bulbs, Nick could make out men with their pants down around their knees, stroking their dicks, being sucked by dark figures kneeling before them or fucking the men crouched in front of them. The air was thick with stale cigarette smoke and the smell of poppers. A hand groped Nick's basket while another squeezed his ass.

"This is it," Tim said. "Just about anything goes here."

The place was stifling hot from the heat of the bodies and the poor ventilation. Nick could feel beads of sweat form along his forehead, trickle down from his armpits, soak his T-shirt. The beat of the hip-hop music throbbed in the air like something tangible, and the darkness pressed down on him like a heavy cloth. Nothing felt real. *Yeah,* Nick thought. *This is more like it.* "Do you still want to get fucked?" he asked.

"Yeah," Tim said. "Sure."

Nick unbuckled his belt and pulled down his zipper. The hip-hop song ended, and the Talking Heads started singing "Take Me to the River." Nick pulled Tim to him and kissed him, pressing his body tight against him, grinding his hips. Tim snaked his tongue into Nick's mouth and slid his hands over Nick's torso, tweaking his nipples with a sharp pinch.

"Yeah," Nick said. "I like it rough like that."

Tim pulled back and fished a small square of cardboard out of his jeans pocket, pressing it into Nick's hand. It was a condom packet. "If you don't mind," he said.

"No," Nick said. "I don't mind." He tugged his jeans down, and his hard dick sprang up. He let Tim slide the condom down his shaft.

"I have lube too," Tim said.

"You're just a regular Boy Scout, aren't you?" Nick said. "Prepared for everything."

Tim gave a brief laugh. "I'm prepared at least for Friday nights." He unzipped his pants and let them fall. Nick stroked his sheathed dick with his lube-smeared hand and wrapped his arms around Tim in a tight bear hug. Other hands stretched out from the darkness and caressed his own naked ass, squeezing and pulling on the muscular cheeks, sliding up his back. Nick ignored them as he slowly skewered Tim.

Tim gave a long, drawn-out sigh, and Nick paused, his dick full in, his body pressed tight to Tim's. Slowly, almost imperceptibly, he began pumping his hips, timing his strokes to the throbbing beat of the Talking Heads. Tim moved his body in response to him, meeting him thrust for thrust. Nick sped up his strokes, his arms still folded around Tim's chest, his hips squirming against Tim's ass in deep grinding motions. He could feel himself slipping away into the act of fucking, all the *thinking* in his head dissolving into sensation. He closed his eyes in relief, welcoming the cocoon of darkness that enveloped them both, the invisible hands that stroked his body, the dark shapes that hovered around him, the music that drowned him in its volume. *Yes, this is what I need.* He slid his dick in all the way and churned his hips. Tim groaned again, louder. Tim squeezed his ass muscles tight against Nick's shaft, and Nick's legs trembled from the sensations this caused. He pulled Tim up and buried his face in Tim's neck, now slick and salty from sweat. Tim twisted his head around, and they kissed awkwardly, his lips fumbling against Tim's. He reached down and wrapped his fingers around Tim's dick. It felt thick in his hand, and its heat flooded into his palm. He stroked the fleshy tube in sync with each thrust of his dick up Tim's ass, and Tim's body writhed and pushed against him.

The hands were all over them both now, stroking them from all sides, pulling at their flesh. One man leaned his naked body against Nick, dry-humping Nick's back. Nick reached behind him and tugged on the man's balls, and after a while, groaning, the man ejaculated. Sluggish drops of come slid down Nick's back into the crack of his ass and down his leg. The man bent down and dragged his tongue against Nick's skin, eating the load he had just deposited.

"I'm getting close," Tim gasped. "I could shoot any time."

"Go for it," Nick growled in his ear. He slid his lube-slicked hand down the length of Tim's shaft just as he thrust his own cock up Tim's ass hard. Tim cried out, and his dick pulsed in Nick's hand, sperm spurting out and down the shaft like white lava as his body spasmed against Nick's.

"Yeah," someone growled. "All fuckin' right!"

Nick felt another load splatter against his back from one of the men behind him. And another after that. Tim was standing with his weight against Nick, breathing heavily, his chest rising and falling. "Damn!" he said.

Nick slowly pulled out of him and peeled the rubber off his still-hard cock. He turned toward the dark shapes beside him. "All right," he said. "Who's next?" A minute later he was slamming the ass of another stranger, his strokes hard and savage. Once again he let the darkness and the heat and the stroking hands around him strip him of everything except raw sensation. Finally! he thought, before he stopped thinking altogether.

He fucked ass all night, one after the other, the dark forms bending down before him and taking his hard dick that refused to shoot. It wasn't long before he was regarded as something of a phenomenon, even to this jaded backroom crowd. His beauty was wasted in the dark, but the men's fingers could feel his muscular body and appraise him, and his relentless dick won an eager admiration. He fucked indiscriminately, without pause, helping to trigger orgasms in one partner after another, even while his own eluded him. He fucked until gray light filtered in around the edges of the leather curtain draped over the front entrance. Now every time someone left or entered, pushing the curtain aside, a pale, feeble light washed in, even as far as the backroom where he fucked. He would catch quick glimpses of his partners, of the men who still surrounded him, waiting their turn, before the light was once more extinguished by the drop of the curtain. "You are fuckin' amazing, man," someone growled in his ear, but Nick ignored him, hell-bent on skewering the ass of the man in front of him.

He fucked until the bartender turned them all out, telling them he had to get some sleep and that they should too. Outside, the early-morning light dazzled Nick's eyes. He had lost his T-shirt somewhere back in the mass of churning bodies, and he drove home shirtless, his mind bruised and sluggish.

When he got back to his apartment, he stumbled into the shower and scrubbed himself clean. He brushed his teeth and gargled with mouthwash, but he couldn't get the metallic taste of sleeplessness out of his mouth. He looked at his bed. He was so exhausted that he had to hold on to the bathroom sink for support, but he knew he wouldn't be able to sleep. Instead he went to his closet and pulled out his suitcase.

He waited at the airport terminal on standby all that morning and afternoon before he finally snagged a seat to Newark on an early-evening flight. He was almost catatonic with exhaustion. *I'll sleep on the plane,* he thought. But after the plane took off, he just stared at the seat in front of him, his eyes burning and dry. A couple hours later he got out of his seat and walked down the aisle to the lavatory. They were flying over Ohio at the time. It was almost midnight, and the passengers were huddled in the dim light into every possible sleeping pose. One man, however, was awake, sitting in an aisle seat toward the rear of the plane. He looked like a businessman: early 40s, dark suit, and red power tie. As Nick passed they locked eyes. Nick paced up and down the aisle a couple of times, to make sure, and each time the man's eyes fixed him in a hard stare.

They fucked in the lavatory, the man hoisted up on the small chrome sink, his legs wrapped around Nick as Nick slammed into him with one hard thrust after another. The man started groaning, and Nick kissed him roughly, more to shut him up than out of passion. It was late at night, and despite the crowded plane, they had the lavatory to themselves. They didn't exit from it until the plane was preparing for its descent into Newark. The man had shot two loads, but Nick's orgasm still eluded him, even though his dick had never been stiffer.

He had telephoned his sister in the San Francisco airport, just before his flight's departure, and she was waiting for him at the terminal. The sky outside the terminal window was still black, but there was a streak of gray in the eastern horizon. This was Nick's second night without sleep. He walked over and hugged his sister as a sleepwalker would.

"You look terrible," she said.

"I feel worse," he replied.

They didn't say anything else until they were in his sister's car on the highway, driving to her home.

"Where is she?" he asked.

"At Duggin's Mortuary. The same one that buried Dad. The funeral's scheduled for Wednesday." Nick didn't say anything, just stared out the window at the oil refineries on their right. His sister glanced at him. "She was in a lot of pain, Nick. This is better."

"Yeah," he said. He leaned back and closed his eyes. It started to rain, and his sister turned on the windshield wipers. He wedged himself into the corner made by the seat and the car door, but sleep still shunned him. He lay there, eyes shut, exhausted, and listened to the rain pelt against the roof of the car.

VISITING SANTA

I pick him out right away in the middle of the crowd, holding the hand of a little girl who's maybe 4 or 5, 6 tops. The place is jammed with parents taking their kids to see Santa. It's a friggin' mob scene. Usually, by this time of day I'm so beaten down by escorting hordes of children through the Candy Cane Forest and down North Pole Avenue, flanked by the elves' houses, that I'm too numb to notice such things. But he catches my eye. He's young, early 20s maybe, and, though bundled up in a down jacket, I can see that he has a good body: the shoulders wide, the torso tapering down to narrow haunches. The little girl cranes her neck up toward him and says something, and he looks down at her and smiles. He's got a nice, open face: the eyes warm, the mouth wide and generous, the hair falling on his forehead in brown curls.

As the two of them make their way to the head of the line, I notice him looking at me more and more. I can only imagine the impression I'm making with my boots with the curled-up toes, the green and brown jerkin, and the candy-striped pointed hat. Still, the way he keeps locking eyes with me increasingly suggests something more than idle curiosity. Maybe he's got a thing for uniforms. Every time I return to the line after escorting a kid to see Santa, we exchange glances that become more and more significant. I know when I'm being eye-fucked, and by the time it's the little girl's turn to see Santa, the tension between us is as sharp and bright as an icicle.

I go into my bit. I look down at the little girl and smile. "Hi," I say. "I'm Sleighbell. What's your name?"

The little girl gives me a look half-shy, half-quizzical. "Linda," she says, after a long pause.

"Well, Linda," I say brightly. "Are you ready to see Santa Claus?"

"No," she says, backing away.

"Sure you are," the man behind her says. I glance up at him. He gives me a wink. Now a wink in this context is a very ambiguous thing, and I'm not about to jump to any conclusions here. The man smiles widely. *Maybe he's just very friendly,* I think. Up close I can see how truly handsome he is. His eyes are wide and chocolate brown, and his cheeks are still high with color from the cold outside. I have zero expectations of anything happening, but, for the hell of it, I heighten the intensity of my gaze and give him my cruisiest stare, the one I reserve for Saturday nights at crowded bars. Damn if he doesn't give it right back to me, his expression all of a sudden sharp and knowing. I look down at Linda again. *I bet your Daddy's just full of secrets,* I think.

"OK, Linda," I say. "Let's go see Santa." I take her hand, and reluctantly she lets me lead her down the path, with Mr. Sexy right behind. Santa is sitting on his Christmas throne, waiting. By the way his shoulders slump and his beard has gone slightly askew, I can tell he's feeling the strain. In the locker room this morning, I couldn't help noticing how beat-up he looked as he changed into his uniform. It's clear that Santa has seen better days.

I glance one last time at Mr. Sexy. He suddenly holds out his hand, and not knowing what else to do, I shake it. "Merry Christmas," he says, as he gives my hand an intimate squeeze and locks his gaze with mine in another, unmistakable eye-fuck.

"Yeah, sure," I say, baffled. I mean, what does he expect to happen? I go back to the next kid waiting to see Santa, leaving him and Linda behind.

The two of them show up in line again about half an hour later. "Well, hi, Linda," I say. "Back to see Santa again?" I glance at the man. His eyes are drilling holes in me. He's definitely in cruise mode.

"It wasn't my idea," Linda says, glancing up at the man. She seems a little put off.

"Oh," I say, looking back at the man. The two of us exchange significant glances above Linda's head. Once more I take in the dark eyes and sensual mouth. I imagine kissing it, with lots of tongue action. My dick quickly stiffens, a fact impossible to hide in my wintergreen tights. *What the fuck—I'll just go for broke here.* "Well, welcome back," I say brightly. "I'm Horny."

"I thought your name was Sleighbell," Linda says.

I look down at her and smile. "That was my twin brother," I say. "He's taking a break right now."

Linda seems to ponder the notion of twin elves. Her expression is dubious. "If you're not Sleighbell," she says. "Then how did you know my name?"

I give the sort of chuckle I imagine elves give. "I was just talking to Sleighbell a few minutes ago," I say. "He told me that he had just met the prettiest little girl named Linda"—I give the man a level look—"and that her daddy was very, very handsome. When I saw the two of you, I just knew you had to be the little girl he was talking about."

"He's not my daddy," Linda says, glancing up at the man and then at me again. "He's my uncle."

"Hi," the man says, grinning. "I'm Horny too."

"No, you're not," Linda says. "Your name is Don."

Don smiles down at her. "Yes, sweetheart. But Horny is my other name. My Christmas name." He winks at me. "And my Friday and Saturday night name too."

"Where's Sleighbell?" the little girl asks me.

I point to the row of elves' cottages a few feet away. They stand about seven feet high and are nothing more than plywood fronts. "He's resting behind those cottages," I say. I lock my gaze with Don's and speak slowly and distinctly. "No one ever goes back there, so it's a nice, quiet place to go if you want a little privacy."

Don nods his head. He places his hand on Linda's shoulder. "Come on, honey," he says. "Let's go see Santa now one more time." He gently steers her down Candy Cane Path. I follow them with my eyes until they make a turn and are out of sight.

It's a slow period right now, so I figure it'd be all right if I take an unscheduled break. I catch the eye of Twinkle (I only know my coworkers by their elf names) and motion him over. "Can you cover for me for a few minutes?" I ask. Twinkle's personality doesn't exactly live up to his name; in fact, he has the "fuck you" attitude of the typical New York punk that I suspect he is during his off-hours.

However, I've covered for him enough times when he wants to go to the men's room and smoke a joint, and he owes me this. It's not long before I'm sneaking behind the elves' cottages, while, scowling, Twinkle leads the children to Santa. I sit down, leaning against one of the wood props. About five minutes later I hear the sound of a throat clearing. I look up and see Don standing next to me. "Hi, Horny," he says, grinning.

I grin back. "Where's Linda?"

"She's with her mom, looking at Barbie dolls."

"I only have a few minutes," I say.

"Well," Don says, unbuckling his belt. "Then we better get right down to business." He unzips his fly and tugs his jeans down. His dick springs out, fully hard, twitching and red. I wrap my hand around it and give it a squeeze, feeling its warmth spread into my palm. It's a handful, all right; thick and long, its head flaring out like a Christmas sugarplum. I give his dick another good squeeze, and a little bead of prejizz oozes out. I lean forward and lap it up, running my tongue around the fleshy knob. Don sighs and pushes his hips forward, and my lips slide down his shaft until my nose is pressed up against his curly brown pubes. I stay like that for a moment, feeling my mouth filled to the brim with cock, which, for me, is about as good as good gets. I cradle Don's ball sac in my hand, feeling its heft, its hairiness, tugging on it gently as my mouth slides up and down his dick shaft. Don sighs again, louder, and begins pumping his hips, fucking my face in long, slow strokes. I reach behind and squeeze his smooth, firm ass cheeks, feeling them clench and relax with each thrust. "Rudolph the Red-Nosed Reindeer" is playing over the sound system, and I hear the voices of kids and their parents just a few feet away on the other side of the backdrop, waiting to see Santa. Everything takes on a surreal quality.

I start sucking on Don's balls, rolling them around with my tongue, locking my eyes with his as he slaps my face with his hard dick. Don's eyes burn brightly, his mouth is half open, and his breath rasps out in ragged gasps. I slide my hands under his shirt, feeling the toned flesh of his lean torso. I find his nipples and twist them. Don gives a low groan. I twist them again, just as I slide my mouth down Don's dick shaft again, my head twisting from side to side. Don groans again, louder, and his body shudders under my hands as his dick squirts its load down my throat, one pulse after another. I drink it greedily, sucking on the meaty tube of flesh, draining it dry. Even after the last squirt has been swallowed, I suck on Don's cock, savoring its taste, the texture of its silky flesh. It's with great reluctance that I finally allow Dan to pull his pants back up again.

"Thanks," Don said. "I needed that."

I give a slight smile. "It's our store's policy. Anything to keep the customer happy."

A few minutes later it's time for my regularly scheduled break. I use it as an opportunity to grab a quick smoke outside. I'm joined by another elf, Chuckles. Chuckles is our oldest elf, well into his 70s. Of all of us, he is the most elf-like: short, almost tiny, with big jug ears and a red bulbous nose. I asked him once why he picked a name more suitable for a clown than an elf. His reply was that I had my head up my ass, his standard answer to any number of comments.

As Chuckles and I suck on our cigarettes, Don, Linda, and a woman I assume is Linda's mom, exit the stores and walk by us, clutching piles of packages. Linda smiles and waves at me. "Merry Christmas, Horny," she calls out.

I glance at Chuckles. "I think she's talking to you," I say. Chuckles looks confused.

The next morning Twinkle and I are standing side by side in the store's locker room, changing into our elf costumes. Twinkle is stripped down to his briefs, and I can't help sneaking admiring glances at him. He's short (which is probably why he got the job as an elf; it certainly wasn't because of his cheerful disposition), with a wiry, compact body, smooth and tightly muscled. Twinkle has the black hair, dark eyes, and the "What the fuck are you looking at?" attitude of a New York Sicilian. He's also a fellow queer; we established our sexual brotherhood on our first day of the job after five minutes of conversation.

"I hear we're getting a new Santa," Twinkle says.

"Oh, yeah," I say. "How come?"

Twinkle gives a derisive snort. "One of the moms complained to store management yesterday afternoon that Santa was tanked. She could smell the booze on his breath."

I remember the tilt in Santa's body yesterday that grew worse as the day progressed. I shake my head. "Where are they going to find a new Santa at this late date?" I ask.

Twinkle's lips curl up into something halfway between a smile and a sneer. "I recommended a friend who needed a job. The guys in management are talking to him right now." There's something about Twinkle's expression that makes me suspicious. "What kind of friend?" I ask. But Twinkle just shrugs. "Come on," I persist. "Where do you know this guy from?"

Twinkle shrugs again. "Just somebody I met at Blow Buddies."

I look at him. "You mean you recommended somebody you met in a sex club to be Santa Claus?"

Twinkle closes his locker door and gives me a hard look. "Don't make such a big deal of it," he growls. "Who the fuck are you, the Virgin Mary?"

I don't meet the new Santa until after I assume my station at the entrance to Candy Cane Forest. It's 5 minutes to 9, and the kids and parents are queued up all the way back to men's haberdashery. Nine o'clock comes around. Then a quarter after 9. The kids are starting to grumble and whine, and the parents are shooting me dirty looks, as if it's my damn fault that Santa is late. To placate them, I go back to Santa Village to find out what's going on. I find Twinkle by the entrance to Santa's home.

"Where the hell is Santa?" I growl. "I'm about to get stoned by the mob out there."

Twinkle shrugs, his expression bored. "He's having a hard time fitting into the uniform."

"Jesus!" I exclaim. "He's too fat for a *Santa* suit?"

"He's not too *fat*," Twinkle says, scowling. "He's too *big*."

I'm about to make a comment when the door leading from the dressing room opens and Santa comes out. I understand Twinkle's distinction now. The guy is fuckin' *huge,* almost seven feet tall, with shoulders you could build a condominium on. His hands stick out of the sleeves with at least four inches of wrist showing. The hands are huge too. They look like they could crush a man's head like a casaba melon.

Twinkle grins. "Yo, Santa!" he says. He glances down at Santa's feet. "Since when does Santa wear snakeskin boots?"

"Since Santa's feet don't fit in the fuckin' boots the store has," Santa growls in a deep baritone. He looks at me, his eyes peering intently between the red cap and the long white beard.

"This is Sleighbell," Twinkle says.

"Yo, dude," Santa says, nodding at me. He keeps his eyes trained on me.

"Well, I better get back to the kids," I say. I'm beginning to feel uncomfortable under Santa's hard scrutiny, and it's a relief to get away. Twinkle walks back with me.

"I think he likes you," Twinkle says, grinning, as we stride through the Candy Cane Forest.

"Lucky me."

"You ought to see his dick. It looks like a fuckin' table leg."

"Jesus, Twinkle," I say, shaking my head. We don't say anything else for the rest of the walk back.

The morning goes smoothly enough, with no major mishaps. I notice that after the kids leave Santa's home they seem unusually subdued. I guess they never pictured Santa as Lurch before. Santa is entitled to one morning break, and the three of us—Santa, Twinkle, and I—share a joint in the employees' men's room. Santa doesn't say much, but once again I feel his eyes trained on me throughout the entire break. I pretend like I don't notice.

"Jeez, does Santa ever have the hots for you," Twinkle says, as the two of us make our way back to our stations.

"No kidding." I say dryly.

"You should be flattered. He's real popular at Blow Buddies."

The three of us work well into the evening. It's two days before Christmas, and the crowds never let up. We're raking in the overtime, and by the time 9 o'clock rolls by and I put the CLOSED sign on the entrance to the Candy Cane Forest, I'm bone-tired.

I walk back to Santa's Village, hitting the light switches as I go. Twinkle is once again at the door to Santa's house. The way he peers at me, shifting from foot to foot, I can tell that something's up.

"How you feelin', man?" he asks.

"OK, I guess." I say, looking at him suspiciously. He's never bothered to ask me that before. "I'm sure as hell ready to call it a day."

"Santa told me he wants to see you before you go," Twinkle says. "He wants to see both of us." He gives me that funny look again.

"What are you up to?" I ask.

"Nothin', nothin'," Twinkle says. He gestures impatiently. "Come on. Let's go visit Santa."

He opens the door, and after a brief pause I follow him into Santa's house. Santa is waiting there on his throne, like I've seen him dozens of times today. The only difference is that this time his red fur-trimmed pants are down around his ankles and he's stroking his dick. My first thought is *Twinkle was right: It does look like a table leg.*

Santa's red jacket is also unbuttoned and open, and the pillow that was stuffed under it has been tossed onto the floor. I take in Santa's massive torso: the swell of the pecs, the swollen, pierced nipples that stand out like miniature fireplugs, the chiseled abs. A mat of chest hair descends down the tight belly before spreading out into the pubic bush, which, unlike Santa's hair and beard, is as black as the coal that bad little boys get in their stockings on Christmas morning. His balls hang low in their fleshy red sac, but it's the monster schlong that commands my attention. Everything about this naked, muscular Santa is on the grand scale, and, seated on his raised throne and surrounded by twinkling lights, he presents an awesome sight: Santa as conceived by Michelangelo. A clear, soprano voice starts singing "O Holy Night" over the sound system, and a chill runs down my spine. I think I'm having a religious moment here.

Santa stirs on his throne. "Why don't you come sit on Santa's lap," he growls, "and tell me what you want for Christmas?"

I glance over in Twinkle's direction. Twinkle has his tights pulled down below his knees, and he's stroking his dick slowly, his bright, shrewd eyes shifting from me to Santa and back to me again. His dick is fat and nicely formed, swelling to a fleshy knob, maybe seven inches, but looking much bigger in proportion to his shortness.

I cross the room, head buzzing, and right when the soprano's voice rises in crescendo—singing "Fall on your knees!"—I take Santa's huge boner in my hand and slowly slide my lips down the shaft. Santa puts his huge hands on either side of my head and starts fucking my face, thrusting his cock down my throat in deep, long strokes. It's a beauty of a dick, worthy of Santa, and I make hungry love to it, twisting my head from side to side, wrapping my tongue around it, sucking on it with loud slurping noises. Twinkle joins me on the other side, and Santa pumps his hips as his dick thrusts up and down between our mouths. I cradle Santa's balls in my hand, feeling their heft, their *meatiness,* imagining the little blizzard of jizz they promise to deliver. I bury my face in them and breathe deeply, smelling the pungent smell of Santa in rut. I take Santa's ball sac in my mouth and roll my tongue over his nuts as Twinkle continues to work over Santa's candy-red dick.

Santa pushes himself off his throne and steps into the middle of the room. Twinkle and I undress him, like attendant elves, pulling off his snakeskin boots ("Be careful with those!" Santa growls), stripping off his jacket and leggings. We leave his red hat on, with the cotton snowball at the tip and, of course, the whiskers. Santa stands naked in the middle of the room, the different colors of the twinkling Christmas lights playing over his muscular flesh. Twinkle and I proceed to worship his body, dragging our tongues over his torso, raising his arms and burying our mouths into Santa's sweaty pits, stroking the hard flesh, running our hands over the twin smooth globes of Santa's ass cheeks. Santa stands there impassively, receiving our adoration, his swollen boner thrust out and twitching. When I start licking his neck, Santa entwines his fingers in my hair, tilts my head up, and plants his mouth on mine. He thrusts his tongue deep down my throat, and I suck on it eagerly as I twist his left nipple ring. "Yeah," Santa growls. "That's a good elf. Play with Santa's tittie."

Santa turns me around so that I'm facing away from him, and wraps his huge arms around my torso in a bear hug. I feel his hard dick push against the length of my ass crack, his body pressed tightly against mine, his whiskers spilling over my shoulder as he nuzzles my neck. He looks down at Twinkle. "Suck Sleighbell's dick," he growls. "Take good care of my little elf buddy."

Twinkle is only too happy to comply. He gets down on his knees in front of me and proceeds to work my dick over. Twinkle is a skillful cocksucker, and I close my eyes and let the sensations play over me: Twinkle's eager lips swallowing my dick shaft, Santa's muscular arms enfolding me, his hands twisting my nipples as his enormous cock slides up and down my ass crack. "The Little Drummer Boy" is playing over the sound system now. Twinkle takes my dick out of his mouth and starts sucking on my balls. His eyes lock with mine, my scrotum in his mouth, and I slap my dick against his face with a loud *thwack*.

"OK, Sleighbell," Santa growls. "Santa going to ride your ass. Santa's going to ride it to the North Pole and back again." He reaches down to his pants and pulls a condom packet out of the pocket, and a tiny jar of lube. He hands them both to Twinkle. "Here," he says gruffly. "Get Santa ready for some hot elf sex."

Twinkle rolls the rubber down Santa's dick and then lubes it up liberally. Santa takes what's left of the lube and squirts a dollop of it into his hand. He reaches down and thoroughly greases up my asshole. He bends his knees, and I can feel his dick head push against my pucker. I lean forward, and Santa impales me, driving his thick dick up my ass inch by slow inch. I groan loudly. "Fuckin' A," Twinkle says, his eyes gleaming, watching the show Santa and I are putting on for him. He leans forward and takes my dick in my mouth again.

Santa starts pumping his hips, plowing his fleshy piston in and out of my ass with thrusts that lift me off my feet each time he drives his dick home, his heavy balls slapping against me. He's sweating hard now, and his flesh slips and slides against me as his hands tug and stroke my body. I can feel his hot breath on the back of my neck, the tickle of his whiskers. The sound of his labored breathing fills my ear, like some workhorse struggling up a hill with a heavy load. Twinkle goes back to sucking me off, and he feeds greedily on my dick as he strokes his own. Santa thrusts his dick full up my ass and keeps it there, grinding his hips against me in a slow circular motion. I give another heartfelt groan that bounces off the walls of the small room.

Santa resumes fucking me with his staccato thrusts, hoisting me up so that I'm standing on my toes. He twists my head back and snakes his tongue into my mouth again. Every thrust now brings a little whimper out of him. The whimpers start getting louder, trailing into moans. I reach down and cup his balls with my hand, feeling how tight they're pulled up now. I know it won't be long before Santa shoots his load. I put a finger between Santa's balls and press hard, just as he delivers another thrust. Santa groans mightily, and I feel his body spasm against mine. His dick pulses in my ass, and Santa proceeds to squirt his load, his body thrashing. I do an involuntary dance as I ride the wave of his orgasm while dangling in his arms. After the last spasm passes, Santa gently lets me down and falls against the wall, breathing heavily.

Twinkle is still working my dick through all of this. Santa stands up again and slides his hands over my body, growling encouragement. He gives both of my nipples a hard twist, and that's all it takes to push me over the edge. "Oh, jeez, I'm coming!" I gasp, as I arch my back and let it rip, feeling my load shoot hard down Twinkle's throat. Twinkle gulps it down thirstily, milking my dick dry. He gives a groan muffled by my dick in his mouth, and looking down, I see his own milky load ooze out between his fingers.

"Fuckin' A," Santa growls. I pull Twinkle up and kiss him, tasting the yeasty froth of my come still in his mouth. The three of us stand there, our bodies pressed tightly together, swaying gently as "White Christmas" plays on the sound system. "Jesus, I hate that song," Santa growls.

Two days later, on Christmas Eve, the three of us turn in our uniforms and draw our paychecks. We go to a neighborhood bar around the corner from the store and toss down a few beers to mark the end of our jobs. It's snowing outside, and as I watch the snowflakes fall against the plate glass and melt, I'm surprised to find I'm feeling a little sad that it's all over. I learn that Twinkle's real name is Lou, short for Luigi, and that Santa's is Bernie. Like me, Lou has no family in the city to celebrate Christmas with. Bernie is Jewish. None of us has plans for Christmas Day. The bar closes early, and when we finally leave the place, the streets are deserted. The snow is coming down harder now. I'm suddenly feeling depressed at the thought of waking up alone on Christmas Day, with no tree or presents. I look at Lou and Bernie. "I've got some primo grass back at my place," I say. "You guys interested in coming over?" I give them each a significant look. "And maybe spend the night?"

Bernie and Lou exchange glances. "Sure," Bernie says.

"I'm game," Lou says.

"Well, all right," I say. The three of us head down the street toward the nearest subway entrance. "Silent Night" is playing over the loudspeaker of a store we pass on the corner.

IN THE ALLEY WITH ANGELO

The naked man stands with his back to the camera, his legs planted far apart in parade rest, his back arched. His back is powerful and muscular, the delts sharply defined, plunging down into a V whose apex is an ass so perfect my eyes water from the beauty of it. I try to imagine what it would feel like to run my hands over those twin half-moons of flesh, squeezing them, molding them with my fingers, prying the crack apart and exposing the sweet pink pucker of the asshole. The guy in the magazine is standing at a slight angle, his face in quarter profile, just revealing the tip of his nose, one eyelid, and the profile of a strong jaw. The shaft of his hard cock juts out beyond the line of his right hip, plunged into the mouth of the equally naked man who is kneeling before him. The kneeling man has his eyes closed, his blissed-out expression saying *This is it! It doesn't get any better than this!*

I close the magazine and stuff it back in the rack, scanning the other covers in front of me. Hot guys with muscle-packed bodies smile back at me, or glare, giving me lots of attitude, clutching their dicks, their eyes challenging me. I would dearly love to buy one these porno rags, something I could smuggle into the bathroom and jerk off to until my gonads dropped off. But the shit would hit the fan if Carol ever stumbled across it; Christ, I don't even want to think about how ugly it could get. I glance at my watch. Six o'clock: the commuter bus is due in five minutes. As I hurry out the door, my gaze meets that of the proprietor hunched behind the counter. He gives me the fish-eye, though I can't really blame the guy. He must be getting tired of seeing me paw through his magazines every day after work without ever buying anything.

There's a fine drizzle misting down, almost more of a heavy fog than actual rain. The bus is already at the stop, and I just barely manage to jump aboard before it pulls away. I squeeze in next to the door and hold on to the overhead railing. I let my mind wander to the pictures I just looked at in the magazines: the muscular bodies, the thick dicks plowing ass, getting sucked, the handsome dudes staring back from the pages. My mind races ahead to the routine I've worked out for myself once I get home: I'll kiss Carol hello, we'll talk for a few minutes, and then I'll excuse myself and go to the bathroom to jerk off while the images are still fresh in my mind. I sigh. *I'm 28 years old,* I think. *Is this all I have to look forward to for the rest of my life?*

We are driving through the rough part of town, winos in doorways, boarded-up storefronts, porno shops, and working girls on the street corners. I count the blocks and when we stop at the light at Jones Street, I crane my neck and look out the window. The bar squats there on the corner like a something out of a combat zone: dingy, paint flaking, the flickering neon sign sputtering and hissing the words THE COCK PIT. For the seven months that I've been riding this bus, I find myself anticipating this corner; it's become the high point of the long ride home. Loud music pours out onto the street and into the bus's windows. Guys lounge around outside, smoking, sometimes talking. I think of the picture of the naked man getting his cock sucked, of the blissful look on the cocksucker's face, and without even thinking about what I'm doing, I push my way out of the safety of the bus and onto the ragged threat of Jones Street.

The bus roars off in a cloud of diesel exhaust, and as it turns the corner and disappears, I'm gripped by disbelief. *What the fuck was I thinking?* The guys outside the bar all turn their heads toward me, their eyes beading on me like tracer missiles, taking in the pin-striped Italian suit and Brooks Brothers raincoat. I glare back at them and enter the noisy bar. Just like outside, the eyes nail me to the wall; I can almost read their thoughts: fair game. I make my way to the bar. The bartender is huge; his flesh spills out under his black T-shirt and over its collar in folds of fat. I order a Seagram's and 7UP and take a deep drink.

I look around the bar. The initial anxiety has receded now, giving way to a powerful curiosity. The guys at the bar are shouting at each other, talking over the din of the rap music pouring out of the jukebox. Other men line the wall, beers and cigarettes in their hands, alone, alert, like they're waiting for something to happen. Several of them are training their hard eyes on me, wasting no energy on subtlety. Some of them are young, and all of them look like trouble. In spite of the rain outside, it's a warm, summer night, and they're dressed in tank tops and shorts, revealing sleek torsos curved with muscle, hard and lean.

I drain my glass and order another drink. The cigarette smoke is making my eyes burn, the music is giving me a headache, but surprisingly I feel myself flying, exhilarated. Mercifully, the rap song comes to an end, and to my surprise, an old Beatles tune comes on. I take another deep gulp and close my eyes.

"Hi," a voice says to me.

I open my eyes. A young guy stands in front of me, Puerto Rican, maybe, or Mexican, with slicked-back black hair and dark, liquid eyes that quickly scan up and down my body. I can almost hear the gears in his brain click and whir. His mouth is wide and the lips full and the body under his fishnet T-shirt is tight and well-defined. "Hello," I say.

His lips pull back into a smile, and his teeth flash. "So what are you doing here, man?" he asks. "Slumming?"

"I'm just having a drink," I say, a little testily.

The guy shrugs, still smiling, his head ducked low, his eyes looking at me sideways. He turns and looks around the room, and for a minute I think he's forgotten about me. But his head swivels around suddenly and his eyes focus full on my face. "You feel like buying me a drink?" he asks.

I give him a long look. "All right," I finally say. I catch the bartender's eye. "Another beer," I say. I glance at the bottle in the guy's hand. "A Bud."

"A Johnny Walker," the guy corrects me. "Neat." He gives me a sly smile. "I only drink beer when *I'm* paying for it."

I smile in spite of myself, and his grin widens. I nod my OK to the bartender. "And bring me another Seagram's and 7, OK?"

The bartender brings us our drinks, and we clink them together. We're getting on like gangbusters.

"What's your name?" he asks.

"Neil."

He sticks out his hand. "Angelo." We shake. His grip is firm, the palms sweaty. Drops of perspiration line his forehead, and his body gives off a thick, musky odor. For the first time, I notice how *hot* it is here, bodies pressed together, bare skin gleaming with a sheen of sweat. And here I am in my suit and raincoat. I feel a drop of sweat trickle down my armpit, and I loosen my tie.

"So what brings you down here, Neil?" Angelo asks.

I shrug. "I felt like having a drink. I saw the bar, so I got off the bus."

Angelo stares at me boldly for a few seconds. He shakes his head and looks away. When he looks at me again, his eyes are sly and his lips are pulled back into a smirk. But he doesn't say anything.

"What?" I ask, feeling the blood rush to my face.

But Angelo just grins and keeps on staring at me. "You didn't come into this bar for no fuckin' drink," he finally says.

"Oh, yeah? Then why *did* I come here?"

Angelo grabs his crotch and tugs on it. "For this, man."

Sweet Jesus, I think, *I'm over my head here.* I stare at Angelo, taking in the muscular brown body, the dark eyes and full lips, the *scent* of him. The image of Angelo naked flashes into my mind, his dick thick and meaty, and suddenly I'm overwhelmed by a surge of horniness. I take a deep gulp from my drink. My hand is shaking, and to my annoyance I see that Angelo notices it.

"Maybe we can work out a deal," he says calmly.

I clear my throat. "I'm listening." I'm holding my glass so tight my knuckles are white.

"Forty bucks for a blow job," he says, all business now. He nods toward the rear of the bar. "Back in the alley behind the bar."

I stare at him. "You mean out in the open? What if we get caught?"

Angelo shrugs. "It's cool. The cops don't go back there. Anybody who's there is looking for the same thing."

My biggest walk on the wild side so far has been having sex with

Carol on the patio in our back yard . Getting blown by another man in an alley behind a bar seems as fantastic as flapping my arms and flying. I shake my head. "No way. Not a chance."

Angelo raises his eyebrows and looks at me. "OK, man," he says, sliding off the stool.

He starts back to the wall.

"No, wait!" I say, my voice sharp.

Men nearby glance at me. Angelo turns. He comes back and resumes his perch on the barstool, his face calm. He looks at me expectantly.

"Maybe we could go to a motel," I say. The music from the jukebox is so loud I almost feel it like a force pushing against my face. My throat is raw from shouting. *If it were only quiet for a few minutes, I could think clearly.* I shouldn't have had that last drink.

"What the fuck!" Angelo laughs. "You think there's a Holiday Inn around the corner?" He tosses down the last of his drink and looks at me with amused disdain. "There ain't no motels in this neighborhood, *Neil.*" He leans forward and puts his hand on my thigh. Excitement races through my body even as I pull back. "It's the alley or nothin'." I don't say anything, and he leans forward, stroking my inner thigh. "Come on, Neil," he croons. "Come on, pretty baby. It'll be fun. No one sucks dick like me. I know I'll really get into it tonight, a hot-looking man like you." His hand slides up and cups my crotch, pushing against my stiff dick. No man has ever done that to me before.

"All right," I say, my voice hoarse. "Let's go."

The fine mist is still coming down back in the alley, and its coolness against my face feels like a blessing after the heat from all the sweaty bodies in the bar. The Cock Pit flanks one side of the alley, facing what looks like some kind of slum residential hotel. Angelo wedges me against a Dumpster and grabs my crotch again. I can't breathe, and I yank off my tie and undo the top two buttons of my shirt. Angelo reaches over and undoes the rest of the buttons. He slides his hands down my chest and flicks his thumbs against my nipples, then squeezes them between his thumbs and forefingers. I groan softly. His hands continue down my torso, kneading the flesh.

"Nice," he murmurs. "Good and solid." He cups my crotch again and lightly kisses me. He pulls back and looks me in the eye. "I like to get paid in advance," he says.

I fumble my wallet out of my back pocket and pull out two twenties. I stuff them in his hand, but before I can pull my hand back he grabs hold of it, turning it over, palm up. He lightly touches my wedding ring. "Bet your ol' lady's wondering where you're at right now," he grins.

I jerk my hand back. "You better change the subject *fast*," I say.

"Easy man, easy," he croons. He reaches down and pulls down my zipper. He unbuckles my belt and slides my pants down. I feel the thin fabric slither down my legs. My hard cock is clearly outlined against the cotton of my Jockeys, a wet spot of precome staining the white cloth. Angelo grins. "Looks like your ready to party, dude."

He hooks his thumbs under the elastic band and yanks them down. My cock springs up to full attention, and Angelo wraps his hand around it. I have never had a man touch my dick before, and the feel of Angelo's callused palm around it is electrifying. He squeezes gently, and a clear drop of precome oozes out. Angelo begins sliding his hand up and down the shaft, pulling the foreskin over the head and then peeling it back again. I suddenly grab his wrist and stop him, to keep from shooting.

"Right," Angelo says, nodding his head. "Let's drag this out a little." He kneels down in front of me and takes my balls in his mouth, rolling them around with his tongue. I groan. Angelo reaches up and cups my ass cheeks with his hands, pulling me closer to him. His eyes meet mine, and I slap his face with my dick, striking his cheeks, his eyes, his nose. Angelo releases my balls and slowly slides his tongue up my dick shaft, leaving a wet path behind it. When he gets to the head, all flared and leaking precome, he tongues the piss-slit, probing the tip of his tongue into it, lapping up the drops of clear fluid. My cock head slides into his mouth and then he works his lips down the shaft, sucking noisily. "Christ," I moan. Angelo starts bobbing his head, sliding his lips up and down my dick, twisting his head from side to side to heighten the sensations of his wet mouth and busy tongue. The rap music is spilling out of the backdoor and (amazingly!) I'm getting into it this time—the driving beat, the hard edge to it. I start pumping my hips to the beat of the music, cramming my dick hard down Angelo's mouth, and then pulling back again until the head rests between his lips. I shove my hips forward again, and as my dick slides between Angelo's lips, I groan again, louder this time. It's clear to me that if I keep this up with Angelo, I'll be squirting my load in a matter of seconds.

I pull out of Angelo's mouth, and he looks up at me expectantly. "Stand up," I tell him. Angelo climbs to his feet and I drop down to my knees in front of him. The image flashes through my mind of the picture in the porno magazine, the blissful look on the kneeling man's face as he sucked on the fat dick crammed down his throat. What I want now, more than anything, is to get a taste of *dick,* find out what it feels like to have another man fuck my face. I unzip Angelo's jeans, and pull his pants down slowly, my heart racing.

Angelo's dick flops half-hard against his thigh, and his balls, swollen from the heat of the summer night, hang low and meaty. I stare for a few moments in silence, taking this all in. I can see why a man's dick is called a root, because that's what Angelo's reminds me of, some kind of brown fleshy tuber with a swollen pink head. His balls are darker, almost black, and they hang in loose folds of flesh. Angelo twists his hips, and his balls sway heavily back and forth like ripe fruit from a tree branch caught in the wind. I breathe in deeply and get a whiff of musk and perspiration and, leaning forward, inhale again. The scent is stronger now, rich and heavy. I bury my face in his balls, and their thick, pungent odor fills my lungs, intoxicates me. No woman smells like this, this is the stink of a *man.* I part my lips and gently tongue Angelo's balls; I open wider and ball meat spills inside my mouth. I roll his scrotum around with my tongue, savoring its silky texture, the raunchiness of its taste. "Yeah, that's right," Angelo croons softly, "Suck on my nuts, juice them up good."

With his balls still in my mouth, I look up, past Angelo's thick, dark meat, across the expanse of his muscled torso, directly into his face. Angelo stares back with half-lidded eyes, the faintest of smiles playing on his lips. My gaze slides down his body until I'm staring at his dick again. It's enormous, filling my vision, swimming in front of my eyes. Everything else has been stripped from me except the hunger to suck cock. I open my mouth and slide my lips down the shaft, slobbering over the thick meat in my mouth, feeling the balls press against my chin. Angelo's dick has swollen to full hardness now, filling my mouth completely. I roll my tongue around it, sucking on it like Angelo did with mine, trying to capture his technique. Angelo holds my head with both hands and starts pumping his hips. His dick pushes hard against the back of my throat, triggering my gag reflex. I pull away, gasping for air and coughing.

"Easy," Angelo says softly.

I look up at Angelo. "Sorry," I say. "I've never done this before."

A small smile plays across Angelo's lips, but it doesn't reach his eyes. "Just some white boy lookin' for new kicks, huh?" he says.

"Yeah," I say, making my voice hard. "Something like that." It's not easy developing an attitude when you're on your knees with your pants tangled around your ankles. It was a mistake telling Angelo I'm new to all this.

"Just do what I tell you," Angelo says gruffly. He takes a step closer so that his erect dick is almost pushed into my face. He twitches it, and it bobs heavily. "Shake hands with it," he says. "Treat it like a friend." I wrap my hand around it and squeeze gently. "Harder," he says. "This ain't fine china you're playing with." I squeeze again, with more force, and a drop of prejizz leaks out. "Now lick it up," Angelo orders. I twirl my tongue around the dark brown cock head, tasting the slimy drop. "OK, now put the head in your mouth." I open my lips and Angelo slides the tip of his dick in. "Put your lips around it and suck on it." As I obey him, Angelo slides his meat in until it fills my mouth. There's still at least three inches to go. "Tilt your head back," he orders. I do so and Angelo pushes his dick all the way in until his balls press against my chin. I feel like I'm suffocating. "Breathe through your nose," he says sharply. "Cause I'm not taking my dick out till I'm good and ready." He reaches back and holds the back of my head firmly. I struggle for a few moments before I get the hang of it. I relax, getting used to the sensation of having a hard dick full in my mouth. Angelo slowly pulls out until just the head is between my lips again. Then he pushes his hips forward again and the cock slides back in. "Suck on it," he rasps. "You want to learn how to suck cock?—well, fuckin' make me feel it!"

I bob my head back and forth now, taking on Angelo's dick as he fucks my face. *This is it! I actually have a dick in my mouth! This is what it feels like!* I feed greedily on the thick tube of meat, slobbering over it, then licking his balls, sucking them into my mouth before returning to sucking cock. I've got one hand around the base of his shaft, while my other hand strokes my own dick lightly, just enough to bring me to the brink of climax without going over the edge. Angelo groans and I look up to see his face flushed, his lips parted. "Yeah," he says. "You're getting the hang of it. Just keep on sucking my dick like that." After a little while he pulls back. "Listen," he says, breathing heavily. "How would you like me to fuck your ass?"

I stare at him and then shake my head violently. "No fucking way."

Angelo pulls a square of foil from his pocket. "I got rubbers, man. You got nothing to worry about."

"No," I say, my voice harder. "Forget it."

"Then you fuck me," Angelo says. "For an extra $20."

I look at him standing there in front of me naked, his thick dick and balls gleaming with my saliva, his smooth, brown body tight and muscled. I squeeze my eyes shut, trying to clear my head. I open them and meet Angelo's gaze. "OK," I say.

I climb to my feet, and Angelo rolls a condom down my hard dick. The mist of rain has thickened to a light drizzle, and the wetness on my face clears my head slightly. I look around at the Dumpster, the trash on the pavement, the walls of crumbling brick on either side of us. I turn back and look at Angelo again. An hour ago I was on a commuter bus heading back to the suburbs. I can't believe any of this is fuckin' real. Angelo spits in his hand and slicks up my dick.

"That'll have to do," he says. "I don't have any lube." He turns around and plants both palms to the brick wall, looking for all the world like a suspect ready to be frisked. His hips are narrow and his ass is a very pretty thing, smooth and dimpled.

I wrap my arms around his torso in a bear hug and press my body hard against his. My dick slides along the crack of his ass, and as I rub up and down against it, Angelo rotates his hips. "Fuck me, man," Angelo growls. "Plow me good."

My cock head pokes against his asshole and Angelo reaches back and guides it in. He groans. I push my hips forward and slide my dick in all the way. Angelo's ass feels like tight velvet against my cock flesh, a sensation distinctly different from pussy. I grind my hips against him, churning his ass good, and Angelo groans again. I pull out halfway and then slam hard inside him again. Angelo reaches behind and squeezes my balls as he meets me thrust for thrust. After a few seconds, we catch our stride, Angelo falling in sync with me. The music continues to pour out of the bar, loud and urgent, the beat pounding. My arms are still wrapped around his torso, and I feel his body squirm against mine, his wet skin slippery and warm. My hand slides down until it wraps around his dick, and I start beating him off, my stroke in sync with the piston strokes of my dick. I raise my head up, eyes closed, and the light rain drips on my face. Our bodies are locked tightly together, skin to skin, and every thrust of my dick up Angelo's ass actually lifts him up hard against the wall, heels raised. I tighten my grip and swing him around so that he's draped over the Dumpster. This angle gives me better access to that sweet, puckered asshole of his, and I shove my dick in hard. Angelo grunts, and I shove again. His dick gives a special throb, and I can tell that it won't take much to push him over the brink. Angelo suddenly squeezes his ass tight against my dick and wiggles his hips. A shock of pleasure shoots through me. Angelo does it again, and the pleasure rises closer to climax. I groan loudly. Angelo reaches back and gives a tug on my balls just as he squeezes his ass for a third time. I cry out as my climax convulses through me, making my body shudder, my load slamming hard into the condom up Angelo's ass. I hold on to his body tight as I ride the spasm out. "Yeah," Angelo groans. "Shoot that load up my ass." I shudder a few more times as my dick pumps out the last few squirts. I collapse on Angelo's back.

We stand like that for a few moments, Angelo draped over the Dumpster, me still clutching his body in a bear hug. I straighten up and Angelo turns to face me. His dick is still hard, and his balls are pulled up and ready to blast out their load of jizz.

"Get on your knees," he growls.

I obey him, almost tripping against my slacks coiled around my ankles. Bits of gravel and grit bite into my knees. Angelo stands over me, pumping his dick furiously. He suddenly groans loudly and a thick, ropy wad of jizz arcs out of his dick and splatters against my face, followed by another, and then another. By the time he's done shooting, my cheeks, nose, and lips are coated with his sperm. He drags his dick across my face, smearing it with the last of his load.

I just stay there for a few seconds in my kneeling position, feeling the light rain drip down on my cheeks and lips, mingling with Angelo's come, diluting it. I wipe my sleeve against my face and stagger to my feet. I pull on my clothes again, my mind dazed. My slacks are smeared with the filth that coats the alley pavement, and my coat is soaking wet and streaked with garbage. My tie is in a crumpled pile at my feet. I bend down and pick it up, noting how filthy it now is. Angelo pulls up his jeans, and I get one last glimpse of that beautiful, thick dick before he zips up his fly. I pull out my wallet and give him his extra $20 for the ass fuck, and throw in another $10 to boot. Angelo says nothing, but slips the money in his back pants pocket. His expression is unreadable.

I walk back into the bar. The men take in my filthy, disheveled clothes and grin derisively. Suddenly, I want nothing more in the world than to get the fuck out of here. I glance at my watch and see that I can still catch the last bus home if I hustle. I turn to Angelo. "Maybe I'll see you again," I shout at him over the music.

Angelo shrugs. "You know where to find me." We lock eyes, and without saying anything else, we both know the chances are slim to none that I'll ever set foot in this bar again. Angelo turns and walks away, disappearing into the cigarette haze. I push my way out the door.

On the bus home I know I have to come up with some plausible excuse for my lateness and the condition of my clothes. Maybe I'll tell Carol that I was mugged. Yet whenever I try to work out the details of my alibi, I find myself instead thinking about the muscled nakedness of Angelo, how his dick felt crammed down my throat, the sensations of his ass sheathed around my own thrusting dick. My body shudders with remembered excitement and I feel my dick stir inside my briefs. I know that tonight I crossed some kind of line. *What am I going to do about this?* I wonder. The rain is heavier now, beating against the bus's window. I absently watch the drops streak across the glass as the bus speeds its way down the highway.

FAMILY VALUES

About halfway under the Bay, the tube shuttle stopped dead. There were some groans, a few curses muttered, but most of the passengers took it in stride. Hell, tube breakdowns were happening all the time lately. Except for a bunch of teenagers talking loudly and laughing in the far end of the car, the passengers all wore their urban stony faces, eyes trained straight ahead, hands in laps, elbows tucked in to avoid contact with anyone else. The monitor overhead showed a scene of a family at dinner, the father carving the roast, the mother beaming, the two blond kids laughing. The music swelled in volume and then silence. "Make family values *your* values," a voice-over said. The screen went dead for a second and then lit up with highlights from today's news. Of course, there was coverage of last night's bombing of the genetic-screening clinic in Oakland. All the media had been on top of it; you couldn't turn around without being confronted with screaming headlines about "homosexual terrorist groups at large".

After a while the news switched to sports and weather, and I stopped watching. I thought about the bombing, wondering if the bombers really were some kind of queer vigilantes. It *was* possible. Ever since last month, when the government had added homo-sexuality to the list of genetic "abnormalities" all fetuses would be screened for, feelings had gotten pretty raw. *Christ, after a few more decades there won't be any more queers around. It's going to be pretty fucking dull.* A few minutes later the shuttle lurched forward, and we were on our way again.

I didn't make it to the club until it was almost midnight. The place was packed, and it took a while to find Stephan. I finally spot-ted him wedged into a nook between the wall and a holo-game

169

machine. "You're late," he said, as I pushed my way out of the crowd. The lights from the demo games washed over his face.

"Sorry," I said, raising my voice to be heard above the music. "Another tube breakdown. I was stuck for almost half an hour." I stared at him. "Why are you hiding back here? I had a hell of a time finding you."

Stephan gave a thin smile. "I thought it'd be a good idea to keep a low profile."

I didn't ask for an explanation. I didn't have to. Gennies weren't very popular in queer circles right now. Even queer gennies. It wasn't fair, but they were such convenient scapegoats. And Stephan *was* something of a celebrity since he belonged to the first group of fetuses the government had ever genetically altered 25 years ago. There were only a few dozen gennies as old as he.

I glanced around the packed room, the far walls lost in the crush of bodies and dimmed lights. The stage and walkway cut across the room, neatly bisecting it. "Did I miss anything?"

Stephan shrugged. "A couple of warm-up solo shows. Nothing much."

There was something off in his tone. I gave him a hard look. "Are you mad at me for being late? I told you it wasn't my fault."

Stephan turned his eyes to me. "No, Jim, I'm not mad, OK?" He gave me another smile, wider this time. It still looked chilly. But then again I was always getting his moods wrong. Fucking gennies. All those faces with those flawless bone structures and perfect features; they were beautiful all right but...inexpressive. You could never tell what a gennie was *feeling*.

"Well, I'm going to get a drink," I said. "I'll be back in a minute." I fought my way to the bar. The bartender was a gennie too, with light blue eyes with the epicanthic folds of an Asian, full African lips, and the sharp hawk nose of a Cherokee Indian. Sometimes the bioengineers got a little carried away. His body was lean and muscular, the skin a pale ivory. He flashed me a smile, his teeth white and perfect. I bought a Pilsner ale and pushed my way back through the crowd toward Stephan.

The lights dimmed when I was halfway there, as a new show started on the stage. I reached Stephan just after the performers had stripped down and were going at it. There were two this time, a gennie and a natural. The gennie was pretty much what one would expect: blond this time, fair-skinned, a perfectly proportioned, beautifully muscled body, a little on the lean side maybe. The natural was something of a surprise, though. He looked like a troll: a squat, muscular body, bandy legs, huge arms, and with the face of a missing link. Beauty and the Beast.

I looked back at Stephan. "So you going to tell me what's bothering you?" I asked.

Stephan turned his gaze toward me. His eyes flashed red and green and blue as the colored lights from the holo-game machine swept over him. "Why don't you just watch the show and get off my back?" he said.

I took a chug from my beer and turned my eyes on the stage. *Fuck you too,* I thought. The blond gennie was on his knees, his fingers squeezing the Beast's nipples, their eyes locked together. A single spot shone down on them both, the angle of the beam sharp, almost vertical, bathing them in white light. Illuminated, the gennie's face looked angelic, the cheekbones high and pure, the sensual lips parted, the blue eyes shining in rapture. Handel's *Messiah* poured out of the sound system, pumped up to a retro disco beat. Whoever had staged this had a wicked sense of humor. As the gennie took the Beast's cock in his mouth, the Beast closed his eyes and groaned. He pressed the palm of each hand against the gennie's temples and started pumping his hips. The gennie reached around and squeezed the Beast's fleshy ass cheeks. The Beast's wide mouth pulled back into a grimace; he looked like a damn *ape,* a knuckle dragger, and it was grotesque to see someone as beautiful as the gennie service him so eagerly. He sped up the tempo of his thrusts, skewering the gennie's mouth savagely, twining his fingers through the gennie's hair and shaking his head like a rag doll's. But no matter what the Beast dished out, the gennie seemed up for it and ready for more. The Beast picked up the gennie and threw him on his belly. The gennie lay on the stage, arms outstretched, body squirming, legs spread apart. The Beast dropped on top of him, spread-eagle, mounting him from behind, with no lubrication, not even spit. He wrapped his huge arms around the gennie's torso and began pumping his hips, baring his teeth and growling noisily, each sound picked by the stage microphones. He was really battering the gennie's ass now, pumping his hips furiously with thrusts that became increasingly more brutal.

All this was making me uncomfortable. S/M was *not* my scene, and the club had never put on a show like this before. I glanced around the room. All eyes were fixed on the stage; conversation had stopped completely. I could tell that the audience was really jazzed, but something was off. The energy wasn't erotic; the vibes I was picking up were more charged. The faces around me were grinning, the eyes bright, but the emotion that crackled through the air was *anger.* And satisfaction. Satisfaction that this gennie, this genetically altered *freak* was being publicly degraded by this big, ugly *natural.* It was just a stupid symbolic gesture, a spit in the face of the government's genetic program, but the crowd was eating it up.

I glanced at Stephan, but his face was expressionless. He just stood there, watching the show. I tugged on his sleeve. "Stephan?" I asked. He turned toward me. He looked perfectly calm. "You want to go?"

Stephan shrugged. "Sure."

Outside the fog had rolled in, and a stiff breeze whipped down the street. I zipped up my jacket as we stood on the street corner in front of the club. I looked up at Stephan. "You're not bothered by how that gennie was treated?" I asked.

Stephan returned my gaze. "Not particularly. All the queers are upset at the new gene-screening policy. It's only natural that they take it out on the gennies."

"You're acting mighty big about this," I said, "considering you're a gennie yourself."

Stephan smiled. "That's me: Mr. Master Race."

There was a billboard across the street, showing a family having a picnic. Although the models were different than those in the tube video, the wife was still beaming, and the children were still blond and laughing. Underneath, of course, was printed MAKE FAMILY VALUES *YOUR* VALUES. Stephan and I started walking. Stephan's detachment to everything was getting on my nerves. A sudden image flashed through my mind of Stephan up on the stage being brutalized by the Beast, and the sharp pleasure I felt at the thought startled me. I glanced at him, taking in the classic profile: the strong chin, the dark, luminous eyes, the thick head of black hair, the powerful neck. He walked with an easy, graceful stride, and I was intensely aware of his body beneath his clothes, its flawless proportions, its muscularity. I worked out regularly, lifted weights, ran, watched what I ate. But I would never come close to Stephan's level of perfection.

"You want to come over to my place?" I asked.

Stephan smiled. "Sure."

I lay on the bed watching as Stephan pulled off his clothes. When he was finally naked, he started toward me. "No, stop," I say. "Just stand there for a moment, OK?" Stephan smiled and obliged me, standing at the foot of the bed, his arms at this side, his left knee bent, his weight on his right hip. As always, my throat constricted with excitement. My eyes slid down Stephan's body, drinking him in: the wide, dark eyes, the full mouth, the cut of the pecs, the powerful arms, the play of muscles down his smooth torso. I wondered if the bioengineers had isolated the gene for dick size and deliberately given Stephan a whopper, or if it had just been a happy accident. "Christ, you're beautiful," I said.

Stephan smiled but said nothing.

"Come over here," I said. I could hardly breathe. Stephan walked over to the side of my bed and climbed in. Later, when the lights were out and I could feel Stephan's body writhe on top of mine, I noticed, as I always did, how *skillful* Stephan was in all of this. He fucked me beautifully, his thrusts deep and strong, his hands and mouth exploring my body with an erotic competence that was quite amazing. And, as always, my body responded to it eagerly, eating it all up, every sensation Stephan pulled out of me. And yet every now and then, in those brief instances between strokes, I'd feel a hot needle of resentment. He was so *perfect* at this. In spite of the pleasure that I knew he was feeling too, there was a *detachment* about him that made me want to smash my fist in his face. When he finally brought me orgasm, it was so sharp and overwhelming that I almost blacked out. Stephan came too, splattering his load on my face, groaning loudly. But it was all theater, almost an elaborate form of masturbation. Stephan collapsed beside me. After a few minutes he began snoring lightly. *Fucking gennies* was my last thought, before I drifted off to sleep.

When I woke up the next morning, Stephan was standing in his boxer shorts, looking out the window. The downward slant of the sun's rays indicated it was late morning. I got out of bed, staggered to the bathroom, took a leak and returned to the bedroom. Stephan was still staring out the window. I turned on the radio and then came up beside him. "What are you looking at?" I asked.

Stephan nodded. "The kids in the playground." The Jesse Helms Elementary School was right across the street from my apartment. It must have been time for morning recess.

My eyes followed his gaze toward the asphalt courtyard where the children were playing. Behind me I could hear a newscaster on the radio talking about the bombing of the gene-screening clinic, something about the police still not coming up with any clues.

"There you have it," Stephan said. "The whole history of the government's genetic program laid out right before our eyes." He pointed over to the basketball courts, where the pre-adolescents were shooting hoops. It was easy to spot the gennies among them: they were quicker and more graceful, taller, and better-proportioned. They were also just a small minority; most of the kids on the courts were naturals, and it was hard not to notice how gangly and awkward they looked. "Those kids were all born around 2019, 2020," Stephan said, his voice matter-of-fact. "Genetic programming was just taking off. Gennies were still a small minority." He pointed to a group of girls skipping rope. They looked to be around nine or 10. "They were born a couple of years later. About half of them are gennies now, the bioengineers were just flexing their muscles. You still got a good cross-section of types: different ethnicities, a wide range of hair and skin color, wide height variations." He nodded to the smaller children playing on the jungle gym. "A couple of years later and nearly all the kids are gennies. No more experimentation in races and ethnicities. The Aryan look is in." And he was right. Nearly every child was fair-skinned and blond. "And finally," Stephan said, gazing at the toddlers playing placidly in the sandbox. "The latest crop. Do you see how none of the kids are squabbling or crying? That was the year the bioengineers isolated and eliminated the gene that controls aggression." He looked over at me. "And now the next wave will be queer-free. I think they've just about covered all the bases with that one."

"I don't see why you're complaining," I said. "You and the rest of your gennie friends came out pretty damn well in the deal."

Stephan turned his head toward me. He gave me a long, level look. I was the first to break eye contact. "So who's complaining?" he said. Half an hour later he was dressed and out the door.

The sound of the doorbell insinuated itself into my dreams, loud and insistent. I stirred and woke up. The doorbell rang again, without a break, someone's thumb pressed hard against it. I glanced at my clock. It was a little after 2 A.M. I climbed out of bed and staggered to the intercom. "Whoever this is," I said, "fuck off."

"Jim, it's me," a voice said. "Stephan."

I hadn't seen Stephan in almost two weeks. "Jesus Christ, Stephan, do you know what time it is?"

There was a long pause. "Jim," Stephan said. "Will you please just let me in?"

There was something in Stephan's voice that brought me fully awake. I buzzed him in. A minute later I heard his knock on the door. When I opened it, Stephan was leaning against the doorjamb. He wasn't wearing a jacket, and the left sleeve of his shirt was soaked in blood.

"Christ, Stephan!"

Stephan just stood there in the doorway. "I think I'm in big trouble, Jim," he said. "You might not want to be a piece of this." His face was drained of color, and his pupils were dilated. He looked like he was about to pass out.

I pulled him inside and shut the door. He stood in the middle of my living room, dripping blood onto my carpet. I sat him down on a chair and pushed his head down between his knees. After a few minutes I took him to the bathroom and pulled off his shirt. In spite of all the blood, the cuts on his arm looked superficial. There were little pieces of glass embedded in the skin, and I brushed them off.

"How did this happen?" I asked.

Stephan looked at me with unfocused eyes. "I jumped through a window," he replied.

"Christ," I muttered. I opened the medicine chest, pulled out some disinfectant and sprinkled it liberally over the cuts. Stephan winced but said nothing. I started rolling bandages around his upper arm. Stephan submitted docilely to everything I did, like a child being tended by his mother. "You want to tell me what you were doing?" I finally asked. He was sitting on the closed toilet seat with me standing above him.

Stephan shook his head. "No." He looked up at me, and I could see the strain in his eyes. And the fear. I hadn't known that he was capable of either. "The less you know, the better for you."

A silence hung in the air. "You didn't kill anyone, did you?" I finally asked.

I had meant it as a joke, but Stephan looked like he was seriously considering the question. "No," he said. "I don't think so." He looked doubtful. He ran his fingers through his hair. "Can I stay the night here?" he asked. "I promise to leave first thing tomorrow."

"That's fuckin' great," I said. "You won't tell me what kind of trouble you're in, and yet you want me to let you stay here."

Stephan stared miserably into space. He climbed slowly to his feet. "OK, I'll go."

"Oh, stay put," I said irritably. "You don't have to tell me anything."

Stephan looked relieved. "If you don't mind," he said. "I'd like to lie down for a while."

I led him to the bedroom, stripped him, and put him to bed. I climbed in too and turned out the light. I didn't know if I would be able to sleep, but I'd at least try. I could hear Stephan breathing raggedly next to me. "Are you all right?" I finally asked.

Stephan didn't answer. After a couple of beats, he pulled me toward him and held me. I wrapped my arms around him and settled into his embrace. This night was getting stranger by the minute; I had never suspected that Stephan would ever need comforting. I stroked his hair, and he lifted his face up to me. We kissed, softly, our lips barely touching. We kissed again, harder, and this time Stephan's tongue pushed into my mouth. His hands slid down my body, caressing me, pulling at my flesh. He reached over and turned on the light. "I want to see your body," he said softly.

We spent most of the night having sex, and it was different from anything I had experienced with Stephan before; there was a raw edge to it that made it more exciting than Stephan's usual technical perfection. After Stephan finally shuddered his orgasm, with mine following soon afterward, we lay together in each other's arms. Stephan pulled me toward him, kissing me lightly. "You don't know how much I needed that," he murmured.

"Things will turn out all right," I said, not knowing what I was talking about. I turned off the light. In the darkness I felt Stephan's heartbeat against my chest. After a while I drifted off to sleep.

When I woke up the next morning, he had already gone. I had no idea what kind of trouble he thought he was in, but in the light of day I couldn't take it that seriously. Stephan was the most capable man I knew. I just didn't think he would do anything stupid or rash.

By the time I was riding to work in the tube shuttle, I had pushed my concerns about Stephan largely aside. My mind drifted toward a report I had to write for work, what arguments I would use to present my points. I glanced up idly at the tube monitor. Stephan's face looked down at me. I listened dumbfounded to the words of the newscaster: "A bombing at the U.C. Berkeley Genetic Research Center. Security guards gave pursuit to a running figure who escaped by jumping out of a first-story window. Genetic printing of blood on the ground outside has identified the suspect as Stephan Clark, who is still at large and considered dangerous..."

I sat there stunned. *Jesus, Stephan. What the hell were you trying to prove?* When I finally looked up, the shuttle was at the end of the line, my stop three stations back. I got off, dialed my office, and called in sick. It wasn't that much of a lie; my stomach was in a tight knot, and I was in danger of losing my breakfast. Outside, it was raining lightly, the drops falling in a fine mist against my face. I walked aimlessly down the streets, hands jammed in my pockets, my mind full of Stephan. I wondered where he was, and the thought of his being hunted down like an animal sickened me. Stephan *was* clever; maybe he would be able to elude pursuit. I shook my head. I hadn't known the guy at all, I hadn't a *clue* that he had taken any of this genetic policy shit seriously. I had thought he had the perfect life, that all he was feeling was...contentment. Yet when Stephan had to choose sides between the queers and the gennies, he had picked the queers.

I stopped at a street corner, waiting for the light to change. A bus rumbled by. On its side was an advertising poster, a family playing on a beach, the surf behind them. MAKE FAMILY VALUES *YOUR* VALUES was written in bold print underneath. The light turned green, and I crossed the street, heading back toward home.

BRAIN FEVER

I lift off the top of the large white box on the table in front of me and look inside, my heart pounding like a wrecking ball. There, nestled among the folds of tissue paper, lie the black square of the mortarboard and, under it, the smooth, cool silk of the graduation gown. I run my hands slowly, reverently, through the gown's folds, feeling the softness of the fabric, the hairs on the back of my hands and wrists erect with static electricity. That's not the only thing on me erect. My dick gives a sharp, hard throb as my fingertips touch the black silk.

I take the gown and mortarboard out of the box and arrange them carefully on my bed. By force of habit, I glance at the pile of porn magazines lying on my bedside table and scan their titles: *Brainy Boys, Gay Geniuses, Nude Professors.* Like a kid reluctant to put away old toys, I pick up the top magazine and open it to the centerfold. It's one of my favorites: a nude model bearing an uncanny resemblance to Albert Einstein lies sprawled on a laboratory bench, a dreamy, come-hither look in his mournful brown eyes. Sweet Jesus, the loads I've squirted over that picture... My hard-on gives another throb, but I resist the temptation to whip it out and wank off. *I'm saving my wad for something better tonight,* I think.

I quickly strip and slip on the graduation gown, leaving it unbuttoned in the front. Its smooth silkiness, crackling with electricity, slithers over my skin caressingly. I adjust the mortarboard on my head, letting the tassel fall to the right side, tickling the upper curve of my ear. I swing open the closet door and stare at my reflection in the full-length mirror. The flared, red head of my dick pokes out between the folds of the gown like some animal peering out of its burrow. "I question the basic premises of your

179

hypothesis," I growl at my reflection, as I wrap my hand around my cock and stroke it slowly. My strokes become faster, my balls swinging in a fleshy blur. "It's clear you're operating from outmoded paradigms"—I gasp at my reflection, pulling my eyebrows down in a frown of concentration. I stop just before squirting. *There's no doubt about it,* I think excitedly. *I look as intelligent as hell! Baby, am I going to score tonight!* If I had any doubts, all I have to do is look at the list of final grades that came in the mail today for my last semester at U.C. Berkeley. *4.0 GPA!* I crow to myself. *Solid A's! What a fuckin' stud I am!*

I think about how I've worked my ass off for the past three years to get where I am tonight, exercising my brain five times a week, rigorously following a strict academic workout routine. Given the way the gay community obsesses on intelligence, it's what you have to do to get laid around here. And now, tonight, I know I'm ready for the final big leap: going in full black silk drag to one of Folsom Street's cap-and-gown bars.

This is a fantasy I've never shared with anyone. I hang out with a pretty vanilla crowd, guys who dis the cap-and-gowners as "a bunch of queens who beneath all their intellectual pretensions have the minds of cretins." Fuckin' hypocrites. Are they any better, parading down Castro Street on a Sunday afternoon, their pastel calculators dangling from their key chains, wearing their Lacoste shirts with $E=MC^2$ neatly stitched above their right pectorals? Or making the rounds at the circuit parties, engaged in Socratic dialogues on the nature of the archetypal forms of the Good, the True, and the Beautiful while buzzing on ecstasy and Special K? *Fuck 'em,* I think, as I clip on the Phi Beta Kappa keys that I bought in a downtown porno shop. I look at myself one last time in the mirror, squeeze my crotch and wink at my reflection before turning out the light and heading out the door.

When I get off my bus at Folsom and 10th, I know exactly where I want to go: Plato's Cave, one of the most raunchy, sex-sweaty, academically-advanced bars in town. The bartender (who goes by the hokey name Gray Matter), is a Stanford Ph.D. physics candidate and one of gay filmdom's hottest porno stars. I've seen Gray's latest video, set in a mock-up of the Lawrence-Livermore cyclotron. The final orgy scene, when all the studs begin shooting their loads while hydrogen ions are being broken down into their component quarks by gamma-ray bombardment, is the talk of the gay community. Plato's Cave is packed.

I cautiously walk into the dimly lit bar, mentally feeling my ground. Black-silk bars have this whole code of behavior, all these dark mating rituals that have to be followed meticulously. Those who don't are contemptuously dismissed as "dilettantes" and promptly ignored. Occasionally, in groups of two or three but mostly solo, young men in their graduation drag line the walls or crowd around the bar. Over the sound system, Madonna is sexily sobbing the periodic table to a driving disco beat.

I push through the crowd as I make my way to the bar. Above the blare of the music, snatches of bar clichés float to my ears. "Haven't I seen you at a Mensa meeting?" "Do you matriculate often?"

"Vanadium," Madonna croons, "chromium, manganese, iron..."

All around me all these courting rites are taking place; the active cruisers are flexing their intellect in front of their desired targets. "Alexander Pope's *The Dunciad* is probably the most lacerating example of Augustan Age mock-epic verse form to be found," a burly tattooed man in shabby black robes whispers pleadingly to a young bored-looking academician. The young man rolls his eyes and walks away.

"Thallium," Madonna husks, "lead, bismuth, polonium..."

Two men on my left are arguing heatedly. Suddenly, one of them in piercing tones exclaims, "Jesus! This queen thinks she knows partial derivatives when she can't even get the Pythagorean theorem straight!"

"Oh, really?" the other hisses. "And just who is it who claims she read *Moby Dick* three times, when the closest she ever got to Herman Melville was Classic Comics?" The two men glare at each other.

"Uranium," Madonna sighs, "neptunium, plutonium, americium..."

Behind the bar, Gray is spellbinding the crowd with the hypothesis that gravitational forces may eventually be discovered to be the products of "gravitons," a so-far merely hypothetical subatomic particle. He reeks of sex, and when he starts talking about how the graviton's existence may eventually turn out to be the missing link to proving Einstein's proposed unified field theory, I can cut with a knife the lust emanating from the crowd. I feel it too and shrug at my reaction. *Fuck it. If I'm just another shallow gay boy who puts brains above everything else, so be it. At least I'm honest about it.*

Gray tears himself away from his admiring audience long enough to give me a beer. I fight through the crowd again, achieve a relatively isolated corner, and gulp it meditatively. For once this attitude isn't a pose; I'm genuinely contemplating my next move. I look around carefully, hunting for a subject on which to ply my lines.

Yet I'm vaguely dissatisfied with what I'm about to do. I'm being too sedate about all this, too guarded, too *routine*. Hell, I'm acting like it's another Saturday night on the Castro, where, after throwing a few lines of Nietzsche out at someone, you take him home and fuck his brains out. This is a night to indulge in fantasy all the way: the first time I've ever gone to a black-silk bar in full cap-and-gown drag. I know what my next move should be.

I nervously shift my eyes toward the back of the bar. Through the smoky haze I can dimly make out a doorless opening leading into a dark hallway. I know from stories I've heard that this is the way to Plato's Cave's well-trafficked backroom. I lick my lips uncertainly; I'm not sure if I'm ready for that kind of scene. As if on cue, the sound system erupts with an old Village People hit. "Brainy, brainy man!" they shout. "I want to be a brainy man." I smile at the timeliness of the song. I square my shoulders. If I back down now, I might as well stick to quoting Monarch Notes synopses of "great books" to the dummies who hang out in the tackier bars on lower Polk Street.

Taking one last swig from my bottle, I push myself away from the sheltering wall and into the crowd. "I'm dean's list material, I'm dean's list material..." I keep repeating to myself as I thread my way across the room. I feel my throat constricting and my heart hammering, and I have to stop and wait until my breathing is better. *I have to be coolheaded*, I think. *My thinking has to be clear. That's crucial.*

I finally make it to the opening and walk down the short hall, trailing my fingers along the wall to guide me in the darkness.

There's a sharp 90-degree turn, and suddenly I'm in my first orgy room. Pools of light feebly spill out from reading lamps haphazardly strung out along the upper wall. In varying degrees of darkness, shadowy figures merge and part. Barely coherent murmurs and moans float in the air, snatches of Hobbes, Shakespeare, Descartes. Someone suddenly comes, gasping out lines from Kant's *Critique of Pure Reason.* The air is hot and fetid, and I feel rivulets of sweat trickling down my back and under my armpits. I've got a roaring hard-on.

As my eyes adjust to the gloom, my attention focuses on a solitary figure standing directly under one of the lights. He's dressed in the full scarlet robes of a Cambridge don, and while some men might have looked hopelessly pretentious in such an outfit, the stranger is able to wear it with a free and natural confidence that radiates pure intelligence. He has a high, in fact lofty forehead; always the size queen, I'm guessing that the man's hat size must be at least an 8¼. The guy's calmly reading a copy of Plato's *The Republic* in the original Greek, seemingly oblivious to the activity around him.

My center of consciousness suddenly drops 2½ feet, and my prick assumes full control. With a boldness found only in the inexperienced and the desperate, I stride across the room, stop next to the stranger, and place my hand upon his left pectoral. He raises his eyes and coolly looks at me but makes no other movement. Emboldened by this, I unbutton the front of the scarlet robe and slip my hands under the silk, stroking the furred chest beneath. "I'm Harry," I say, as I squeeze the man's nipples. "What's your name?"

The stranger looks at me silently. "Rocco," he finally growls. His nipples are fully erect now under my fingertips. He continues staring at me, waiting.

Time to start flexing the brain muscle, I think. "I see you're reading *The Republic,* Rocco," I say, "where Plato traces the journey of the soul into a spiritual immersion in the Eternal One." My hands descend slowly down Rocco's hard, furry abs.

Rocco keeps his level gaze aimed at me. When my fingers are a couple of inches above the bulge of his cock, Rocco's hand darts out and grasps my wrist. "Fuckin' A," he growls. "Of course, Plato's model of a purely ascending creative force was eventually adopted by Saint Thomas Aquinas to describe God as the Unmoved Mover."

I smile at the easy trap Rocco has set for me. "I believe you're mistaken," I say calmly. "Aquinas's Unmoved Mover was inspired by Aristotle, not Plato." I free his hand and wrap my fingers around Rocco's fat cock. I start stroking it slowly, pulling the silky foreskin up and down the thick shaft. I pull out my own dick and wrap my hand around both our cocks, stroking the twin dick shafts together. Rocco leans back and closes his eyes as I murmur, "Aristotle envisioned a purely ascendant God, but Plato's Ultimate Good also embraces the descent into the manifest."

I feel a hand slide down my back and squeeze my ass. I turn to see a young street punk standing next to me, his black silk gown falling open to reveal a smooth, tightly muscled torso and a heavy horse-dick swinging half-hard between his thighs. His eyebrows and left nostril are pierced, and he sports a tattoo on his bulging left biceps that reads BORN TO STUDY. "Yeah," the punk growls. "But Plato was fuckin' ripping off Parmenides, who first came up with the model of an Ultimate Good that descends into the realm of the manifest a full century before Plato ever did." Before I can respond, the punk drops to his knees and takes my cock in his mouth.

I sigh as I feel the warm, wet mouth expertly work my dick. I being pumping my hips, fucking the punk's face with long, slow strokes. Rocco's hands are working my body now, tugging on the smooth, hard flesh. I pull Rocco to me and kiss him fiercely, my tongue pushing deep into his mouth, as the young punk sucks and slobbers over first my dick and then Rocco's and then back to mine again. The punk opens his mouth wide and swallows my fleshy balls, rolling his tongue around them. I look down, and the punk meets my gaze, his mouth full of my ball sac. "Yeah, fuckin' suck those balls," I growl as I slap my dick across his upturned face. "You might be right about Parmenides," I add, "but big fuckin' deal. The Buddhist sage Nagarajuna came up with the concept of the divine in the manifest world centuries before any of the Greeks."

"Not to mention the teachings in the Bhagavad Gita," Rocco adds, his voice low and guttural. "And, before that, the Hindu Upanishads. They all were making the same fuckin' point." I'm still stroking Rocco's massive dong, fast enough to make his balls bounce heavily, and Rocco's eyes burn with a feverish light. It's so fucking hot to watch him leaning against the wall, his hips thrust out, the light from the reading lamp spilling onto his hairy, muscular torso.

"Bullshit!" the punk growls as he slides his tongue up the length of my wanker and rolls it around the purple flared head. "You can't compare the Greeks to the Buddhist philosophers. The Buddhists were preaching dependent origination, where no object in the universe exists by itself." He slides his hands down my ass cheeks, squeezing them, running his fingers over the smooth skin. "Whereas the Greeks believed that every object could be traced back to an ideal form." His hands work their way up my torso again, and he gives each nipple a hard squeeze.

"OK, OK," I gasp, as the punk burrows his head down between my legs. I feel my ass cheeks being parted, and the punk massages my asshole as resumes licking my ball sac. "Damn!" I groan, distracted. With an effort, I collect my thoughts. "So what if Plato didn't fuckin' *originate* the concept of the divine in the manifest? It was how he developed the concept that mattered."

"Yeah," Rocco grunts. He pulls his massive boner down and releases it, letting it slap against his hairy belly. His heavy ball sac swings from side to side, like ripe fruit on a windblown tree branch. "Plato set the prototype model of the One Source and Ground for all the other Western philosophers, from Plotinus right up to Spinoza and Hegel. So fuckin' lay off him, OK?" With a quick shrug, he slips his scarlet robes off his shoulders and lets them fall to the floor. He stands before me buck naked, his ponderous dong bobbing heavily between his beefy thighs, begging to be sucked. It's an offer I can't refuse, and I bend down and take Rocco's engorged cock in my mouth and greedily suck it as the punk continues to play with my asshole.

I can't get enough of Rocco's fat dick, and I feed on it voraciously, first circling my tongue around the bulbous red head and then sliding my lips down the shaft until my nose is pressed hard against Rocco's black, crinkly pubes. The punk is now corkscrewing a finger up my ass, inch by slow inch, as he strokes my dick with his other hand. I close my eyes and let the sensations sweep over me: Rocco's hard dick shoved deep down my throat, the punk's finger working my ass while he's stroking my dick. The air in the room seems to close in on us, and I feel streams of sweat trickle down my body and splash onto the floor below. Others in the room watch the show we're putting on with hard, feverish eyes, beating off to the sight, offering counterarguments between fondles or collaborative evidence accented with stroking and heavy sucking.

A huge bearded giant of a man breaks free from the crowd and approaches us, his monstrous, condomed dong swinging heavily between his massive thighs. He pushes the punk aside, spits on his dick, and proceeds to slowly impale my ass. "Of course, Freud was a Neoplatonist," he growls, as he slowly skewers me. "The two major forces in the human psyche that Freud identified as Eros and Thanatos are just other names for Plato's ascending and descending spirits."

I pull Rocco's cock out of my mouth and turn my head toward the giant. "That's horse shit," I gasp, relaxing my ass muscles and breathing deep to accommodate his huge prick. "Freud's forces of the psyche never ascend into the transpersonal realm like Plato's, and thus they cancel each other out rather than reinforce each other. That's why Plato was an optimist and Freud essentially a pessimist." I begin pumping my hips, meeting the giant's thrusting cock, stroke for stroke. I squeeze my ass muscles tight as the giant pulls his dong out, and he gasps with pleasure. "Yeah," Rocco grunts, as he crams his dick back down my throat again. "Freud was a classic reductionist, keeping all forces of the psyche confined to the prepersonal realms. What an asshole." He reaches over and squeezes the giant's left nipple, twisting it hard.

The giant glares at him with hard, bright eyes. "Of course, Jung committed the opposite fallacy," he grunts, his face bathed in sweat, "by elevating all psychic forces to the transpersonal realm." He thrusts his ramrod dick full in me, slapping his balls against my ass, and then slowly grinds his hips.

I give a mighty groan and take Rocco's cock out of my mouth once again. "I hear you, man," I gasp. "All those archetypes Jung was talking about deal with states of consciousness that take place before the development of the ego. Jung had his head up his ass when he called them transpersonal." The giant has his arms wrapped tightly around my torso in a bear hug, and I feel the weight of his body press down on me as he drives his fleshy piston in. I go back to gobbling on Rocco's pulsating dick meat.

I feel the dicks of the two studs impale me from both ends, Rocco's pushing down my throat while the giant's is shoved deep up my ass. It's like being spitted by one giant cock that runs through the entire length of my body, and I close my eyes and sink into that thought. Rocco and the giant keep on plowing my orifices as they continue their discourse. Meanwhile, the punk has crawled down under me and is dragging his tongue over my stiff, fat cock and balls. I'm immersed in sensation, dicks and mouths and hands exploring every inch of my body, quotes from Hobbes and Hegel faintly buzzing in my ears.

The giant is increasingly punctuating his arguments with low groans and trailing whimpers. He gives one final hard thrust of his dick up my ass, and I feel his legs tremble against me. "Shit, I'm coming!" he cries out. He gives a mighty groan as his body spasms, and his dick pulses deep inside me, pumping his jizz into the condom up my ass in one spurt after another. With one final deep sigh, the giant pulls out and collapses to the floor, mumbling something about Retro-Romantics and the pre/trans fallacy.

Rocco's thrusts are coming deeper and faster, and I'm having a hard time accommodating his huge dong full down my throat. I start sucking on his low-hanging balls, rolling them around with my tongue, as I stroke his spit-slicked man-root. Rocco looks down at me with glazed eyes, sweat pouring down his face, his mouth open. "Yeah, you sexy, brainy stud," he growls. "Wash those balls. Stroke that dick. Make me come." I pump my hand up and down Rocco's humongous tube of meat a few more times, and then he groans loudly as his body trembles against me. "Oh, shit, I'm coming!" he cries out. His dick throbs in my hand, and the first volley of spunk arcs out and splatters hard against my face, followed by another and then another. By the time Rocco's done shooting, my face is drenched with his dick-slime. I feel it drip sluggishly down my cheeks and chin, mingling with my sweat. Rocco bends down and slowly laps it up, like some thirsty jungle cat.

The punk is working my dick hard with his mouth, and I fuck his face energetically, meeting him thrust for thrust. He's a skillful cocksucker, and I feel my load being slowly pulled out of me. "Talk dirty to me," I growl to Rocco.

Rocco bends over and whispers the Heisenberg uncertainty principle in my ear as the punk continues to work my dick. That does the trick for me, and I feel myself slip over the edge into the orgasm. "Fuckin' A!" I groan, as I shoot my load deep down the punk's throat. He drinks it thirstily, sucking on it like a baby on its mother's tit, feeding on my spermy cream. Rocco plants his mouth over mine and kisses me hard as my body spasms. I collapse on the floor with the other men, ours arms and limbs intertwined together, our sweaty bodies pressed together. I close my eyes, lost in post-sex catatonia, listening to someone across the room slowly chanting the three laws of thermodynamics. Minutes pass, and I begin to feel chilly as the sweat evaporates off my back. I slowly get up and pull my soiled and crumpled graduation gown back on. The other men do the same.

Rocco and I walk out of the bar together, leaving the others in the orgy room. Neither of us talk, silently realizing that any further conversation could only be anticlimactic. I smile wanly at the pun. When we reach the street corner, Rocco pulls me to him and kisses me one last time. "You fucking genius," he growls in my ear. "You fucking intelligent stud." Then he turns and walks away.

I stand quietly on the corner for a few seconds, watching Rocco's receding back. Then, numb to the bone with fatigue and joy, I strike out in the opposite direction. I begin to sing softly. "Brainy, brainy man. I want to be a brainy man."

VAMPIRE

You wouldn't believe how fuckin' hungry I get when I first wake up. It's always like this, no matter how much I feed the night before. I crawl out from inside the refrigerator carton I found two weeks ago behind an appliance store and sit on the floor, scratching my head. I look around. Fourteen days in this rented room hasn't warmed me up to it; the place still looks like a junkie's nightmare. I never was like one of those affected Anne Rice vampire queens, all that tragic posturing and Louis Quatorze decor, but I do have some appreciation for the finer things. I can remember nice apartments with fireplaces and bay windows overlooking parks and furniture bought new from Italian showrooms. And honest-to-God coffins, for chrissake, made out of mahogany, with satin linings and bronze fittings. I stare at the ribbons of paint peeling from the walls, the ratty, Salvation Army furniture, the orange-crate tables. The psycho case in the room next door is screaming at his crack-addict girlfriend about something, and she's screaming back. This is all so depressing. If I could afford it and if I could find a shrink who practiced at night, I'd get therapy. I have some real quality-of-life issues, here. Immortality is not what it's cracked up to be.

My belly growls, and I realize that I've got to take care of business. I assess the situation. *What do I feel like tonight?* I ask myself. *Tex-Mex? Thai? Italian?* No, definitely not Italian; I had that last night. I think his name was Gino. I stretch and climb to my feet. Tonight I feel like *seafood*.

I hail a cab outside and tell the driver to take me to the waterfront. It's winter, the evenings start early this time of year, and the cab darts and weaves through rush hour traffic. The store windows are lit with Christmas decorations, and the sidewalks are crowded

189

with shoppers. I stare glumly out the cab window. *When was the last time I celebrated Christmas?* I wonder. I can't remember. Certainly not since I joined the ranks of the undead. As the cab nears the docks, the Christmas decorations get more beat-up until they're reduced to an occasional string of lights in some shabby shop window. The cabbie's got the radio on, and "The Little Drummer Boy" pours out of the back speakers. "Can you turn that down?" I ask irritably. The cabbie looks at me in the rearview mirror and after a couple of beats twists the volume knob to low.

We drive down streets flanked with dark warehouses and empty loading docks. It must have rained during the day, while I was sleeping in my cardboard box, because there are pools of water in the potholes, catching the reflection of the occasional streetlamp. The traffic has thinned to next to nothing, but I notice one car seems to be dogging us. I feel my throat tighten. *Van Helsing!* I think, feeling the old dread. It can't be. I've painstakingly covered my tracks since our last encounter two weeks ago, there's no *way* that old bastard could have found me again. But I know enough never to underestimate him. I wait a couple of blocks before I dare sneak another glance out the back window. The street behind us is now deserted, and I let myself relax a bit. But only a bit. You never can tell with that son of a bitch. It really sucks belonging to the last minority it's OK to oppress.

I can only see the back of the cabbie's head—the greased-back black hair, the thick neck—and the muscular forearms resting on the steering wheel. The eyes that glance at me in the rearview mirror are brown and melancholy. I glance at his ID on the dashboard and notice that his name is Vaslo. *Hungarian?* I wonder. *Polish?* I consider feeding on him, and I toy with the image of his body's hot fluids flooding into my mouth, how they would taste before I swallowed. Sweet Jesus, but that's a delectable thought! But with him driving, I can't maintain eye contact long enough to hypnotize him. *Let it go,* I think. *There are plenty of others.*

Vaslo drops me off at the entrance to a waterfront bar. As I pay him, I look him straight in the face, taking in once more the sad eyes, the sensual, well-formed mouth, the strong chin. Out of habit I hold his gaze as I pull my wallet out, and after a few seconds his eyes glaze and his mouth falls open. The hunger roars through my body. But we're on a public street, cars are cruising by, and I can see pedestrians half a block away. My hunger is tempting me to take dangerous risks. I throw the bills on the front seat. "Here," I snarl. "Now beat it!" His body jerks, and he blinks his eyes. I tear myself away and walk to the door without looking back.

The bar's a dump, but I'm not one to let aesthetics get in the way. I stand in the doorway, my eyes doing a slow sweep of the place. Because of the cold night outside, the room is overheated; the warm air rushes up to my nostrils, heavy with the scent of cigarette smoke, stale beer, and unwashed bodies. Saliva pools in my mouth.

I settle on the two sailors leaning against the bar, talking. My eyes scan them as I approach the bar: The one on the right is short and dark, with a tight, muscular body and angry eyes that dart around the bar as he drinks his beer. I can tell he's a firecracker. His buddy is taller and leaner, with sandy hair and a mild expression. They strike me as unlikely companions.

When I'm beside them, I motion to the bartender. "Whatever you got on tap," I say. "And fresh drinks for my two friends as well."

The sailors turn their heads and look at me, the shorter one suspiciously, the other merely curious. After a beat, they give their orders to the bartender. By the second round, they start warming up to me, and on the third, we're all the best of friends. The sandy-haired guy is Luke, and his angry little buddy is Nick. I focus my thoughts as we talk, gently probing their minds, setting things up to hypnotize them. I stop. *Hell,* I think, *I bet I can take these guys on without cheating.* There's always more sport to simple seduction.

I smile and pour on the charm, feigning interest while they fill me in on the sailor's life: how the Hong Kong girls compare to Thais, which ports have the best whorehouses, the stories behind their various tattoos. Subtly at first, but then with increasing blatancy I nudge the conversation along toward sex. They both are only too willing to follow that thread, and soon there's a tension among us that starts to crackle like ozone before a lightning strike.

"It must be tough on you guys," I finally say, "being at sea for weeks at a time. I bet by the time you hit a port, you're ready for whatever it takes to get your rocks off."

Nick and Luke both shoot me a hard look. They can sense that we've crossed a line, that we're not just making idle conversation anymore. "Yeah," Nick says slowly. "It gets to be a real problem sometimes."

I let the silence hang in the air for a moment. "I can take care of your problem, if you want." I say carefully. My eyes dart to Luke's face and then back to Nick's. "For both of you."

Nick and Luke exchange glances. Nick raises one eyebrow, and after a beat, Luke gives a small nod. They both turn their eyes on me again. I jerk my head toward the back door beyond the pool tables. "Follow me," I say. My tone is calm, but the hunger is pounding inside me like a wrecking ball.

We walk out the bar's backdoor into the alley behind it. The cold winter night bites into us. I don't waste time on preliminaries but drop to my knees in front of the two sailors. I reach up and unbuckle first Luke's belt, then Nick's, unzip their flies, and then pull down their trousers. The two men watch me, Nick's dark eyes narrowed, Luke's gaze more calm and steady. I pull back slightly and take in what's for dinner tonight. Nick's dick swings heavily between his muscular thighs: thick, dark, uncut, and meaty. Luke's is pinker, blue-veined, with a fleshy red dick head and balls that hang low and ripe.

I start with Luke, burying my face into his balls, smelling their pungent odor of musk and sweat, feeling their hairs tickle my nose. I open my mouth and slide his dick in, slowly bobbing my head up and down. Luke's dick soon swells to full hardness, filling my mouth impressively. Luke sighs and begins pumping his hips, fucking my face with slow, easy strokes. I reach up and twist his nipples, not gently. Luke groans, and his dick gives a sharp throb in my mouth.

I spit in my other hand and start beating Nick off, sliding the silky foreskin up and down the shaft. Nick's dick is thick and fleshy, and I can barely get my fingers around it. I pull Luke's dick out of my mouth and beat off both men together, a dick in each hand. Luke's low-hangers swing heavily between his legs, but Nick's are pulled up tighter, closely hugging the base of his dick shaft. I look up at the two sailors as I stroke their cocks, probing into their minds, tickling the pleasure centers in their brains.

Nick gives a startled gasp of pleasure and Luke's knees buckle. They stare down at me, astonished, and I grin back at them.

I alternate working over the two dicks in front of me, sucking on Nick's for a while, teasing him, bringing him to the brink, and then switching back to Luke's. I slide my hand under Nick's shirt, feeling the hard bands of his abs, the smoothness of his skin under my fingertips, the rough little nubs of his nipples, stiff from the cold. My other hand squeezes the muscles of Luke's ass, feeling them clench and unclench as his dick slides in and out of my mouth. I've got the two of them wound up tighter than a top, and their cocks twitch in front of me, wet from my saliva, arcing up, just about as hard as cocks get. Every time my mouth sweeps down their cocks, I stare up into their eyes and enter their minds, tickling their pleasure centers with increasing intensity. Luke gives off a little whimper with each downward slide of my mouth, and Nick groans loudly when I switch my attentions to him. I feel like I'm drawing music out of the two instruments of flesh in front of me, working them both with the skill of a virtuoso.

Their excitement ripples into my mind, I can *sense* it, feel its pulse in my brain, ratcheting my hunger to higher and higher levels. It's hell for me as well to tease them like this, to bring them to the brink of shooting, only to draw them back again, but the self-torture excites me, whips me into a frenzy of expectation. Nick pumps his hips frantically, his moans bouncing off the alley's brick walls, and when I switch to Luke's dick again, Nick whimpers in frustration. Soon Luke is groaning again, tremors shaking his body as I work his dick ravenously while Nick watches us with feverish eyes.

I reach the point where I can't take the torment of the hunger any more. I slide my mouth down Luke's dick shaft as I push into his mind with the one word: *now!* Luke gives a mighty groan, and his body spasms. His dick throbs in my mouth and I feel his hot load gush down my throat. I suck on his dick like a baby on its mother's tit, squeezing every last drop out, savoring the thick, sweet cream of his load; it's like a milk shake, and I close my eyes with the sheer, sharp pleasure of it. Strength flows into my body as Luke crumples to his knees.

Nick is next. I skin back his dick and run my tongue around the flared head as my other hand slides under his shirt, squeezing the hard muscles of his torso. I leave his dick full in my mouth for a moment, my nose buried in his crinkly black pubes, his heavy balls pressed against my chin, the balls that hold that sweet, sweet load of his that will soon be gushing down my throat. I squeeze his nipples again, and he groans. "Yeah," he croons, "That's right. Play with my titties." I reach behind and run my hands over his ass, feeling the firm flesh under my fingertips. I pull his cheeks apart and worm my finger up his asshole at the same moment that my mouth slides down his dick. Nick's body shudders and he cries out as his hot sperm splatters down my throat to join Luke's load. It's hot and spicy, with just the faintest undertaste of chili and basil, and I gulp it down thirstily.

I'm sucking out the last drop from Nick's swollen dick when the door leading to the bar is suddenly flung open. Light streams into the alley, silhouetting the bodies of three men crowded in the doorway. I recognize Van Helsing and his gang immediately. *Shit!* I jump to my feet, shoving Nick aside, and run down the alley. "Grab that cocksucker!" I hear Van Helsing shout, and then there are the sounds of footsteps in pursuit.

I fling the garbage cans down behind me; there's the crash of someone falling over them, but I don't look back. The entrance to the alley is ahead of me, it seems to stretch out at an impossibly far distance, and the footsteps are gaining. I still feel groggy from my recent feeding, my coordination is off, and I stumble and fall. Someone lunges out toward me, and I kick out, landing my foot in his belly. He grunts and doubles over, and I scramble to my feet again, lurching forward. *I'll never get away,* I think desperately.

I stumble out of the alley, and miraculously there's a cab by the curb, with the door open. "Get in," someone shouts, and I dive into the backseat. The cab roars off, tires squealing and the door still open. I look back and see Van Helsing standing on the curb, his face twisted in rage.

I reach over and slam the door shut as the cab races down the street. Vaslo's eyes glance back at me in the rearview mirror. He winks, then shifts his gaze to the road ahead. I'm too dazed to say anything for a while. I lean back into the cab's seat and smooth my hair down. A glance out the rear window shows that the streets are empty, but I keep my optimism in check. Vaslo tears down streets and back alleys, the car weaving from side to side. My stomach clenches, but I don't ask him to slow down. He finally careens into a dark alley and slams on the brakes. I lurch forward, grabbing hold of the seat in front of me. Vaslo turns his head toward me, grinning. "I think we lost your friend," he says. He speaks in a heavy Eastern European accent.

I pull myself up. "Don't be too sure. He has a habit of popping up unexpectedly."

"Yeah, I know. I know all about Van Helsing."

I stare at Vaslo, letting a few beats go by. "You're just full of surprises," I finally say. I take a deep breath and let it out. "What else do you know?"

"I know you're a..." Vaslo spits out some unintelligible word.

"What the hell does that mean?"

"It's Romanian. It means 'sperm eater'." Vaslo stretches his arms above his head. "One of the lesser known types of vampires. The ones that don't feed on blood." He pauses and risks a quick glance at me. "The ones that don't kill their prey."

"Jeez," I mutter. I give a humorless laugh. "And I thought I was so good at passing."

"I knew after you paid me," Vaslo says calmly. I notice that he's not looking me in the eyes as he talks, but over my left shoulder. *This guy's no dummy,* I think. *He knows I need eye contact to hypnotize him.* "I know what it's like to be hypnotized by a sperm eater." He reaches into his shirt pocket, pulls a cigarette out and lights it. He inhales deeply and lets out a cloud of smoke. "I was the lover of a sperm-eater once. Back in Moldavia. I was always his first. I'd wait by his coffin when evening first started coming on, and he would wake up and drain me dry." Vaslo's eyes soften in memory. "The best blow jobs I ever had." He risks another quick glance at me and grins. "That little mental trick you sperm eaters have, pushing into a man's mind right when he starts shooting, is fucking amazing."

"What happened to him?" I ask.

Vaslo's eyes harden. "Van Helsing killed him. His men cornered him and locked him in a room until he starved. I was in the local pub when Van Helsing came in days later and bragged about it."

"Jesus," I say softly. I let a couple of seconds go by. "Van Helsing killed my last lover too," I finally say. "In the same way. His name was Miguel."

Vaslo takes another long drag from his cigarette and exhales. We don't say anything for a long time. I hear a TV blaring from one of the windows facing the alley. "I can understand killing the blood drinkers," he finally says. "They're a public menace, and it's either us or them. But the sperm eaters harm no one." He shakes his head. "But Van Helsing is fanatical about vampires. He wants them all dead."

"No shit," I say. "The bastard's been tracking me for months. He's inhuman."

Vaslo gives a bark of laughter. "You're one to talk."

To my surprise, this stings. "Hey, I may be one of the walking dead," I say, "but I've still got feelings."

Vaslo doesn't seem to notice my injured tone. "When I saw him walk into the bar with his goons, I knew it was you he was after. That's why I waited with the door open and the engine running."

"You know, you can look me in the eye," I say. "I won't hypnotize you. I promise."

Vaslo turns his gaze toward me. "What's your name?" he asks.

"Joe." Vaslo raises his eyebrows, and I laugh. "We're not all named Dracula, you know."

Vaslo reaches down and starts the engine. "Let's go," he says.

"Where?" I ask. I find Vaslo's habit of taking charge disconcerting.

"To my apartment," Vaslo says. "I'm willing to bet Van Helsing has your place staked out. It won't be safe to go back there." I can't dispute the logic of this and say nothing. "Besides," Vaslo grins, cupping his basket. "I imagine you'll want another chance to feed."

In spite of my recent feeding, hunger still flicks lightly through my body. "Why do we have to wait until we get back to your place?" I ask.

Vaslo shoots me a sharp look. He grins. "No reason at all." He switches off the engine and gets out of the cab. In less than a minute he's in the backseat with me, with his pants down around his ankles.

I bend my head down toward his lap, but he stops me. "Kiss me first," he says. "Let's put a little romance in this. I'm not a fast-food joint."

I look at him, startled. "All right," I finally say.

Vaslo cups the back of my neck with his hand and pulls me toward him. He slips his tongue into my mouth as his lips work against mine. Soon I feel his hands sliding over my body, tugging my flesh, tweaking my nipples. I run my tongue down the length of his torso and swallow his dick. It's like a torpedo: a sleek, small head that swells out into a fat tube; I pull back the foreskin and slide my mouth down it until my nose is pressed against his pubes. I hold that position for a few beats, letting myself get acquainted with the size and texture of his dick, how it fills my mouth, how the head pushes against the back of my throat. Vaslo starts the action, pumping his hips slowly, twining his fingers through my hair and gently tugging my head back and forth. I wrap my hand around his balls and give them a good tug as my mouth swoops down his thick shaft. I look up, and when my eyes meet Vaslo's I probe into his mind until I find the pleasure center. I give it a sharp push. Vaslo gasps. "Sweet Jesus," he murmurs.

I quicken my pace, bobbing my head rapidly, sliding my lips down the velvety skin of Vaslo's dick. Vaslo thrusts his hips up to meet each descent of my mouth. He shifts his body, and now he's on top of me, his dick still thrusting in and out of my mouth, his balls slapping against my chin. His hands clasp the sides of my head, holding it still as he impales my mouth. He gives a deep thrust and leaves his dick full down my throat, triggering my gag reflex. I reach up and tweak his nipples hard. Vaslo groans and resumes fucking my face.

When I sense by the throb of Vaslo's dick and the tightness of his balls that he's ready to shoot, I give another hard push into his mind. Vaslo cries out, and his body shudders. His dick pulses in my mouth, pumping out his thick load as I suck mightily. I close my eyes with pleasure from the taste of it: currants and cinnamon, oranges and honey, with a slight hint of cloves.

Vaslo lies wedged in the corner of the taxi's backseat, panting. A last drop of come seeps out of his dick head, and I bend down and lick it off. Vaslo runs his fingers through my hair, and I look up into his eyes. "What about you?" he says. "Don't you want to come too?"

I shake my head. "The only time a sperm eater comes is when he's creating another sperm eater. By fucking a mortal and shooting a load up his ass." I look at Vaslo. "Didn't your vampire boyfriend explain this to you?"

Vaslo shakes his head slowly. "I'd ask. But he refused to talk about it."

"I'm not surprised," I say. I give a short laugh. "I'm giving away a trade secret here, Vaslo. It's considered bad form for a vampire to reveal this to a mortal."

"Let's go," Vaslo says. He climbs back into the driver's seat and backs out of the alley.

Vaslo drives us through a maze of streets, until we wind up on a dark, tree-lined street bordering Dolores Park. He slows to a crawl. "I just live a little farther down, at the end of the block," he says.

The street seems deserted all right, but I feel a nagging sense of dread. I tell myself it's just my frayed nerves. Vaslo cruises down past a line of parked cars, and the dread explodes like a sunburst in my brain. "Get us out of here!" I snarl. "We're in danger!"

Lights suddenly blaze on all around us, and I hear the sound of car engines roaring to life. "Shit!" Vaslo exclaims. A van pulls out in front of us and jackknifes across the street, blocking us. Vaslo throws the cab into reverse, but two police cars come tearing up behind us, sirens screaming and lights flashing. Vaslo guns the accelerator and plows into them. There's the sound of metal crashing on metal, and I'm thrown hard against the side of the car.

"Get out!" Vaslo shouts. "Make a run for it!"

I yank open the door, but before I can even place my feet on the ground, I feel hands grab my arms and pull me out of the backseat. Three men descend upon me, and in a matter of seconds I find myself pinned down on the street, face up, helplessly struggling. I try to stare into their eyes, but my attackers know enough to avoid eye contact. Behind them, two of Van Helsing's men are beating the shit out of Vaslo. He slumps to the pavement.

A man walks slowly up to me. He stops and squats down. "Hello, Joe," he says.

I look into Van Helsing's face, but like the others, he carefully avoids eye contact. He straightens and nods to the men. "Put him in the car." Vaslo groans and props himself up on his elbow. One of Van Helsing's men kicks him, and Vaslo doubles over with a grunt. "That's enough!" Van Helsing snaps. "He's human. Save that for the vampire."

"Look," I say, making my words fast and urgent. "It'll be daylight in a couple of hours. Just keep me laid out here until the sun rises. Make it quick."

Van Helsing chuckles, and he looks at me with an expression that seems almost affectionate. "Joe, my friend," he says softly. "I've invested way too much time and energy on you to finish you off so quickly." He lays his hand on my cheek. "We're going to drag this out as long as possible."

I'm squeezed into the back of Van Helsing's car between Van Helsing and one of his thugs, a blond giant of a man with muscles that squirm under his T-shirt like rats in a canvas sack. Blondie wears a crucifix around his neck, and on his left biceps there's a tattoo of Jesus' head bleeding from a crown of thorns. Another crucifix dangles from the rearview mirror. All that's missing is a dashboard Jesus. The driver's dark, Greek maybe, or Sicilian, with a thick mustache, black curls, and liquid, soulful eyes. Van Helsing has a habit of surrounding himself with handsome men; I've always suspected him of being as closeted as a fundamentalist preacher.

The dashboard clock says it's a little after 5 in the morning. We have about half an hour worth of darkness left. I silently pray (yeah, vampires pray too) that Van Helsing has miscalculated, that we'll still be on the streets at sunrise. The odds are strong that frying in the backseat of this car would be an improvement over whatever Van Helsing has cooked up for me. Van Helsing seems to pick up on my thoughts. "Hurry," he mutters to the driver.

The driver takes the Army Street exit and turns off onto Bayshore Boulevard. We drive past empty factories and tire yards, and it's not long before we're deep in the Hunter's Point section of San Francisco.

"Where are you taking me?" I ask Van Helsing.

"Shut up," Blondie says. He speaks with a German accent. Van Helsing ignores the both of us and stares out the car window.

The car stops at a red light. I glance at the deserted street outside and make a swift calculation of the distance between me and the backseat door. "Don't even think about it," Blondie says, his voice bored. He tightens his hold around my bicep. Van Helsing gives a smile as thin as a razor's edge.

We eventually pull up in front of a ramshackle brick building. The driver turns off the engine and climbs out, and Blondie opens the door and pulls me out after him. I'm not tall (5 foot 9), and both men tower over me. They escort me into the building, a hand under each armpit, my feet barely touching the ground. Van Helsing follows close behind.

I'm half dragged down a long, narrow corridor, flanked on both sides by closed doors. I have no idea what this building once was, but it looks deserted now, the floors thick with dust, the light fixtures festooned with cobwebs. After a while they stop at a door no different from any of the others. Van Helsing pulls out a key and fumbles with the lock.

If ever I'm going to get a chance, this is it. I turn to Blondie and give him a sharp jab in the side with my elbow. "Hey, cocksucker!" I yell. Startled, he turns and looks me full in the face, and with that brief eye contact I enter his mind and push *hard*. My only trick is giving pleasure, not pain, but I let him have it with both barrels. His eyes widen and his jaw drops open as the mental orgasm jolts through him. I tear out of his loosened grip and push him against the driver. Both men stagger against the wall, and I make a run for it, dashing down the dusty hallway.

Footsteps ring behind me, but I keep my eyes focused on the stretch of floor in front of me, pumping my legs as hard as I can. Sweet Jesus, I wish the myths about vampires were true, that I could shift my body into the form of a bat and just tear out into the night. As it is, I can barely keep ahead of the bastards; I hear them panting right behind me.

I turn a corner, and there's the front door straight ahead, like the gate to heaven. I fling myself against it, it bursts open, and suddenly I'm out in the winter's night again, the cold air rushing against me like a kiss from God himself. The exhilaration I feel does me in; I get careless and don't notice the pile of broken lumber directly ahead of me. I plow right into it and go flying, hands outstretched, boards tossed into the air. I barely hit ground before Van Helsing's men pile on top of me, cursing and pelting me with their fists, snarling like wolves in a *Wild Kingdom* segment. I give the fight everything I'm worth. Hell, I've got nothing to lose, and I snarl along with them, kicking and punching savagely. It's a lost cause, though. They're bigger and stronger, and it only takes a few minutes before they've got me facedown on the ground with my arms wrenched behind my back. I can turn my head just enough to look up. Van Helsing has caught up and stands in front of me, panting, his eyes wild with rage. He turns to Blondie. "You stupid asshole!" he snarls. "You almost let him get away!" Blondie's face darkens, but he doesn't say anything.

There's nothing left in me anymore. The men drag me back to the door where I staged my escape, and Van Helsing opens it this time without incident. To my surprise, the room is completely ordinary (I don't know what I was expecting, a stone dungeon maybe, straight out of a grade-B horror flick). All it is is some kind of storage room: a concrete floor with empty, metal shelves lining the walls. Pipes rise out of the floor on the far end, run along the wall, and exit out the ceiling.

"Handcuff him," Van Helsing snaps. Blondie pulls out a pair of handcuffs and secures me to the thickest of the pipes.

Van Helsing is finally regaining some of his composure. He turns to me and smiles grimly, making sure his gaze misses my eyes by a couple of inches. "You won't need a coffin in here, Joe," he says calmly. "There's no way any daylight could penetrate inside this room." I don't say anything. I know he's not doing me any favors. "We're going to leave you now, " he continues. "For a long time, actually." He sighs. "Typically, a vampire starves within four days if he doesn't feed." He gives a small laugh. "But some of them, the strong ones, can drag on for over a week." His gaze wanders down my body. "What do you say, Joe? You feel like trying for the record?"

I laugh. "All this just because you want to suck my dick but can't admit it." I shake my head. "Jesus, you're pathetic."

Van Helsing clamps his jaw shut tight. He forces another smile, but I can see I scored a hit. "I've got one last surprise for you, Joe," he finally says in a tight voice. He turns his head to the two men behind him. "You know what to do," he snaps.

The two men step forward. I slide to the floor and curl into a half-fetal position, expecting another beating, but to my surprise they stop a few feet in front of me. In unison, both men unbuckle their belts, unzip their flies, and let their pants slide down their legs. They start jacking off, their faces blank, their eyes focused off somewhere in the distance as they conjure up whatever fantasies it takes to get their nut off. At another time, I might have enjoyed the show. Blondie's dick lives up to the promise of his giant's body; it's a club, thick and red and uncut, its head flaring out into a meaty little fist. The Italian's (Greek's?) dick is in proportion to his tight, compact body: dark and roped with veins. His balls swing low between his thighs with every stroke, a fleshy, ripe sac full to bursting with jizz. I can just imagine the tasty load in them, and in spite of myself, my mouth waters.

Blondie's hand slides up his powerfully muscled torso, pulling the skin, tweaking each nipple. His hips pump with quick, savage thrusts, and his dick head winks in and out of his fist. The driver's strokes are slower, more sensual. He spits in his hand and slides it down the shaft of his dick, closing his eyes as the sensations this creates sweep over him.

I glance at Van Helsing. He's standing directly behind the men, his eyes fixed on their naked asses. It's not hard to spot the little tent his dick has made in his slacks. I laugh. "Why don't you come over here and sit by me, Van Helsing?" I sneer. "You'd get a much better view." Van Helsing's face darkens again, and his jaw clamps down hard enough to crack teeth.

Blondie's the first to shoot. With a groan, he arches his back as his load pulses out and splatters against the floor a few feet away from me. His body spasms with each spurt. When he's finally done, he shakes the remaining come off his fingers onto the little spermy pool at his feet. The driver quickens the pace of his strokes. Sweat beads his forehead, and his balls pull up tight. He gives a long, trailing whimper when he finally comes, the drops of his spermy load joining that of Blondie's on the floor in front of me.

Both men silently pull up their pants and buckle their belts. Without looking at me, they walk out of the room. "Sweet dreams, Joe," Van Helsing sneers.

"Bite me," I sneer back. Yeah, it's a lame retort, but the circumstances aren't exactly conducive to sparkling wit.

Van Helsing turns off the light and closes the door. I sit in the darkness, trying to keep my mind blank. The scent of the spermy loads the two men left behind wafts up to my nose, rich and tantalizing, and I feel my belly cramp with hunger, in spite of my earlier feedings. I reach over as far as the handcuffs will allow, but the puddles of jizz are just beyond the reach of my outstretched fingers. Now I understand why Van Helsing had his men jerk off. I cover my nose with my hand, trying to block out the sex odor, but it seeps between my fingers and into my nostrils. I close my eyes and think about how Vaslo's vampire lover died. And Miguel. Of all the ways to kill a vampire, starvation is the worst.

After a while I completely lose track of time. I lie there in the darkness, sinking more and more into hunger. Images play through my mind, men I have fed on, dicks I have sucked, loads I have swallowed. I think about the two sailors, Nick and Luke, the taste of their loads as they pumped down my throat. And of Vaslo's. I remember telling him about when vampires fuck. I think about my last lover, Miguel, and the night I turned him into a sperm eater...

"You sure you want to go through with this?" I ask. Miguel and I are lying naked on a bed in a Mexico City pension. Sounds of traffic and the come-on calls of the working girls float up from the street below.

"Yeah," Miguel says. "I'm sure."

"I think you're fuckin' crazy."

Miguel raises an eyebrow. "Crazy for wanting to be immortal?"

I give a sharp laugh. "Immortality is overrated. Take it from one who knows."

"I've made up my mind," Miguel says.

I don't say anything.

"We'll be buddies," he adds, his voice coaxing. "Forever. On the prowl, sucking cock together."

I still don't say anything.

"You owe me, Joe," he adds, his voice taking on an edge. "Big time."

"Yeah," I say quietly. "I know." I look at him and sigh. "Can I feed first?"

Miguel smiles. "Sure." He slides his arm under me and pulls me toward him. I don't resist. We kiss, tentatively at first, and then with greater force. He reaches down and wraps his hand around my cock, stroking it. It doesn't take long before I'm hard. There's a jar of lotion on the table by the bed; Miguel takes a big dollop of it and greases up my stiff dick. I close my eyes, feeling his slicked-up hand slide down my shaft. I open them again and look at him.

I roll on top of him, seizing his wrists and pinning his arms above his head. As we kiss, I grind my body against his, feeling the warmth of his mortal flesh flow into mine. Miguel breaks free from my grasp and wraps a hand around both our cocks, dick flesh against dick flesh, balls against balls. I slowly fuck his fist, our dicks sliding together, the skin of my torso squirming against his. Miguel twists his head and sticks his tongue in my ear and then nibbles on the lobe. I nuzzle against his neck, gently nipping it, aping my blood-drinking vampire cousins. My mouth slides down to Miguel's chest. I flick his nipples lightly with my tongue and then suck on them, pushing my face into Miguel's body. Sweet Jesus, but I love his flesh! Miguel combs his fingers through my hair, murmuring obscenities. I take another scoop of lotion out of the jar and run my fingers down the crack of Miguel's ass, probing for the pucker of his asshole. When I find it, I push in, first one finger, then two. Miguel sighs and then gives a low laugh. His dick is as hard as dicks get, and I bend down and take it in my mouth.

This will be Miguel's last orgasm for what could be a very long time, and I want it to be especially good. I work his dick with my mouth, sucking on it, licking it, making love to it as my fingers slide in and out of his asshole. Miguel groans mightily and writhes on the bed. He raises his head and our eyes meet. My lips slide down his dick shaft as I push into his mind's pleasure center, and Miguel cries out loudly. I keep the mind link intact as I suck and slurp over his dick, pushing through the flood of thoughts and images, whipping his brain up into something hot and frenzied. My tongue slides down to his balls and washes over them, their hairs tickling the inside of my mouth. As I tongue the fleshy sac, my spit-slicked hand continues to strokes his shaft. I'm doing an all-out pleasure assault on Miguel's body, working it over with my mouth and hands, diddling with his mind. Sweat streams down Miguel's face and makes his muscular torso gleam in the faint light that pours in from the outside window. He arches his back as he thrusts his dick down my throat, his breath coming out of his open mouth in ragged gasps. I can sense his readiness. Once more I look into his eyes, probe deep into his mind and push. Miguel gasps, and his body shudders. His dick throbs in my mouth and his sweet, thick load pulses down my throat. Miguel thrashes in the bed like a wild man as I feed off his load, sucking his thick dick, draining those plump balls dry. When I've finally done feeding he collapses back down on the mattress. "Christ!" he groans. I roll the last of his load over with my tongue, savoring the taste of it, its smoothness and flavor, so distinctively Miguel's. It'll be the last time I'll ever be able to do so, and I feel a pang of sadness.

I lie next to him, gently stroking his chest, my thumb and forefinger idly massaging his nipples. "I can promise you a lifetime of terrific orgasms, Miguel," I say. "Are you sure you want to give that all up?"

He turns his head toward me, and I can see the determination in his eyes. "Yeah," he says. "Stop trying to talk me out of this."

"All right," I say. "Then here goes."

I push his knees apart and hoist his legs up around my torso. His asshole is still greased from our last session, but I add an extra dollop to it. "I haven't done this for a few decades," I say. "I don't make a habit of creating vampires. I may be a little rusty."

"It'll be like riding a bike," Miguel answers. "You'll do fine." He pulls my head down and kisses me again. Slowly, inch by inch, I push my dick inside him. When I'm fully in, I stay there, motionless, staring into his eyes. Miguel looks back at me, lips parted, his eyes bright with excitement, and I bend down and kiss him again. I start pumping my hips, and Miguel moves in response, matching me thrust with thrust. I feel his hands slide down my back and squeeze my ass cheeks, pushing me deeper inside him.

"Yeah, that's right." Miguel groans. "Fuck me hard. Make me immortal."

Miguel squeezes his ass muscles tight each time I pull out, and ripples of pleasure wash over me. "You're good!" I laugh. My dick feels like it's encased in tight velvet. "Real good!" Miguel laughs back and kisses me, his tongue *pushing deep into my mouth. I increase the tempo of my thrusts, slamming into his ass with deep, hard strokes. I can feel Miguel's load inside my belly, energizing me, filling me with strength. Miguel reaches down and tugs on my balls, not gently. I bend down and bite his lips, snarling, and Miguel wraps his arms around me in a tight bear hug. It has been so long since I've fucked ass! As each thrust of my dick sends me to another level of pleasure, I feel the wildness surge through me. Miguel's dick is hard again, pushing up against his belly, red and still wet from my saliva.*

I'm getting close. I give another deep thrust and feel myself taken to the edge. "Miguel," I gasp. "I'm ready to shoot. We can still stop before it's too late."

"Fuck that!" Miguel growls. "Give it to me." He twists my nipples, and I shove my dick hard up his ass, as deep as I can penetrate. My body spasms and the orgasm washes over me, picks me up and carries me on its crest, higher and higher. I cry out as my load shoots out deep into the warm, velvety darkness inside Miguel. Miguel holds on to me tightly, his legs clamped securely around my hips. I collapse on top of him, panting, my dick still full up his ass.

We lie like that without talking, even moving, except for the rise and fall of Miguel's chest against mine. Two hookers are having a fight on the street below, and their shrill voices rise up into the room. I raise my head and look at Miguel. He's staring up at the ceiling, his mouth open.

"Miguel?" I ask.

"Something is happening to me," he says. "I can feel it."

"You're turning into a vampire, Miguel," I say. "Like you wanted to."

I hold on to him for the next few hours as he works through the transformation, thrashing and shuddering in my arms. It's well after 2 in the morning before the last of what's mortal about Miguel has died. Miguel lies still in my arms, his eyes still trained on the ceiling.

"Miguel," I whisper into his ear. "We only have a few more hours before daybreak. We have to feed."

Miguel turns his head and looks at me. He licks his lips. "OK," he says.

"Are you sure you're up to it?"

Miguel gives me a thin smile. "Do I have a choice?"

I shake my head. "No," I say. "You don't."

I help Miguel climb unsteadily to his feet. He stands in the middle of the room, swaying slightly, as I dress him. I button his shirt for him. "It gets easier after the first night," I say. "That much I remember."

Miguel nods his head. "I sure as hell hope so."

I kiss him gently, and then we walk out into the warm tropical night, looking for dick to suck.

I thought Miguel and I would be partners throughout eternity. Two months later Van Helsing killed him, and I was forced to flee.

Someone is shaking my shoulder. I'm only dimly aware of it, the sensation is dwarfed by the hunger that rages through me. "Joe," I hear a voice say. I try to raise my head, but can't quite manage it. I open my eyes. The lights are on, and Vaslo is leaning over me, his face anxious. "Joe," he says again. "Wake up. We've got to go."

"Wh...what?" I ask. I can't focus my thoughts. *How long have I been here?* I wonder.

Vaslo glances worriedly toward the door and then back at me. "They'll be here any minute," he whispers urgently. "We have to get out of here." He unlocks my handcuffs. "Can you get up?"

I try to push myself up, but collapse back onto the floor.

"Shit!" Vaslo mutters. He unzips his jeans and pulls out his cock. "Here, Joe," he says. "I got something for you." He cradles my head in his arm and sticks his dick in my mouth. My instincts take over, and I begin sucking on it weakly. Vaslo's dick grows to hardness, and he starts pumping his hips, sliding his dick in and out of my mouth. He shifts his position until he's sitting on top of me, his legs straddling my chest, his hands still supporting my head. He fucks my mouth with quick, deep strokes, slapping his balls against my chin. "That's it, Joe," Vaslo murmurs. "Take it in." He's breathing heavily now, and his thighs clamp tightly against me. A shudder runs through his body, and he gives a sharp gasp. His dick throbs, and suddenly my mouth is full of his come. Dear God, how sweet it tastes! I gulp it eagerly, feeling the load pulse down my throat, drop by delicious drop. Strength flows back into my body, and I keep on sucking, coaxing out every stray drop. "Easy, easy," Vaslo says gently. He pulls his dick out of my mouth. "That's it, Joe," he says. "You're going to have to make do with that."

I struggle to a sitting position, and look at Vaslo. "How did you find me?" I ask.

"I have friends all over. One of them drove Van Helsing's blond hoodlum here this morning in his cab." He bends down and helps me to my feet. "Listen, we have to get out of here."

He wraps my arm around his shoulder, and we stagger out into the hallway. Blondie is trussed up like a luau pig, with adhesive tape over his mouth. He glares at us as we hurry by, and Vaslo snarls something at him in Romanian.

Vaslo has a van parked outside, and he shoves me into the passenger seat. The cold bite of the night air cuts through my grogginess; I take a deep breath and sigh gratefully. As Vaslo starts the ignition, I glance at him. "How long have I been...?" I ask.

"Three days," Vaslo says grimly. He puts the van in gear and drives off. "I'll give you another feeding in a few minutes," he adds. "Just give me time to recharge the batteries."

We whip past dark buildings in deserted streets. I glance at the dashboard clock; it's a few minutes past midnight. Vaslo turns on the radio, and rock music fills the van. About 20 minutes later he pulls into a deserted lot and parks behind a pile of old tires, the engine still idling. He looks at me, his mouth curled up into a slight smile. "Dinnertime," he says, unbuckling his belt. He lifts his hips up and tugs his jeans down below his knees. There's a streetlight on the corner of the lot, and its faint light pours over Vaslo's body. His dick flops heavily against his thigh, half hard, and his balls are pulled up tight from the cold. Vaslo reaches over and cranks the heater up another couple of notches. "It's fuckin' freezing in here," he mutters. He glances at me and jerks his head behind him. "Let's go back."

We crawl over the front seats and stretch out full length in the back of the van. I pull off Vaslo's boots, followed by his jeans and shorts, and then bury my face between his thighs, breathing in the sharp, musky smell of his crotch. I nibble my lips down his shaft, feeling it swell and harden in my mouth. I look up, and we stare into each other's eyes. Vaslo holds my head with both hands and thrusts his dick deep down my throat. By now, I'm getting a very intimate knowledge of the shape and size of his cock, the ridge that runs the length of the shaft, how the head swells up, the loose ring of foreskin. I cradle his balls in my hand and squeeze them gently, feeling the tickle of their hairs against my skin. Vaslo, my rescuer, my lover, my nourisher...

Vaslo shifts his body, pinning me against the side of the van as he energetically fucks my face. I twist my head from side to side, sliding my tongue up his shaft, reaching up with both hands and twisting his nipples. Vaslo sighs deeply. "Fucking vampires," he murmurs. "They're so damn good at sucking cock."

I slide my hands over his torso, tugging at the skin, feeling the play of his muscles beneath my fingertips. My fingers run down the ridge of his spine, across the rise of his smooth, hard ass. I pry the cheeks apart and push against Vaslo's asshole. He shifts his hips to provide me access, and I slide a finger inside him, slowly twisting it. Vaslo sighs. I finger-fuck him as I suck him off, synchronizing the downsweep of my lips with each thrust of my finger. I look up into his eyes and enter his mind, pushing hard against his pleasure center. Vaslo sighs again, louder, the noise trailing off into a low groan. "Yeah, baby," he whispers. "Keep on doing what you're doing."

I suck and tease his dick, work it over, bringing him closer and closer to the brink of orgasm. Vaslo's breaths come out in little whimpers. Soon the whimpers become louder, longer; in spite of the cold, sweat beads his forehead. "I'm almost there," he gasps, and gives a long, thrust of his dick down my throat just as I shove my finger up his ass to the third joint. I flood his mind's pleasure center with sensation. Vaslo cries out loudly, and once more, the second time in less than half an hour, I feel his thick load gush down my throat. I suck voraciously, savoring the taste of Vaslo's jizz. Even when he's drained dry and his dick has begun to soften, I keep sucking on it, gently, lovingly, straining for that last stray drop. Vaslo lies on his back, his mouth open and his arm over his eyes, as I work him over.

A couple of minutes later he pulls his dick out of my mouth and props himself up on his elbow. "We've got to go, Joe," he says softly. His eyes are still dazed, and he focuses them with effort. "Van Helsing will be looking for us."

"All right," I say.

We wind up on Highway 5, heading south. I'm still hungry, but the hunger is manageable, at least for the time being. Vaslo's eyes are fixed on the road. "Where are we going?" I ask.

Vaslo glances at me. "How does Mexico sound? Van Helsing doesn't have a vampire extradition arrangement with them like he does here. You'll be safer there."

I settle back into the seat and stare out the window. "OK," I say. I'm still weak and a little dazed, and I'm quite willing to let Vaslo make the decisions for the time being.

I let a few minutes go by. "Vaslo," I say cautiously. "Feeding off you won't be enough. I'll need others too."

Vaslo keeps his eyes trained on the road. "Look in the glove compartment," he says. I open the compartment and pull out a sheaf of papers. Written on it is a list of rest stops, parks, public toilets. I look at Vaslo quizzically. He returns my stare and grins.

"I downloaded that from the Internet," he says. "It's a list of all the gay cruising spots between here and the Mexican border. You don't have to worry, Joe. We'll make lots of stops. You'll feed like a king." He winks. "There's a trucker's rest area just 20 miles ahead that we can start with."

I shake my head and laugh. "You're fucking amazing, Vaslo."

Vaslo grins. "Just remember. You always feed on me first."

I smile back. "Consider it a promise," I say.

Vaslo turns the radio back on, and we tear down Highway 5, heading south to Mexico.

BROTHER JOHN'S TRAVELING SALVATION SHOW

It's his eyes that give me second thoughts about climbing into his car. They flick around like houseflies, never settling in one place for longer than a couple of seconds. His gaze meets mine once, for a micro-instance, and then goes bouncing off like a ricocheting bullet. I balance uncertainly, one foot in the car, the other on the shoulder of the highway.

"How far down the road you headed?" I ask.

With a great effort, he forces himself to look me full in the face. His eyes are filled with fear and excitement. I don't like this one bit. "Oh, a ways," he says, waving his hand vaguely in the air. "I'm not going anywhere in particular. I'm just driving around." He pats the passenger seat with his hand. "Hop in." He's smiling, but his glance is anything but friendly.

I make a quick assessment of him. He's about 40, slender, and other than this *nervousness* he's giving off, he's totally ordinary-looking. If he turns out to be some kind of psycho from hell, I'm sure I can take him down. And I've been stuck on this fuckin' highway for almost five hours without a ride. I'm willing to take the risk.

I throw my duffel bag in the backseat and climb into the car. "I'm headed for Kansas City," I say.

He nods his head, grinning. "I can take you there. No problem." He makes no effort to put the car in gear. He opens and closes his fingers around the steering wheel, staring straight ahead.

I wait. He just sits there, clenching and unclenching his fingers. "Is there a problem?" I finally ask, putting an edge to my voice.

He turns and faces me. "I'll take you to Kansas City if you let me suck your cock," he blurts out.

I look at him for a few seconds, then turn my head and look out the window. There's a cornfield next to us, bathed in sunlight, and I can see the crows wheeling over it. I pull a pack of Marlboros out of my shirt pocket and shake a cigarette free. I light it, looking him full in the face.

"You mean it about taking me all the way to Kansas City?"

He nods his head vigorously. "Hell, yeah! I'll take you to St. Louis if you want." He licks his lips. "That is, if you, you know..."

"Let you blow me?" I finish his sentence. I inhale deeply and blow out a stream of smoke. "OK," I say. "It's a deal."

The man blinks and opens and closes his mouth. He wears the expression of someone who thinks he's closed a deal too soon. "You have to come too," he says, the words falling out of his mouth. "I won't take you anywhere unless you shoot a load for me."

I shrug. "OK."

"And let me kiss you too," he adds hurriedly. "On the mouth." I open the car door. "All right, all right, forget about the kissing." His voice is suddenly panic-stricken. I close the door again. Silence. "Well, all right," he finally says. He clears his throat. I keep my eyes trained on the circling crows. "All right," he says again. He puts the car in gear, and we drive off.

He finds a dirt road that branches off into the woods. He pulls behind a stand of pines and looks over at me. *Well, I guess that's my cue*, I think. I unbuckle my belt, pull down my zipper, and tug my jeans down below my knees. I hitch my thumbs under the elastic band of my briefs and pull them down too. I lean against the car door and look at the man.

His forehead is beaded with sweat. "Take your T-shirt off too," he says in a low, strangled voice.

I peel off my T-shirt and toss it on the car floor. The man just sits there, his eyes scanning up and down my body. "Beautiful," he murmurs. He reaches out and lightly touches my chest. His fingers slide down my torso, kneading the muscles. The ache in his face is almost too painful to watch. "Just fuckin' beautiful," he whispers.

He leans forward and presses his lips against my left nipple. His tongue darts out, swirling around the pink flesh, making it hard. He does the same with my right nipple, this time biting it gently as well. I look down at the bald spot at the back of his head. Physically, he does nothing for me, but all this attention he's showing me *is* turning me on. I feel like I'm a fuckin' rock star. His face moves down my torso, his lips kissing my abs. My dick has swollen to a half-erection. He takes it in his hand, cradling it in his palm. He gives it a long look. It stirs under the naked worship of his gaze and swells to full hardness. "Sweet Jesus in heaven," he says softly.

He bends down and takes my dick in his mouth. He starts bobbing his head, and I pump my hips in sync with his lip-strokes, fucking his face with short, fast thrusts. He holds on to my balls and tugs on them. "Easy, easy," I murmur. He is not a tidy cocksucker; he slobbers and drools and makes grunting, slurping noises. I hold on to his head with both hands and plow his mouth good. He's got his own dick out and is stroking it hard.

I close my eyes and let the sensations sweep over me, feeling my load churn in my balls with each downward plunge of his mouth. He buries his nose in my pubes like he's rooting for acorns, my dick shoved deep down his throat. He reaches up and twists my nipples with both hands. My body shudders, and he takes my dick out of his mouth, stroking it furiously. I arch my back, and my load squirts out, splattering against his face. "Oh, yeah!" he groans. His body suddenly twitches, and he gives a long, trailing moan. I see his own jizz ooze out between his fingers. When he's finally done, he collapses against the seat, panting.

We sit there for what seems like one helluva long time. Except for a breeze moving through the treetops and an occasional birdsong, it's utterly quiet. I'm the first to stir. I retrieve my T-shirt and slip it on. "Can we go now?" I ask.

He nods, my jizz smeared across his face. He pulls out a handkerchief and wipes it off. A few minutes later we're dressed and back on the main highway. It's late afternoon now, and the shadows from the trees fall long across the asphalt. Neither one of us says anything. After about a half an hour, he pulls off onto an exit. "I got to get some gas," he says, his voice flat. He won't look me in the eye.

We pull into an Amoco station. I climb out. "I'm gonna take a whiz," I say. He nods but says nothing, his face expressionless. It's gonna be a long ride to Kansas City.

I do my business and wash my hands. I look in the mirror. I'm surprised at how tough and mean the face that looks back at me is. I splash water on my face and run my fingers through my hair. *OK,* I think. *It's only two hours to Kansas City. Let's just get this over with.*

When I get back to the gas pumps, there's no one there and my duffel bag is leaning against a case of motor oil. I look down the highway and see the last of the bastard's rear bumper disappearing into the horizon. *Well, shit!* I stand there for a minute, as if by just looking at the highway I can will that son of a bitch to turn around and keep his part of the deal. The sun is low on the horizon now; it'll be dark in a couple of hours. The highway stretches off in both directions, straight as a plumb line and empty of cars. Across the road lies a series of low hills. There are a couple of trucks, a few cars, and a bus parked on the top of the nearest one, and I can make out men moving around.

I walk into the station. Some old guy is perched behind the cash register, watching me with half-lidded eyes. "What's the nearest town from here?" I ask.

"Coopersville," he says. "Six miles north."

I walk to the door and look out. If I'm lucky, I can hitch a ride into town before nightfall. *Yeah. And then what?* I watch the men on the hill. "What's going on over there?" I ask.

"A revival meeting," the man says behind me. "Brother John's Traveling Salvation Show. He comes by here every year."

I watch them for a few minutes more and make a decision. I shoulder my duffel bag and head out across the highway. When I get halfway up the hill I can see that what the men are doing is pitching a giant tent. The canvas is stretched out on the ground, and the work crew is hammering in stakes. Two men are standing by the nearest truck, talking. I walk up to them.

"Howdy," I say.

They look at me and nod.

"You need any help setting up?" I ask. "In exchange for a meal and a place to sleep?"

The man closest to me shakes his head. "Sorry, son. We got everything taken care of."

Well, what do I do now? Nothing comes to mind. "OK," I finally say. "Thanks anyway," I turn to go.

"You live in these parts?" the other man asks. His tone is quiet, but there's something about his voice that snags my attention. I glance at him, and his dark brown eyes meet my gaze calmly. He's younger than the other guy, mid 30s, maybe. He has the body of a day laborer: tall, broad shoulders, powerful arms, a massive chest, but his face is mild and thoughtful.

"No," I reply. "I'm just passing through. I'm trying to get to Kansas City."

The man seems to consider this. "What's in Kansas City?" he asks. "Family?"

"No," I say again. "Nothing's in Kansas City. It's just a place to spend some time in."

The man nods, as if this makes perfect sense. He turns to the other man. "Hank, find him something to do." He walks off.

Hank looks exasperated. "OK," he finally says, "I guess you can help set up the tent."

I stare after the retreating form of the other man. "Who was that?" I ask.

"That's Brother John," Hank says curtly. "Now come on and follow me if you want work." He's already hurrying off, and I have to run after him to catch up.

The gospel choir is belting out "That Old Rugged Cross," swaying their bodies in rhythm to the song, and the audience is clapping and stamping their feet. The place is *jumping*. Strings of electric lights run along the tent's ceiling; I can hear the hum of the diesel generator outside during the rare periods of quiet between songs. Hank has me standing along the side of the tent toward the front, a sort of combination usher and security guard. "Things get a little wild sometimes," he says, "and I want you handy if I need any help in crowd control." He fixes me with a hard glare. "You don't do *nothing* unless I give you a signal. If I see you roughing anybody up, I'll come down on you so hard, you goin' to wish your daddy had kept his pecker in his pants the night you was conceived."

The choir finishes its song, and the lights dim until the tent is plunged into gloom. Out of the darkness the choir starts singing "Amazing Grace" softly and slowly. The audience is dead silent, spellbound. The lights are turned up slowly, revealing the silhouette of a man, then shot to full brightness, and we all see that it's Brother John. He's dressed simply: dark slacks, a white cotton shirt open at the throat, revealing a strong, bull neck. He stands before the congregation, his eyes sweeping over us calmly. For a split second his gaze meets mine, and I feel like I'm being greeted by an old friend welcoming me home. Something in me stirs, and then his gaze moves on. *Christ, he's good!* I think. He smiles, his mouth open just enough to show a flash of white, even teeth; his dark hair curls down across his forehead. I'm suddenly struck by how *handsome* he is. I'm amazed I hadn't noticed this the first time we met. The choir finishes the song with a surge of voices blending together on one high note. A shiver goes through me even as I fight to resist it.

Dead silence, except for the hum of the generator and the sound of crickets singing in the summer night outside. "Brothers," Brother John says, his voice soft, and yet, in the silence, filling the tent, "and sisters." He raises up his arms, his hands outstretched. *"Welcome!"*

It's well after midnight before I finally stagger out of the tent. Brother John's voice is still ringing in my ears, even though he's finished for the night and presumably has gone to bed.

All night he's been talking, sometimes low and pleading, sometimes his voice ringing out into the night air, praying for us, rejoicing with us, grieving with us, yelling at us. I have never seen such a performance. He had the crowd twisted around his finger. Me included.

Hank comes up to me, a paper bag in his hand. He looks me hard in the face, and though he isn't smiling, his eyes are sympathetic. "How you doin', son?" he asks.

"I don't know," I say, shaking my head. I look back at the tent, now empty and dark. "That was...amazing!"

Hank grins. "I know." He puts a cigarette in his mouth, and

lights it. "Ol' Brother John can sure kick ass when he gets a steam up." He lays his hand on my shoulder. "I got a bedroll set up for you in the bus."

Someone calls out to Hank, and he goes over to the man. They talk together for a while, and then Hank comes back, frowning. "There's a problem with the lights I got to tend to," he says. He hands over the paper bag he's been holding. "Do me a favor, will you, son? Take this over to Brother John. He's in the trailer by the bus."

"Sure," I say. "No problem." Hank goes back toward the tent and I make my way to the trailer. I glance in the bag. Inside is a pint of Jack Daniel's.

I knock on the trailer door, but nobody answers. I try the doorknob, and the door swings open. I stick my head in. There's a small room out front: a couple of chairs, a bed, a table, a rack with clothes hanging from it, not much more. The place is empty, but I hear the shower running on the other side of what must be a bathroom door. The water turns off.

"Brother John?" I call out.

Silence. "Who's out there?"

"It's me, Jim," I shout through the door. "The guy you gave work to this afternoon."

The door suddenly opens. Brother John comes out wearing a white terry-cloth robe. He's toweling down his hair. "Hi, Jim," he says, smiling. "Have a seat."

I remain standing. I hold out the bottle to him. "Hank asked me to give this to you." When he makes no effort to take it, I put it on the table. I turn toward the door.

"What's the rush?" Brother John grins. "Sit down. Have a drink with me." He raises his eyebrows. "Unless it bothers you to see a preacher man take a snort."

"Hell," I laugh. "I don't care." I sit in one of the chairs. Brother John gets out two glasses and fills each of them with three fingers of whiskey. He hands one to me and sits in the other chair, opposite me.

He holds his glass up. "Here's to the Lord's will. Which moves in mysterious ways." We clink our glasses together, and I take a gulp of whiskey. Brother John looks at me. His face is still flushed, his eyes bright. Once again, I'm struck by how handsome a man he is. "Damn, I'm pumped!" he says. He looks at me and laughs. "It takes a while for me to wind down, Jim. These shows are one hell of an adrenaline rush."

"I never saw anything like it," I say. I look him full in the face. "You were incredible."

Brother John grins broadly. "Why, thank you, Jim," he says. He reaches for the bottle on the table beside him, and his robe falls open, revealing a chest furred with dark hair, one pink nipple peeking out. He refills my glass and pours another shot for himself. He takes a gulp from it and sighs. He slides his body down in the chair, slouching, his legs spread apart. His brown eyes regard me frankly. "So what the hell is in Kansas City for you?"

"Nothing much," I say. "I'm just kind of bumming around."

Brother John stretches, and the sash of his robe becomes undone. The robe falls open, but he doesn't seem to notice. "Seems like kind of an aimless way to live, Jim," he says mildly. His dick is thick and dark and hangs heavily against his thigh.

"Yeah, well, I'm just taking some time off," I say, my mouth feeling suddenly dry. I try to keep my eyes trained on his face, but they keep wandering down his body. Brother John's torso is heavily muscled, the pecs firm, the abs nicely cut. I take another gulp of whiskey. "I guess I'm just seeing what the world's like."

Brother John's dick slowly hardens. I glance at his face, but his expression is still calm. "Well, just be careful, Jim," he says. "A man's got to have some purpose to his life. He can't just go wandering around forever."

I don't say anything. Hell, I don't know what I *could* say. The only noise I hear is the chirping of the crickets outside. Brother John's dick is fully erect now, sticking straight out in front of him. I stare at it openly.

"Why don't you come over here, Jim," Brother John says softly, "and help me work off some of this energy."

I don't have to think twice about his offer. Before you can say "Hallelujah," I'm down on my knees between his outstretched legs; that thick, meaty dick of his crammed down my throat. I slide my hands up his torso, running my fingers through the chest hairs, kneading the hard flesh. I find both his nipples and squeeze hard. "Yeah," Brother John grunts. "That's it. Squeeze 'em good. Make me feel it."

Standing, he puts his hands on either side of my head and shoves his hips forward. His dick slams against the back of my throat, his balls pressing against my chin. I bob my head up and down, running my tongue over that thick column of flesh, feeling its shape and size. My hands slide up his torso, feeling the smooth, ripped belly, the swell of the pecs. Brother John sighs. My hands knead his shoulders, run over the hard mounds of his biceps and, sliding down his back, cup his smooth ass. I feel the cheek muscles clench and unclench with each thrust of his hips. I burrow my face into Brother John's balls, inhaling deeply, breathing in the faint scent of musk that's still there even after his shower. I wrap my hand around his dick and squeeze it, watching the fleshy knob turn from red to dark purple and then back to red as I loosen my grip. I slowly slide my lips down the shaft. Glancing up, my mouth full of dick, my gaze sweeps across the muscular, hairy torso until my eyes meet his. Brother John beams down at me, his smile generous. "Oh, yeah, Jim," he murmurs. "That feels so damn *good.*"

He bends down, hooks his hands under my armpits, and pulls me to my feet. Holding my head in his hands, he kisses me tenderly, his tongue sliding into my mouth as easily as if that were the only place on earth it *could* be. He wraps his powerful arms around me and pulls my body tight against his, his hard dick thrusting against my belly. I cup his ass with my hands, my fingers probing into his crack, spreading the cheeks apart, pushing against his bunghole. Brother John undresses me. When I'm finally naked, he spits in his hand and then wraps it around my cock, stroking it slowly. I groan as the sensations sweep over my body. With his arms still around me, he guides me to the bed, and when we're beside it, he topples the both of us on top of it.

Brother John stretches full on top of me, his naked flesh writhing against mine, my wrists pinned above my head by his strong hands. He kisses me again, long and hard, and then pulls away, looking down at me. "You going to let me taste that sweet cock of yours, Jim?" he croons.

"Oh, yeah!" I murmur. "But only if you let me keep on sucking yours."

Brother John grins. He pivots his body around so that his dick and balls hang right above my face. I feel his warm, wet mouth slide down my dick shaft, and I raise my head, tonguing his scrotum, rolling those heavy, ripe balls around in my mouth. I reach up and squeeze his dick. A clear drop of precome oozes out of the slit, and I rub it over my fingers, slicking them up. I start beating him off, my come-slicked hand working his dick in long, slow strokes.

Brother John's lips work their way skillfully down my shaft, nibbling it, sucking on it. *This is the second blow job I've received today,* I think, amazed. Maybe right now, even as I'm fucking Brother John's face, the man who gave me the ride this morning is beating off, thinking about our encounter, getting all hot all over again. Brother John is now tonguing my balls, sucking on them, rolling them around in his mouth as his spit-slicked hand strokes my dick. He burrows his fingers inside my ass-crack. I feel him push against my asshole, play with, and then, finally, enter it. He worms his finger up my ass slowly, one knuckle at a time, rotating it, pushing against my prostate. I cry out and my body shudders. If my dick were any harder, it could drill through granite. "You like that, Jim?" Brother John croons. "You want more of the same?"

"Oh, yeah," I groan. "Don't stop!"

Brother John slides in another finger, and I groan again. "Would you like me to fuck you, baby?" he asks, his eyes feverish. "Really plow your sweet ass good?"

"Hell, yeah!" I gasp. "Go for it!"

Brother John opens the drawer of his bedside table and pulls out a condom package and a jar of lube. I can't help but be a little startled. "Jeez," I laugh. "Just how often do you do this?"

Brother John's mouth curves up into a slow grin. "Not that often. Certainly not often enough. But I like to be ready whenever the Lord hands me the opportunity."

I laugh again, not sure whether or not he's joking. "Do you think the Lord sent me to you?"

Brother John's smile widens. "I don't doubt it for a second, baby." He rolls the condom down his dick and hoists my legs around his torso. "I think you're just what the Lord thought I needed right now."

He thrusts his hips forward, and I feel him slowly skewer me, working his way inside me inch by inch. I take a deep breath and hold it. Brother John's face is inches above mine, and his eyes are full on me, watching me carefully.

"Easy...easy," I gasp. Brother John stops for a moment and then slowly, with infinite patience, works his way full in. We stayed poised like that for a few beats, and then he gently begins to pump his hips. I feel his dick shaft move in and out, and I relax into it, letting my breath out.

"Yeah," Brother John croons. "That's right, Jim. Settle into it. Accept it." He quickens his strokes and I move my hips to meet him, pushing down as he thrusts up. "Oh, Jesus," he groans. "You do that so well."

I feel the fullness of his dick in me, loving the sensation, and I reach down and cup his furry balls in my hand, squeezing them gently. Brother John lowers his head and kisses me tenderly, his tongue thrusting down my throat at the same moment that his dick thrusts up my ass. Brother John wraps his hand around my dick and starts stroking it in sync with the thrusts of his hips. The rhythm our bodies have settled into comes together with increasing smoothness. We're doing that old horizontal dance I fuckin' love so well: Brother John's dick in my ass, my dick in his hand, his tongue in my mouth, the thrust and recede, the stroke in and stroke out, the give and the take. I clamp my ass muscles hard against his dick just as he plunges it full up the chute. Brother John gives a long, trailing groan and then unexpectedly laughs.

"What's so funny?" I ask, grinning.

Brother John shakes his head. "I was just thinking of the old Bible story, about Jacob wrestling with the angel." He seizes the back of my neck and shakes it playfully. "That's us, baby."

"Oh, yeah?" I smile. "Which one of us is Jacob and which one the angel?"

Brother John thrusts his dick hard up my ass and grinds his hips. I gasp with pleasure. "That's the beauty of it," he says. "We're each both Jacob *and* the angel." He thrusts again, and I reach back and squeeze his balls. I feel the shudder sweep over his body. He cries out, heaving his body off the mattress, and I hold on for dear life as his load splatters into the condom up my ass. Even after the first waves of the orgasm have swept over him, his body is seized by small tremors every few seconds. He looks up at me, his eyes filled with exhaustion and joy.

"Sit on my chest," he urges, "And squirt your load on my face."

I slide up his torso until my dick is right above his face. Brother John tongues my balls as I jack off with quick, urgent strokes. I rub my dick over his handsome face and then continue my strokes. Once again, I feel Brother John's finger work its way up my ass, and he pushes hard against my prostate just as I trigger my orgasm. I cry out as I shoot my load, my come raining down on his eyes, his cheeks, his chin. By the time I'm done, his face is caked with my load; it drips down his face in thick drops. I bend down and lick it off tenderly, ending with a lingering kiss on his mouth.

We sleep together in Brother John's bed, his arms wrapped around me. When we wake up the next morning, we repeat last night, only this time I get to plow Brother John's ass. By the time I finally start dressing, the sun is high in the sky and pouring through the window.

Brother John watches as I pull on my boots. "So what are you going to do now?" he asks. "Hitch to Kansas City?"

I shrug. "I guess so."

He doesn't say anything for a long time. Whenever I glance at him, I see his eyes on me. His expression is impossible to read. Finally, while I'm at the mirror, combing my hair, he comes up and wraps his arms around me. He kisses my neck. "You want a job working in my show? One of our guys quit when we were in Wichita, and we could use another hand. Odd jobs, manual labor, help with the crowds, that kind of thing." His hands are sliding up and down my torso.

I look at his reflection, my eyes meeting his, saying nothing. "You wouldn't try to convert me or something if I took the job, would you?" I finally ask.

Brother John grins. "No, Jim. I promise."

"All right," I say. "Maybe for a few weeks." I laugh, shaking my head. "Hell, I never figured I'd wind up working for a revival show."

Brother John laughs too. "Like I said, the Lord works in mysterious ways, Jim." His hands knead my flesh, and I feel his hot breath on the nape of my neck.

BLIND DATE

He's standing in the theater lobby, leaning against the wall just by the entrance. I do a classic double take as I push through the door, first a quick glance and then the snap of the neck as I take a longer look. He's younger and much better-looking than the average clientele here, and I find myself wondering if he's here to audition for a job as a dancer. Guys drift in and out of here so often. I take in the bomber jacket, the tight chinos, the T-shirt one size too small stretching across a tight torso, and I think, The guy is hot. The dark glasses, though, are a bit much; the lobby is dimly lit and it's hard enough to see in it with normal eyesight. *Terminator chic,* I think, until I noticed the folded white cane in his right hand. With a start, I realize that he's blind.

Rusty's in the ticket booth, counting out ones for the till. It's all part of a closed loop. The customers get the ones as change for larger bills, they stuff them in the dancers' socks for a little extra attention, and the dancers exchange them for tens and twenties after their shows. Rusty has told me that he's getting to know each bill intimately now, he's been handling the same ones over and over for so long.

I go over and lean against the half door that separates the booth from the lobby. "Hi," I say.

Rusty glances up. "How ya doin', Mike?" He speaks in the barest Alabama drawl.

I shoot a look up the stairs that lead to the dressing room. "Is Kevin here yet?"

Rusty nods. "He came in about 10 minutes ago."

Kevin and I are tonight's two-man show. He's easily my favorite dancer to work with: a nicely muscled body the color of dark mocha, an easy, sexy smile, and that fleshy, thick dick of his that just begs to be sucked. I never have to fake arousal when I'm on stage with him.

I glance at the clock in Rusty's booth; five minutes until show time. Plenty of time to get ready. I turn my head and stare at the blind guy. He's only a few feet away, and his head is tilted as if he's straining to listen to us. "Are you tonight's entertainment?" he suddenly asks.

"Half of it," I answer carefully, "at least for the 8 o'clock show."

"Good," he says, nodding. "I like your voice. You sound sexy." Stretching his arm before him, he makes his way across the lobby and opens the theater door. Music spills out into the lobby, the standard bass beat of your generic suck-and-fuck flick. The door swings closed behind him.

I look at Rusty. "What the hell is a blind man doing in a movie theater?"

Rusty shrugs. "I don't think he's here for the movie."

Kevin and I have performed together often enough that we have the routine down cold. We wait in the dressing room stripped to our jockstraps until the music comes on. Tonight it's a tape of Gregorian chants revved up to a disco beat. We both amble out onto the dark stage and strike our poses, Kevin with his arms crossed against his chest and legs apart, me with my back to the audience, fists on hips. The lights turn up slowly. After a few beats, we turn toward each other and kiss, pressing our bodies together, grinding our pelvises against each other in a slow circular movement. I slide my hands over Kevin's firm ass and squeeze his cheeks as my jock-encased dick rubs back and forth against his. I don't see the audience out there as much as *feel* it, this *presence* in the dark, watching us.

I slip my thumbs under the elastic band of Kevin's jockstrap and yank it down. Kevin's meaty dick spills out, half-hard, and sways heavily against his thigh. Always the pro, he turns so that everyone out there can get a good look at what he's got. I kiss his neck, flick his nipples with my tongue, then drop to my knees and take his dick in my mouth, nibbling down the thick shaft. I feel it stir and grow hard in my mouth. I always get a buzz sucking cock in front of an audience, the *brassiness* of it, the knowledge that all those guys out there have paid money to watch me do this. I whip my own dick out and start stroking it, slowly, easily, teasing it into hardness. My other hand kneads the tight muscles of Kevin's torso, playing across the ridged abs, the hard pecs. I cup Kevin's balls, tugging on them gently, as he pumps his dick in and out of my mouth. The stage lights prevent me from seeing beyond the first couple of rows, but the guys up front all have their dicks out and are pounding their puds like there's hell to pay.

After about a minute of this, Kevin hooks his hands under my armpits and pulls me up. We kiss again and then kick ourselves free of the jockstraps dangling below our knees. We walk to the front of the stage. We're both jerking off now, not seriously, just enough light strokes to keep our boners hard. I give Kevin's firm rump another hard squeeze, and he flashes me a grin. He really is a sweet, sexy guy. I'd love to throw him onto a bed someday and have some real honest-to-God *sex* with him. *Yeah, me and every other guy,* I think. The only action I ever get off of him is here on stage in front of an audience. Kevin has a boyfriend and limits his extracurricular sex to his performances. This is how he defines monogamy.

It's time to work the audience. Kevin and I step down off the stage and into the central aisle that runs down the length of the theater. I go left and Kevin goes right. The first row is filled with what looks like Japanese businessmen, all neatly dressed in suits and ties. These guys just love us decadent Americans, and they tip big. I stand in front of the first one, stroking my dick, giving him my friendliest smile. He bends down and stuffs a dollar bill in my sock. Madonna is on the sound system now, and her high voice pours down over me as the man's hands travel over my body, massaging my flesh, his fingers flicking my nipples. One hand drops back to his cock, the other wraps around mine. He strokes both our dicks with a quick, excited tempo. After a few seconds of this, I squeeze his arm and move on to the next one. By the time I've worked the row, my socks are bulging with bills. I glance over Kevin's way. He's climbed up onto the armrests of two seats, hands behind his head, his dick swaying heavily as he swings his hips in time to the music. The man in front of him stares up, mouth open, eyes glassy. He's stuffing bills in Kevin's socks, buying time, urging Kevin to stay a few seconds longer, so that he can continue to drink in the sight of that black cock swaying inches from his mouth. He takes a hit of poppers and stuffs another bill in Kevin's sock. Kevin smiles benignly down at him and squats down low, dropping his balls into the man's eager mouth. Technically, we're not suppose to let the patrons take such liberties with us, but every now and then, when we're feeling generous, we bend the rules a little.

It's not until I work my way over to the fifth row that I spot the blind guy again. I had forgotten all about him. He's sitting in the middle seat, his head cocked. I touch his cheek with my hand and he jerks his face toward me.

"Howdy," I say above the din of the music.

He doesn't say anything, just reaches up and touches my torso with his fingers. His touch is light, not so much a grope as a fixing of my position. I swing my leg over, straddling him. His fingers are less tentative now. They knead my flesh, explore my upper body and arms.

"You have a great body," he says. He pulls a bill out of his pocket and holds it out to me.

"That's a twenty," I tell him, figuring he's made a mistake. I mean, hell, I don't want to take advantage of the guy.

"I know," he says. "How about giving me $20 worth of your attention?"

I stuff the bill into my sock, and then take his hands and place them back on my torso. His fingers slide over me quickly, lightly tugging and massaging me. There's something hesitant about his touch, like he doesn't know how far he's allowed to go. I help him out by grasping his wrist and dragging his hand down to my cock. His fingers play up and down the shaft, exploring it, gauging its size. They wrap around it and start stroking. His other hand cups my balls. "Sweet Jesus, but your cock big!" he says. "What are you, nine inches?"

"Eight, actually," I say. "It's the thickness that makes it seems bigger."

He lets go of my balls and pulls his zipper down. He fishes out his own dick and begins pumping his fist with it. "Let me help you out," I say, replacing his hand with mine. His dick has a good heft to it and fills my hand nicely. He leans back against the chair, mouth open, hips thrust forward as I beat him off. He's breathing heavy now, his chest rising and falling rapidly. I spit in my hand and slick his dick up good. He gives a loud groan.

He's keeps stroking my dick while his other hand explores the rest of my body. His fingers squeeze my nipples and then slide up to my face, lightly pushing against my chin, my cheeks, my eyes and forehead. "I bet you're a hot-looking stud," he pants.

"Yeah," I grunt. "I'm a fuckin' heartbreaker." Actually, I'm only average. My eyes are too close together, and my nose is too big. I got this gig because of my muscles and big dick. But if it turns this guy on to think I'm drop-dead gorgeous, I'm willing to play out the fantasy.

I quicken the pace of my strokes and tweak his left nipple hard. That does the trick. A shudder runs through his body, and he groans loudly. He arches his back, and jizz squirts out of his dick, splattering against my chest and belly. He thrashes around for a few seconds and then collapses back into his chair, panting, his shades tilting at an angle on his nose. I squeeze his arm. "See you around, buddy," I say.

He holds on to my wrist. "What's your name?"

I look around. The other patrons in the theater are looking at me, waiting for me to continue on with my rounds. I've spent more time with this guy than I should have. Kevin has already worked his way toward the rear of the theater. "Mike," I say, a little abruptly.

"I'm Carl," the guy says. "Thanks, Mike." He lets go of my hand, and I move on to the next guy. A few minutes later, I join Kevin back on the stage. We face the audience, pounding our puds to the beat of the music over the sound system. Kevin's dark skin gleams with sweat under the spotlight, and I reach over and gently squeeze his balls. He flashes me a big grin as his load squirts out over the front row. I follow quickly after him, thrusting my hips out, shooting my wad as I give out a loud theatrical groan. When my dick's done squirting, I shake the excess come off my hand and wave at the audience. Everyone breaks into applause. The spotlight's in my face, and I can't make out Carl. I can only assume he's clapping too. I find myself hoping that the fucker had a good time.

I run into Carl a week later, in the Safeway where I have my daytime job. I'm at the dairy shelves putting in a fresh supply of milk. Out of the corner of my eye I see someone standing to my left, hovering over me. I turn my head and see that it's Carl. I almost didn't recognize him: he's dressed casually in jeans and a blue flannel shirt, a far cry from his cholo-biker look he was sporting in the theater. Only the shades are the same.

"Excuse me," he says. "Can you hand me a half-gallon of nonfat milk, please?" His head is turned at a slight angle, his blind eyes trained over my left shoulder. I pull out a carton and hand it to him. "Thanks," he says.

"No problem, Carl," I answer.

That stops him in his tracks. He turns back to me. "Do I know you?"

I look around to make sure no one is in earshot. "We met last week. At the Tom Cat theater. I was one of the dancers."

Carl tilts his head, taking this in. "Mike?"

I put the last carton of milk on the shelf and stand up. "In the flesh."

"Not as much as when we last met," Carl grins. He shifts his basket to his other arm. "You shopping here too?"

I clear my throat. "Well, actually, I work here. I stock the shelves."

"Hot damn!" Carl laughs. "I don't fuckin' believe it."

I laugh too. "It doesn't exactly conform with the fantasy, does it?" I check out Carl again—the tight, compact body; the dark, curly hair, the strong jaw and wide mouth. The memory of his thick dick in my hand flashes through my mind, and I find myself wondering what he looks like naked. The blindness doesn't detract from the fantasies playing in my head; it just gives them an exotic touch.

"It's too bad you're working," he says. "Otherwise, I'd offer to buy you a beer."

I push a stray strand of hair out of my face. "I get off in 15 minutes. You feel like waiting?"

"Hell, yeah!"

We go to a beat-up neighborhood bar around the corner from the store. I order a pitcher of draft and fill both our glasses. We clink them together, Carl spilling some of his beer on the table. He doesn't seem to mind. "Here's to chance encounters," I say.

"A-fucking-men," Carl replies.

I take a pull from my beer. "So was that your first time in a porn theater?"

Carl shrugs. "Yeah." He grins. "My little walk on the wild side. A friend told me about the live dancers that worked the audience. I was feeling horny and frustrated, so I decided to give it a shot." He holds his hands out, palms up. "For once, the reality out-stripped the fantasy. I've been beating off all this last week think-ing about you."

"Oh, yeah?" I say. I finish off my glass and pour another one. I see that Carl's is almost empty, and I refill his as well. "It's nice to know my work is appreciated."

He shakes his head. "It blows my mind that I just ran into you like this." He takes a pull from his glass. "It's kind of hard picturing you stocking shelves."

I give a little laugh. "Well, us nude dancers have to live too, you know. We certainly can't make it on what they pay us at the theater. Even with tips."

Carl sits back. "It's a hot fantasy, thinking about dancing naked in front of an audience, jerking off while everyone is watching. What's it like to do something like that?"

I shrug, a gesture wasted on Carl. "After a while, it's just another day at the office."

We sit in silence for a few seconds. I look at the hairs peeking out above the top button of Carl's shirt, and think about slowly unsnapping the buttons one by one. It's a lazy summer afternoon, the type of day that feels so nice when you're in bed naked with another man. Unexpectedly, I feel lonely, even a little sad.

"Would you like to go up to my place?" Carl suddenly asks. "I just live a couple of blocks away."

"Yeah," I say slowly. "I'd like that a lot."

Carl lives in a small one-bedroom apartment that overlooks a back alley. The place is sparsely furnished and excruciatingly tidy. There's a bench press over in the corner of the living room, the weights neatly stacked in piles around it. A few chairs, a table, a couch, that's about it. One of the walls is lined with shelves filled with audiocassettes. Photographs are mounted on the wall above the sofa: Carl blowing out the candles of a birthday cake, group shots of what looks like a family reunion, Carl on a beach blanket with three other guys, all laughing. I wonder who looks at these pictures. Certainly not blind Carl.

By the window there's a small end table bathed in a shaft of sunlight. Something gleams, catching my eye. I look more closely and see a syringe laid neatly along the table's edge. Carl goes over to a box of compact discs and runs his fingers along their spines until he stops and pulls one out. He pops it into a CD player, and the Talking Heads start singing "Take Me to the River."

"You want some unsolicited advice?" I ask him.

Carl turns and faces me. "Yeah?"

"You shouldn't leave your works out for anyone to see. It might get you into a shitload of trouble."

Carl cocks his head. "My works?"

I clear my throat. "Your syringe, I mean."

Carl gives a thin smile. "I don't do drugs, if that's what you think. At least not illegal ones. I use that syringe for insulin shots. I'm a diabetic." He pauses. "That's how come I'm blind."

"Oh," I say, embarrassed. "Sorry."

Carl walks cautiously toward me, tracking me by my voice. "Don't be." I hold out my hand and touch him lightly on the shoulder. He takes off his shades and places them on an end table next to us. I notice with relief that his eyes are normal-looking: gray, fringed by long lashes. I don't know what I was expecting, something shrunken and disfigured perhaps. He reaches out and lightly runs his hands over my torso, anchoring my coordinates, just like he did in the theater. I pull him toward me and we kiss, gently at first, and then not so gently, our tongues pushing into each other's mouths. Carl's hands slip under my T-shirt and slides over my torso, pulling on my flesh, kneading the muscles of my torso. His fingers find my nipples, and he pinches them. I cup his ass with my hands and pull him hard against me, rubbing my crotch against his. We kiss again and then Carl pulls back. "Just stand there," he says. "I want to take your clothes off."

I'm more than willing to oblige him. Carl pulls my T-shirt over my head and tosses it to the floor. He runs his hands again over my naked torso, gently this time, his head tilted as if in concentration. His fingers feel like feathers; they barely touch my skin. Carl kneels down and pulls off my sneakers, then my socks. Still on his knees, he rubs his face against my jeans, like some great cat. I run my fingers through his hair as he presses his mouth against the bulge of my hardening cock, his tongue licking the denim, leaving a dark smear across my crotch. He reaches up, unbuckles my belt, and pulls my zipper down. His fingers hook into my waistband, and with killing slowness, he tugs down my jeans and briefs. I kick them off when they're around my ankles, and stand naked in the middle of the room. A slight breeze comes in from the half-open window and plays across my skin.

I bend down to kiss him, but Carl gently pushes me away. "Don't do anything," he says. "Just stand still."

I oblige him, my feet slightly apart and my arms at my sides. I'm used to *performing* when I'm naked; it feels strange to just stand so passively. Carl reaches out and wraps his hand around my cock. He doesn't stroke it, just squeezes and touches it, his fingers exploring the shaft. His other hand cups my balls gently, cradling them in his palm, the fingers massaging them. He looks up at me with his blind eyes. "Tell me about your dick and balls," he says. "What color are they? What do they look like?"

I stare back down at him. "They're dark," I say. "I'm half-Italian, and I've got some Puerto Rican blood in me too. My dick's the color of old oak; the head flares out and is even darker. My balls are almost black. As you can probably tell, they tend to hang low, the right ball more than the left. My nut sac is pretty fleshy. My pubes are black and crinkly."

Carl listens with his head cocked attentively, as if he were expecting to be quizzed on this later. His hand strokes the shaft of my cock. I can feel it start to swell out, grow hard under his touch. "Is your dick as beautiful as it feels?" he asks.

"Yeah," I answer truthfully. "I'd say so. I get a lot of compliments on it."

"I don't doubt it," Carl says. He buries his nose into the flesh of my nut sac and sniffs. "I love the smell of your balls," he says. Holding my dick in his hand, he sniffs along the shaft. He bends his head and presses his lips against my dick with a pressure that is not quite a kiss, and then drags his tongue slowly up the shaft and swirls it around the head. My body tingles with sensation. Carl suddenly plunges down and takes my whole dick in his mouth, his nose pushed up hard against my pubes. I groan and start pumping my hips, fucking his face with hard, quick thrusts. Carl spits in his hand and slicks my dick up good. I groan again, louder. He reaches behind and grabs my ass, squeezing each cheek.

I bend over and pull him up by his armpits. "It's time you got naked," I say. I pull off his clothes, kissing each patch of bare skin revealed. Carl's skin is smooth and pale, the torso nicely defined, the nipples wide and pink. It's clear that he uses his weight set often. The pecs are hard, the abs are cut beautifully, and his biceps bulge impressively. I put my mouth over his left biceps and kiss it.

Carl bends down and presses his face in my hair. "Let's go to bed." he murmurs.

Back in Carl's bedroom, I suck Carl's cock as he lies on his back, face upturned to the ceiling. His dick is pink and fat and fills my mouth nicely. I nibble down the shaft, sliding my tongue over it with great slurping noises. I squeeze his nipples with one hand, alternating from right to left to right again. My other hand slides under his firm, tight ass, kneading the cheeks, exploring the crack. I feel the pucker of his asshole, and I brush my index finger against it. Carl sighs deeply. I worm the finger in, knuckle by knuckle, twisting it inside. Carl's sighs get deeper, turn into groans.

"Turn your body around," he growls. "I want to suck on your dick while you do that to me."

I pivot around and straddle Carl, and we fuck each other's faces as I continue to work his ass. Carl's hands are all over me, sliding up and down my back, tugging on my skin, stroking, kneading. He twists his head from side to side as he bobs it up and down, and the sensations this produces on my dick radiate out through my body like warm electricity. I push my finger hard up against Carl's prostate and he groans mightily.

"I want you to fuck me," he says. "Just really plow my ass good."

The drawer in Carl's nightstand is well-stocked with condoms and lube. I sheathe up and grease up and drape Carl's legs over my shoulders. Carl reaches down and guides my dick to the pucker of his asshole. I carefully impale him, working each inch in with painstaking attention. I start pumping my hips, first slowly and then with increasing tempo. My face hovers inches above Carl's, and I stare down into his blind eyes. His eyelids are pulled back and his wide, blank stare gives him a look of amazement, even shock, like he can't quite believe this is happening to him. His forehead is dotted with perspiration, and his lips are parted, increasing the illusion. This both unsettles and excites me. I shove my dick hard up his ass and churn my hips against his. He groans loudly, and I plant my mouth over his, biting his lips.

Carl wraps his arms tight around me and rolls us both over. He sits on my dick now, leaning forward, working his ass, his mouth still glued to mine. I reach down with a lube-smeared hand and begin jacking him off, sliding my fingers up and down his grease-slicked dick. Carl goes wild, bucking and snorting like a bull in heat. The bedsprings creak and groan under the combined weight of our thrashing bodies.

Carl reaches back behind him and tugs on my balls. He squeezes and relaxes his ass muscles as he rides up and down my dick, winding me up like a clock. With each slide down my dick, he ratchets me up another level of pleasure. I stare at him astonished. "Where the *hell* did you learn to fuck like this!" I gasp.

Carl beams a wide smile, his face turned to the wall behind the bed. He has the happy, excited expression of a kid riding a roller coaster. "I'm just playing this by ear, man," he laughs. He bends down and we kiss again, Carl thrusting his tongue deep down into my mouth. I suck on his tongue, like I did his dick a few minutes ago. I feel myself getting close, the climax building up to the trigger point. I pull my dick out of his ass, up to the head, then thrust in all the way, going for broke. That does the trick for me. The orgasm sweeps over me as my load squirts out into the condom up Carl's ass. I cry out as I ride the waves out, one after another, my body jerking as each one crashes over me.

When the last spasm subsides, I wrap my palm around Carl's thick, greased dick and start stroking. Carl slides up my chest until his balls are right above my mouth. I run my tongue over them eagerly, sucking on them, giving them a good washing. With my other hand I reach up and squeeze one of his nipples. Carl groans, and his body trembles. The first squirt of his load splatters against my face, followed by others, all raining down on my cheeks, my eyes, my mouth. I close my eyes and let the come squirt down on my face in hot, sticky drops.

Carl rolls over and collapses onto the bed. "Damn!" he groans. I slide my arm around his shoulders and pull him to me. We kiss lightly, Carl's tongue flicking over my face, licking it clean. We lie together in silence for what seems a long time, our bodies pressed together. I can feel the pounding of Carl's heart against my chest.

"You know what I miss most?" Carl says suddenly. "I mean about being blind."

"What?" I ask, lightly stroking his back. Sunlight slants through the bedroom window, lighting up the dust motes in the air.

"It's not the sunset or the movies or some goddamn view on a mountain." Carl's face is turned to the ceiling, his voice matter-of-fact. "What I miss most are men's bodies, their faces, their fat, hard dicks. Jesus, I would love to take a long, hard look at your long, hard dick!"

"Not so hard right now," I say. "You took care of that."

Carl doesn't say anything. The room is getting dark. After a couple of minutes I prop myself on my elbow. "I gotta go, Carl," I say. "Show time in an hour."

Carl shrugs. When I'm dressed, he walks me to the door. We kiss, and he puts a piece of paper in my hand. "My phone number," he says. "In case you feel like calling."

"I will," I say, meaning it. We kiss again and I walk out the door.

That evening as I work the audience, I watch the men watching my naked body, their faces hungry, their eyes bright. Their hands wander over my torso, pull on my dick. I close my eyes and remember the feel of Carl's hands just an hour ago. When I'm back on stage, stroking my dick along with Kevin, I shoot a load that makes it to the second row. *For you, Carl,* I think. The audience claps loudly as I grin and bow. "You're feeling frisky tonight," Kevin whispers, grinning. I grin back, my eyes sweeping over his naked body, a drop of jizz dangling from his still-stiff dick. "Did I ever tell you how much I enjoy looking at your body?" I say. I pick up my jockstrap and walk off the stage, the guys still clapping and whistling.

TONY'S BIG ADVENTURE

Ever since I was a kid, I've been letting my older cousin, Guido, tell me what to do. Even now, when I'm 18 and grown-up, things haven't changed all that much. Guido has balls of brass; he can pull off the most outrageous shit. As kids we'd be in some record store, and when we were back out on the street he'd show me all the CDs he'd crammed into his jacket pockets and the albums he'd stuffed under his shirt. He's always ripping stuff off: clothes, beer, radios, any shit you could think of. My folks think he's bad news, the bad seed of the family, and tell me to stay away from him. Me, I think he's pretty cool, and I hang out with him whenever I can ("Like a stray mutt," he tells me, but he grins while he's saying it). Guido seems to like having me around; every now or then he swipes a CD I want or a pair of jeans my size and tosses them to me. He even lets me fuck his old girlfriends sometimes.

So when he tells me he's going to break into the electronics store over on Franklin Street 'cause he needs a new CD player, I just figure that's Guido being Guido. But then he gives me this look. "And you're coming too," he says. "I need a lookout."

Well, shit, I wasn't expecting that. "I dunno, Guido," I say. "Maybe you should find somebody else."

"It's a cinch, Tony," Guido grins. "Grandma could bust inside this joint." He puts his arm around my shoulder. "I'm letting you in on this 'cause you're my main man, dude. Like Tonto. And you're family. Now there's some quality shit in that store, but I need someone outside to keep an eye out." He gives my shoulder a squeeze. "You could use a new sound system, couldn't you, Tony? Something state-of-the-art instead of that piece of shit CD player you got."

"Guido," I say. "This is an *electronics* store you're talking about, for chrissakes. They'll have security systems up the ass there."

But Guido just laughs. "Tony, there ain't a security system I can't get around. Just leave it to me, OK?"

Well, anyway, let's just say that Guido shows me the logic of his thinking. Around midnight, still not quite sure what the fuck I'm getting myself into, I find myself at the head of the alley behind the store, keeping an eye out for trouble while Guido jimmies open the backdoor. A couple of minutes later, I hear him rummaging around in there. He pokes his head out the door. "Tony, come in here and help me carry this stuff out," he says in a loud whisper.

I look behind me and then walk inside. Guido's got TV sets, VCRs, tape decks, CD players, a couple of computers all lined up by the door. "Jesus, Guido," I say. "I thought you were going to take just a couple of things, not the whole goddamn store!"

Guido gives me a smile that doesn't quite make it up to his eyes. "You thought wrong, Tony. I'm not going to pass up a deal like this. Now help me carry this stuff out."

Well, I don't like this shit at all. As I begin piling the boxes into the back of the pickup truck Guido borrowed, I think how this wasn't such a hot idea after all. Guido's still inside, rooting through what's left to see if he didn't miss nothing. Maybe a nickel fell from the cash box today or something. I hoist a VCR up to toss in the flatbed, shaking my head.

Suddenly a high-beam flashlight turns on, catching me full in its light. "This is the police!" a voice barks. "Put your hands up!"

Oh, shit, I think. I drop the box and raise my hands. I feel like I'm going to throw up.

Guido picks that moment to walk out the back door, his arms loaded. He sees me pinned in the flashlight beam. "What the fuck..." he says. The beam swings over to him, and as soon as it does, I bolt down the alley.

The light swings back toward me again. "Stop or I'll shoot!" one of the cops yells after me. But I keep on going, zigzagging to make a harder target. A gun goes off and a bullet whizzes by my left ear, chipping off part of the brick wall next to me. I hear footsteps on the pavement behind me, but I don't look back to see how close the cop is. I finally reach the main street and hightail across. A car screeches on its brakes and plows into a trash can. Horns are blasting. I snatch a glance over my shoulder and see a cop on the sidewalk behind me, waving down a patrol car half a block down the street. *Oh fuck, oh fuck, oh fuck, oh fuck,* I think as I turn the corner.

I know if I don't get off this street *now,* my ass is grass. Off to my left is a revolving door of what looks like a tony hotel. Without thinking twice, I plunge through it hard enough to make the sucker spin like a top. It's a big hotel with a big lobby, packed with people coming and going. The carpet feels soft and plush beneath my feet, and the chandeliers above look like a bunch of glass wedding cakes. I slow down to a walk and try to blend in, which is a joke, me dressed in torn jeans, old sneakers, and a greasy, stained T-shirt. One of the dudes behind the check-in counter gives me the fish-eye and then turns to the guy next to him. They both stare at me. I say a prayer to the Blessed Virgin, promising that if I get out of this all right, I'll be a fuckin' altar boy. I sneak a glance at the front entrance just as a couple of cops walk through the door. Their eyes begin scanning the lobby.

A hand grabs my shoulder. I jump up and whirl around, fists cocked and my heart pounding hard enough to crack a rib. I face a guy a few years older than me, blond, well-built, dressed in a sports shirt and a pair of jeans like mine, only cleaner and not torn. "Hey, easy, buddy," he says, taking a step back.

I squint my eyes, giving the dude my meanest look. I have never been so fuckin' scared in my life. "Yeah, what?" I snarl.

But blondie just kind of laughs. "You do 'street punk' real good. The client will eat it up." I don't say nothing. Blondie raises an eyebrow. "Charlie *did* send you, didn't he?"

I don't know what the fuck he's talking about, but I figure I stick out less hanging out with him than by myself. "Yeah," I say. "That's right."

Blondie's eyes scan my body appreciatively. "I got to hand it to Charlie. He's finally coming up with some quality merchandise." He sticks out his hand. "I'm Bill."

Because I don't know what else to do, I shake it. He looks at me, waiting. "I'm Tony," I mumble.

"A little piece of advice," Bill says, his tone friendly. "Next time you have a gig at a hotel, try to dress up a little more. The staff doesn't like trade to be too obvious." He smiles, but his eyes drill holes in me.

"Yeah," I say. "I'll keep that in mind."

Bill's eyes sweep up and down my body again. I shift my weight to my other foot, not liking the way he's looking at me. "This is going to be fun," he says. "Charley did explain the gig to you, right?"

I clear my throat. "Well, actually, he didn't really get into the details..."

Bill cracks a tight grin. "That's Charley for you. Leaves you to fend for yourself." He glances at his watch. "Well, we're due up in Mr. Keating's room in a couple of minutes so I'll make this brief. He just likes to watch, so all we have to do is put on a show for him. There's $100 in it for each of us, but if he likes what he sees, he'll probably tip us something extra." He gives me that look again. "You a top or a bottom?"

I look at him. "A top or a bottom what?"

Bill raises an eyebrow. "Do you like to fuck or get fucked?" he finally says, his voice patient.

I don't say nothing for a few seconds. "What the fuck are you talking about?" I finally ask.

There's a light in Bill's eyes I don't like at all. "Do we have a problem here?" he asks quietly. I don't say nothing. "Just what did Charley tell you about tonight?" Bill is developing an attitude now.

A cop is getting closer, scanning the lobby with his eyes. He looks over in our direction. I turn my back to him. "Charley didn't tell me squat," I say, the words falling out of my mouth. My heart is pounding like a jackhammer. "He just said to show up here for a gig and you'd explain what to do."

Bill's blue eyes narrow, and for a second I'm more scared of him than of the cop. "Charley is such an asshole," he mutters. He wraps a hand around my left biceps, and I can feel his fingers dig in. "What we're going to do," he says in a low growl, "is go up to the client's room, get naked, and put on a show. That means we're going to suck cock, fuck ass, shoot as many loads as we can work up, and each leave $100 richer. If we put on a good enough show, there's possible future work with this client. If you pull out, you can just tell Charley that he's in deep shit."

I glance behind me. The cop is now talking to another cop. They both look our way and start walking in our direction.

"Who said anything about pulling out?" I say. I shake my arm free from Bill's grip and walk toward the elevator. "Let's go," I say. "The dude's waiting for us!" Bill finally follows after me. As the elevator door closes, I see the two cops watching us suspiciously. However, they stay put. Bill is my only ticket out of here, and I know there's no backing out now.

Bill pushes the button for the 32nd floor. The ride up is tense, with Bill staring off into space. I sneak a look at him, my eyes sliding down his body, taking in the muscles pushing against his tight T-shirt. *What's it going to be like to suck his cock?* I wonder. Surprisingly, I'm not that bugged by the idea. In fact, as I get the picture of Bill deep-throating me, I feel my own dick start to get hard. Go figure.

We get off the elevator and Bill leads the way down one of the hallways. He moves like he's been here before, and I catch myself wondering how long he's been in this line of work. He's a good-looking guy, clean-cut and in shape. At first glance, he looks like one of those underwear models in a Sears catalog. But looking closer, there's something a little sleazy about him, maybe the way his eyes are always looking around or the looseness of his mouth. He reminds me of Guido. *I wonder where Guido is now.* That asshole. If it weren't for him, I wouldn't be in this mess. Still, it's strange that I'm not that upset. The main thing I feel is curiosity.

We stop at one of the doors and Bill knocks on it. "It's open," a voice from inside calls out. Bill pushes open the door and we walk in.

This is the first hotel room I've ever been in, so I got nothin' to compare it with. But it looks fuckin' *swank*: high ceilings, thick rugs, plush chairs, and a bitching view of the city skyline outside. The lights are turned down low, but I see a bed off on the other side of the room. From where I stand, it looks as big as a handball court. Our "client" is standing in the middle of the room wearing a bathrobe, his hands jammed in his pockets. I figure him for about mid 40s: tall, thinning hair, still in shape. I look at him closely, curious about what kind of guy would blow $200 watching a couple of hustlers suck each others' cocks. But the guy just looks like any other joe you'd see on the street.

"Good evening, Mr. Keating," Bill says, flashing a big smile.

Keating nods his head. "Hello, Bill," he says. His eyes shift over toward me, sweeping up and down my body like a prison searchlight. "Who's your friend?"

Bill puts an arm around my shoulder. "This is Tony." His smile widens. All of a sudden he's the nicest fuckin' guy in the world. "Tony's kinda new to this game. I'm breaking him in."

Keating's eyes light up with a new interest. I know that stare he's giving me. I've seen it on Guido's face a million times. I can almost hear the wheels spinning in his head as he tries to figure what he can get from me. There's a CD player in the corner, and Keating walks over to it, slipping a disc in. Something cool and jazzy starts playing.

"Why don't you gentlemen just get started?" he says. He pulls up a chair and sits down in it, facing us.

Bill don't waste any time. He pulls me to him, hugging me tight, rubbing his hips against mine. He smiles at me, but the look in his eyes says, *Fuck this up and you'll be sorry.* But that ain't nothing I don't already know. I think about the cops looking for me in the lobby and what life would be like in the slammer. I nuzzle my chin against his neck and press my lips to his skin.

A saxophone bleeds music from the speakers, and I close my eyes. I feel my dick stirring, getting hard. Bill feels it too. He smiles at me again, only this time it seems more real. Some of the strain eases from his face. For a second I kinda sympathize with the guy. This is what he does to survive, and he just doesn't want me to screw it up for him. He plants his mouth against mine, pushing my teeth open with his tongue. I stiffen with surprise but then ease into it. I never kissed a man before, and the feel of his whiskers against my face is fuckin' strange—but not in a bad way. In fact, it's making me hot.

Bill pulls off my T-shirt and then peels off his own. I feel his skin rub against mine, his body hard with muscle. The dude must work out. He's got a long, rangy torso, smooth and tight, the nipples a light pink against his pale skin. He bends down and runs his tongue over my left nipple as he slips his other hand down in my jeans and cups my ass. His fingers pry open the crack and rub against my bunghole. I sneak a glance at Keating. He has his bathrobe open now; he's naked underneath and is stroking his stiff cock, his eyes glued on us. It's a turn-on being watched while I do sex things I never done before, and I find myself wanting to put on a good show for him. I bend down and stick my tongue in Bill's ear. I know that drives women wild, and it seems to have the same effect on Bill. He takes my nipple between his teeth and bites it, just enough to tease.

Bill unzips my fly and tugs my jeans down around my knees. His hand slides inside my jockeys from behind, and his finger pushes up my hole to the third joint. My dick is as stiff as a fuckin' tire iron and bumps hard against the piss-stained cotton. Bill drops to his knees and licks the cloth, his tongue getting my briefs sopping wet. He pulls them down and my dick swings up, slapping against my belly. Bill sucks my balls into his mouth and rolls them around, teasing me with his tongue as he jacks me off. The finger of his other hand finds its way back inside my ass, and he starts finger-fucking me slow and easy. I pump my hips to meet his strokes, my dick leaking precome. He suddenly plunges his head down and swallows the whole shaft, at the same time jamming two fingers hard up my ass. I cry out and shove my dick down his throat, until my balls are pressed tight against his chin.

As I fuck Bill's face, I turn my head and watch Keating. He returns my stare, floggin' his hog so fast his balls are a blur. He smiles at me, but I keep my face cold, giving him my best cowboy squint. His eyes eat me up; the hunger in them is so big that I half expect him to shove Bill aside and go down on me himself. But he just sits there, watching me, his mouth half-open, his eyes like needles. I flex my arms for him, pumping my biceps up as big as grapefruit. Keating gives a long sigh that trails off into a groan. "Look at that hot Italian punk getting sucked off," he growls softly. "Ramming his thick brown dick down that blond stud's throat. Fuckin' sexy, arrogant bastard. Maybe having a big dick shoved down his throat would change his attitude a little."

Bill looks up at me, my dick still in his mouth. I can tell he wants me to pick up on Keating's hint. I shake my head but find myself wondering what a dick in my mouth would feel like. Bill's eyebrows pull down and his eyes shoot daggers at me. I almost laugh. It's pretty hard to give someone the evil eye when you're swinging on his dick.

Bill takes my dick out of his mouth and stands up. He wraps his arms around me and pretends like he's nuzzling my ear. "Come on, Tony, do this for me, OK?" he begs softly. "Keating won't pay either of us if he's not happy with the show." I pull back and look into Bill's face and see something close to desperation in his eyes. And I think about my own problems too. If Keating kicks us out, I got to face those cops down in the lobby again. Besides, my curiosity is getting the best of me. *What would it feel like to have a hard dick in my mouth?* I wonder. To my surprise my own cock gives a sharp throb at the thought.

What the hell—I start to drop down to my knees. "No," Keating says. "You two do it on the bed." A few seconds tick by before Bill takes my arm and leads me across the room. He climbs onto the bed, props himself up with his elbows and spreads his legs out into a wide "V". I kneel before him and wrap my hand around his dick.

I have never touched a man's dick before (except my own, of course), and I give Bill's a light squeeze, feeling its warmth spread out into my palm. His dick is a little longer than mine but not as thick, pink and cut where mine is brown and uncut, with a big ol' red cock head just dribblin' precome. His balls hang low and ripe in their sac and are lightly furred with blond fuzz. I've had my dick sucked a number of times by various girlfriends, and I know what kind of blow job feels the best. I bend down and slurp my tongue across Bill's nut-sac and up the shaft, swirling it around his cock head. The precome tastes slick and a little salty in my mouth. I begin nibbling down the shaft, twisting my head from side to side like that Chock full o' Nuts waitress did to me a couple of weeks ago back in the restaurant storeroom. Bill groans loud, but there's something a little *theatrical* about it; I suspect he putting on a show for Keating. As for me, I'm just wondering whether or not I like having a dick in my mouth. I decide it's too early to tell, and so I keep sliding my mouth up and down Bill's shaft, trying to figure out how I feel about it.

"Swing around," Bill whispers. "Let's get a little sixty-nine action going."

Hey, that sounds OK by me. I pivot my body around so that my dick juts right above Bill's face. As he keeps pumping his dick down my throat, he sucks my balls into his mouth and rolls them around with his tongue. He spits in his hand and then starts stroking my dick, slicking it up nice and slippery. Goddamn, does that feel good! I burrow my nose into his balls and breathe in that ripe, musky smell, so different from a woman's. We fuck each other's faces for a few minutes, our sweat-slicked bodies slapping together, me forgetting all about Keating for the time being. Bill's mouth slides up to my ass, and I feel his tongue wash my bunghole. The fucker's just setting my body on fire!

Bill pulls his head away. "I want you to fuck my ass, Tony," he growls.

"No problem," I grin. I swing around again and grab each of Bill's ankles, hoisting his legs up high.

"Hold on a second," Bill grunts. He reaches over to the nightstand by the bed. There's a jar of lube and a pack of rubbers lying on top. He tosses them to me, and it's only a couple of seconds before I got my dick sheathed and greased and plowed to the balls up his ass. Fucking is something I'm damn good at, and if Keating wants a show, I'll give it to him. I slide in faster than Bill wants me to—I can tell, but I don't care. Then I slowly pull my dick out, right to the head, and just hang there in space for a second before plunging in hard, grinding my hips against him. Bill groans loudly, and this time the motherfucker sounds like he means it. I slam his ass hard again and then get down to the serious business of fucking the holy hell out of that boy. Bill's eyes lock with mine, and his lips pull back into a snarl. He thrusts his body up to meet mine, tightening and untightening his ass muscles around my dick. It's hard to say if this is better than pussy, but it's funner than hell in its own way.

Bill and I wrestle together in the bed, sometimes me on top, sometimes him, both our bodies pumping away, me plowing his ass like it was springtime in Kansas. I can see how Bill can make a living out of this. He's a goddamn wildcat, and he knows how to play my body like a tenor sax: wrapping his legs tight around me, twisting my nipples, pushing me to the edge of coming and then backing off again, over and over. I bend down and plant my mouth over his, shoving my tongue so deep down his throat that I half expect to bump against my dick coming the other way. I wrap a lube-smeared hand around his dick and he fucks my fist to the same tempo that I fuck his ass.

"Goddamn, you boys are *hot!*" Keating exclaims, but we ignore him, too wrapped up in what we're doing to each other. Bill thrusts against my slammin' dick like the pro he is, and I feel myself being drawn again close to the edge. I groan mightily, and the sound of my voice bounces off the high ceiling.

"Yeah, baby," Bill croons. "Whip it out so we can all watch you squirt your load."

I'd rather just shoot inside Bill's ass, but I remember that I'm playing to an audience. I pull out and rip the rubber off, just as my dick starts spewing jizz. My spunk squirts across Bill's belly, caking his body with ropy wads as I holler loud enough to bring the ceiling down on us. Bill groans, and then I feel his load shoot into my hand and ooze between my fingers. I wipe my hand across his face, and he licks his sticky jizz off my fingers, one by one. By the way Keating is moaning and carrying on, I guess he's shootin' too, but neither one of us pays much attention to him. I sit with my legs straddled across Bill's body and grin down at him. He grins back, and a little spark of buddyhood flashes between us for a second.

After Keating pays us and we're in the hall outside, waiting for the elevator, Bill reaches up and squeezes the back of my neck. "We make a great team, Tony," he says, smiling. "Maybe we could work another gig together sometime soon."

"Sure," I say. "Just call Charley. He knows how to get a hold of me." We don't say nothing in the elevator down. Out in the lobby I shake Bill's hand, say goodbye, and walk out the hotel door. As I walk down the street, I think about Guido, wondering what happened to him. He's most likely in the slammer now and will be there for a good long time. I was damn lucky to get away. It's funny how sometimes a night turns out so different than you expect. Over in the east, the sky is turning light; it's time I went home and caught some shut-eye. I put my hands in my pockets and start whistling as I walk down to the nearest subway station.

GIVING PHONE

"Welcome to Sex Talk, the all-gay phone line that allows you to connect with hot men all over the San Francisco Bay Area. If you're familiar with how we work and want to get right into the action, press 1."

Click

"To keep your previously recorded profile, press 1. To record a new profile, press 2."

Click

"You have up to 30 seconds to record your profile. When you here the beep, begin talking."

Beep

"Yeah, this is Tony. I just got home from work, and I'm sitting here with my jacket and tie on and my pants down around my ankles, and I'm strokin' my fat 8½-inch uncut dick while watching some of my favorite porn, my huge bull nuts bouncing with each stroke. I'm 25, 5 foot 11, 170 pounds of hard, tight muscle. I work out five, six times a week, totally buffed, masculine. Buzz cut, 'stache, goatee, pierced nipples, smooth body. Looking for a horny J.O. buddy to talk dirty to me while I stroke my wanger and squirt my hot load all over my chest."

"To listen to your profile, press 1. To save your profile, press 2. To rerecord your profile, press 3."

Click

"Your profile has been saved. To begin listening to the other callers on line, press 1. To advance to the next profile, press 2. To leave a message for a particular caller, press 3."

Click

"I'm a total party pig. Love to get nasty, worship some big cock

248

any way you want it done. Love fuckin' getting my face pounded, licking up your hole, man, getting my hole totally pounded. I'm 29, 5 foot 8, 150, clean-cut. Contact me. You'll be happy you did."
Click

"Hey, looking for some hot, horny oral top. I'm a total oral bottom—hot pussy mouth, deep throat, great tongue action, 35, 6 feet tall, 180, shaved head, goatee, real hungry, need to be fed. So if you want to get your dick worked on, let me know."
Click

"Two nasty, verbal guys partying and playing. Dominant top and versatile bottom, both in good shape. Looking for a submissive party pig, a kinky pussy-boy slut, a real bitch boy who likes to deep throat dick, eat ass, get fucked."
Click

"Yeah, hot and horned-up bi stud looking to get off with other guys who are into sharing pussy, group scenes, showing off, anything kinky and perverted. I'm 6 foot 2, 185, Latino, black hair, brown eyes, got 8¼ inches uncut, 6¼ around, low-hanging balls, nice hairy hole, and a real fuckin' dirty mind. Give me a call if you're into getting your rocks off."
Click

"Hi, I'm Andy, and, like, I'm new to the gay scene, and I'm looking for, like, maybe a boyfriend. I'm 22, 5 foot 8, really cute, with a nice smooth body and blue eyes. I like to cuddle, and, uh...play around, and I'm really into video games, and I think Ricky Martin is *soooo* hot."
Click

"Hey, guys, are you horny as fuck and looking for an alternative to the same old shit? How about talking with an exceptionally hot buddy man who's really got what it takes to make you blow that load over the phone? My name is Tom, and I guarantee you ejaculatory fireworks and a good fucking time. Ex-cop, ex-trucker, 6 foot 1, 180, big pecs, furry chest, nipples like pencil erasers, tattoos, hairy crotch and ass. Call me."
Click

"At the sound of the beep, leave your message."
Beep

"Yo, Tom, fuckin' got really turned on by your message. You sound really hot. My name is Tony, and I'm just kicking back, strokin' my 8¼-inch salami, fingerin' my hole while I watch some porn. I'm all sweaty and stinky now, looking to pop a load while talkin' dirty with a horny J.O. buddy. Let me know if you're interested."

Click

"Your message has been sent."

(Silence)

"You've got mail."

Click

"Hey, Tony, got your message. You sound like a fuckin' stud. I'm whacking off to porn too. I'd fucking love to drain my balls and squirt a load while talking nasty to you. Punch 5 and let's connect."

Click

"Tom?"

"Yo, Tony. How you doin', man?"

"I'm doin' just fine, man. Just sitting back with my favorite cowboy porn video on, stroking my dick, getting it all juiced up. Got some prejizz oozing out of my dick head, making my pole all nice and slippery."

"Sounds hot, dude. Just got back from the gym, haven't showered yet. Kickin' back on my sofa, naked, smelling my stinkin' pits, sliding my hand up and down my fat dick, my other hand tuggin' on my nipples. Watchin' a video of this little pussy boy getting plowed by three hot studs."

"Shit. I wish I was there to smell those pits of yours, man."

"Oh, yeah? What would you do?"

"Well, you know, Tom, I'd climb up on top of your hairy naked body, lift your arm up, and bury my face in your smelly pit, really givin' you lots of tongue. Then I'd lift up your other arm and do the same thing, nuzzling into the pit, lapping up all that sweat. Then I'd plant my mouth on yours and kiss you hard, frenching you good, so you could taste your sweat on my tongue. While I'm doing this, I'm grinding my hips against yours, dry-humping your belly, getting both our dicks real stiff."

"Shit, Tony, then while we're still kissing, I'd wrap my hand around both our dicks and start jacking us off together, dick flesh against dick flesh, feeling your dick *throb* against mine, my low-hanging bull nuts pressed against yours, your skin against mine, our bodies slippery with sweat, sliding all over each other."

"Yeah, Tom, and while you're jacking the both of us off, I'm chewing on those fireplug nipples of yours, working them over with my tongue, nipping on your hard, hairy pecs. With my other hand, I'm reaching down beneath those low-hangers of yours, (*beep*) playing with your hairy hole, corkscrewing my finger in, fuckin' you with it slowly, while we're still kissing (*beep*). Shit, man, that's my call waiting. Can you hang on while I get rid of whoever's calling?"

"Yeah, sure, man. But hurry back. You've fuckin' got me all worked up."

Click

"Hello?"

"Hello, Tony? This is your mother."

"Hey, Mom, this isn't exactly a great time to talk right now. Can I call you back in a little while?"

"This will only take a second, Tony. What time are you coming by with Aunt Pauline's cake?"

(Silence)

"What are you talking about, Mom?"

"I knew you'd forget all about this! I just knew it! Tonight is Aunt Pauline's surprise birthday party! I talked to you about this last week, Tony! You're suppose to swing by Eppler's Bakery and pick up the cake and bring it over."

"Mom, this really isn't a good time to talk. I'm in the middle of something right now."

"Well, Tony, that's just too bad, but I want to make sure this time that you understand what you're supposed to do. I've already ordered the cake, so all you have to do is pick it up. Eppler's closes at 7:30, so don't be late."

"Yeah, yeah, I'll pick up the cake, OK? Now can I go?"

"Tony, you could at least *pretend* you enjoy talking with your mother. Just make sure that Eppler's got the right message written on the cake. It should read HAPPY BIRTHDAY, PAULINE. You got that?"

"Yeah, yeah, 'Happy birthday, Pauline.' I gotta go. Bye."

"Wait a second, Tony! And check to see if it has a strawberry-cream filling, like I ordered. I had to pay extra for that filling, so I want to you to make sure that's what they're giving us."

"Yeah, OK, strawberry cream. I'll take care of everything. Bye, Mom."

Click

"Yo, Tom, you still there?"

"Hey, man, I was just about to give up on you."

"Sorry about that, dude. Now where were we?"

"We're kissing. I'm jacking us off together and fingering your hole."

"Yeah, that's right, dude. You're working my ass good, fuckin' it with your finger, and I'm feeling your dick flesh against mine as you stroke our cocks together. And they're both leaking prejizz now—it's oozing out of our piss slits, slickin' up our shafts, making our cocks all slippery. And then you sit up, and I got some strawberry-cream cake, and I grab a handful of it and rub it all over your fuckin' torso, man, just all this gooey, sweet icing smearing your body, and you grab my head and shove my face against you, and I start licking the icing off you. Yeah, man, and now my face is all smeared with it too and you bend down and kiss me again, stretching your body against mine, smearing me with all that cake and gooey icing."

"Yeah, that's right, Tony, and then I sit on your chest and drop my balls in your mouth, and you start licking them clean, while I rub my hard dick all over your face. And you look up into my eyes, my ball sac in your mouth, and you watch me watching you tonguing my balls. Then I start fucking your face nice and slow, that big tube-steak of mine sliding in and out of your pussy mouth."

"Yeah, Tom, I can feel that fat dick head of yours banging against the back of my throat, my tongue rolling around it, playing with it, tasting the prejizz that's leaking out of your come-slit, my nose buried in your pubes."

"Yeah, baby, and then I climb off you, and we go into the shower and start washing all that strawberry goo off, and I'm soaping off your body, getting a lather all worked up, and I wrap my soapy hand around your stiff Italian salami, and you're doing the same to me. I turn you around so that the water is spraying on your face and down your chest and belly, and with my soapy hand I start lathering up your asshole too, while I'm still stroking your fat cock with my other hand."

"Yeah, Tom, and now you start finger fucking me again, only this time you're using both fingers, working them up my chute knuckle by slow knuckle, twisting them, until you're pushing against my prostrate. And you're fuckin' *driving me wild!*"

"Yeah, Tony, you got a nice, dirty mouth on you, don't you, baby? And then I take my fingers out, and I hold onto your hips, your back still to me, and I start sliding my thick, juiced-up dick up and down your soapy ass crack. And the whole 8 inches of my dick (*beep*) is squeezed in your crack, between your tight, muscular ass cheeks, my big round bulbous dick head pushing against your pink pucker, just the head pushing against it (*beep*), pokin' it, teasing it. And you're moaning, and squirming, and beggin' me to (*beep*)...shit, man, is that your fuckin' call waiting again?"

"Hey, Tom, man, I'm sorry. Just give me a second, I swear I'll get rid of whoever's calling and get right back to you."

Click

"Yeah?"

"Tony, what are you going to wear to your Aunt Pauline's party?"

"Jesus H. Christ, Mom!"

"Nice mouth you got on you, young man."

"Mom, I told you this wasn't a good time to talk. Can I just call you back in a little while?"

"Tony, this will just take a second. Just tell me what you plan to wear tonight."

"I dunno, Mom. A T-shirt and jeans, I guess."

"You're going to wear T-shirt and jeans to your Aunt Pauline's surprise birthday party? Why don't you just spit in her face?"

"OK, Mom. I'll wear a shirt with buttons. Can I go now?"

"What you'll do is wear a sports jacket, slacks, and tie. What about that nice brown tweed jacket of yours. And those beige slacks?"

"Fine, fine. Whatever you want, Mom. I'll wear a fuckin' tuxedo, if you want."

"*What* did you just say to me?"

"Nothing, Mom."

"How *dare* you use that kind of language to your mother!"

"Look, I'm sorry, OK?"

"I didn't raise you to be such a garbage mouth, young man! Is that how you talk to your friends?"

"Yeah, Mom, as a matter of fact it is. Look, I gotta go. I hear fire engines and I think the apartment house is on fire."

Click

"Yo, Tom? You there?"

"Yeah, man. I've been waiting."

"Sorry about that, man. OK, we're in the shower, and you're pushing that big juiced-up cock head against my asshole."

"Yeah, Tony, only I don't penetrate you, at least not right away. I just press my cock head against your pussy ass, make it throb, make it tingle. And I'm tweaking your nipples hard, man, pinching them good. I got you all lathered up, with the hot water pounding your face, streamin' down your body while I push and poke my soaped-up dick against your asshole."

"Listen, man, could we move this back into the bedroom? I want to be lying down with legs spread when you finally skewer my asshole."

"Sure, Tony, we're back in bed, and I got you on your back, your legs hoisted up and over my shoulders, your pretty pussy ass spread wide and open, and it looks so fuckin' hot I just have to go down on you and eat that pretty ass, all squeaky-clean from the shower. And I roll my tongue over it, lap it up good, munch on it while I'm stroking your fat cock."

"Yeah, Tom, I feel you eating my asshole out, and it's fucking making me crazy! I feel your tongue slurping all over my pussy pucker, getting it all juiced up and ready for your fat dick, and I push my hips up and thrust my ass hard into your face and you take it, man. You take it like a man, your nose and mouth buried in my crack."

"Fuckin' A, dude! I love eating ass. But now that I've got your bunghole all sloppy wet, I sit up and grab some lube to grease you up right."

"Yeah, Tom, you squirt out a big fuckin' dollop into your hand and then start rubbing your fingers against my asshole, all around it, inside it, greasin' me up like a fuckin' pig."

"That's right, Tony, 'cause that's what you are: a fuckin' pig—a pig for dick."

"Yeah, Tom, that's me, all right: a real dick pig. I can't get enough of dick! And I'm feeding at the trough tonight with your fat red juiced-up dick. So I'm on my back, with my legs up in the air and spread wide, and I wrap them around your torso, wrap my hand around that monster dong of yours and guide it to my asshole."

"That's right, Tony, and I'm poking my dick head against your pucker, and my dick head is really fat and bulbous, and there's this tension as I push against you, stretching open your asshole. Your asshole resists at first—it's not sure it can take in my huge crank, and then it loosens just a little and with a little pop I'm inside. And you give a groan, 'cause you're not used to such a slab of meat inside you. So I stay real still, not moving, letting your asshole get acquainted with my cock, shake hands with it, so to speak. And we're both looking at each other, our eyes locked together, breathing hard, and I slide my massive tool a couple of inches inside you."

"Yeah, Tom, and I let out this big mother of a groan, but not so much because it hurts but because it feels so...fuckin'...good!"

"That's right, baby. So I slide a couple of more inches in, stretching your asshole good, because my cock widens out at the base, and you groan again, half with pleasure, half with pain. And now your eyes are locked onto mine, you take a deep breath, and as you let it out, I slide in the remaining four inches all at once, nice and easy, like butter on a hot skillet."

"Oh, yeah, Tom, and it feels so fuckin' good to have my asshole filled to the brim with cock!"

"Yeah, Tony, your asshole's completely stuffed with dick. And we lie together on your bed, not moving again, except we're both breathing really deep, and I start pumping my hips nice and slow, real gentle-like, just the littlest bit of friction."

"That's right, and I move my hips in time with your strokes, and I clamp my ass muscles down hard so that when you pull out, you can fuckin' feel the walls of my asshole against your stiff prick."

"Yeah, baby, you clamp down tight on my dick, and your asshole feels like velvet, so smooth, so warm. And I speed up my strokes, going faster and deeper. And I turn you on your belly and start really pounding your ass good. I got my arms wrapped tightly around your torso in a big ol' bear hug, my muscular, sweaty body slipping and sliding against yours, my dick thrusting deep and hard inside you, slamming your pussy ass good, my balls slapping against you, you on your belly, eating the pillow, groaning every time I slam into your asshole."

"Yeah, Tom, and then I pivot around again, 'cause I want to watch you as you fuck me. So now I'm on my back, legs wrapped around you, and you're fuckin' pounding me, nice and hard, grunting with each thrust, sweat pouring down your face and dripping onto me, your teeth bared, your blue eyes drilling into me."

"Actually, they're brown."

"OK, your *brown* eyes drilling into me. And I'm jacking off as you're slamming my ass, sliding my lubed-up hand up and down my dick in time with each of your strokes, and with my other hand I reach up and twist your nipple, *hard*!"

"Oh, baby, I love it when you do that!"

"Yeah, Tom, and you bend down and we kiss again long and hard, my tongue pushing deep down into your mouth, you never missing a stroke. And I reach down and I start tugging on your nuts. They fill my hand so nicely, those big low-hanging bull nuts of yours."

"Yeah, and my nuts are shaved, so they feel nice and smooth in your hand."

"Ah, no, man, I really like the feel of hairy balls a lot better."

"OK, Tony, my nuts are *not* shaved. They're as furry as you want them to be. Only they're pulled up real tight now, 'cause I'm getting *real* close to squirting my load."

"Oh, yeah? For real?"

"Yeah, Tony, I'm right there surfin' the edge of the wave, buddy. A couple of strokes and I'll pop my cork for my sure. How 'bout you? You close?"

"Oh, yeah. I could shoot any time. I've been holding back 'cause I like listening to your dirty mouth so much."

"You want to go for it, Tony?

"Yeah, baby. Let's do it!"

"OK, I'm pumping your ass hard now, really slamming into you..."

"Yeah, and I reach up and give your nipple a good hard twist just as you slide that fat dick of yours full up my ass."

"Yeah, yeah, oh yeah, Tony, and that does the trick. That pushes me over the edge—oh yeah, here it comes. Ah, ah, oh shit, I'm coming! Aaaarrrgggh! Oh yeah! Fuckin' A, I'm *shooting*!"

"Oh, yeah, OK, I'm just about there, too—oh yeah, oh yeah, here it comes, yeah, yeah, oh shit! Aaaahhhhh! I'm coming too! Ahhhhh!"

"Yeah, that's right, baby, squirt that load, shoot it good!"

"Ah! Ah! Oh, *shit*!"

"Fuckin' A!"

"Ahhhh." (Laughs) "Ah, yeah. Damn!"

(Laughs) "Damn is right!"

"Whew! Shit, Tom!"

"You liked that, Tony, baby?"

"Hell, yeah. That was a fuckin' monster orgasm. I squirted all over my face. Damn near blinded myself."

(Laughs) "Yeah, me too. I got jizz dripping"—(*beep*)—"all over me."

"Man, I'd love to do that again with you some"—(*beep*)—"other time, Tom, my friend."

"Yeah, cool. I'm on the sex line a lot. Catch me next time." (*beep*) "That fuckin' call waiting of yours."

"Yeah, I know. Um, maybe you can give me your number?" (*beep*) "That way we wouldn't have to leave it up to chance."

"Uh, let's just leave it the way it is. I'll catch you on the line some other time." (*beep*) "You better get your other call."

"Yeah. Right." (Pause) "You sure you don't want to give me your number?"

"Look, I'm sorry. I don't do repeats on the sex line. I like to keep things simple."

"Right." (*beep*)

"Hey, Tony, you don't have to cop an attitude."

"Yeah. Well, I better get that call."

"OK, man. Sorry."

"Don't be."

Click

"Tony, you weren't serious about your apartment house being on fire, were you?"

"No, Mom. I was just kidding."

"What's wrong? You sound funny."

"Nothing, Mom. Skip it. So why did you call this time?"

"I forgot to tell you how much Aunt Pauline's cake will cost. It'll be $26 and some change. So be sure to bring enough money. I'll pay you back at the party."

"Yeah, all right."

"Are you sure you're OK?"

"I'm fine, Mom. Don't badger me, OK? I'll see you at the party."

"Remember, Eppler's closes in an hour and a half. Don't be late."

"I won't. Talk to you later. Bye."

Click

"Welcome to Sex Talk, the all-gay phone line that allows you to connect with hot men all over the San Francisco Bay Area. If you're familiar with how we work and want to get right into the action, press 1."

Click

"To keep your previously recorded profile, press 1. To record a new profile, press 2."

Click

"You have up to 30 seconds to record your profile. When you hear the beep, begin talking."

Beep

"Yeah, this is Tony. I'm sitting here, strokin' my fat 8½-inch uncut dick, my huge bull nuts bouncing with each stroke. I'm 25, 5 foot 11, 160 pounds of hard, tight muscle. I work out five, six times a week, totally buffed. Buzz cut, 'stache, goatee, pierced nipples, smooth body. Looking for a horny J.O. buddy to talk dirty to me while I stroke my wanger and squirt my hot load all over my chest..."

INCUBUS

Every year I do it, in spite of all my best intentions: I put off my Halloween shopping until the last minute, right when the crowds are the worst. Macy's is packed with a screaming, ugly mob, Halloween carols are blaring out over the loudspeakers, there's a lady dressed up as a witch in front of the store, ringing her bell for the Salvation Army. I go to the gourmet section of the store, where I can get the freeze-dried henbane for Aunt Lucy and a canister of newt eyeballs, imported from Italy (at $24.99 a pound, for Gaia's sake!) for my brother, George, who's majoring in hexes and spell-casting at UC Berkeley and needs them for his midterm project. I'm able to snag one of the last of the Cabbage Patch voodoo dolls in the children's toys section for my niece, Suzie, a minor miracle since they're *the* hot ticket item for all the kids this year. I'm coping all right until things take an ugly turn at the potions department. The saleslady at the counter there is giving me a lot of attitude, deliberately ignoring me while she waits on customers that have *clearly* arrived after me. Normally, I would just let it ride, but I'm tired, my nerves are frayed, and I let myself get pissed. Glancing on both sides to see that no one's looking, I mutter a quick incantation, gesture with my left hand, and, even though she's a good 10 feet away from me, give her a good, sharp goose. She lets fly with a yelp, the hex alarms go off, and the Macy's warlock patrol shows up before I can beat a hasty retreat. They grab me under each armpit and escort me unceremoniously out the store, tossing my packages after me. How embarrassing.

The bus ride home is a nightmare, packed with shoppers, everyone pissed off and thoroughly sick of the holidays (Halloween spirit, what a laugh!). A couple of old ladies are yammering away next to me about how commercial Halloween has become, how there's nothing religious about it anymore, it's just the worship of the almighty buck. In the back of the bus a couple of street punks break out into a hex fight, with the other passengers yelling at them to knock it off. The bus driver finally has to stop the bus and throw them both off. By the time we finally make it to my stop, my head is pounding like a fuckin' sledgehammer. When I get to the doorstep, I find that I don't have my keys. I lose it for a moment. There's a stray cat on the fence nearby, and it takes every ounce of my willpower to keep from frying it with a blasting spell just to vent a little of my rage.

I ring the bell. Fortunately, my roommate, Kevin, is home. He answers the door naked, with blue runes painted on his body. I hear chanting in the background.

"Goddamn it, Kevin," I snap. "I thought we agreed that you'd hold your coven's Halloween orgy somewhere else!"

Kevin looks apologetic. "I couldn't help it, Sam. Somebody screwed up at the Temple of Isis. You know what a bunch of airheads they are over there. There was a double booking and we got the boot. We didn't have anywhere else to go."

I accept this news sullenly. "All right," I finally mutter, "But could you at least ask them to keep it down? I've had a rotten day."

"Sure," Kevin nods. "No problem. We're just about done with chanting anyway." He gives me a friendly smile. "You're welcome to join us in the orgy, if you want."

Kevin really is a sweet guy. He knows that I broke up with my own coven a couple of months ago, and that I'm spending the holidays alone this year. I feel a pang of guilt for being so short-tempered with him.

"That's real nice of you," I say. "But I wouldn't want to butt in."

"Don't be silly. We'd love to have you." Kevin raises his eyebrows. "You don't want Halloween to go by without attending at least one pagan orgy, do you?"

I have plans all right, but I don't want to tell them to Kevin because I know he'll try to talk me out of them. "I'm just going to go upstairs and watch *The Andy Williams Halloween Special* on TV," I lie.

"Oh, that sounds exciting," Kevin says. He grimaces impatiently. "Come on, Sam. The guys are waiting for me. Don't make me drag you in by force."

The idea does sound enticing. I've met Kevin's coven a number of times, and some of the guys are pretty hot. And what I'm planning upstairs can wait a bit. "Well, all right," I say.

"Great!" Kevin beams. He puts his arm around my shoulder and leads me into the living room. His coven is gathered in a circle, around a makeshift altar. Like Kevin, they're all naked with painted runes all over their bodies. "Hey, guys," he says. "Sam's going to join us for the orgy, OK?"

There are murmurs of greetings and the circle opens to include me. I shuck off my clothes and join them. I only know the guys by their coven names. Sunhawk is standing next to me, and he gives my ass a playful squeeze. "Merry Halloween," he says, smiling.

"Thanks," I say, grinning back. I hold his gaze for a few seconds, staring into those beautiful blue eyes of his. I take in the shaggy blond hair, the friendly smile, the nicely muscled body, and feel a rush of gladness that I decided to join in on the fun. I've always had something of a hard-on for Sunhawk. It seems like he feels similarly, because his dick slowly lengthens and stiffens against his thigh as he looks at me. I glance at it and back at his face again. "You got a little Halloween treat for me, Sunhawk?" I croon in his ear.

"Not so little," he says, smiling. "You'll see soon enough." He leans over and gives me a long lingering kiss, his tongue pushing into my mouth. I feel his hand wrap around my dick and start stroking it.

"Hey, guys," a voice to my left says. "How about sharing the action?"

I turn and see Lobo next to us, grinning, his warm brown eyes shining. He wraps an arm around each of our shoulders. Lobo looks damn good, much better than when I saw him a month ago. He must be working out: His body is beautifully muscled, the pecs nicely cut, his belly showing the classic six-pack. His dick seems bigger than I remember, thicker, fleshier. I look into his face, and

I swear he looks 10 years younger. Suddenly, I'm suspicious. I'm willing to bet he didn't get that body from any gym. Lobo is wearing an amulet around his neck, a very complicated piece of work, covered with runes and hex signs.

I hold it in the palm of my hand. "You sneaky bastard," I grin. "You're casting a spell of illusion, aren't you?"

Lobo grins back, a little sheepishly. "Just a minor one. To spruce up the looks a little." He runs his hands down my chest. "You like it?"

"Yeah," I say, "I do. A lot." I pull Lobo to me and plant my mouth over his, grinding my groin against his. Our two hard dicks rub over each other, and I wrap my hand around them and begin stroking them together. Lobo is looking very hot right now, and I'm not overly concerned over what's real and what's not.

Sunhawk embraces me from behind, his hands kneading the muscles of my torso, his hard dick poking against the crack of my ass. Kevin has put on a CD of Patti LuPone singing Isis cultic chants, and the three of us sway slowly to the music, our bodies pressed tightly together, flesh on flesh, hard cocks pushing against each other. The smell of sandalwood incense is thick in the air, and I close my eyes, letting the sensations roll over me. Slowly, dreamily, I drop to my knees. I reach up and wrap hands around the two dicks twitching above me, stroking their foreskins up and down the thick shafts. I lean forward and tongue Sunhawk's nut sac, rolling his balls around in my mouth, sucking on them, getting familiar with their texture and taste. After I've given them a good washing, I do the same to Lobo's. With his spell of illusion, he's given himself a pair of meaty low-hangers, ripe and heavy; I flick my tongue over them, open my mouth wide, and let all that ball meat spill in. I look up, my mouth full of scrotum, across the expanse of muscled flesh and gaze into Lobo's handsome face. He grins down at me, and slaps his dick against my cheek with a loud *thwack*.

I slide my tongue up Lobo's shaft, flicking it across the swollen glans, lapping up the clear pearls of prejizz that leak out his piss slit. Sunhawk stands next to him, his furred chest complementing Lobo's smooth muscularity so nicely. I spit in my hand and start jacking Sunhawk off, my strokes slow and sensual, as my mouth slides up and down Lobo's dick. The two men bend forward and kiss as I play with their pretty dicks, sucking off one and then the other, teasing them both to the brink of shooting and pulling back at the last instant and then bringing them close to the brink again. It doesn't take long before I have them both worked up to a level of high excitation, Lobo giving off little whimpers of frustrated pleasure, Sunhawk groaning loudly.

I look up at them both and grin. "You boys having a good time?" I ask.

"Sweet Gaia, how you can suck dick!" Sunhawk says, his eyes wide, his forehead beaded with sweat.

I glance around the room. Kevin is busy plowing the ass of some humpy little redheaded bantam cock, short but packed with muscles, his smooth skin dusted with freckles. Others in the room are split up in groups of two or three, sucking, fucking, and jacking off. There's a faint breeze stirring through the open window, and the altar candle flames flicker, throwing shadows on the walls and ceilings. Patti keeps wailing on the tape, belting out those pagan gospel songs she does so well. The incense sticks are burning low now, and the room is filled with their scent, thick and sweet, almost cloying. Looking at the writhing naked bodies around me, I'm suddenly struck for the first time with a warm Halloween glow. I know it's sentimental to say this, almost corny, but there's nothing like a good old-fashioned orgy to put one in the true spirit of the Holidays.

I look up at the two naked men standing in front of me, kissing, stroking each other's bodies, their saliva-slicked dicks gleaming in the warm glow of the candlelight. *What a beautiful sight!* I think. I go back to sucking them off, alternating as before between Sunhawk's thick red cock and Lobo's illusion-enhanced monster schlong. Once more, through my mouth and hands, I bring them both to the brink. Sunhawk gazes down at me, his eyes glazed with lust, his mouth open, his chest rising and falling. Lobo is so distracted by the state I've brought him to that he's having difficulty concentrating on his spell. His features shimmer and blur for a moment before he regains control and locks the illusion back into place. I reach up and stroke their bodies, tweaking their nipples, squeezing their asses, pulling on the flesh of their torsos, all the while feed-ing on the two hard dicks that twitch above me. All around me the room is filled with groans and soft whimpers as the members of Kevin's coven begin to release their loads.

Sunhawk is the first of the two men to shoot. With a long, ragged moan, he lets his load fly. It arcs across the air and splatters hard against my face in a thick, spermy rain. But before his first volley of spunk is out, Lobo joins him, his dick erupting into a Vesuvius of jizz, his load slamming below my left eye, joining Sunhawk's as it slides down my face. He cries out, and I pull down on both their balls, milking their orgasms out of them. Their loads drip sluggishly down my cheeks and hang in thick drops from my chin. Lobo and Sunhawk both drop to their knees, and we collapse onto the floor in a tangle of arms and legs.

Sunhawk spits in his hand and starts jacking me off. "I want to see you shoot too, baby," he croons. Lobo joins him, bending down and sucking on my balls.

I gently disengage myself. "Thanks, guys," I say. "But I've got other plans for my load tonight." I kiss them both lightly and stand up. The orgy is pretty much winding down, a few stragglers still shooting, but most of the coven sprawled on the floor in happy exhaustion. I raise my hand to them in the Warlock Salute. "Good night, everybody," I say. "Happy Halloween." The guys call out to me, and I leave the room, grinning.

The scene with Kevin's coven has whetted my appetite for what I've planned as tonight's pièce de résistance. I bound up the stairs to my room, shut the door behind me, and push all the furniture aside until I've cleared a wide space. I pull a weather-beaten book out from under my bed, the cover stained and torn, the pages as dry and fragile as old leaves. I can just barely make out the title: *Fundamentals of Hexology: Conjuring Spirits*. I bought this book last month in a back alley from some grubby little guy with shifty eyes and shaking hands. It's strictly contraband; only licensed hexolo-gists are allowed to have access to this kind of stuff. With my heart hammering, I turn to the chapter titled "Succubae and Incubi, Basic Incantations." My brother, George, is a natural at this kind of stuff, but frankly, I never had much of a talent in this direction. Only because it's Halloween, when the veil between the spirit and material worlds is the thinnest and even the weaker spells can bust through to the astral plane, do I stand even half a chance of succeeding. That, plus the satellite dish I bought last month at the Good Guys to boost the spell power. It's these fucking incantations that make conjuring spirits so hard. They're all written in backward Latin, and they're so goddamn complicated. If I mispronounce one piss-ass syllable it'll ruin the whole spell, and I'll have to start all over again.

I light a candle, place it on the floor, take a pinch of saffron, and drop it in the flame. The flame flares up in blue fire, sizzling loudly, and then subsides back to its original state. That should get the spirits' attention. I sit in front of the candle with my legs crossed. *OK, concentrate,* I tell myself. I put on the earphones, plug the headset into the jack linked to the satellite dish, and start chanting the words printed in the book. Sweet Gaia, there are five pages' worth of spells, single-spaced and small type! I keep screwing up, but finally, around midnight, I get through the whole incantation. I wait. Nothing happens. I crank up the amplifier 'til the needle's in the red zone and repeat the spell, carefully working my mouth around each syllable. I wait again, watching the full moon slowly sink in the night sky. Still nothing. I must have mispronounced one of the spell words without knowing it. Damn, I got to sign up for one of those Berlitz classes on Speaking Latin Backward in Three Easy Weeks.

I consider chanting the spell again. *Fuck it,* I think. *It's late and I'm tired. I'm going to bed.* My good spirits are dashed to hell, and I'm really pissed that I didn't just shoot a load when I was fooling around with Sunhawk and Lobo. In spite of my sleepiness, I'm feeling horny and on edge and more than a little depressed. Halloween just won't be complete without a good, come-splattering orgasm with a lust-crazed incubus. I finally drift off into sleep.

I dream I'm at a ball game. The New York Zoroastrians are playing the San Francisco Druids and are trailing by three runs. The stadium is packed with people whipped up into a frenzy of excitement. I buy a Polish sausage from a hot dog vendor. It sticks out of the bun, plump and greasy, a few drops of fluid oozing out of the end. I'm ravenous, and I wrap my lips around it, but I don't bite down. I start licking it, sliding the thick tube of meat in and out of my mouth, squeezing it, rolling my tongue around it. *Wait a minute!* I think. *This isn't a dream!* I open my eyes and see the dark form of a man sitting on my chest, leaning forward, his arms propping him up as he fucks my mouth with slow, easy strokes. I struggle to a half sitting position and turn on the bedside lamp. "What the hell do you think you're doing?" I cry out.

The man straddling me gives me a slow, easy grin. "Hello, Sam," he says. "Happy Halloween!" There's a light blue aura around him; it seems almost to crackle with electricity.

"Sweet Gaia," I say. "You're the incubus I summoned!"

The incubus leans back, his stiff dick wet with my saliva, his balls hanging low and ripe. He laughs and winks at me. "In the flesh."

I rub the sleep out of my eyes. "You sure took your sweet time getting here."

He rolls his eyes. "You're lucky I was able to make it at all! Your spell pronunciation really sucks, Sam. It took me hours to break through."

I'm wide awake now. I take a long, hard look at him: the dark, liquid eyes, the sensual mouth, the crisp, black curls of hair falling against his high forehead. His smooth body is the color of teak and flawlessly muscled, the pecs cut like fine crystal, the stomach chiseled. His dick lies heavily against my belly, thick, veined, its head flared like a fleshy mushroom. My throat tightens and my heart hammers like a fist inside my chest trying to punch its way out. "What's your name?" I ask.

"Balthazar," he says, grinning.

I reach up and slide my hands down his torso. His skin feels like velvet under my fingertips. "Goddess damn," I groan. "You are so-o-o fuckin' beautiful."

Balthazar smiles a slow, randy smile. "Well, I'm all yours, baby," he croons. "At least for the night. You conjured me, you get to play out any fantasy you want."

"Scoot up," I say. "Drop your balls in my mouth." My voice cracks, and I swallow hard.

Balthazar's balls are like meaty eggs, hanging low in a sac lightly furred with soft down. I roll them around with my tongue, sucking on one and then the other, trying unsuccessfully to fit them both in my mouth at the same time. As I feed on them, Balthazar rubs his fleshy dick over my face, against my nose and cheeks, my eyes and forehead. I look up into Balthazar's face. It blurs briefly, and now he's a blond Viking, his eyes as blue as the early-morning sky, his face fierce and masculine, his massively muscled body furred with dark blond hair. His dick is as thick as before, but it's pink now, lined by blue veins snaking up the shaft and crowned by a head the color and size of a ripe plum. I reach up and squeeze his rose-pink nipples, rolling them between my thumbs and forefingers, pulling on them, tweaking them. My hands roam over his body, feeling the play of muscles that push out against his skin like bands of vulcanized rubber. I cup his ass cheeks in my hands, squeezing them, feeling their muscularity.

"Turn around," I say hoarsely. "Suck on my dick while I suck on yours."

Balthazar swivels his leg around and turns so that his face is above my cock. He lowers his head and I feel his lips work their way down my dick shaft, nibble by nibble, the tongue licking against it furiously. His cock sucking technique is indescribable; sensations flicker over my body like fire, shooting up from my groin, tingling into the rest of my body, growing stronger in intensity with each swoop of his head. His hard, thick dick pulses above me, and I take it in my mouth, feeding on it hungrily. Balthazar pries my ass cheeks apart, and I feel his finger burrow into the crack, pushing against my bunghole. I spread my legs wide apart and push up with my hips, giving him freer access. Balthazar slowly impales my ass with his finger, twisting it up knuckle by knuckle, crooking his finger inside. I give a mighty groan, muffled by his thick dick crammed deep into my throat.

Balthazar's body blurs again for an instant, and now I find myself sucking a thick, black dick. Balthazar's skin darkens to the color of wet, fertile earth; his body lengthens and grows leaner, the skin smoothens. His balls sway heavily above me, their pouch creased and midnight dark. Balthazar turns his head and looks back at me, his full lips stretched back in soundless laughter, flashing dazzling teeth, his chocolate-brown eyes gleaming with amusement. "You having a good time, Sam?" he asks, in a low baritone voice. But I just grunt, while I gobble down on his dick, feeding on it voraciously. His dick is the one constant in all these changes: Whether inky black or candy pink, it is always long, thick, and hard as rebar.

Balthazar pulls his dick out of my mouth and turns around so that he's facing me. He grabs both my ankles and pulls them apart, exposing the pucker of my asshole, bends down, and runs his tongue across it. I writhe in the bed, thrashing my head from side to side on the pillow. He does it again, and I clamp my legs around his head and squeeze his face into my ass crack. Balthazar goes bunghole diving, slobbering it up good with his spit. He breaks free and looks up at me again. "What you need, Sam," he growls, "is a serious fucking."

"Oh, yeah?" I growl back. "You think you're man enough to give me one?"

Balthazar laughs at that one. "Well, I know I'm *incubus* enough." His grin grows sly. "The real question is, Are you *man* enough to take it?" He blurs again for an instance, and now he's a redheaded street punk, short, his body muscle-packed and heavily tattooed, his arms, legs, and face heavily dusted with freckles, his dick crowned by an orange-red pubic bush. His thin lips curl up into a sneer and his slate-gray eyes squint at me menacingly. "All right, fucker," he croons, in a tenor Dublin brogue, "Get ready for the plow of a lifetime."

I sneer back, playing out the fantasy. "Talk is cheap."

Balthazar laughs. He spits in his hand, slicks up his pink, freckled dick, and with excruciating slowness slides it up my chute. I swear, he must be making his dick grow bigger with each shove he gives it. "Easy," I groan.

"Just take it as you get it," Balthazar snarls. His face is directly above mine, and I can see the malicious gleam in his eyes. *Sweet Gaia,* I wonder, *what the hell have I gotten myself into?*

Balthazar starts pumping his hips, and I lose the thought in the sensations that sweep over me. He plunges his dick full in, and leaves it there, grinding his hips against mine. I groan from the sharp pleasure. He pulls out and then thrusts in again, with greater force, and I cry out loudly. He resumes his strokes, deep and slow at first, building in speed with each new thrust of his hips. I slide my hands down his back and over his smooth, muscular ass, squeezing the cheeks as they relax and contract. Balthazar spits in his hands and wraps it around my dick, jerking me off in strokes that match each thrust and withdrawal of his dick. His mouth is open and his breath comes out in ragged gasps, punctuated from time to time with a low whimper. Sweat beads his forehead and his eyes still gleam with that same sly amusement.

I pull his head down and kiss him, forcing my tongue deep down into his throat. Balthazar's body squirms on top of mine, his skin slick with sweat (*Do incubi sweat,* I wonder, *or is this too part of the illusion?*), and his mouth feels like a flame against mine. I can't get enough of him. Every thrust of his dick, every stroke of his hand, the play of the muscles of his body against mine, the feel of his lips, just fires up the hunger, stokes it, makes me crave more. We roll around on the bed, snarling, cursing, laughing, Balthazar plowing my ass, me fucking his fist, our flesh so entwined that I can no longer tell where my body ends and Balthazar's begins. I have never felt anything like this. I didn't even know pleasure could be this intense, and yet there's nothing satisfying in it. All I want is *more,* for Balthazar to fuck faster and deeper, for his huge dick to fill my ass *more,* for his tongue to bury itself *farther* into my mouth. "Crank it up!" I cry out. "Give me everything you got!"

Balthazar shape-shifts now at every thrust of his hips: Samurai warrior; slender, blond boy; blue-eyed college jock; unwashed construction worker; corporate power broker; older brother; tattooed marine...every fantasy I've ever entertained, every man I've ever lusted after, they writhe in my arms, cram their dicks up my ass, carry out every sex act I've ever hungered for. The faces that hover above me blur and solidify into a kaleidoscope of features, and yet through all this whir of change, this frenzy of bodies dissolving and shifting in my arms, the amusement in Balthazar's eyes is always there. I feel the orgasm building up, but somehow it never gets triggered. My dick is swollen almost painfully hard, my balls are pulled up tight against my body, the levels of pleasure keep ratcheting up, but the release never comes. Finally, with a loud groan, Balthazar pulls his dick out of my ass and starts beating off. He lifts up his head and bellows just as the first squirt of jizz gushes out and slams into my face with the force of a slap. Another load follows, then another, the creamy spunk splattering against my face and chest, dripping down my cheek, running down my torso in thick, viscous streams. Balthazar's body heaves and bucks, his blue aura blazing, his dick just spewing out its load as if there were no end to it. When, after an impossibly long time, it's over, Balthazar slowly lowers his head and looks at me. Even then, the amusement is still in his eyes.

"Your turn, Sam," he says softly. He starts beating me off again, his hand moving up and down my dick in long, sure strokes.

The pleasure sweeps over me once again, higher, stronger, more intense than ever. Balthazar presses down hard between my balls and the orgasm is finally triggered. My load spews out of my dick, splattering against my torso, mixing with the pool of Balthazar's spent jizz. I keep expecting the orgasm to end, but the intensity just mounts, the load keeps shooting out. "Balthazar," I cry out, "when's it going to stop?"

Balthazar laughs. "Happy Halloween, Sam," he says, before disappearing in a blaze of light. I pass out eventually, the orgasm still pulsing through me undiminished.

When I wake up, it's daylight and Kevin is standing over me, his face stamped with anxiety. "Sweet Gaia, Sam," he says. "Are you all right?"

I try to prop myself up on my elbow, but find I'm too weak to move. "What time is it?" I ask.

"Three o'clock," Kevin says. "Tuesday. You've been unconscious for two days."

I'm too wasted to be astonished.

Kevin holds up the battered spell book and shakes it at me. "You damn idiot!" he yells. "You could have got yourself killed, conjuring an incubus! Don't you know how dangerous that was!"

I don't have it in me to argue. "I'm sorry, Kevin," I say meekly.

Kevin immediately relents. "You scared the hell out of me, Sam," he says.

"I'm sorry," I say again. "I won't do it again." I pull the blankets up. "I think I'll try to get some sleep now."

Kevin gives me a searching look, but apparently decides it's OK to leave me alone. He walks out of the room, shutting the door softly behind him. I stare at the ceiling, remembering that wild, ecstatic ride with Balthazar. *Nothing could ever top that,* I think. *Any other sex will just pale by comparison.* I feel so *drained;* I seriously wonder if I'll ever shoot another load. But when I close my eyes, Balthazar's images pass through my mind, all the faces, the bodies, the hard, thrusting dicks of every shape and color. My dick stirs and slowly stiffens. *Well, I'll be damned,* I think, as I drift off to sleep, a silly-ass grin plastered on my face.

CALLS FROM MIKE

At a quarter after 4, Nick tells me to carry a load of two-by-fours up the ladder to the journeyman carpenters on the third level. I stare at him. "Can't it wait till tomorrow, Nick?" I ask. "It's almost quitting time."

Nick's mouth curls into a lazy grin. I know I'm not going to like his answer. "Sure, Rossi," he says, his voice low and easy. "I'll tell the new apprentice, the one who's going to replace your ass if you don't do what I tell you, to do it first thing tomorrow morning." He raises his eyebrows. "Is that what you want?"

"No," I say quietly.

"Good," Nick says. "Then I suggest you get your ass in gear." I stare at his back as he walks away, my eyes shooting daggers at him. But that doesn't stop me from checking out the easy strut of his body, the butch little pivot of his ass, as he makes his way to the foreman's trailer.

I don't get home until after 6. The muscles in my upper torso ache, my shirt is plastered to my back, and my pits are ripe and smelly. I pull a beer out of the fridge, pop it open, and fall back onto the couch. The beer pours down my throat like the jizz of God, and I close my eyes and savor the sensation. When I open them again, I glance to the side table where the phone and answering machine sit. The message light is blinking, and I push the play button.

"Surprise, surprise, Tony. This is Mike." The voice is loud and pissed. Surprise is right; my name's Angelo. "I bet you didn't think I'd find you, but I got your number from Carol." *Carol who?* I think. *I don't know any Carol.* Angry laugh. "You know she can't keep a secret. Anyway, you had your little fun and games, and you better get your ass back here *tonight*!" There's a bang as Mike slams down the receiver. *What was that all about?* I wonder. I don't know who the fuck Tony is, or Mike either for that matter, or how this Carol wound up giving him my number. As I eat my dinner and watch the evening news, I find my mind wandering back to the message, wondering about the little drama behind it. Maybe Tony owes Mike money. Maybe Tony's been fucking around with Mike's girl-friend. Hell, maybe Mike and Tony are lovers, and Tony's tomcat-ting with someone else. I guess I'll never find out.

The next day when I come home from work, the message light is blinking again on my answering machine. I push the play button. "Tony, Tony," Mike says, his voice low and anguished. "Don't do this to me, baby. You're ripping my heart out." His voice breaks on the last word. There's a long silence. "I'm sorry we fought, man," he says. I have to strain to hear him. "Come home, baby." He hangs up.

I sit down and stare at the machine. This is getting pretty heavy. For the rest of the evening, I keep thinking about Mike and Tony, about what the story might be with them. Since dumb-fuck Mike didn't leave a number, there's no way I can call him and straighten him out. There's something about his voice that snags my interest, a roughness to it. I'm not good with accents, but I'm guessing blue collar Jersey. I try to picture what he looks like. I see tattoos, a stubbled chin, a torn T-shirt with a pack of Marlboros rolled up in the sleeve. This gets mixed up with images of the guys at the construction site: Danny with his sleepy, half-lidded eyes, Carlos with his muscle-packed torso, even that son of a bitch, Nick, with his lop-sided smile and easy strut. My dick stirs and pushes up against my jockeys. Even when I go to bed and drift off to sleep, I find myself wondering about Mike and Tony.

I wake up to the phone ringing like there's hell to pay. The clock on the bedside table says a little after 2. I fumble for the receiver, finally find it, and put it to my ear. "Hello?" I mumble.

"Tony?" a voice on the other end asks.

Shit! I think. "Tony's not here."

"Oh, yeah? And who the fuck are you?" Mike's words are slurred. He sounds drunk.

"I'm nobody," I say. "Stop calling here. You got the wrong number."

"Don't give me that shit! Get Tony on the line or I'll rip your fucking lungs out!"

I laugh. "You don't even know where I live. Good fuckin' luck!"

A pause. "You fucking Tony?" Mike asks. "You swinging on his dick? Because if you are, you're dogmeat, fucker! Do you hear me? *Dogmeat!* Just say your fuckin' prayers if you're fucking my Tony."

"Look," I say. "Will you listen to me? There's no Tony here. You got the wrong number."

"Just say your prayers, dogmeat!" Mike shouts in the phone. He slams down the receiver.

Christ! I think. I hang up the phone and pull the covers back over me. But as I lie in bed, I find myself thinking about Mike. He sounds like an asshole, major bad news. *Oh, yeah?* I think. *Then why's my dick hard right now thinking about him?* After a couple of minutes I wrap my hand around it and start stroking, conjuring up Mike's voice again, his rough, raspy baritone. The fantasies blend to the guys at the construction site. I finally shoot my load with the image of Nick cramming his dick down my throat, growling obscenities while Carlos fucks my ass. I don't bother to wipe my jizz off and drift off into sleep with it crusting on my belly.

Two days go by without any messages from Mike. Maybe Tony finally went back home, or Mike gave him up for a lost cause. I tell myself I'm relieved it's all over, but I can't explain away the little throb of disappointment I feel. On the third night, though, there's another message from Mike.

"Hello, Tony, it's me," the voice says. Instead of the usual drama, Mike's voice is subdued, almost calm. I hear voices and glasses clinking in the background. "I know you're sitting there, listening to this message. Will you please pick up the phone?" Long pause. Mike sighs. "OK, have it your way. I'm over at the Cinch Bar on Polk Street. I just want to talk with you face to face. I'll behave

myself, I promise." Another pause. "Tony, you motherfucker!"
Mike snarls. "You owe me this. You've fuckin' lived with me for two
years. You can at least give me a half-hour of conversation before
you kiss me off. I'll be here till 10." Mike slams down the phone. I
glance at my watch. It's 8:30. *Well, I can either blow this off or do
something about it.* It's not much of a struggle to make up my mind.
I want to see if Mike lives up to the fantasies I've been weaving
around him.

I walk into The Cinch with Bonnie Raitt singing "Let's Give
Them Something To Talk About" on the jukebox. The place is
packed. It's going to be tough picking Mike out in this crowd. I
slowly swing my head, searching for men sitting alone and looking desperate. Which turns out to be about half the bar.

I see him hunched over a well drink at the bar, eyes glued to
the door. They shoot over toward me, do a quick scan, and then
flick away. The guy is a couple of years older than me: mid 20s
maybe, clean-cut, short red hair, and a tight, muscular torso
straining against a polo shirt one size to small. He doesn't look
desperate, just grim, his mouth pulled down in a slight scowl, his
eyes hard and dull.

I walk over to him. "Excuse me," I say. "Are you Mike?"

The eyes shoot at me, pinning me down like an insect on a
specimen tray. "Yeah," he says. "What of it?" There's a pause. His
gaze flicks up and down my body. "Did Tony send you?" His voice
is taking on an edge. I see that it wouldn't take much to push him
into full rage.

"No," I say. "I came here to tell you there's been a big mistake."
His eyes are pale blue, as best as I can guess from the light of the
bar. With his square jaw and the spray of freckles across his face, he
looks like the original all-American Boy. That is, the all-American
Boy bent on murder. The fucker is very sexy. I feel my dick stir
and push up against my 501s.

"There's been a mistake all right. You made it, fucking my Tony."
Mike's tone is level and cool, his eyes hard.

"Jesus," I laugh angrily. "You're a real piece of work. I can see
why Tony left you."

Mike's jaw is clenched so hard I half expect him to start spitting out broken teeth. A vein pulses in his forehead.

"Will you calm down?" I say. "I just want to tell you that Tony's not—"

"What did Tony say about me?" Mike demands. He slides off his stool and faces me, fists clenched. I can feel the heat from his body, smell the fresh sweat. My dick is fully hard now. I find myself wondering what it'd be like having sex with this punk, how it would feel wrestling naked in bed with him, his muscular, tight body pressed against mine.

"If you're thinking about slugging me," I say. "You'd better think again." I glare back at him, staring him down.

After a moment, Mike relaxes. He climbs back on the stool and regards me coldly. "What's your name," he asks.

"Angelo," I say.

Mike shakes his head. "Fucking Italians. All they do is cause me grief." His eyes sweep up and down my body. "So Tony's hanging out with his own kind now, huh? He doesn't like Irish boys anymore?"

I don't say anything. It would be so simple for me to set Mike straight, to tell the dumb, sexy fuck that he's been dialing the wrong number. All I have to do is open my mouth. But something inside me suddenly wants to play this out, keep the conversation going. "Is Tony *your* type?" I ask.

Mike glares at me. "What the fuck kind of question is that?" His voice is low and raw. He takes a steady pull from his vodka and soda, and shoots me a hard look. I meet his gaze, and after a few beats Mike's shoulders drop and he gives a short, bitter laugh. "Yeah," he says. "In spades. That was always the problem. Tony can pull the most outrageous shit with me, and the son of a bitch knows he'll always get away with it." He gives a long sigh and stares out the window as if he expects Tony to walk by. I seize the opportunity to take a longer look at the bulge pushing against the frayed denim of his jeans. When I raise my eyes, Mike is looking me in the face.

"Yeah," he says. "It *is* a lot bigger than Tony's." He flashes a nasty smile. "Tony's a little deficient in that department, in spite of all his other plus points." His smile widens, his eyes gleam maliciously.

"But then you must already know that, don't you?" I don't say anything. Mike takes another sip from his beer. "Does Tony know you've got a roving eye?" he asks, his tone conversational.

"Jesus," I say. "You're making a hell of a big deal over a little glance."

Mike gives a hard laugh. "Yeah, well, we both know where those little glances lead to, don't we? Tony's big on little glances too. " He regards me shrewdly. "You'll find that out soon enough, if you haven't already." Some rap song starts playing on the jukebox, its volume deafening. Mike grimaces. "Look," he says. "It's too damn noisy here. How about continuing this conversation somewhere else?"

I give a short laugh. "What's there to talk about?"

Mike shrugs. "Oh, I dunno. I still got a few things to get off my chest." I'm uneasy about his sudden calmness. He nods toward the door beyond the pool tables. "Maybe we could step out into the back alley for a while."

I shake my head. "No thanks. The last time we talked, you said you were going to rip my lungs out. I like it better with people around."

Mike raises his eyebrows. "Don't tell me you're *afraid* of me?" he laughs. There's nothing mocking in the laughter; he seems genuinely amused. I don't say anything. His eyes sweep down my body and back up to my face. "A big guy like you, with all those muscles...hell, you could mop up the street with me." He slides off his stool, and stands in front of me, arms outstretched and hands open. "Look, Angelo, no concealed weapons." I still don't say anything. "Come on," he says. "I'm sick of shoutin' over the fuckin' jukebox. Let's step outside." He walks toward the back door of the bar without looking behind. After a few seconds, I reluctantly follow him outside.

The alley behind the bar faces a crumbling brick wall lined with garbage cans. There's a streetlight at the far end, dimly lighting the place. Music and conversation pour out from the bar. "So what do you want to talk about?" I ask.

Mike doesn't say anything. He reaches down and gives my crotch a squeeze and then backs up against the brick wall. He calmly unbuckles his belt, unzips, and tugs his jeans down. He's not wearing any underwear, and his half-hard dick flops against his thigh.

"Are you crazy?" I say. But my eyes are riveted on his dick. It's a beauty, all right, thick and long, the head flared, veins snaking up the shaft. My own dick starts pushing against my zipper, hollering to be let out.

Mike leans against the wall and starts beating off, his strokes slow and sensuous. His mouth is curled up into a small smile. "I just figured you'd want a break from Tony's stubby little dick," he says. "Maybe swing on something with some *meat* on it." He works his T-shirt up and tweaks his nipple. His torso is beautifully muscled, cut to perfection.

Well, before my brain even has a chance to think about it, I'm on my knees, slobbering over Mike's dick, working my lips up and down that beautiful thick shaft. Mike grabs my head with both hands and starts pumping his hips, thrusting his dick deep down my throat. I reach up and grab his ass, squeezing tight. The flesh feels smooth and hard under my fingertips. I drag my tongue down his dick and burrow my face into his balls, breathing in their ripe, musky smell. I open my mouth and suck them in, rolling the scrotal flesh around with my tongue. I yank down the zipper of my fly, pull out my own hard dick, and start stroking.

Mike slaps his dick across my face with a loud *thwack*. "Yeah," he growls. "That's good, baby. Juice those balls up nice."

I look up at him, his balls in my mouth. Mike's face is hard, his eyes skewering me. They gleam with malice. He pulls his balls out and stuffs his dick back down my throat. He proceeds to fuck my mouth in long, savage strokes, slamming his dick in like he's trying to drill a hole through the back of my head. *That's OK, Mike,* I think. *I can get into playing rough.* I take his hard thrusts eagerly, twisting my head from side to side, as my tongue wraps around the thick shaft. I work a finger up Mike's asshole, knuckle by knuckle, and then start sliding it in and out. Mike groans. I wiggle it again as he plunges down my throat, and Mike groans again, louder. His balls are pulled up tight. and his dick is solid rebar. He whips it out of my mouth. "Get up!" he says. "I want to fuck your ass."

"I don't have a condom on me," I say.

Mike's eyes burn. "Yeah, well, I do." He bends down and pulls one out of his back pocket.

I stay on my knees, my gaze locked with his. Finally, I nod my head. "All right," I say. I climb to my feet as Mike rolls the condom down the length of his dick. He spits in his hand, sliding it up and down the shaft, and then wraps his arms around me from behind, pulling my body tight against his. I can feel the muscles of his torso press against my back, his dick thrusting up against me, probing into my ass crack. He shoves me toward the garbage cans, using the weight of his body to push me over them.

I break out of his hug and turn to face him. "Yeah, you can fuck me," I say. "But you're going to do it the way *I* like it. Face to face, me watching you as you shove your dick up my ass."

Mike gives me a grin that doesn't quite make it to his eyes. "Sure, Angelo. Anything you say." He lifts me on top of the garbage cans and hoists my legs over his shoulders. I hold onto his waist as he pokes his dick against my asshole and then slowly, inch by inch, slides it in. Mike's face is right above mine, his teeth bared in a fierce grin, his eyes burning holes in mine. "How do you like that, baby?" he growls. "I bet that fills you in a way Tony never could."

I slide my hands up his torso, tugging on the hard flesh, feeling its smoothness, flicking his nipples with my thumbs. "Yeah," I say. "But can you fuck as good as Tony?"

Mike thrusts deep into my ass and I cry out. "Well, we'll just have to see, won't we?" he says. He starts pumping his hips, his thrusts fast and vicious, his grip on me as hard as iron. I reach up and pull his face against mine, biting his lips. Mike shoves his tongue deep down my throat as he skewers my ass. He grinds his hips against me, rotating them, driving his dick even deeper inside, churning my ass with it. I squeeze my ass muscles tight and push up against him. Mike's eyes widen in surprise, and he gasps with the sudden rush of pleasure he feels. "Sweet Jesus, but you're a hot piece of tail," he says. He spits in his hand and starts jacking me off, timing his strokes with each thrust of his hips.

The metal handles of the garbage can lids dig into my back, and the smell of ripe garbage fills my nose. I can hear Bruce Springsteen singing "Pink Cadillac" inside the bar, and the murmur of voices just a few feet away through the door. Mike starts fucking in time to the beat of the song. I reach up and twist his nipples hard, and he groans again. The air in the alley is closed and stifling, sweat beads Mike's forehead and splashes onto my face. Mike varies the way he plows my ass: a series of long, easy strokes punctuated by a savage burst of piston thrusts. He pulls out and slams me with a particular viciousness. I lose my balance, and the garbage cans tip over. We crash down amid a heap of spilled garbage: coffee grounds, banana peels, bottles and cans. I roll over on top of Mike and pin his shoulders down as he continues to slam his dick up my ass. I reach back and cradle his balls in my hand. They're pulled up tight and swollen, ready to pump out their load of jizz. I press my finger hard between them, and that's all it takes to push Mike over the edge. He cries out as his body trembles under me, and I feel his cock throb as it squirts its hot load into the condom up my ass. I ride out his orgasm, the bucking of his muscular body under me, garbage scattering everywhere. It just takes a few quick strokes of my hand to trigger my own orgasm. I groan as my jizz squirts out, splattering against Mike's face, dripping down his cheek in thick, sluggish drops. When the last of the spasms passes through me, I collapse on top of Mike.

We lie there in silence, the music from the bar's jukebox filtering out into the stale, reeking air in the alley. Mike is the first to move. He wipes his arm across his face, climbs to his feet, and pulls his pants up. They're stained with garbage, dark spots splattered against the denim. He brushes them off in a futile effort to clean them, and then straightens up and looks down at me.

I struggle to get up, but Mike plants his foot on my chest and pushes me back down. "Of course you realize," he says calmly, "that as soon as you leave, I'm going to call Tony and tell him I just fucked his new boyfriend in the alley. You're going to have some explaining to do when you get home."

I push Mike's foot off me and clamber to my feet. "I don't know Tony," I say. "I never met him in my life."

Mike looks at me with narrowed eyes. "What the fuck are you talking about?"

"Just what I said," I say, brushing bits of eggshell off my shirt. "This Carol friend of yours gave you the wrong number. Your friend never stayed at my place. That's why I came out here. So I could tell you, since you were too fuckin' stupid to leave a number for me to call you."

Mike gives me a long, long look. I return his gaze calmly. "Is this a joke?" he finally asks.

I shrug. "I'm afraid not."

There's another long silence. Mike suddenly laughs. "You know, I think you're telling the truth." He pulls his shirt down and runs his fingers through his hair. His eyes scan my face again. "You son of a bitch, you *are* telling the truth!" He shakes his head. "I guess the laugh's on me." He flashes me a broad grin and holds out his hand to me. "You must think me one big dope. You want to shake hands and be friends?"

I smile back. "Sure." I take his hand. Mike tightens his grip and pulls me toward him. His other hand arcs through the air and smashes into my jaw. I go crashing down among the overturned garbage cans. Mike looks down at me. "You still laughing, Angelo?" he asks. He spins on his heel and walks back into the bar. After a couple of minutes, I pick myself up and follow after him. Mike is gone. I go to the john and splash water on my face. My jaw is beginning to swell, but it doesn't seem to be broken. It's going to hurt for the next couple of days, though.

When I walk back into my apartment, the message light is on. I push the play button. "That was a funny trick you pulled on me, Angelo," Mike says. "You shouldn't hold that punch against me. You had it coming." Pause. "I've been thinking about our little good time in the alley. You got the right name, Angelo. You fuck like an angel. If you want, next time I'll plow you on an honest-to-God bed. I'll call you in a couple of days."

I take a couple of aspirin and go to bed, nursing my sore jaw. I lie there, wondering what I'm going to say to Mike when he finally gets around to calling again.

FIRESTORM

I never plan to have sex with Nick in the firehouse; it just seems to happen. The first time was in the shower room at 3 A.M. after putting out a two-alarm fire in an east-side apartment house. Then there was that early Saturday morning when Nick walked into the locker room and caught me polishing my boots; it wasn't more than five minutes later that I was plowing his ass in the alcove behind the condom machine. And the time right in the dorm, when Nick came over to my bed around midnight to discuss the duty roster and ended up giving me a blow job while all the other firemen around us were sawing wood.

The funny thing is I'm not like this normally: taking risks and doing crazy things that could get my ass fired. I'm a solid, dependable, salt-of-the-earth kind of guy. There's just something about Nick, that wild gleam in those beautiful dark eyes, that cocky smile, that loose-limbed easy way he walks, just shy of a strut—he lights a fire in me that just rages out of control. And it's only when I get to squirt my hose, either while slamming his sweet perfect ass or deep-throating his handsome face, that I can finally put that fire out and get some peace of mind.

Anyway, I was in the firehouse locker room giving Nick a blow job when the five-alarm bell rang. I already had a condom in my hand and couldn't wait to slip it on. Startled, I took Nick's dick out of my mouth and stared up at him. He looked back at me, eyes wide, and I almost burst out laughing. In the year that I've known Nick, I have *never* seen him show shock, even with buildings burning down around our heads and us smashing our way out side by side with our fire axes. But I can't blame him. In all the years I've been on the force, we have never had a five-alarm fire before.

Fires of that intensity are the stuff of legend.

I clambered to my feet, stuffing the condom in my back pocket, and Nick quickly pulled his pants up. Not a second too soon, as the other firemen on duty came bursting in from the dorm. Jake was the first one in. I grabbed his arm as he rushed by. "What the hell is going on?" I asked, shouting above the sudden din of the other voices and the sound of locker doors slamming.

Jake's eyes still had the half-focused look of a man suddenly roused from sleep. "I don't know," he replied. "All I heard was that the hills outside the city are in flames." He yanked his arm free and ripped open his locker door to get his gear.

Nick and I exchanged quick glances, and right away I could see the excited gleam in his eye. I scrambled through the crowd of men to my locker and started pulling my own equipment out. As I tugged my coat on, I sneaked another worried look Nick's way. He was getting his gear out too, his fingers zipping up his suit and strapping on his helmet with a quick, efficient economy of movement. Once again his eyes met mine. The only other time I've seen his face like this was when he was plowing my ass and working himself up to a bodacious orgasm. *Shit!* I thought. *I bet Nick's dick is rock-hard now!* That was the problem with Nick. He was too fuckin' crazy to be in this line of work; in spite of his skill, it made him dangerous. For me, fighting fires was a way to make a living. For Nick, it was a goddamn religious experience, something as good as sex. Maybe better. He had this *thing* about fire that was more than a little wacko. It made him take risks that no fireman had any business taking.

In a matter of minutes we were on the fire engine, heading for the city outskirts, sirens screaming. Even though it was early morning, the sky was surprisingly dark, like a storm was rolling in. I looked up at Nick in the tiller seat. "Maybe we'll get lucky and get some rain," I shouted.

He rolled his eyes. "Guess again, Tom," he shouted back.

I checked out the sky again and saw what he meant. Those weren't rain clouds. That was *smoke,* like I've never seen it before, blowing in from the east, plunging the city into darkness. My eyes scanned the direction it was coming from. All I saw was blackness, churning out into the eastern horizon. For a second I saw a flicker of red light that must have been flame, but then it was lost again behind that curtain of smoke. *Holy shit! Are we ever in for it today!*

The police had cordoned off the roads leading up to the hills, and we slowed down as we made our way past the barricades and the mobs of people pressing against them. Things weren't any calmer on the other side of the police line; the area had become a war zone. Cars were careening down the narrow streets from the hills above, weaving dangerously among streams of running people clutching pets and possessions in their arms.

We got as far up the hill as the Claremont Hotel. Smoke swirled around its white Victorian towers, but it was coming from farther up the hill, and from the north. At least for now the hotel didn't seem to be in any immediate danger. A base of operations had been established in the parking lot. Other engines had pulled up into it, and there were uniforms everywhere, firemen to be sure, but also cops and even some National Guard.

Chavez, who was up front driving, pulled to a stop and we all jumped off. I recognized Chief McCabe over by the far end of the lot, already talking to two teams of firemen. He saw us and motioned us over to him. "The fire is sweeping down toward Grizzly Peak Boulevard," he shouted at us over the noise of the crowd. "We got two pumper trucks up there already, and the last I heard we still have pressure in the water mains. We've already made a couple of sweeps through the area with a bullhorn, telling people to evacuate, but there are still some damn fools up there trying to save their homes. I want you guys to do what you can to keep the fire from jumping the boulevard. And for God's sake, tell any civilians you see to get the hell out of there!"

"OK, men," Chavez barked. "You heard him. Let's move!" We raced back to the truck and piled on. Chavez activated the siren and we roared up the hillside. I glanced up at Nick still in the tiller seat, but he was staring straight up the hill, with parted lips and bright eyes. He looked like he was about to cream in his jeans. I looked up too, and this time I could see the flames roaring up into the sky. Somebody's mansion along the ridge crest collapsed in an explosion of flying embers and smoke. The houses on either side of it were blazing like jamboree bonfires. And we were heading right for it.

After a couple of minutes we came abreast of one of the pumper trucks. The houses around us had not caught fire yet, but we could see the flames sweeping down the hillside toward them. Without a word, we dismounted and hooked up a couple of hoses to the truck. We all grabbed them and aimed high, toward the nearest bank of fire. It hissed and sputtered, and fresh smoke poured out into the sky.

Chavez came up to me and grabbed my arm to get my attention. He tugged on Nick's sleeve as well. "I want you two to grab a hose and go up that street", he said, pointing to our left. "Find a hydrant and start dousing the area. The wind is shifting to the west and carrying embers down in that direction. Do what you can to keep any new fires from starting." I started to pull away, but he held on to my arm and tugged me back. "And for God's sake, don't wander off too far from the truck! Any sign of trouble, get your asses back here pronto!" Beneath the soot, his face was grim. Nick and I nodded. We grabbed a hose and scurried off in the direction Chavez had pointed.

After about a block, we found a hydrant and hooked up to it. Chavez was right about the wind shift. Burning embers were falling down among us, sometimes winking out, occasionally starting small brush fires. We hosed them down whenever one started, but the embers kept coming down at increasing frequency. It looked more and more like a losing proposition.

Nick pointed further down the street. "There's more smoke coming down from there," he said. "I wouldn't be surprised if there was another bank of fire coming our direction." He didn't seem overly concerned about this. "Let's go check it out."

The son of a bitch has a death wish, I thought. "Hell, no," I said. "We're in no way prepared to take on another fire by ourselves. We're heading back to the truck right now!"

Nick didn't say anything, but just kept staring off down the street toward the smoke. I was prepared to strong-arm him and drag him back. He pointed ahead and toward the left. "Looks like we're not alone," he said mildly.

I looked toward where he was pointing. And I saw it too. A figure was silhouetted on a housetop, about a block away, hosing down his roof. "Sweet Jesus," I groaned. "We got to get that idiot down from there fast!"

"Let's go, then," Nick said. He started running down the street toward the man on the roof. I followed after him, cursing.

By the time we got there, the smoke had surrounded us and visibility wasn't more than 15 or 20 feet. The house was a split-level ranch, one story only, and the man on the roof was just a few feet above us.

"Get down from there!" I shouted up at him. "The fire's going to be here any minute now!"

The man turned and looked down at us, and I saw with a shock that he was just a kid, early 20s max. He wore the same stunned, disbelieving expression I had seen on the faces of the other refugees fleeing from the flames. "I got to save this place!" he shouted back. "It's my folks' home." A burning ember fell on the roof a few feet away, and he quickly hosed it down.

The flames were visible now behind the smoke. A half a block down an electrical transformer exploded. A little farther away auto alarms started blaring as the cars parked in the street ignited. "Get the fuck down from there!" I screamed at him in my best drill sergeant's voice. That did the trick. The young man scurried across the roof and down a ladder propped up against the wall. "Is there anybody else in this house?" I barked. The young man shook his head. "Then let's go!"

The three of us started running down the street toward the direction where the fire truck was parked. I began to feel the heat on my back, and the smoke swirled around us thicker than ever. There was a muffled roar behind us, like a crowd at a World Series game witnessing a grand slam home run. I had no idea how much farther we had to go, but it was clear that the fire was gaining. Another electrical transformer exploded, this time directly behind us.

"We're not going to make it back to the truck in time," Nick shouted. He was breathing heavily but his face was still calm. *What does it take to get a rise out of this guy?* I thought.

"You got any ideas?" I shouted back, trying to match his calm. I was suddenly aware that I desperately had to piss.

Nick looked around. There was a brief shift of wind, and the smoke thinned slightly. "Over there," he pointed. "Is that a swimming pool?"

I trained my eyes in the direction he pointed. We were looking at a low sprawling home. Part of its back yard was visible, and I could just barely make out what looked like a strip of concrete and a chrome ladder. "Yeah, I think you're right!" I shouted back. I glanced at the kid. His eyes were glassy with terror. "Come on!" I shouted at him. "Follow us!"

The three of us bolted across the front lawn, down the grass strip that flanked the house and into the back yard. Flames were almost goosing us. There, surrounded by a low mesh fence and strip of concrete, a swimming pool stretched out before us like a vision from heaven. We vaulted over the fence and jumped in.

The neighboring house burst into flames and we felt a rush of heat roll over us. Nick looked at me. "I don't know about you but I'm getting out of this damn gear. I feel like I'm roasting." It wasn't a bad idea, and I followed his example, shrugging out of my heavy coat and helmet. I turned to the kid to see how he was doing.

"You all right?" I asked.

He nodded but didn't say anything. For the first time I really looked at him. My earlier impression was right; he was young, all right, maybe still in his late teens. He had a thatch of sandy hair, light blue eyes, and a face that belonged on a Wheaties box. Under the UCLA T-shirt and cutoffs he was wearing, his body was tight and fit. He wasn't beefy, but his arms, chest, and legs had a muscularity about them that made me suspect he was a jock.

I made an attempt at an encouraging smile. "What's your name?" I asked.

Flaming embers were raining down on the house behind us. The roof started smoking. The young man turned and stared at me with unfocused eyes. For a second I thought he wasn't going to answer me. He licked his lips. "Dave," he mumbled.

I squeezed Dave's arm. Even in all this danger I couldn't help noticing the impressive bulge of his biceps. "We'll get out of this

OK, Dave," I said. Once again I pasted a smile on my face. If it looked as phony as it felt, I imagine Dave found it anything but reassuring. Dave looked past me. The expression on his face changed to surprise.

I looked behind me. Nick had stripped down to his bikini briefs, and now was in the process of tugging them down.

"What the hell are you doing?" I asked, stunned.

Nick grinned at me and his eyes shined with excitement. His face was fearless, lit with joy. He looked almost deranged. "I'm just getting comfortable," he laughed. He kicked off his briefs and tossed them further down the pool. His dick was half-hard and rapidly growing. Flames were now crackling on the roof of the house behind us, and a trail of fire was making its way down the exterior walls. The houses on either side of us were yellow-orange fireballs. Nick tossed back his head and laughed. "Ain't this a bitch!" he shouted. He threw back his head and gave a long wolf howl. "I am the God of Hellfire!" he sang.

I glanced over at Dave. His face was almost a caricature of shock, his mouth hanging open, his eyes almost wide enough to pop out. "Is this guy really a fireman?" he asked, awed.

All at once the shock, the adrenaline rush, the terror, the *weirdness* hit me like a thunderclap. I threw back my head and laughed. Dave's eyes bulged out even further, something I didn't think possible, and that just made me laugh all the harder. Nick joined in, and then, amazingly, so did Dave. The roof of the house behind us collapsed with a loud roar, and we laughed even harder. It was all tinged with hysteria of course, at least for me and Dave, but there was something exhilarating about all this as well. All bets were off now; there was nothing any further we could do to save ourselves, and I was ready for anything. Nick pulled me over to him, and we kissed long and hard, our tongues crammed deep down each other's throat. *What the fuck,* I thought. *This is probably the last time I'm ever going to get off. I might as well go out with a bang.* I wrapped my hand around Nick's dick and began to stroke it. I always loved the way his cock filled my palm, sliding in and out of my curled fingers like it had a mind of its own. Nick pulled his body close to mine and ground his hips against me. He unzipped my fly and pulled down my pants. Liberated, my cock sprung to full attention, slapping hard against my belly. I shrugged off my shirt and stepped out of my pants. Waves of heat played upon my naked skin.

I felt a hand squeeze my ass and I turned around, surprised. Dave stared back at me with wild eyes. He had already whipped out his cock and was beating off with quick short strokes. He stopped for a second, peeled his shirt off, and tossed it over by Nick's fire-engine-red briefs, floating in the deep end of the pool. His body was hairless and tanned, the color of rich mocha, and ripped in a way that spoke of weeks spent working out in the university gym. His hand slid down between the crack in my ass, and I could feel his finger rubbing up against my bunghole. I didn't know if he naturally swung toward guys, but I guess there's something about facing imminent death that will encourage you to take whatever's available. Nick dropped down to his knees in the shallow water and took my dick in his mouth. His lips slid up and down the shaft, and he twisted his head from side to side for maximum sensory effect. Nick always did know how to give terrific blow jobs. He threw himself wholeheartedly into sucking cock, like just about everything else he did.

Dave wrapped his arms around me from behind, sliding his strong hands up and down my torso. He rubbed his thumbs over my nipples, then squeezed them hard. I groaned loudly. I reached behind and cupped his balls in my hand. They had a meatiness and heft to them that gave my dick an extra throb. Dave pressed his body tight against mine, his thick cock sliding up and down my ass crack. I turned my head and we kissed hard, our tongues wrapping around each other. I closed my eyes and let the sensations caused by Nick's mouth and Dave's hands and tongue sweep over me. Fire-heated pool water lapped around my thighs and each breath I took seared my lungs. The flames around us were consuming most of the oxygen and I felt dizzy from the lack of it. It gave the sex a dreamy, unreal quality, nightmarish but exciting at the same time.

Dave's cock head poked against my bunghole, and I knew he meant to fuck me. "Hold on a second," I said. I reached for my pants, pulled the condom out of my back pocket, and handed it to him. He stared at it stupidly, like I had just given him a rubber chicken.

Nick took my cock out of his mouth and laughed. "I don't believe it!" he said.

"Believe it," I replied.

Nick shook his head and grinned. "You're like the guy in front of the firing squad who won't smoke a last cigarette because it's bad for his health."

"We still might get out of this," I said sharply. I thrust the condom into Dave's hand. "You want to fuck, put it on."

Without argument, Dave unrolled the condom down his dick shaft and spat in his hand. He stroked his cock a couple of times for extra hardness and then pushed it between my ass cheeks. I bent over to make it easier for him. With excruciating slowness he worked his dick inch by inch up my ass. I closed my eyes and grimaced from the pain, momentarily forgetting about the fire. I made a vow that if ever I survived this, I would include a tube of lube in my standard fire-fighting kit. Dave began pumping his hips, sliding his dick in and out of my chute; the pain subsided and soon was replaced with the exquisite sensation of having my ass full of cock meat. I began moving my body in sync with Dave's, meeting him thrust for thrust. Dave groaned his appreciation. I felt my dick regain its hardness and I started beating off. Nick made a motion to resume sucking me off again.

"No," I gasped. "Stand up. I want dick in both ends."

Nick straightened up, grinning. His dick thrust out in front of him, thick and implacable, the head flared, demanding to be sucked. The heat of the fire around us had made his balls hang loose and heavy; I rolled them gently in my hand as I slid my mouth down his shaft. Since my first taste of it in the firehouse shower room, Nick's dick has always felt like it was made for my mouth; the fit seemed almost too perfect to be an accident. My tongue played on it, teased it, working it back into the deeper reaches of my throat.

Nick starting pumping his hips, deliberately synchronizing his thrusts with Dave's. *Thrust in,* and I was stuffed with dick meat from both ends, *pull out,* and I was left empty and greedy for more.

Nick reached over and squeezed Dave's nipples, never falling out of the rhythm the two of them had set. They were dancing together, using me as a conduit to have sex with each other as well as me. My dick gave an extra throb just thinking about this, and I felt my balls pull up in anticipation of the load I was about to blow.

Dave started moaning, and I felt the grip of his arms around my torso get tighter. "Yeah," Nick grunted. "Shoot that load up his ass." Dave quickened his thrusts, and suddenly his body began to shudder. He cried out as I felt the pulse of his dick squirting his come into the condom up my ass. As if on cue, Nick suddenly pulled his dick out of my mouth and a gush of jizz spewed onto my face, and then another and another. It dripped down my cheeks and chin, thick and viscous. I wiped my hand across my face, then wrapped my come-drenched fingers around my dick again. A few quick thrusts into my fist and I was off and running too, squirting come into the heated pool water as if it were on fire and I was hell-bent on putting it out. The flames around us roared and smoke filled our lungs. I could feel the skin on my face begin to blister from the heat. We collapsed into the deeper waters of the pool and waited, exhausted, for whatever was going to happen to go ahead and take its course.

As it turned out, we survived. Through the quirk of a wind shift, the fire marched on to the north and left the yard around the pool unscathed. It was only after the fire around us had subsided to smoldering rubble that we finally risked leaving the safety of the pool. The hot coals on the ground soon burned through Dave's tennies, and Nick and I had to cut pieces of our coats off and wrap them around his feet. But we made it back to safety eventually. The other guys in our team had given us up for dead and were stunned when we finally showed up. To his acute embarrassment, Chavez started bawling like a baby.

The miraculous survival of two firemen and a college kid is the kind of story the media loves. We made the front pages of all the local papers and even a sidebar in *Time*. It was clipped and posted on the firehouse locker room bulletin board, with the words "Local Heroes Make Good" scrawled on top.

Nick and I read it together. It was late at night, and we were just turning in from our shift.

I turned to Nick and grinned. "If they only knew the whole story, Christ, would that ever knock their socks off!"

Nick laughed. He glanced into the darkened dorm room. "It looks like everyone's asleep," he said. His mouth curved up into a sly grin.

"Cut it out, Nick," I laughed, shaking my head. "We got to start acting like responsible adults."

But Nick just pulled me toward him and planted his mouth on mine. After a few seconds I reached down and unzipped his fly. "Come on," I growled. "We haven't done it by the watercooler yet."

PHYSICAL THERAPY

The doors of the ambulance swing open, and the two guys in white jump out. As they roll the gurney out, one of them loses his grip and it comes down hard on the asphalt. My leg explodes in a shock of pain. "Jesus fuck!" I cry out. Black spots burst across my vision. I think I pass out for a while, because the next thing I'm aware of is a fluorescent light overhead and faces peering down at me. Voices fade in and out. "It was a hit-and-run," I hear a man's voice say. "A pickup truck slammed into his cycle hard, and according to witnesses this dude went *flying*." Someone bends down over me and shakes my shoulder. "Can you hear me?" he asks.

My vision is swimming, and the face above me shifts in and out of focus. I squeeze my eyes shut and open them again. "Yeah," I mutter.

"You've been in an accident," the voice says. "You've got a badly broken leg, and you may have a concussion as well. Do you have any family or friends we can contact?"

The room is spinning around again, and I struggle to stay conscious. "No," I manage to say. "Not in this city. I'm just passing through." I grab the arm of the guy leaning over me. "What about my chopper?" I ask. "Is it OK?"

The guy gives a sharp laugh of surprise. "Your chopper's only good for scrap, buddy," someone behind him says. I think it's the ambulance driver.

"Ask him if he's got any health insurance," a woman's voice says.

I fall back onto the gurney. *Goddamn, shit, fuck, piss,* I think. I pass out.

The nurse wheels in a rolling rack loaded up with trays. Feeding time at the zoo.

There are five other guys here in the ward, all charity cases like myself: two knife fights, one DUI that ended up wrapped around a telephone pole, a shooting, and a fall out of a three-story window. At least I got the bed next to the window, along with its view of the brick wall opposite us. The drugs they gave me are wearing off, and my leg is throbbing like a son of a bitch. Every pulse shoots up my body to my fingertips, my head, even my damn *teeth*. The nurse comes by with my lunch tray and places it on the stand next to me.

"Can you give me something more to kill the pain?" I ask her, keeping my voice as low and polite as I can manage.

She turns her eyes on me. She looks like she's looking at a piece of furniture. "I can't give you any more medication for another two hours," she says.

I feel the rage rise up, and I push it back down. "You don't understand," I say slowly, drawing out the words. "I can't wait for two hours. I need something *now*."

"I'm sorry. Doctor's orders." Her eyes look like ball bearings. "Why don't you finish your lunch and not make any more trouble?"

I sweep the tray off the table and it goes flying onto the floor with a loud clatter. Food splatters everywhere. "All done," I say. We glare at each other for a few moments. She wheels around on her heel and stalks off. I fall back onto the bed, my eyes closed.

The guy across from me, the one who got shot, laughs. "What an asshole," he says.

"Eat shit," I reply, without much conviction. I turn my head and stare out the window at the brick wall.

I don't know how much time's gone by, a few minutes maybe, when I hear footsteps approach. I don't look to see who it is. "Looks like you had a little accident here," a man's voice says. I turn and see a dude dressed up in an orderly's smock, holding a mop and pail. The fucker towers over me like an oak tree. He looks Hispanic, Mexican maybe: dark skin, brown eyes, mustache. He's got arms like tree trunks and a chest as wide as a semi's front grille. A black plastic tag is pinned to his shirt, the word MIGUEL engraved on it in white.

"It wasn't an accident," I say, glaring at him, waiting for him to give me a ration of shit. But Miguel just looks at me calmly. He bends down and picks up the tray, mops up the floor, and then walks out the room, clutching the mop, pail, and tray in his giant hands.

The throbbing in my leg wakes me up. The clock on the bed stand says 2:17, and I know I'm not due for another dose of pain-killers until 4. I lie there, staring up at the ceiling. *Today is Monday, the day I was due at the construction site in Chicago. Two days ago I was a high-rise iron man. Now I'm dogmeat.* A faint light streams in from the hallway outside, and I look around. My roommates are all sawing wood, sleeping the sleep of the painless, the sons of bitches. I reach over and grab my crutches. When the doctor gave them to me yesterday, he told me to use them only for trips to the john. But if I don't get out of bed, I'm going to go out of my fuckin' skull.

The hospital corridors are dimly lit and empty. I hobble down them, my crutches squeaking against the linoleum. After about 20 minutes of this, I turn a corner and see a sign on the wall reading AIDS WARD. My armpits are killing me, and I can feel the sweat on my forehead dripping down into my eyebrows. But it feels good to use my body; I keep pushing on. All the rooms are dark; all the patients seem to be sleeping. I hear a noise, what sounds like a groan. *Another poor slob in pain,* I think. The noise is coming down the hall, from a room up ahead and to my left. A faint light streams from it. As I pass by, I glance in. I stop, my mouth dropping open, all thoughts about my aching leg forgotten.

Miguel is standing next to the bed of a patient, his shirt hiked up over his chest, his pants and jockeys tangled down around his ankles. He's jerking off, pulling on his dick with slow, deliberate strokes, his eyes watching intently the face of the man in bed. His body is beautifully muscled: the pecs sharply defined, the abs sculpted into a neat six-pack, the biceps rounded and veined. The torso is as brown and smooth as polished oak, his nipples two dark acorns. But it's his dick that finally commands my attention. It lives up to the promise of his giant's body: thick and uncut, its dark, round knob the size and color of a ripe plum. Miguel slides his fist up and down the shaft, his hips pushing forward slightly with each downstroke of his hand, the plum head winking in and out of the foreskin. His balls hang loose and heavy, swaying gently in their folds of scrotum flesh. He stands there in a pool of light, darkness all around him. The patient raises a thin arm and slides his hand across Miguel's body, kneading the flesh of his torso. Miguel's expression is calm and tender; his face looks like that of one of the plaster saints I used to see in church as a kid.

Miguel spits in his hand and slicks his dick up. I can see beads of sweat forming on his forehead, and his breath is coming out in ragged gasps. Suddenly his body shudders. Miguel groans and closes his eyes as his load oozes out between his fingers. His body spasms repeatedly as the orgasm sweeps through him and then finally passes. He stands there for a moment, his muscular body glistening with sweat, his jizz dripping down his hand, his thick, long dick slowly softening. I feel my own dick stir at the sight, making a tent out of my hospital gown.

I suddenly realize that all Miguel has to do is raise his head for him to see me. I back off slowly toward a less conspicuous position. Bad mistake. My left crutch slips out, and I go crashing to the floor. The pain is like a sunburst in my head, and I cry out. I lie there stunned for a few moments, unable to lift my head, unable even to breathe.

Miguel's face hovers over me. "Are you all right?" he asks. He's pulled his pants up, but his fly is still open.

I take a couple of deep breaths. I want to curse out a string of obscenities, but no sound comes out. I shake my head. The pain causes my eyes to brim with tears.

Miguel bends down and picks me up in his arms. He walks down the empty corridors in long, even strides. When he gets to my room, he lays me gently on the bed. He pushes the call button, and after a couple of minutes the night nurse shows up. "He slipped while going to the toilet," Miguel says. "He's in a lot of pain. Can you get him something?"

The nurse shakes her head. "Not till 4 o'clock."

But Miguel just smiles. "Jesus, Susan, we're talking half an hour here. I won't tell anybody." He winks at her.

The nurse relents and brings me two pills of Demerol. Miguel lifts my head and holds a glass of water to my lips. I swallow the pills. The nurse leaves, and Miguel sits by the bed, watching me.

I close my eyes. After a while, the pills kick in, and I fall asleep.

The next day Miguel comes by with a washcloth and a basin of soapy water. "I'm here to give you a sponge bath," he says. His tone is matter-of-fact, as if our encounter last night never happened. He draws the curtain around us. I look up at him with curiosity as he pulls down the bedclothes and removes my hospital gown. "How are you feeling?" he asks.

"Better than last night," I say, watching his face for a reaction.

But Miguel merely nods his head. "Good," he says. He squeezes the sponge in the basin and then proceeds to soap down my chest. He rubs the sponge against my torso in slow, widening circles. I wait for him to say something, some explanation perhaps, or plea for my silence, but he says nothing. Finally, he glances up at my face. "You have a nice body," he says. "Do you work out?"

This catches me off guard. "Yeah," I say. I nod toward my leg. "At least before this."

Miguel continues soaping down my body. After a while, I can't stand it anymore. "What the hell were you doing last night?" I ask, my voice low so that the others outside the curtain can't hear me.

Miguel regards me calmly. "What the hell do you think?" he asks, smiling slightly.

I don't say anything for a couple of beats. I plaster a nasty little smirk on my face. "A special form of physical therapy?"

Miguel is washing out my armpits now. "You could say that," he says, ignoring the sarcasm in my voice. His gaze holds mine. "I was just trying to help the guy feel like a human being again. Instead of an 'AIDS patient.'"

Miguel scrubs my face and neck. I close my eyes, conjuring up the memory of Miguel fucking his fist, his muscular body gleaming in the light of the bedside lamp. I feel my dick stir, and I deliberately stoke the flames, grabbing onto any sexual fantasy I can think of. It only takes a few seconds before I'm sporting a full hard-on. I take a hold of Miguel's wrist and place his hand on my dick. "How about giving *me* a little physical therapy," I ask.

But Miguel just looks amused. "Knock it off," he says. He takes his hand away and sponges down my right leg, the one not in a cast. I don't say anything else. After he's done, he drops the sponge into the basin. "What's your name?" he asks.

I hold his gaze. "Al."

"Look, Al," Miguel says. "What I was giving that patient last night is not what you need right now. If it were, I'd do it."

"Oh, yeah?" I say. "What do you think I need?"

Miguel smiles. "A friend."

"Thanks," I say. "But I don't take charity." I wait for Miguel to point out the obvious fact that that's all I *am* taking, here in this charity ward. But he just shrugs and says nothing. He finishes up and leaves a couple of minutes later.

I see a lot of Miguel the next couple of days. He wheels me down the hall to the hospital sunroom. He cleans me up. He brings my food to me. I find myself looking forward to whenever he next shows up; he's the only person in the fuckin' hospital who treats me like a human being. Once, while taking me down to get X-rays, he asks me what I'm going to do when I'm released from the hospital.

I don't say anything for a long time. "I don't know," I finally answer.

"Don't you have any family? Friends?" he asks.

"I have a brother somewhere," I say. "I lost track of him a few years ago. I have some friends back east, I guess." I put my hands on the wheels, stop the chair, and turn to face him. "I'm a construction worker," I say. "I work on high rises, traveling around the country looking for gigs. I'm never in one place long enough to make real friends. I was traveling to Chicago for a job when this happened. I've been out of work for five months, and this job was going to get me on my feet again."

"What did you do for the five months you were out of work?" Miguel asks.

I give Miguel a long, level look. "I hustled," I finally say. "Sometimes I hung out at a porn video store in the Combat Zone in Boston. For 20 bucks, a john could take me in a booth and suck my dick. For an extra 10, I'd suck his." I glance down at my leg in the cast and give a laugh with precious little humor in it. "I can't fall back on that this time, though. No john wants to make it with a gimp." We don't talk any more for the rest of the ride down.

The next day I wait for Miguel to show up with my breakfast. I'm hoping we can talk for a few minutes; I find that I miss his company. When 8 o'clock finally rolls around, some guy I never saw before comes in with my tray. "Where's Miguel?" I ask.

The guy puts the tray on the stand next to me. "You mean that big Mexican guy?" he asks. He shrugs. "He got fired."

I bolt up to a sitting position. "Why?"

The guy gives a smutty little grin. "He got caught jerking off with one of the patients in the AIDS ward last night. Sick, eh?" He turns and walks out the door.

Later that day, the doctor comes in and tells me I'm being discharged from the hospital first thing tomorrow.

"I suggest you make arrangements for your home care, Mr. Pulaski," he says. "It's going to take a while for your leg to heal."

I spend the afternoon staring at the ceiling, weighing in: a broken leg, no money, no job, no bike, no friends... *So I'm finally hitting bottom,* I think. *I always wondered what it'd feel like.* I don't feel particularly bad. Just numb. After a while, I ask the nurse for a telephone book. I turn to the city government listings and look up "Social Services." A couple of phone calls later, I have a list of all the city's homeless shelters.

After a week at the shelter, I feel that I've pretty much got the hang of the system. The people who run it kick everybody out at 9 A.M. I hang out in a nearby park with the dopers and drunks; it's one of the few places I can get to on crutches. There's a Baptist mission a block away that runs a soup kitchen, and I get my meals there after listening to a sermon about Jesus. I don't think or feel much of anything. I've had the vague hope sometimes of my leg healing and me getting another job, but lately I don't even think about that much. Sometimes my fellow bums pass around a bottle of Thunderbird, and I take a swig. I usually don't talk to anybody.

I've just finished my dinner at the mission and I'm hobbling back toward the shelter (they open the doors again at 7). I've gained an intimate knowledge of the stretch of street between the mission and the shelter, every fuckin' liquor store, bar, and adult video store

BOB VICKERY

(I've tried hustling back among the booths of a couple of these, but found no takers; I was right when I told Miguel that the johns don't want gimps). I turn the last corner before the shelter. Miguel is standing there in front of the door. We look at each other.

"Well, this is a surprise," I say.

Miguel smiles. "I've still got friends at the hospital. I heard you were discharged, and I've been looking for you." His eyes travel down the length of my body. "You look like shit, Al." He wrinkles his nose. "You smell like it too."

"Thanks."

Miguel takes me by the elbow. "Come on. My car is parked just a block away."

I pull back. "Where are we going?"

"Back to my place." Miguel says. "And I don't want to hear any argument."

I have to laugh at that one. "You honestly think I'm going to argue?"

Miguel lives in a small apartment over a garage behind a duplex. The first thing he does after we walk in is pull out a basin from under the sink. He starts filling it with hot water. He looks at me over his shoulder. "Take off your clothes," he says. "I'm going to give you a bath." I don't argue with him. I pull off my jacket and T-shirt, drop my jeans and kick them off. When I'm naked, Miguel nods toward the bed. "Lie down."

I obey. Miguel sits down on the side of the bed, placing the basin beside me. He drops a washcloth in it, squeezes it, and starts bathing my chest. We don't talk. I keep my eyes focused on Miguel's face, but he just looks down at the parts of my body that he's washing. He washes my armpits, my arms, each finger. The washcloth travels down my torso. He washes my dick and balls. The feel of the warm, wet cloth on them gives me an instant hard-on, but Miguel pays no attention. He washes my asshole; I push up my hips to give him better access. He washes my right leg and both feet, working each toe like he did my fingers before. When he's finally done, he drops the washcloth in the basin. Only then does he look me in the face. He bends down and kisses me, his tongue pushing into my mouth. I break away.

"Is this more physical therapy for a needy patient?" I ask.

Miguel looks down at me. "You know what your problem is, Al?" he says. "You talk too damn much." He kisses me again, and this time I tongue him back. I pull on his shirt, fumbling with the buttons.

"Get naked," I say.

Miguel stands and pulls off his clothes. When he's finally naked, he slips into the bed beside me and wraps his arms around me. "Maybe you can give *me* some physical therapy," he murmurs. "I've had a helluva week myself." I look hard at him, and for the first time I notice the lines of strain in his face, the anxiety in his eyes. I remember that he just lost his job.

Miguel takes my face in his hands and kisses my mouth tenderly, then my eyelids, my cheeks, my hair. He shifts lower in the bed, and I feel his tongue on my left nipple, licking it, working it over. I sigh. He takes the nub between his teeth and nips softly. My sigh turns into a low groan. Miguel does the same with my right nipple, working the nub, making it stand erect. I close my eyes and let the sensations tingle through my body. It's been so long since I've been in bed with another man...

Miguel drags his tongue down my torso, sliding it across the abs, into the forest of my pubes. He works his way down the bed so that his head is positioned beneath the V of my legs. I feel his tongue slide across my balls, and then he opens his mouth and sucks my scrotum in. He looks up at me, my balls in his mouth, and I hold his gaze as I run my fingers through his curly hair. Miguel reaches up and twists my nipples as he rolls my balls around with his tongue. His tongue works its way down to my asshole. I feel its warm wetness as he probes against it.

"Christ Almighty," I groan.

Miguel wraps a hand around my dick and squeezes it. "I love your cock, Al," he says, looking up at me. "It fills my hand so nicely." He starts stroking it, sliding his hand up and down the shaft, his tongue working on my balls again. He presses his lips against the base of my dick and then moves up, kiss by kiss, to the head. His lips open, and he plunges down, taking my dick full into his mouth. His head starts bobbing up and down, and I push my hips up to meet him. I've got my fingers entwined in Miguel's hair now, anchoring his head as I skewer his warm, wet mouth with my dick.

"Swing around," I say.

Miguel pivots his body around so that his dick juts out a few inches above me. His balls hang low and heavy, like ripe fruit; I raise my head and bury my face in them, breathing in their musky pungency. I open my mouth, and Miguel's ball sac drops in. As I continue to fuck Miguel's face, I suck on his balls, rolling them around with my tongue, savoring their fleshiness. I spit in my hand and curl my fingers around his dick, sliding them up and down the shaft. Miguel groans, his voice muffled by my dick down his throat.

Miguel pulls back and swings his legs around so that he's straddling my torso, facing me. He pumps his hips, pushing his fat dick hard against my belly. He leans back, and his dick sticks out in front of him, proud and hard. I drink it in with my eyes, how thick it is, how dark, how the veins run up the shaft, ending in that purple plum on top. I wrap my hands around both our dicks and squeeze them together. I've got the red working-class dick of your average Polack, much lighter in color than Miguel's, cut, maybe not as long, but certainly nothing to be ashamed of. I love the feel of Miguel's dick against mine, the two warm, blood-engorged shafts of meat touching each other. I start stroking them together, pulling the foreskin over Miguel's cock head. A drop oozes out of his piss slit, and then another. I run my fingers over the clear little pearls of prejizz, slicking up my palm with them so that my strokes slide down both our cocks like butter across a hot skillet.

Miguel looks down at me, his body towering over me like a wall of muscle, his dark eyes burning, his mouth slightly open. I can see the excitement in his eyes, and the hunger. I feel it too, perhaps even more so. Miguel reaches down and smoothes my hair from my forehead. "It is so goddamn nice to have you in my bed, Al," he says. He bends down and kisses me again, wrapping his huge arms around me in a bear hug, grinding his body against mine.

"You feel like fucking me, Miguel?" I ask. "Just plowing my ass good?"

Miguel's grin broadens. He opens the drawer to his nightstand and pulls out a condom and a jar of lube. "That's just what I had in mind."

He scoops out two fingers worth of lube and slides them into the crack of my ass. I can feel the fingers work their way to my bung-hole, massaging it, playing with it. One of them penetrates me, sliding inside until it's completely in. I push up with my hips, exposing my asshole even more to Miguel. He crooks his finger and pushes against my prostate; I give a laugh, just from the sheer pleasure of the sensation.

Miguel pulls his finger out, rolls a condom down his dick, and slathers it with more lube. I take his dick in my hand, and as Miguel hovers over me, I guide it to my asshole. Miguel penetrates me slowly, inch by patient inch, his eyes intent on my face, watching my reaction. "Let me know if I'm hurting you," he murmurs, but I just shake my head, my eyes never leaving his. When he's fully in, Miguel just lies motionless on top of me for a moment, his arms wrapped around my torso, his face buried against my neck. He starts pumping his hips, slowly at first, with short thrusts. I pull his face down to mine and kiss him hard. Miguel's thrusts become deeper, faster. I slide my hands down his smooth back, squeezing the hard muscles of his ass, feeling them clench and unclench with each push of his hips. Miguel's torso writhes against mine, and I can feel his muscles, like steel embedded in hard rubber, flex against my body.

We roll over, and now I'm on top, my plastered leg carefully positioned. I sit erect so that I can look down at Miguel. I run my hands over his torso, squeezing his nipples, flicking them, pinching them. Miguel's lips are pulled back into a snarl, and his eyes have a fierceness that I've never seen before. There's an *electricity* passing between us, a connection that crackles with energy. I squeeze my ass muscles tightly, just as Miguel thrusts his dick hard up my ass. Miguel groans softly. I do it again at his next thrust, and Miguel's groans rise in volume. He looks at me with startled eyes.

"Where did you learn to fuck like this?" he asks, wide-eyed. But I just laugh. I reach back and hold his balls in my hand, squeezing them gently. They've pulled up tight against his body, and I know it won't be long now before he shoots. Miguel's huge hand, slicked with lube, is wrapped around my dick, stroking it in sync with each thrust of his hips. He pulls his dick out, its head just inside my sphincter, holds the position for a second, and then plunges in hard, his shaft sliding full up my chute. I feel his body shudder, and he cries out sharply. The orgasm sweeps over him one spasm after another, and I ride it out on top of his thrashing body, feeling his hot load pump into the condom up my ass.

Miguel continues stroking my dick, and I feel myself getting close. "Slide down," he says, "and let me suck on your balls."

I move down his chest and drop my balls in Miguel's mouth. He tongues my scrotum as he continues stroking my dick. I lean back, eyes closed, feeling Miguel draw me to the brink. When I do come, I groan loudly, my load squirting out, splattering against Miguel's face in a thick white rain of jizz. I collapse onto the bed beside Miguel. We lie there silently, our bodies pressed together. After a while, I prop myself on my elbow and look down at Miguel.

My load drips down his face. I kiss him, tasting my jizz on his lips. "Jesus, you're a mess," I say, grinning.

Miguel laughs and pulls me to him again. We lie in bed for what seems like a long time. I watch the patterns of sun and shadow move across the ceiling. "Miguel," I finally say. "What did you have in mind when you found me and brought me here?"

"We don't have to talk about it now," Miguel says.

"I don't have any money. It'll be a while before I can work again. Do you realize what you're taking on?"

Miguel pulls me tighter against him. "Just shut up, OK?" he says gently. "I can handle it, believe me."

We don't say anything else. After a while, I can tell by the steady rhythm of his breath that Miguel is sleeping. *Let it go. Whatever happens, happens.* I close my eyes, and it doesn't take long before I drift off into sleep myself.

UNPLANNED STOP

"Mommy?" Karen's voice pipes up from the back. "I don't feel so good."

Linda turns around. "What's the matter, honey," she asks. "You carsick?"

Karen gives a whimper for an answer.

Oh, Jesus, I think. "Try to hold it in, sweetheart," I say. "We'll find a place to pull over in a few minutes." We're on a stretch of highway with nothing but trees on either side. A sign up ahead says the next exit is 28 miles away. *This is just fucking perfect.*

Karen answers by retching loudly. "Gross!" Kenny says, rolling down a window.

Mark giggles. "Karen just puked." He turns to Karen. "Way to go, pukeface." Karen starts wailing.

"Knock it off, Mark!" I snap.

"Yeah," Kenny says. "Shut up!" In the rearview mirror, I see him reach over and slug Mark in the shoulder. Mark slugs him back. Soon I hear the sounds of punches and kicks in the backseat. The headache I've been courting for the past 60 miles has escalated to a dull series of contained bomb blasts.

"If you kids don't behave yourself," I say in a low, murderous voice, "I'm going to pull onto the shoulder and give you all spankings so hard you won't be able to sit down for a month."

Linda has turned around and is draped over the front seat, trying to clean up Karen's vomit with a wad of tissue.

"Karen," I say. "Roll down your window so that Mommy can toss out the dirty tissue."

"That's littering, Daddy," Karen protests.

"That's all right, darling," I say between clenched teeth.

305

"Sometimes it's OK to litter. Now roll down your window."

"No!" Karen says.

"Christ," I mutter to Linda. "Why can't these kids for once just do what I tell them to?"

"She's right," Linda says. "It *is* littering." Karen giggles.

I keep my eyes trained to the highway, stung by this betrayal, gripping the steering wheel so tight that my hands hurt. *Jesus, Jesus, Jesus,* I think. I'm not sure whether I'm swearing or praying. Kenny and Mark are still fighting, and I'm just too damn tired to break them up. Far up ahead I spot the back of a truck, one of those 18-wheelers that go cross-country. When we pass it, I glance up through the windshield, catching a glimpse of a tanned, muscular arm hanging out of the cab window, a barbed-wire tattoo encircling his biceps. I spot a flash of a profile: a beard, shades, a black cowboy hat, and then we're past him.

I hear the smack of a fist against flesh, and suddenly Kenny starts bawling. I rub my eyes. *Sweet Jesus, when will it ever end?* I look in the mirror, not at Kenny and Mark, but at the truck behind us. It's fallen way behind, now; it doesn't look like the driver's in any hurry. I let my thoughts wander, fantasizing that I'm riding shotgun with him—no wife, no crying kids, just a couple of buddies out on the open road who are shooting the shit, laughing at each other's jokes, throwing good-natured insults at each other.

We pass a sign that says COOPER'S JUNCTION 1 MILE. I turn my head toward the backseat. "Anyone here need to make a bathroom break? Next exit won't be for anther 34 miles."

Nobody says anything. I see the exit coming up. "This is your last chance, folks," I call out. "After this, it's a long haul before the next restroom." Silence. We drive past the exit.

Two miles past the exit Karen pipes up. "Daddy, I have to go to the bathroom."

My hands spasm around the steering wheel. "Why didn't you say so when I asked, honey?" I ask, gritting my teeth.

"I don't know," Karen says, her voice rising in petulance.

"Well, you're going to have to wait till the next exit."

"I can't," Karen whimpers. "I have to go *now!*"

The blood is roaring in my ears, and I can feel a vein throbbing in my forehead. I look at the concrete median strip that divides the highway. It's not very high, a foot at the max. I slam on the brakes, and we all pitch forward.

"Just what the hell are you doing, Jim?" Linda asks, her voice shrill with alarm.

"Getting Karen to a bathroom," I say. I yank the steering wheel to the left and the two front wheels bounce over the divider. Linda and the kids give a collective gasp of shock. I gun the engine, and there's a sickening noise of metal against concrete. One final pump of my foot on the accelerator and the rear wheels clear the divider as well. Suddenly we're on the other side of the highway, heading back toward Cooper's Junction.

"I'll get you to a bathroom in just a minute, honey," I call back at Karen. At that moment the oil warning-light blinks on. I glance out the rearview mirror and see a slick forming on the highway behind us. "FUCK!" I scream at the top of my lungs.

There's a stunned silence. "Daddy said the *f* word," Mark says.

"No, he didn't, honey," Linda says, glaring at me. "It just sounded like he did."

By the time we limp into Cooper's Junction, smoke is coming out from under the hood. We have just barely enough momentum to coast into a run-down garage on the edge of the town. Linda opens her mouth to say something, sees the expression on my face, and closes it again.

I climb out of the driver's seat and walk into the station. Nobody's in the office. I walk through the door leading into the garage. There's a radio blaring, but I don't see anyone in there either. Eventually, I spot a pair of legs sticking out from under the body of a pickup truck.

"Excuse me," I say, raising my voice to be heard above the music. The mechanic wheels out from under the truck, his face and arms smeared with grease. There's a pack of cigarettes rolled up in the left sleeve of his stained T-shirt. He props himself up to a sitting position. "Yeah?" he says. He's just a kid, barely out of his teens, and I can tell right away he's a punk. Something about the sneer he's wearing and the hard glint in his dark eyes. I adopt an aggressive posture: feet planted wide apart, hands clenching and unclenching.

"I got some engine problems," I say. "I wonder if you could look at it."

The mechanic looks at me for a good 15 seconds without saying anything. I match him, glare for glare. I'm just spoiling for a fight. "I'll get to you in a minute," he says. He rolls under the truck again.

I stand there, stupidly looking at his legs. After a while I go back to the car. Linda looks at me. "Well?" she asks.

"The mechanic will be here in a little while," I say tightly.

Twenty minutes later he saunters over to our car. He looks at the trail of oil on the road behind us. "It looks like you got a busted oil pan," he says. "What'd you do, drive over a tree stump?"

"Can you fix it?" I ask.

"Maybe," he shrugs. "Not today, though." He rolls down his shirtsleeve and flips open the pack of cigarettes. Only after he pulls out a cigarette and lights it does he bother to look at me again. "I don't have the parts you need, and I'm the only one here." He inhales deeply and then blows out the smoke. "Maybe tomorrow I can find someone to drive over to Vernon and see if they have a spare oil pan."

He wants me to beg, I think. *I'd rip out my tongue first.* "Is there someplace my family and I can spend the night?" I ask.

The mechanic scratches his head. "We got a couple of cabins behind the garage for when truckers come by. I could put you up in one."

"Fine," I growl.

"It ain't the Ritz," he says. He's not smirking, but he's damn close.

"Well, we don't have a fucking choice, do we?" My growl is getting close to a snarl.

The mechanic's mouth curls up into a slow smile. "No, I guess you don't."

We eat dinner in Cooper Junction's one restaurant, a greasy spoon with a picture of Jesus over the cash register and flypaper hanging from the ceiling. My mind keeps wandering over toward the mechanic. *What an asshole,* I think. But I find myself thinking about his muscular torso under the tight, filthy shirt, the curve of his biceps, his pretty-boy, surly face. Through the plate-glass window I can see the lights on in the garage. He must still be out there, working.

On the way back to the cabin I notice a truck pulled up in front of the gas pumps. The mechanic is standing alongside the cab, talking to the driver, grinning. I can't see the driver from where I'm standing, just a muscular arm hanging out the cab window, a barbed-wire tattoo around his biceps. The trucker says something, and the mechanic laughs. I can hear the tenor sound of it carry across the space separating us. He's not a punk right now, just some guy hanging out with a buddy on a warm summer evening.

Later, in the cabin, I lie in the darkness, staring at the ceiling and ticking off all the different ways this day has wound up sucking shit. Linda is snoring gently beside me, and the kids are stretched out on the floor in their sleeping bags. I can't sleep; after a while I don't even try anymore. I get up, fumble around in the dark for my clothes, and quietly get dressed. Linda stirs. "What are you doing?" she asks.

"I'm just going for a walk," I say.

Outside, the evening has cooled a bit, but the night air still has a balmy feel to it. Off in the distance, Cooper's Junction is dark, all shut down, but I can see there's still a faint light shining in the back window of the garage. I glance at my watch. It's almost midnight. *The mechanic can't still be working this late at night,* I think. I wander toward the garage, curious. The truck is still parked in front of the pumps, but there's no sign of the driver. The garage's sliding door is closed and the office is dark. I twist the doorknob and, seeing that the door's unlocked, step inside the office. I can just barely make out the counter, the rack of candy bars, the cash register. A faint light streams in from under the crack of the door leading into the garage. *This is trespassing,* I think, but I shrug the thought off. I turn the knob, and the door swings open.

A trouble lamp hanging from a pipe overhead provides the only illumination. Directly underneath it, bathed in a pool of light, a muscular, bearded man leans against the pickup truck, both arms stretched out on the hood, his head thrown back. His jeans are around his ankles, and the mechanic is kneeling in front of him, enthusiastically sucking him off. I stand in the doorway, taking in the details. The man's wearing a red and black flannel shirt, unbuttoned now, revealing a powerful torso packing about 10 pounds more than it should. The pecs swell out, each one topped by a nut-brown nipple peeking through a forest of curly brown hair that descends down across the curve of his belly. His legs are short and thick with muscle. There's a barbed-wire tattoo around his left biceps. *Well, at least that answers where the trucker is,* I think. The mechanic is on his knees before him, working the trucker's dick, sucking on it, slurping noisily as his mouth slides down the shaft. He's whipped his own dick out as well, and he strokes it with his right hand as his left tugs on the trucker's balls.

My throat's so tight my breaths are coming in shallow and fast. My dick is threatening to bust my fly open, and I'm too damn excited to worry about what this is saying about me. The mechanic is now chewing on the trucker's fleshy nuts, sucking them into his mouth as he slides the foreskin up and down the thick dick. The trucker lolls his head from side to side. He gives a long groan, opens his eyes, and suddenly we're staring at each other.

He taps the mechanic's shoulder. "We got company," he says.

The mechanic turns his head. "Christ!" he exclaims, jumping to his feet. His hard dick sticks out from his fly, and he makes no effort to tuck it back in his jeans. He looks annoyed more than anything else. "We're closed," he says.

"I saw the light shining from the garage window," I say. "I was just checking to see what was going on." I realize how lame this sounds.

"Nothing that's any of your damn business," the mechanic says. "Go back to your wife."

"Maybe he doesn't want to," the trucker says. His eyes are still trained on me, eyes that are slate-gray and pushed up into narrow squints by his high cheekbones. He's going bald; what hair he has is cut boot-camp short. His thin lips curve up into an easy smile. "Maybe he wants to hang out with the guys for a while."

The mechanic looks at him, then at me, then at him again. "Christ, Curtis," he mutters. He looks at me again and shakes his head. "Jesus H. Christ!" He spits on the floor in disgust.

"You talk too much, Billy," Curtis says. He slowly begins to stroke his dick, his eyes never leaving my face. His dick is uncut, and I watch the red bulb of his cock head wink in and out of sight as he skins the foreskin back and forth. "You like what you see?" he asks me. I don't say anything. My mouth is too dry to speak.

"I don't want any trouble," Billy says. He eyes me warily, but there's a new speculation in his expression.

Curtis's eyes are still trained on me. "You're not going to cause any trouble, are you, Mister?" he asks.

I run my tongue over my lips, still watching Curtis's hand slide up and down the meaty shaft of his cock. His balls hang heavy in their wrinkled sac, swaying with each stroke of his hand. After a long pause, I shake my head. "No," I say softly.

Curtis grins broadly. "I didn't think so." There's another long moment where the only sound in the garage is the wet slapping noise of Curtis's spit-slicked hand working his dick. "Why don't you just come over here and join us, buddy?" he finally growls.

"Jim," I say. "My name's Jim."

Curtis nods his approval. "OK. Why don't you come join us, Jim?"

"All right," I hear myself say.

I walk across the length of the room, my mind buzzing with unreality. When I reach the two men, Curtis reaches out and hooks the back of my neck with his hand. He pulls my face against his and kisses me fiercely, his tongue thrusting into my mouth. It is so fucking *strange* to feel whiskers against my face! He reaches down and cups my crotch with his hand.

I pull away. "Listen," I say. "I can't go through with this."

Billy snickers. "Shut up, Billy," Curtis says, his eyes never leaving my face. His hand squeezes my dick through the rough fabric of my jeans. "Your dick's telling me something else, Jim," he says softly.

"Christ, I'm a married man. My wife and kids are just next door."

"Everything's OK, Jim," Curtis says softly. He slips his other hand under my shirt and slides it against the skin of my torso. I close my eyes. "Nobody has to know anything," he croons. "You're just taking a little break." He pulls me close again. I try to pull away, but he plants his mouth over mine and frenches me hard. I struggle. I stop struggling. It only takes a few seconds before I'm frenching him back, pushing my tongue deep into his mouth. I push up hard against him, my hands squeezing and tugging at his flesh. Curtis takes my hand and lays it on his hard dick. I wrap my fingers around the shaft and start stroking.

"Billy," Curtis growls. "Take care of him."

Billy reaches over and unbuckles my belt. He slowly pulls down my zipper. My heart is pounding hard enough to crack a rib. Billy hooks his thumbs around the waistband of my jeans and pulls them down. The BVDs are next to drop. Then I feel his warm, wet mouth slide down the shaft of my dick, and I sigh loudly.

"Yeah," Curtis growls. "Feels nice, don't it? If there's one thing Billy knows how to do, it's suck dick." Curtis's hands slide under my T-shirt, massaging the flesh of my torso, stroking it, pulling it. He takes both nipples between his thumbs and forefingers and squeezes, not gently, just as Billy's mouth slides full down my dick shaft.

"Sweet Jesus," I groan.

"That's right," Curtis breathes. "Sink into it." Billy is sucking on my balls, rolling them around with his tongue. Curtis pulls my shirt over my head and tosses it onto the floor. I offer no resistance. His hands slide behind me, squeezing my ass cheeks, the rough calluses of his palms scratching against my flesh. I can feel his fingers, feather light, move up my back and then across my shoulders. He suddenly grabs me by the scruff of my neck and squeezes, holding me so that I'm fully facing him. "You ever suck cock, Jim?" Curtis growls, his eyes bright and fierce.

I shake my head as much as his grasp will allow. "No," I say.

Curtis's mouth curls up into a sly grin. "Well, congratulations," he says. "'Cause you're going to now."

He pushes down hard on my shoulders, forcing me to my knees. I put up a token resistance and then give it up. Curtis wraps his fingers around my hair and tugs my head back. My gaze meets his, my eyes wide, my lips parted. Curtis squats down and drops his balls into my mouth. The fleshy pouch spills in, and instinctively I begin sucking on it. "Yeah, " Curtis croons. "I can tell you're a natural at this." I roll his balls around with my tongue, exploring the texture and taste of the silky sac, their hairs tickling the inside of my mouth.

Christ! I've got the balls of another man in my mouth! I think. I drag my tongue across them until they gleam with my spit. My own dick is rock-hard and throbbing.

"OK, Jim," Curtis says. "It's time for the big enchilada." He pokes the head of his dick against my lips. It's a small fist of flesh: red, flared, meaty, weeping precome.

I part my lips, and Curtis slides his dick full down my mouth. I gag, and Curtis pulls back, but only a little. "Breathe through your nose," Curtis says softly. "Relax your throat." I do what he says. "That's right, baby," he continues in his soft baritone. He slides his dick deeper down my throat. I gag again but shift the angle of my head and forge on. Before long, I've got the entire tube of flesh inside my mouth, my nose pushed into Curtis's crinkly black pubes.

Curtis holds my head between his two large hands, not forcibly, but with enough pressure to steady me as he proceeds to fuck my mouth. I feel the thick shaft of flesh slide down my throat and then out again, over and over. I look up at Curtis across the expanse of hairy, muscle-packed torso into his calm gray eyes. He gives me a wolfish smile. "You having a good time, Jim?" he asks and then thrusts his dick so hard down my throat that his balls slam against my chin.

Billy clambers to his feet and stands next to Curtis, his dick hard and twitching. Without thinking about it I wrap my hand around it and stroke. Billy bends his knees slightly and starts pumping his hips, fucking my fist in quick, short jabs. His body is lean, supple, each muscle of his torso beautifully defined. A streak of grease cuts down across the six-pack of his belly, and its darkness accents the pale smoothness of his skin in a way that makes my boner throb. Unlike the trucker, his dick is circumcised and thrusts up into a proud curve, its blue veins snaking up the pink column of flesh. I pull away from the trucker and slide my lips down Billy's shaft. Billy grabs my head and shoves his hips hard enough against my face to make me gag again.

"Easy, Billy," the trucker growls.

"Shit!" Billy says in disgust. But he lets go of my head. Billy's balls are plump and hang up tight under the base of his cock; I slide my tongue down and nuzzle my face against them, breathing in deeply their musky scent. Ball meat surrounds my nose, pushes against the skin of my face, as Billy's hard dick lies against my forehead. I go back to sucking Billy off, then Curtis, and then Billy again, comparing the heft and weight of one dick against the other.

The trucker pulls me to my feet, and the three of us kiss, with lots of tongue action, our mouths wet and slobbering. My face is soaked with trucker and mechanic drool. Curtis's and Billy's hands slide up and down my body, and I soon feel the trucker's fingers burrow into the crack of my ass, pushing the cheeks apart, probing down toward my asshole. His finger pushes against my pucker and then enters me slowly, knuckle by knuckle.

"Whoa," I gasp. "I don't think I'm ready for this."

"Sure you are," Curtis growls softly, his face inches from mine. "Just relax. Sink into it." I look into his eyes and see the excitement. I relax my ass muscles, and the trucker slides a second finger in. He pushes in hard and deep.

"I feel like I have to piss," I say.

Billy snorts. "This guy is such an amateur."

"That's just me pressing against your prostate," Curtis says. "Don't pay it, or Billy, any mind." He pulls his fingers out, bends down, and fishes a foil packet out of his jeans pocket. "OK, Jim," he says. "It's time for your next lesson." He tears open the packet and sheathes his dick with the condom. He steps behind me and wraps his powerful arms around me. I feel his hot breath on my neck, and his hard dick poking along the length of my ass crack.

"Curtis..." I begin.

"Easy, baby, easy," Curtis croons into my ear. "Trust me, you'll love this." He spits into his hand and lubes his sheathed cock with the gob of saliva. I feel his cock head push inside me, followed by an inch of shaft.

"Ahhhhhh," I groan.

"Relax," Curtis whispers. "It only hurts if you're all clenched up." He stops briefly and then slides in another few inches. I feel the fur of his chest against my back, the encircling embrace of his arms, and the pain starts giving way to an electric tingling radiating from my asshole. Curtis slides all the way in, and I groan again, this time half in pleasure. "That's it, baby," Curtis whispers. "Let it happen."

He begins pumping his hips, and the slide of his thick dick in and out of my ass sets my body humming.

Billy is on his knees in front of me, sucking on my dick, twisting his head from side to side. The air is full of our groans and sighs and grunts, of the sound of skin slapping against skin. My body is soon drenched in sweat; I feel it trickle down my arms, my forehead, my belly; it makes my back slippery against Curtis's bull torso. Curtis grinds his hips against me, his cock full up my ass, and I lean back against him, eyes closed. He buries his face into my neck, squeezing my nipples as his dick continues to pump in and out of my ass. I twine my fingers through Billy's thick hair and skewer his mouth with my dick as Curtis skewers me. Billy feeds on my cock hungrily, sucking on it, licking it, teasing my load out of my balls, drawing me to the brink of orgasm. By the increasingly loud groans Curtis makes and the furious way that Billy is pounding his pud, I can't believe they're very far behind me.

Curtis gives my nipples another hard squeeze as he slides his dick full up my ass. I give a long, trailing groan, and Billy whips my dick out of his mouth just as it starts to squirt. I cry out loudly. Hot pellets of jizz splatter against his face, one volley after another. "Yeah," Billy growls and then groans as his load pulses out into his closed fist and oozes between his fingers. Curtis gives one more long, hard thrust, and his body shudders against mine, thrashing like a bull in a slaughterhouse, heaving and bucking as he shoots his load in the condom up my ass. His body gives one final spasm and then is quiet, his weight leaning against me for support.

When I finally get back to the cabin, it's almost 2 A.M. Linda and the kids are still sound asleep. I go to the bathroom, close the door behind me, and turn on the light. Part of my load is caked to my belly, and I can feel the sweat of the mechanic and the trucker on me. I take a quick shower and as I towel off, I look at the reflection staring back at me. *Well, you've been wondering what'd be like to have sex with a man,* I think. *Now you know.* I slide into the bed next to Linda's sleeping form and after a couple of minutes, drift off into sleep.

By the time we all wake up and stir out of the cabin, Curtis is already on the road. Billy is gone too but comes back shortly afterward with a new oil pan he was able to locate in Vernon. He installs it while the morning is still early, insisting that we only pay him for the parts. He really is a nice kid, not a punk at all like I first thought. Linda seems suspicious of this sudden largesse on his part but is not about to queer the deal. We're back out on the road by 10 o'clock.

Linda switches on the radio and turns the dial until she finds a rock-and-roll station. Bruce Springsteen comes on, singing "I'm On Fire." She looks at me and smiles, remembering our first date when we necked in my car to this song. I force myself to smile back. My ass is still tender from the pounding Curtis gave it last night, and images of my wild time with the trucker and the mechanic are running through my mind in an endless loop. *What the fuck am I going to do about this?* I wonder. Nothing comes to mind. Linda is staring out the window, and the kids are quiet in the backseat, playing Nintendo and drawing in their coloring books. *What the fuck am I going to do?* We pass another truck, and even though I know it's not Curtis's, I still crane my neck to catch a glimpse of the driver. He looks down at me and nods. I gun the engine and pass him, speeding down the highway toward home.

FANTASIES

The building's one of those converted Victorians, all the fancy woodwork stripped away and the facade covered with badly painted stucco. The steps are scattered with your standard-issue urban litter: flyers for pizza parlors and Chinese takeouts, yellowing newspapers—that kind of thing. I take them two at a time, and when I get to the top, I pace up and down the stoop, breathing deeply. I'm getting an adrenaline rush like you wouldn't believe; my heart's pounding like a racing-car piston, and my brain's buzzing so much that I feel like I'm about to burst a blood vessel. *OK, focus,* I tell myself. *Channel the energy.* After I've calmed down a bit, I bend over and read the names on the strips of cardboard beneath each mailbox. "Vinnie Castelloni" is scrawled on the far right strip, with "Vinnie" written in bold strokes, "Castelloni" all scrunched together. I push the doorbell.

I wait. My hand begins to cramp, and I look down and see I'm holding my Bible so tight my knuckles are white. I loosen my fingers. *Relax,* I tell myself. *Get into this.* I shut my eyes and take another deep breath. By the time the front door finally opens, I'm ready for bear.

The guy on the other side of the door eyes me suspiciously. He's in his mid to late 20s, too old for the street punk attitude he's giving off. His black hair is greased back, there's a two-day-old stubble on his face, and a cigarette dangles from his surly mouth. The tank top he wears hugs a torso packed with muscles. There's a tear in it, above his left pectoral exposing a nipple with the color and chewed toughness of an old pencil eraser. His gaze flicks up and down my body and then settles on my face. He has the eyes of a fallen angel: dark, liquid, but burning with a hard, cynical light.

Mingled with the smell of old sweat is the unmistakable stench of the hell-bound sinner.

"Yeah?" he growls.

I clear my throat. I glance at the name card under the mailbox and then back at his face again. "Good morning, Vinnie." I say, making my voice loud and hearty. I raise my eyebrows and beam him my friendliest smile. "It *is* all right if I call you Vinnie, isn't it?" Vinnie just glares at me with narrowed eyes, saying nothing. "I'm here to share with you some wonderful news," I plunge on, "about how you can lay down the burdens of life and let Jesus into your heart." I tug on the knot of my tie and inhale deeply. "I wonder if you'd be willing to give me a minute of your time?"

Vinnie just stands there in the doorway, staring at me. He takes a deep drag from his cigarette and then flicks the butt down the front steps. His full lips curl up into nasty little smile. "Sure," he says, opening the door wider, "Come on in." I push through before he gets a chance to change his mind.

The apartment's small and dark: cheap thrift-store furniture, a threadbare rug, a beat-up old TV set. There are beer cans and news-papers scattered around the floor, and the kitchen sink is stacked with dirty dishes. A *Hustler* magazine lies open on the floor beside the couch, the centerfold model posed with her legs spread wide open, showing pink (*Just what was Vinnie doing when I rang the bell?* I wonder). I turn my head away and catch Vinnie watching me, smirking. He pulls a chair out from the table and straddles it, his forearms resting on its back. I sit down on the couch. I make a point of sliding my foot under the *Hustler* cover and flipping it shut. "So what did you want to talk to me about?" he asks.

I run my tongue over my lips and put both hands on my knees. I'm feeling *pumped*. "Have you taken Jesus into your heart, Vinnie?" I ask.

Vinnie raises his arms above his head and stretches, like some big jungle cat. The muscles of his torso ripple under his tight shirt. "No," he says calmly. "I can't say that I have."

I look directly into his beautiful dark eyes. "Did you ever stop to think that there may be a better way to live your life? Do you ever worry about your soul?" I raise my arm and shake my Bible at him. "The Bible says 'Believe on the Lord, Jesus Christ and thou shalt be saved.'" I realize I must look more like I'm trying to exorcise him than convert him, and I lower my arm.

Vinnie gives a little bark of laughter. He picks up a pack of cigarettes from the table next to him and shakes one loose. He looks at me over the flame of his match. "Do you really believe all that stuff?" he asks.

"Yes, I do," I say. "And it's worth your soul for you to believe it too."

Vinnie looks amused. "What'll happen to me if I don't?"

I hold up my Bible. "It's all in here, Vinnie. If you don't believe, then you're just opening the door and letting Satan rule your life."

Vinnie seems to consider this. He takes a deep drag from his cigarette and exhales a stream of smoke. "Does Satan have a big dick?" he asks. "Do you ever wonder about things like that?"

"Well, if you're going to go on like that..." I say.

"Does he?" Vinnie interrupts, his voice louder. He doesn't look amused now. His eyes drill into mine. "Is it thick and long? Do his balls hang down low?" He stands up so abruptly his chair topples back with a crash. He takes a step forward. "Do you ever wonder what it'd be like to suck it?"

I don't say anything for a while. "Is there a point you're trying to make?" I finally ask.

Vinnie's grin is boyish, but his eyes are two hard chips of stone. He walks over and stands before me, his crotch inches from my face. I can't help noticing the sizable bulge under the frayed denim of his jeans.

"Just answer the question," Vinnie says, his voice louder now. "Do you ever think about giving Satan head?"

There's nothing I can say to that. I close my eyes and start praying, the words spilling out of my mouth in a steady stream.

Vinnie hits me across the face, not hard, and with an open palm. It's a blow not meant to hurt, but to get my attention. It works. I stop praying and glare up at him. "I wouldn't do that again if I were you," I say.

"Do you wonder about how Satan's cock would feel crammed down your throat?" Vinnie sneers. "Or shoved up your ass?" He's clenching and unclenching his fists now. "Is that what you want, to get fucked by Satan?"

"Sweet Jesus, but you've got a filthy mouth."

"I do, huh?" Vinnie growls. "Well, then what about me? Maybe you'd like to chew on my dick for a while." With a quick movement, he unzips his fly and yanks his jeans down. His hard dick springs out in front of him, inches from my face. "How about it?" he sneers. "How do I measure up?"

I stare at the thick shaft of flesh before me. "I've seen bigger," I lie.

"Bullshit!" Vinnie snarls. He grabs my shoulders and pins me on the couch. I struggle, but I don't have enough purchase room to break free. Vinnie straddles my torso, his meaty red cock looming above my face. He grabs hold of it and slaps it hard against my left cheek, with a loud *thwack*. "Aren't you supposed to turn the other cheek now?" he jeers.

"Why are you doing this to me?" I cry out. "I came here to help you!"

"Shut up!" Vinnie snarls. He glares down at me. "You Jesus boys make me want to *puke*! Goddamn hypocrites!" He stands up and kicks off his sneakers and jeans. He pulls his tank top off last; I watch as it slides up over his body, revealing a hairless torso packed with muscles. I stare at his naked body, the sharp cut of the muscles; the smooth, chiseled abs; his meaty, dark cock jutting straight out before him. "I want you to get on your knees before me like you're going to pray," he says, "and lick my balls. Lick them for Jesus."

I don't move. I can't take my eyes off his body. With a snarl, Vinnie pulls me off the couch and onto the floor before him. He yanks back my hair, and when I open my mouth to protest, he drops his balls in. The fleshy scrotum fills my mouth, and as if it had a mind of its own, my tongue starts bathing it, rolling it around, savoring the taste and heft of his ball meat.

"Yeah," Vinnie growls, "that's it. Give those balls a good washing."

I burrow my nose into his crotch and inhale deeply, breathing in the pungent, ripe scent. The smell travels down into my lungs, intoxicating me. It has the stench of Satan: raw, animal, musky. I can't get enough of it! I wrap my hand around his dick and begin stroking it, feeling the living tube of flesh throb in my palm. I look at it hungrily, tracing the veins up the shaft, noticing how the head flares out, red and angry. If I were to picture Satan's dick, it *would* look like this, just as meaty, just as dark and threatening. I slide my tongue up the fleshy shaft and swirl it around the cock head. Vinnie grunts his approval. I squeeze his dick and a clear drop of prejizz oozes out. I lap it up and then swoop down, taking Vinnie's dick deep down my throat. Vinnie gasps, and I feel a tinge of smugness that I've knocked him down a peg. I begin bobbing my head up and down, sliding my lips along the thick shaft. Vinnie seizes hold of my head with both hands and pumps his hips savagely. His cock rams hard against the back of my throat, slamming down it. I grab his ass cheeks with both hands and give them a good squeeze, feeling their smoothness and muscularity. I tug down my zipper and pull my own stiff dick out. I started beating off furiously, timing my strokes to Vinnie's thrusting hips.

We quickly settle into a fast-paced rhythm of cock sucking and pud pounding. It's been too long a time since I've had a dick in my mouth, and the old hunger sweeps over me again. Vinnie is relentless; he plows my face with his dick like there's hell to pay, but as brutal as he tries to be, I take it all in eagerly. Old skills that I haven't used for some time come back now, and I give Vinnie what I'm willing to bet is a truly righteous blow job. Vinnie's breath comes out in ragged grunts, then low whimpers. I look up and see the sweat dripping down his face, his eyes glazed, his mouth open. My lips slide down his shaft, and I bury my nose in his pubes, keeping his dick thrust deep inside my throat, working it with my tongue. I cup his fleshy balls in my hand and squeeze them. Vinnie groans and his legs begin to tremble. I take his dick out of my mouth and stroke it quickly. Vinnie's groans rise in volume; he throws back his head and bellows as his jizz shoots out, splattering against my face, coating my cheeks, my mouth, my eyes with his creamy load. His body shudders a few more times and then grows still. A few quick strokes with my hand is all I need before I feel my own load pulse out, oozing between my closed fingers. I groan loudly. Vinnie bends down and kisses me, pushing his tongue deep inside my mouth. He wraps his arms around me and holds me until the last of the spasms pass through me.

We lie like that for a few moments, Vinnie propped up against the couch, me lying in his arms. I can feel his chest rise and fall as he breathes. He looks down and our eyes meet. There's a moment of silence, and then we both laugh. Vinnie runs his finger along my cheek, scooping up a dollop of his come. "Jeez, what a mess!" he grins.

I laugh again. Vinnie disentangles himself and walks out of the room. He comes back with a towel, which he tosses to me. I wipe his load from my face. "Well, did you enjoy yourself?" he asks.

"You have to ask?" I grin. I toss him back the towel. "I think that was our best fantasy yet. Better than the TV repairman. Even better than the census taker."

Vinnie laughs again but says nothing. He picks up the fallen chair and puts it back by the table. I just lean back against the couch, watching his naked body. Even after just squirting a load, I feel myself getting turned on again, he's so goddamn handsome. "You're a natural at this—playing out these little fantasies I set up," I say. "You should go into acting."

Vinnie shakes his head. "No thanks. The escort business pays better."

Vinnie lets me use his shower. When I'm cleaned and dressed, I hand him the $100 I owe him. "I'll give you a call in a couple of weeks," I say, "after I work out another fantasy. Maybe something involving a cop next time."

Vinnie shrugs. "Whatever you want, Gary." Now that he's out of character, he's amiable and relaxed. He's actually a sweet guy when he's not acting out some role.

He walks me to his door. Next to it stands a side table cluttered with envelopes, notepads, and an appointment calendar. There's also a framed photograph on it I hadn't noticed before. I glance at it briefly. Vinnie and another man are standing on the deck of a cabin cruiser, the sea and a sunny sky behind them. Both men are laughing and have their arms around each other. Vinnie's friend has those all-American good looks found in milk commercials: wavy red hair, a boyish face, a compact, muscular body. The two of them make a very handsome couple, and I feel a pang of envy at how *happy* they look.

I pick up the picture for a closer look. "Your friend's a good-looking guy." I glance toward Vinnie. "Where was this taken?"

Vinnie gives me a polite smile, but there's a tightness to it that wasn't there before. "Cancún," he says. He takes the picture from my hand and puts it back on the table. "Well, good night."

I can take a hint; we shake hands, and I leave.

About a week later, I run into Vinnie on Castro Street. Well, 'run into' isn't exactly right. I see him on the other side of the street, waiting in line in front of the Castro Theater. A re-edited version of *Blade Runner* has just been released, and there's a good crowd of people queued up. It's a little after 9 on a Saturday night, and the neighborhood is just beginning to come alive. The restaurants are full, and the music from the bars spills out onto the sidewalks. It's a warm evening, unusual for San Francisco, and the uniform of the night seems to be tank tops and shorts. Vinnie's no exception, and the gym shorts and T-shirt he's wearing show off his muscular body to good effect. Vinnie's with someone; in fact he's got his arm draped around the other guy's shoulder. The gesture is too casual to be erotic, but it's that very casualness that makes it look so intimate.

I'm in no rush, and because I'm a nosy little fucker, I stop and watch them from the doorway of a doughnut shop. There's something familiar about the guy with Vinnie, but I can't quite place him. I look at him closely and suddenly make the connection. He's the man I saw in the picture with Vinnie. Only I can see now that the photo was incredibly flattering; in real life he isn't nearly as good-looking. In fact, he's actually kind of scrawny and worn around the edges. This surprises me. A guy with Vinnie's looks could easily do a lot better. Hell, he could get anybody he wanted. Vinnie's friend says something to Vinnie, and Vinnie grins. Once again I'm struck by how fuckin' beautiful Vinnie is; it breaks my heart just to look at him. After a while I move on.

Later, in a bar, as I'm talking and laughing with friends, that scene with Vinnie and his friend flashes through my mind. *What does Vinnie see in that scrawny little fucker?* I wonder. But someone says something to me, and I let the thought drop.

The phone rings and rings, and I start to wonder if Vinnie's out. It's been over two months since we acted out our little Jehovah's Witness fantasy, and my dick is hard and juicin' with the thought of him naked in bed with me. I'm a regular client, and I usually don't let so much time go by between sessions, but with business trips and a two-week vacation in Hawaii, things just got in the way. But now I'm ready to make up for lost time—no fantasies, no role-playing, just down-home, sweaty, gruntin' sex.

Someone finally picks up the phone. "Hello?"

"Yo, Vinnie," I say. "It's Gary."

"Hi," Vinnie's voice sounds oddly flat.

"How have you been?" I ask.

"OK."

There's a long silence. I begin wondering if for some reason Vinnie's put off with me. Last time I told him that I'd call in a couple of weeks; is he pissed because I've taken so long?

"Is everything OK?" I ask. "You sound kind of funny."

"I'm fine." Another pause. "So what's up?"

I clear my throat. "I was wondering if we could get together again tonight. Nothing fancy, no fantasies this time, just a regular roll in the hay."

There's a long silence on the other end of the line. For a moment I wonder if we've been disconnected. "All right," Vinnie finally says. "What time?"

His tone is really putting me off. He sounds so *remote*. "Around 10 o'clock maybe?" I say. I hear my own voice taking on a certain coolness, matching his.

"Yeah, that'll be fine," he says. He hangs up without saying goodbye.

I sit there with the phone still in my hand. *That was weird,* I think, as I return the receiver to its cradle. Vinnie's usually a friendly, charming guy.

I go through the evening thinking about that conversation and getting more and more annoyed. A large part of Vinnie's charm as an escort comes from his being a friendly, down-to-earth guy, a rare trait for someone in his line, especially if they're as hot as he is. If he's going to suddenly start copping an attitude with me, that'll kill the mood for sure. I begin thinking about the possibility of canceling with Vinnie and finding someone else. God knows the city's full of handsome guys willing to turn a trick if the price is right.

The latest issue of the local gay rag is on my coffee table. I pick it up and start flipping through the pages toward the back section, where the escorts and sex masseurs advertise. I find myself in the obituaries and I'm about to turn the page again when one of the notices catches my eye. I recognize the picture immediately: it's Vinnie's red-haired friend; in fact, it looks like the photo's been cropped from the framed picture I saw on Vinnie's side table. I sit and read the obituary, all the way to the end. The man's name was Steve Benson; he was 26 when he died, cause of death: "complications due to AIDS." The obituary ends by saying that Steve is survived by his mother, his father, a sister, and his loving partner, Vincent. I see that the funeral was today.

I look at the picture of the laughing man for a few seconds more and then close the paper. *Oh, shit!* I think. *Poor Vinnie.*

Vinnie answers the door in his bathrobe. He smiles apologetically. "Hi, Gary," he says. "I'm running a little late. I just got out of the shower." He stands aside and motions for me to enter. I walk in and sit on the couch. "Do you want a beer or something?" he asks. I shake my head, watching Vinnie closely. He seems pretty normal, a little subdued maybe. As always, I'm struck by how handsome he is. I think of the naked, muscular body under that terry-cloth robe and feel my dick begin to stiffen.

"It's been a while," I say.

Vinnie smiles. Some of his old charm comes back into his face. "Yeah, I've been wondering what happened to you. Everything OK?"

I nod. "Sure. Things are all right." I let a few seconds go by. "How about you?"

Vinnie shrugs. "Yeah, things are fine."

Both of us are silent for a few seconds. Vinnie finally walks over to the couch and slips off his robe. It falls to the floor, around his feet. I sit back and look at him, the beautifully sculpted body, the thick dick hanging between his thighs. "What a handsome man you are," I say.

Vinnie gives a small smile. "Let's go back to the bedroom."

I undress by the nightlight Vinnie keeps going next to his bed. Vinnie is already lying on top of his bedspread, his legs splayed, his hands behind his head. Once I'm naked, I slip in beside him, kissing him lightly on the lips. My mouth travels south, against his neck, stopping for a moment at each nipple, then down across the hard, rippled expanse of his belly. Vinnie lies motionless. I rest his dick in my hand and kiss it too; even soft, it has an impressive thickness. I put it in my mouth and started sucking, twisting my head from side to side for maximum effect. I flick my tongue over it, and then suck some more. Vinnie's dick stays limp in my mouth. After a couple of minutes I give it up. I look up at Vinnie's face.

Vinnie's staring somewhere over my shoulder, his expression unreadable. "Vinnie," I say softly. He turns his head toward me and looks me full in the face. His eyes have the stunned, baffled look of plane-crash victim. Beneath the shock, all I see is despair; he's drowning in it. I have never seen so much grief in another person's face.

"Ah, jeez, Vinnie" is all I can say. I reach up and stroke his cheek. After a few seconds I add, "I saw his obituary in the paper."

Vinnie stares at me for a long time, saying nothing. Suddenly, unexpectedly, his eyes brim with tears. He reaches down and pulls me up against him. We lie in bed, our naked bodies pressed together, my face against Vinnie's neck. My hands stroke his back, up and down, kneading the skin. There's nothing erotic in my intent; it's just the only way I know to comfort him. I feel his hands rub against my back as well. We lie together like that for a long time, his heart beating against my chest.

I'm not quite sure exactly when it happens, but there's a subtle change now in the way Vinnie's holding me, a newly purposeful tightness to the embrace. I look at him, and he returns my gaze. He slowly lowers his head and kisses me, pressing his lips gently against mine. He does it again, more passionately, this time slipping his tongue inside my mouth. His pelvis starts grinding against mine, and I can feel his dick thickening, getting harder. He starts dry-humping my belly, pushing his now-erect cock against my body. My own dick is stiff and ready for action.

He breaks away and opens the drawer of the nightstand, pulling a condom package out. I take it from him, tear it open, and roll it down his dick. Vinnie pulls a tube of lube out of the drawer and squirts a dollop on his palm. He reaches down and massages my ass, probing into my crack, pushing a finger up my bunghole. I groan. When I'm nicely lubed, he wraps me in his arms again, rubbing his body against mine. He works his thick, hard dick between my legs, and I take over from there, holding it with my hand, guiding it in. I breath deep, letting myself relax, welcoming the sensations of Vinnie's dick pushing its way up inside me.

Vinnie wraps his arms around me again and begins to pump his hips slowly. His hands travel over my torso, kneading the flesh, stroking it. With his eyes closed, he bends down and kisses my face, his lips gently pressing against my mouth, my eyes, my hair. He has never been this tender with me before. His thrusts pick up speed, and I move my body in time to them. Vinnie sighs his gratitude. I squeeze my ass muscles hard around Vinnie's thick root, and Vinnie sighs again. He kisses me again, shoving his tongue once more down my throat. I wrap my tongue around his, holding his face between my two hands. Vinnie's eyes are still closed, and it doesn't take a rocket scientist to figure out who he's pretending is in bed with him now.

With a quick movement, Vinnie flips me on my back and lies on top of me. His muscular torso, slippery with sweat, squirms against mine. He plows my ass with deep, quick thrusts now, his dick pulling almost completely out and then plunging all the way in, working its way deep inside me. Vinnie grinds his hips against mine, his balls pressed tight against my ass, his thrusts pushing me hard against the bed board. And yet, even with the tempo of the sex sped up, the tenderness remains. His hand is wrapped around my dick, greased by the lube, and he beats me off with long, slow strokes. I reach down and cup his balls in my hand. They're pulled up tight against his body, and I know that it won't be long before he blows his load. He pulls out again and then skewers me, his hips churning. I feel his body shudder, and I pull his face down to mine, kissing him hard. Vinnie cries out as the first wave of jizz slams into the condom up my ass. His hard torso heaves and bucks against mine with each succeeding spasm. Vinnie's strokes take me closer and closer to climax, and then suddenly I'm shooting too, squirting my load into his hand, my groans covered by Vinnie's mouth over mine. Our bodies strain and push against each other and then fall apart.

I glance over at Vinnie. He's lying on his back, staring up at the ceiling, his softening dick still encased in the rubber. I finally get up and pull my clothes on. Vinnie doesn't say anything or make a movement. For a moment I think he's fallen asleep, but when I look, his eyes are still open.

When I'm finally dressed, I pull my wallet out of my back pocket and fish out a wad of twenties. I sit on the edge of the bed and shake Vinnie's shoulder. He turns his head and looks at me, saying nothing. The misery in his eyes hasn't changed. I never know what to say in moments like this. "Here's the money I owe you," I say, feeling very awkward.

Vinnie pushes my hand away. "Forget it." He manages a small laugh. "Tonight it's on the house." I squeeze his arm, but I can't think of anything to say. "Good night, Gary," Vinnie finally says.

I stand. "Good night, Vinnie." I walk out the bedroom door. When I'm in the living room, I glance at the picture of Vinnie and his lover, Steve, laughing on the cabin cruiser. I slide the money under it and leave the apartment.

Outside, I see that the fog has rolled in over Twin Peaks, and the night has turned chilly. So much for our Indian Summer. I zip up my coat and jam my hands in my pockets. It's late and nobody else is out on the streets. *The last time I was with Vinnie, I was a Jehovah's Witness. Tonight I was his dead lover.* I decide that I just might take a break from fantasy for a while. I climb into my car and drive down the deserted streets toward home.

BIRDS

It's a quarter after 10, I'm already 15 minutes late for my appointment, and I can't find a damn house number that will tell me where I am. It looks like I'm lost; the city planner who laid out the streets around here must have been tripping on acid. I hate being late; it's so unprofessional, something amateurs that hustle in porno video booths do. The radio is tuned to KFOG and was playing rock until just a moment ago. Now the news is on: a teachers' strike in Sacramento, a tornado in Abilene, something about birds in Bodega Bay. I turn the dial until I find a classic rock station. "Well, don't you know about the bird? Everybody knows that the bird's the word!" a gravelly voice sings. *What's this shit?* I think, switching off the radio.

By the time I find the place, it's almost 10:30. I just hope the client is in a forgiving frame of mind. And Tony too, when I show up late after I'm done with "work." I race up the concrete walk, taking the steps two at a time, and ring the bell. "Yeah?" somebody says on the intercom.

"Hi," I say. "It's Nick."

"You're late." He doesn't sound happy about the fact.

"I'm sorry. I got lost."

There's a long pause. I'm beginning to wonder if he's going to call the whole thing off. Some clients are jittery the first time, and it only takes something small to spook them. But he finally buzzes me in, and I push open the door into the lobby. There's a mirror that runs the length of the right-hand wall. I check out my appearance, running my fingers through my hair, straightening my leather jacket, practicing my James Dean squint. I should be able to turn this guy's mood around in no time.

When I make it to his apartment, the door is ajar. I push it open and walk in a couple of steps. "Hello?" I call out.

"Over here," a voice answers.

I walk into the living room. The guy is standing across the room by the window, the San Francisco skyline fanning out behind him. He's got the lights on dim, but a quick glance tells me all I need to know: he won't be a problem. He's in his early 40s, trim, tall, with thinning blond hair that lightens to gray at the temples. His eyebrows are blond too, blending in with his tan, giving his face a smooth, bald look. "Hi," I say. "I take it you're Steve."

The guy nods, his expression noncommittal. "And you're Nick."

I grin. "In the flesh." I look around the room. Steve goes for the exotic look. There are Balinese masks along one of the walls, a Tibetan mandala on another, Mayan figurines on the mantle, potted plants everywhere. A standing cage with a red and yellow parrot inside inhabits a niche by the window. "This is nice," I say. Actually, the place looks like a Cost Plus Imports showroom.

Steve smiles. He's beginning to warm up. "Do you want a drink?"

"Sure. A beer if you have one."

"No problem." Steve exits through a swinging door into the kitchen.

I walk over to the window and check out the view. I'm beginning to relax now, settle into the situation. The parrot gives a loud squawk. "How ya doin?" I say softly. I stick my finger between the cage bars and wiggle it at him. The parrot cocks his head and looks at it. With a loud squawk, it throws itself against the bars and digs its hooked beak into my finger.

"Jesus Fuck!" I cry out. I jerk my hand away. There's a ragged gash down the length of the finger. Blood oozes out and begins to drip on Steve's off-white shag carpet.

Steve rushes into the living room, a beer bottle in one hand, a glass of red wine in the other. "What's wrong?"

"Your parrot just bit me!" I exclaim. I hold my dripping hand out for him to see.

Steve looks put off. "What were you doing to it?"

Now I'm really getting pissed. "I didn't do anything!" My finger is beginning to throb, and the blood drips down the length of

my hand, past the heel of my palm and over my wrist. I cup my
other hand under the bright red trickle, trying to catch the flow
before any more of it stains Steve's fucking carpet. "I just wiggled
my finger at it."

Steve looks at the wound. "That's a pretty deep gash," he says.
He leads me into the bathroom and holds my hand under the sink
faucet. After the blood is washed away, he looks at the wound
more closely. "I don't think it'll need stitches." He opens the medicine cabinet and pulls out a bottle of iodine. "This is going to
sting." He splashes some iodine on the cut. Sting is an under-
statement. I bite down on my lip, and my eyes brim with tears.
Not quite the butch punk image I was trying to convey. Steve
wraps my finger in gauze and leads me back to the living room. I
sit down on the couch and glumly sip my beer as he cleans my
blood off the carpet.

Steve looks up and gives me a tight grin. "This isn't going too
well, is it?"

"Not really," I say.

He sits down beside me and takes a sip of wine. "Maybe we
should just call it off."

Yeah, right, I think. *I'm going to walk out of here empty-handed after
all this aggravation.* "No, no," I say hurriedly. "It'll be OK. Let's
just give it a chance." I put my hand on Steve's thigh.

Steve gives me a hard look. I can almost hear the gears in his
brain click and whir as he weighs the pros and cons of going
through with this. His blue eyes sweep down my body and up to
my face again. I smile at him. *Come on, Steve,* I think. *Don't start copping an attitude with me.* He allows himself to smile back. "You're
very handsome," he says.

OK, now things are finally settling into familiar patterns.
"Thanks." I slide my hand up and down Steve's thigh, increasing the
pressure. There's an expectant pause. When Steve doesn't do anything, I lean over and kiss him, gently at first, my mouth barely
touching his, and then with increasing pressure. Steve relaxes his
mouth, and I slip my tongue in. His hands slide under my T-shirt,
kneading the muscles of my torso, tweaking my nipples.

Steve pulls away. "Why don't you get naked?" he asks quietly.

"No problem," I smile. I climb to my feet and turn toward him. I kick off my shoes, pull off my socks, unzip my fly slowly, my eyes never leaving Steve's. My jeans drop down around my ankles, and I step out of them. Steve leans back against the couch, his arms along the back, his eyes attentive. I hook my thumbs under the elastic bands of my Jockeys.

"No," Steve says abruptly. "Not yet. Just stand there."

"OK," I say. I start posing for him, flexing my arms, twisting my torso so that the light catches the ripple of my muscles.

Steve slides off the couch and onto his knees before me. His hands once more play over my torso, working their way across my belly, brushing lightly against my cock, squeezing my thighs. His eyes take on a dreamy look. "You're skin feels like silk," he says. "I love smooth, muscular bodies." He squeezes my hardening cock through the cloth of my briefs. A drop of precome stains the white cotton, and he leans forwards and presses his lips against the moist spot. His mouth opens, and he drags his tongue against the shape of my cock. The entire front of my briefs is wet with saliva and precome.

"I bet you've got a beautiful dick," he murmurs. He slides his fingers under the elastic waistband of my briefs, and slowly, lovingly pulls them down. My dick, bent down by the descending cloth, is revealed inch by inch. When the briefs clear it, it springs up and sways heavily in front of Steve's face. Once we get to this point, I'm home free. My dick is thick and meaty and red, with a head that flares out like a cobra's. My clients *always* love it.

Steve gazes at it with worshipful eyes. "Holy shit," he says under his breath.

"It likes being touched," I say.

Steve reaches up and wraps his hand around it. He gives it a squeeze, and another drop of prejizz oozes out. Steve coats his thumb with it and then rubs the clear fluid between his thumb and forefinger. His other hand cups my balls and gently tugs on them. "I love the way your balls fill my hand," he says. He leans forward and buries his face in them, and then pulls back and reaches behind him for his wineglass, still almost full. He presses the cool glass against my belly, slowly tipping it. Wine trickles down through my pubes, across my dick, dripping off my balls. Steve positions his face upward, between my legs, catching the red liquid in his mouth, his tongue lapping it off my wine-drenched ball sac. Wine dribbles down his chin and splashes onto the carpet below. *His carpet's getting a workout tonight,* I think.

Steve is sucking on my nuts now, rolling his tongue over them, licking every drop of wine off. His tongue works its way up the underside of my dick, licking it like a meaty popsicle. When he gets to the head, he swirls his tongue around it, his eyes never leaving mine. He slides his mouth down the length of the shaft, his lips nibbling all the way. He doesn't stop until his nose is buried in my pubes.

I begin pumping my hips, slowly at first and then with increasing speed. My dick slides in and out between Steve's lips, pushing against the roof of his mouth. I reach over and cradle his head in my hands, not forcing him, just steadying him as I fuck his face with my long, deep strokes. Steve is no slouch at cock sucking; his tongue plays along the shaft skillfully, and he angles his head so he can take in the full eight inches. He reaches behind and grabs my ass cheeks with both hands, squeezing them like cantaloupes he's thinking of buying.

He breaks away and looks up at me. "Let's go to the bedroom," he says.

"OK," I say.

The bedroom is small and boxy and dominated by a queen-size brass bed. A wide-screen television is mounted on the wall facing the bed. It's turned on, but the sound is turned down so that the images flicker noiselessly. Steve catches my questioning glance toward it.

"I always leave it on," he says. "It keeps me company."

"You've already got company," I say.

"I always leave it on," he repeats.

Whatever, I think. I jump onto the bed and prop myself up on my elbows. My legs are spread apart in a V, and my dick lies hard against my belly. I give it a couple of twitches for Steve's benefit. Steve stands at the foot of the bed, his eyes scanning up and down the length of my body. He pulls off his clothes, his eyes never leaving me. When he's finally naked, he crawls in between my legs and takes my cock in his mouth again. I sink my head into the pillow and let the sensations of his warm, wet mouth sweep over my body.

"You feel like fucking my ass?" Steve asks.

I open my eyes and look down at him. I smile. "Sure. If that's what you want."

Steve pulls out a condom and a jar of lube from the drawer of the night table next to the bed. I watch, my hands behind my head, as he rolls the condom down my dick. He leans forward and kisses me again. I scoop out a dollop of the grease and run my hand between the crack of Steve's ass. I find the pucker of his asshole and work a finger up inside, knuckle by knuckle. Steve closes his eyes, and then opens them again, smiling. "Oh, yeah!" he sighs.

I pull my finger out, and poke the head of my cock against his asshole with teasing jabs, not penetrating him yet. Steve sits astride my hips, his hands flicking my nipples as I slowly enter him. "Jeez, that feels good," he groans. I wrap my greased hand around his dick and start stroking. Steve's body is firm and furry, his chest lightly dusted with a patch of sandy hair that trails down his belly before thickening once more in his pubes. Leaning forward, he starts riding my dick, and we begin our little horizontal dance, moving our bodies together, getting the feel of each other's rhythms. We fuck well, pacing ourselves nicely, and I find I'm actually enjoying myself. Steven notices this and looks down at me and smiles. It's nice when this happens, when the client has some finesse about him. I start making sex noises, some of my groans and sighs genuine, some of them theater for Steve's benefit.

I speed up my hand strokes on Steve's dick. He gives a little gasp with each downward plunge of my hand; after a while, the gasps become trailing whimpers. His balls are pulled up tight; it won't be long before he's ready to blow his load. I thrust my dick hard up his ass and keep it there, pivoting my hips. Steve groans loudly. I'm getting close too, and I know that with a little maneuvering I can time it so that we come together. The clients always appreciate that when it happens and often show it in their tips. I thrust again, feeling my load getting pulled up from my balls. Another stroke and I'm almost there—I glance behind Steve and happen to look at the flickering TV screen behind him.

"Holy shit!" I exclaim.

"What's wrong?" Steve asks, alarmed. He catches the direction of my gaze and looks behind me at the television. The 11 o'clock news is on, and the television shows a picture of pure chaos, what looks like a small town under attack by...birds! Seagulls, there must be *thousands* of them, are dive-bombing the downtown section, smashing into windows, plummeting down on people trying to find cover. A man staggers past the camera with at least a dozen birds perched on him, pecking savagely. Birds dive directly at the camera, which wheels crazily around, showing a glimpse of store-fronts: a diner, a hat store, a shop with the sign BODEGA BAY PHARMACY mounted above. The camera jerks around again, and focuses briefly on a phone booth with a young blond woman trapped inside, seagulls smashing into the glass sides. Flames shoot out from buildings in the background. More gulls plunge at the camera, and the picture suddenly goes dark. The news anchor comes back on air. Steve searches for the remote, lost somewhere in the bedclothes, but by the time he finds it, the station has cut to a commercial.

"That was weird," I say.

Steve shrugs, and I know he's annoyed. I can't blame him; my timing was lousy, interrupting our sex right at the moment when we were both about to shoot. Hardly the actions of a professional. "Now where were we?" I ask, smiling, trying to salvage the moment. We wind up jacking each other off, Steve shooting his load on my face, a liberty I don't usually allow my clients to take. He licks it off, slowly, his tongue dragging across my cheeks like a cocker spaniel's. I lie in bed with him, holding him longer than normal. When I leave, Steve pays me the $150 he owes me, but doesn't tip me.

In the car, I play back the events of the evening. *Tonight has been weird!* I think. I glance down at my hand on the steering wheel, the index finger wrapped in gauze, still throbbing like a motherfucker. *Maybe I should have a doctor look at it.* Suddenly, without warning, something crashes into my windshield. For a second, I think someone threw a rock, but then I see the small, crumpled body of a sparrow slide down the glass, smearing it with blood and rolling off the hood. Slowing down, I check out the windshield; there's a small crack right at the point of impact. *What the fuck is going on with all the birds?*

I drive down Geary Boulevard, threading through the late-night traffic, until I reach the Cliff House restaurant, perched on a spit of rock overlooking the Pacific. I pull into the parking lot, jump out of my car, and walk briskly to the restaurant. The moon is nearly full and leaves a long, wavering trail across the ocean. A few seagulls wheel overhead in the night sky, calling to each other. *I didn't know gulls flew at night,* I think. I take the steps up to the restaurant door two at a time.

Tony sits at an empty table in the main dining room, now dark except for a single wall sconce on the far side of the room. I hear the kitchen crew in back, still cleaning up, talking to each other in Spanish. Tony does not look like a happy camper. "You're late," he says.

"Yeah," I say. "I've been getting that a lot lately." I walk over to him and bend down to kiss him. Tony turns his handsome head away. "Don't be like that, baby," I say. "I couldn't help it. I got held up at work."

"Work," Tony snorts. We usually avoid talking about how I make my living. He glances down and notices my bandaged hand. "What happened to your hand?" he asks.

"The client had a parrot," I say. Tony gives me a long, hard stare. "Don't give me that look," I say, exasperated. "It was a pet, for God's sake. It wasn't part of the sex act."

Tony stands and pulls his jacket off the back of his chair. "Let's get out of here."

We walk silently down the restaurant stairs. The night feels balmy, almost tropical, a rare occurrence in San Francisco. I reach down and take Tony's hand in mine. He doesn't resist, but his fingers don't give mine an answering squeeze. I tug his arm gently toward the cliff face. "Let's just take a walk, baby," I say. "It's such a nice night."

"It's late," Tony says. "And I'm tired."

"Just a short walk," I urge.

Tony relents. We walk along the cliff's edge, listening to the surf below. The moon looks like a searchlight. I notice more gulls than normal are wheeling around overhead. "There's something strange going on with birds tonight," I say. Tony doesn't say anything, but I feel the stiffness in his hand easing up. I let go and gently squeeze his neck. "Don't be mad at me, Tony," I say. "I fuckin' love you." I pull Tony to me and we kiss, gently at first, our lips nibbling together, then with greater intensity. I slide my hands under Tony's shirt, feeling the warm, smooth hardness of his torso. I flick my thumbs across his nipples and then squeeze them. Tony sighs and presses his body against mine. I feel his hard dick thrust up against me through the denim of his jeans. He slides his hands across my slacks and squeezes my dick.

"You got something there for me?" he asks. "Or did you use it all up on your *client?*"

I give a low laugh. "Baby, the pump is always primed for you."

We find a flat grassy spot not far from the cliff edge and stretch out on it. I slowly undress Tony, unbuttoning his shirt, pulling off his shoes and jeans. He does the same for me, and I wrap my arms around him, feeling his naked skin against mine. The restaurant is totally dark now, and the only light comes from the moon washing over us. Tony's skin looks like marble in its light. He is so fuckin' beautiful, it breaks my heart.

Tony lies naked on the grass, propped up on his elbows, watching me roll a condom down my stiff dick. I hoist his legs around me and penetrate him slowly, my mouth planted on his. Tony groans softly. We lie together on the grass, motionless for a minute, my dick full up his ass, my body pressed tightly against his. I start pumping my hips, slowly at first, and then with greater intensity, my mouth planted on his. Tony thrusts his hips up to meet me, and I give a muffled groan of gratitude. We settle down into the serious business of fucking, and I proceed to plow Tony's ass with long, deep plunges.

This is the second time I've fucked in less than an hour, and even in the heat of the action, I can't help but notice the difference in the sex. Steve was all right, but Tony knows my body well; he knows which little pulls and thrusts drive me crazy, and the sex with him ratchets up to a peak I could never reach with a client. Tony's eyes drill into mine. He's gasping now, stroking his dick in sync with every thrust of mine; his tight, muscular torso squirming against mine. *This is so fine!* I think The night breeze from the ocean plays over my body. I hear the palm fronds rustle overhead and seagulls crying to each other. Loudly. I give one final deep thrust and feel myself slowly fall over the edge into the orgasm, like some great boulder crashing down a hillside. My body trembles and I groan loudly.

"Pull it out," Tony growls. "I want to see you shoot your load."

I pull out and whip the condom off. My dick throbs in my hand as my load squirts out, one pulse after another, splattering against Tony's face: his cheeks, his chin, below his eyes. "Yeah," he growls. "That's right." He groans as his own load squirts out between his fingers.

I look down at him, grinning. Drops of my come slide down his face. "Jeez, you're a mess," I laugh. I bend down and drag my tongue across his face, lapping up my load.

I hear a whirring noise, and something strikes me against the back of my head.

"What the fuck?" I exclaim. I jerk my head around just in time to see a seagull dive into my face. I duck and feel its beak tear along the side of my head. Something wet and sticky trickles down my head. I touch my head and see that my fingers are red with blood.

Suddenly the sky is alive with gulls, fluttering directly over-head, crying raucously, wings whirring as one by one they swoop down on us.

"Holy shit!" Tony cries out. We jump to our feet, our arms beating off the attack.

"Run for it!" I shout. "Get to the car!" Tony reaches for his jeans. A gull swoops down and rakes his face with its talons. He cries out. "Forget the fuckin' clothes!" I shout. "Just run!"

We hightail it naked along the cliff's edge, the gulls dive-bombing us, screeching like banshees. By the time we make it back to the car, we're both streaked with blood. I say a quick, silent prayer of gratitude that I hadn't locked the car doors. We jump in and slam the doors behind us. The gulls start smashing against the windshield.

"Let's get the fuck out of here!" Tony says. His eyes are wide with shock. Blood streams down his face.

I look at him. "How do you propose I do that?" I ask. "The car keys are in my pants pocket back by the cliff."

"Shit," Tony mutters.

We sit there naked in the front seat, watching the gulls do their kamikaze attacks against the windshield. It's only a matter of minutes before the car's hood is piled deep with their crumpled bodies. The windshield is a constellation of stars from the shattered glass, and we jump every time another gull splatters against it. I glance at Tony and wonder if I look as scared as he does.

"If they smash through the windshield, we're dogmeat," Tony says in a low, quivering voice.

"Thanks for sharing," I say.

And then, just as suddenly as it began, the attack is over. The gulls wheel around the car a bit more and then take off toward the ocean, their bodies silhouetted by the moonlight as they skim off into the distance. Tony and I sit in the car for a long time without speaking. It takes a few minutes more before I finally work up the nerve to get out of the car and dash back to the cliff's edge for our clothes. I swoop them up into my arms and race back to the car. I fling them into Tony's lap, as I dive back into the front seat. "Get the car key," I snap.

Tony fishes it out of my pants pocket and thrusts it into my hand. I jam it into the ignition and shift down into first. "Can't we get dressed first?" Tony says.

"Fuck that!" I say. "We'll get dressed when we've got a few miles between us and this goddamn place." I roar out of the lot and tear down Geary Boulevard.

The dashboard clock says it's a little after midnight. The neighborhoods we pass through seem normal enough, people out on the street, windows lighted. I have to drive with my head out of the window because I can barely see through the broken, blood-smeared windshield. We pass by the Balboa Theater, dark now, its marquee announcing a Hitchcock double feature. The scene at the cliff seems like a bad dream, but I don't need the crusted blood on my face or smashed windshield to remind me otherwise.

"It's the environment," Tony mutters. "We've been fucking around with Nature all these years, and now she's getting back at us."

My head is throbbing, and I still feel badly shaken. "Look," I say irritably, "just spare me your crackpot theories right now, OK?" I glance at Tony. His mouth is drawn into a tight line. I reach over and squeeze his hand. "Sorry, baby," I say.

I glance up at the telephone wires that flank the street. More pigeons than I have ever seen in my life are roosted on them, bodies pressed tightly together, the wires sagging under their weight. One by one they start fluttering up into the night sky. "Shit," I mutter. I press my foot hard against the accelerator and tear down the road toward home.

HITCH COCK

Phil and I hang out all afternoon in the head of the Statue of Liberty, waiting for the crowd to thin. I spend most of the time staring out the windows, like James Stewart in *Rear Window*, only, unlike James, I don't witness Raymond Burr slicing up his wife, just the tugs and freighters steaming up and down the East River. Seagulls wheel around in the sky above, swooping and rising like the crows dive-bombing Tippi Hedren and the schoolchildren in *The Birds*. Phil is pacing back and forth, growing more and more tense, his eyes shifting nervously like, like...John Hodiak in *Lifeboat*? Farley Granger in *Strangers on a Train*? Henry Fonda in *The Wrong Man*? No, I decide, definitely most like Robert Cummings in *Saboteur* when he's hiding out with the sideshow freaks in the circus train as the feds search for him car by car. This is very fitting, since the fantasy we're about to act out comes from the same movie.

Phil glances at his watch and then at me. He really is a handsome man, his dark eyes snapping with intensity, his sexy mouth pulled down in a worried scowl. "This place is going to close in less than an hour," he says in a low voice. "If we're going to pull this off, we'd better do it damn soon."

He's right, of course. I look around. There's been a steady stream of tourists since we first arrived, but a group of school kids has just left, and now there's just us and three others. This might be as close to a chance as we're going to get. I sidle over to the exit door and look down. The stairs are narrow and steep, and I feel a wave of acrophobia, like James Stewart in *Vertigo* when he's chasing Kim Novak up the bell tower. For the moment, I don't see anyone. I catch Phil's eye and jerk my head. He nods, picks up his gym bag, and we race down to the first landing. The main stairs continue on down from here through the trunk of Liberty to the exit below. But a wire mesh fence with a padlocked door separates us from a ladder that ascends up Liberty's arm to the lamp she's holding.

We both glance up and down the stairs. Still nobody in sight, but we can hear footsteps below, ascending. More sightseers, most likely, and they'll be up here in less than a minute. Phil quickly unzips his gym bag and pulls out a pair of bolt cutters. It takes just a couple of seconds to slice through the padlock. The sound of steps is louder now; the people will be here any second. Phil and I slip through the door and close it behind us. I replace the padlock so that, unless someone looks at it closely, it still seems securely locked. Phil and I scramble up the ladder.

We push open a small door in the base of Liberty's lamp and find ourselves outside, on the tiny balcony that rings the flame. My heart is pounding with excitement. Phil opens his mouth to say something, but I quiet him with a gesture; I want to soak in this moment in the proper silence. This is where Robert Cummings corners and accidentally kills Norman Lloyd, the Nazi assassin and bomber, in the final scene in *Saboteur*. A slight breeze blows in from Staten Island and ruffles through my hair. The sun is low in the sky, squatting over the Meadowlands and the apartment buildings in Bayonne. I glance over toward Phil. He's watching me, his eyes amused, his mouth curled in a sly grin. "We don't have much time," he says. "Let's get this show on the road."

"All right," I laugh. I pull Phil toward me and plant my mouth over his. Phil is a good three or four inches shorter than me, a bantam cock of man with a wiry, compact body, and I have to bend my neck downward to kiss him. His tongue pushes through toward the back of my throat, and he starts grinding his crotch against mine. I reach behind him, cup his ass with my hands, and pull his body tight against me. I can feel his stiff dick push through the rough fabric of his jeans and rub against me. I slide my hands under his T-shirt and across the smooth muscles of his torso. I find the stiff nubs of his nipples and tweak them hard. Phil groans softly. He reaches down, unbuckles my belt, and pulls down the zipper of my fly. In a matter of seconds, my pants and shorts are down around my ankles. I step out of them, pull off my shirt and stand naked by Liberty's torch. It only takes a couple of moments to strip Phil naked as well.

Phil reaches down and wraps his hand around both our dicks, squeezing them together. I look down at the solid mass of dick flesh encircled by his fingers: my cock, pink and fat, leaking pre-come, pressed tight against Phil's dark, blood-engorged prick. Phil may be short in stature, but he's prodigiously hung, his dick thick and long, blue veins snaking up the meaty tuber. It is so damn exciting to be bare-ass naked with my good fuck buddy Phil out in the open on top of one of Hitchcock's most famous settings. A film buff's ultimate sexual fantasy. Phil starts jacking us off slowly, his hand moving up and down the twin columns of dick flesh.

I sink down to my knees, the pitted copper of the old balcony biting into my skin, and bury my face into Phil's fleshy ball sac, inhaling deeply, breathing in the ripe scent. I open my mouth and let his ball meat spill in, rolling it around with my tongue. Phil takes his stiff cock and slaps my face with it. "Yeah," he growls. "Suck on those balls. Juice them up good." I hold his cock at the base and squeeze it, watching it darken in color, its engorged head taking on the color and size of a small plum.

"Beautiful," I murmur. I slide my tongue up the fleshy shaft slowly, lovingly, and when I get to the head, I open my lips wide and take the whole cock in my mouth. Phil groans again. He holds my head with both hands, his fingers entwined in my hair, and starts pumping his hips with quick, staccato thrusts. I reach behind and grab his ass, squeezing the muscular cheeks as his dick slides in and out of my mouth. My fingers burrow into his ass crack and massage his bunghole, teasing and playing with the pucker of flesh. Phil sighs.

Far off in the distance I hear the low moan of a tugboat horn. It's followed shortly after by the higher pitched call of the Staten Island Ferry. As I feed on Phil's dick, I find myself wondering what kind of show we're providing for the traffic in the East River. Can the ferry passengers make out any details, or are we too distant to be noticed? I like to think that people are lining the decks, their binoculars trained on us, watching me give Phil head.

Phil's legs start to tremble. His balls are pulled up tight and his dick throbs in my mouth. The fucker's just about ready to shoot. I take his dick out of my mouth and start jacking him off. Phil groans loudly, his body spasms, and suddenly his jizz spurts out, splattering against my face, pelting my eyes, my nose, my cheeks. Another spasm sweeps over him, and then another. By the time he's done, his load is sliding down my face in thick, sluggish drops.

I wipe my hand over my face, sliming it up with his jizz, and start beating off. Phil pulls me to my feet, his hands playing up and down my body, pulling on my flesh, tugging my balls, stroking me all over. I close my eyes and arch my back as my jizz squirts out over the low copper railing into the empty air below. I find myself wondering if any of it splattered against the windows in Liberty's head.

Phil wraps his arms around me and kisses me. He breaks away, laughing. "Well, chalk up another Hitchcock landmark," he says. He glances at his watch. "Jesus! We got to get out of here. It's closing time."

We throw on our clothes. I reach up and touch Liberty's torch one last time before climbing down the ladder back to the main stairs. When we clamber into the lobby in the Statue's base, the guard looks at us with wide eyes. "Where the hell did you guys come from?" he asks. "I already checked for stragglers."

Phil shrugs and gives him his blandest expression. "I guess you missed us," he says.

Later, while standing on the deck of the ferry, we watch the Statue recede into the distance in the growing twilight. The lamp suddenly flashes on. Phil laughs. "If we were up there right now, can you imagine what kind of shadow show we'd be putting on?"

That night we watch *Psycho* sitting in the back row of a Greenwich Village movie house. Phil and I have our zippers down and dicks out even before Janet Leigh has driven out of Phoenix with the stolen $40,000. We jack each other off slowly, teasingly, as the film rolls on. As I sit back in my movie seat watching a Hitchcock film with Phil's thick, hard dick throbbing in my hand, I think, *Life doesn't get any better than this.* I finally shoot my load during the shower scene, my jizz squirting into Phil's hand as poor

Janet gets hacked to death by Anthony Perkins in his psychotic-mother drag.

The next day we fly out to Rapid City, South Dakota. We rent a car at the airport, drop off our bags at a Motel 6, and head out toward the Mount Rushmore Visitors' Center. The place is packed with tourists trying to milk the most out of their last remaining days of summer. Through the wide windows of the center I can see Mount Rushmore looming over us, the four presidents gazing benignly into the distance. Just like the scene where Eva Marie Saint shoots Cary Grant in *North By Northwest.*

When it's my turn at the counter, I check out the ranger behind it. The guy could be a poster boy for the National Park Service: mild blue eyes, a strong jaw, neatly clipped blond hair, broad shoulders underneath his crisply starched uniform. He looks like a Midwestern Swede, one of those corn-fed, earnest young farmers' sons that only the Bible Belt can produce. The name tag pinned over his right pec reads JOHANSON.

Ranger Johanson flashes me a polite smile. "Can I help you?" he asks.

I give him a cruisy smile in return, more of a knee-jerk reaction than a genuine effort to seduce. "You got any trail maps? My buddy and I are looking for some good trails to hike."

He pulls out a few maps from below the counter. I turn up the wattage of my smile. Ranger Johanson's eyes flick up and down my body, so quickly that if I weren't on the alert, I might have missed it. "Here you go," he says, his voice pleasant and detached.

I take them and join Phil over by the viewfinders. "You're such a dick pig," he says.

"I just smiled at him," I say. I pull out the maps. "It's going to be a real ball buster hike tomorrow. We're going to have to get up extra early." Phil doesn't say anything.

That evening, armed with our *Spartacus Guide to Gay America,* Phil and I explore the gay side of Rapid City. Slim pickings, at best. We wind up in a place called the Rendezvous Club, something straight out of the '50s, right up to the crepe wallpaper, the wall sconces with crystal pendants, and the Patsy Cline records on the jukebox. I buy a pitcher of beer and join Phil at a table at the far end of the room, over by the cigarette machine. I feel uneasy. Try as I can, I can't conjure up a Hitchcock scene this bar might evoke.

"This place depresses me," I say. "Let's blow."

"Relax," Phil says. "We've got nowhere else to go. Would you rather hang out in that dump of a motel?"

I shrug and say nothing. I gloomily watch the pool game in progress a few feet away. After a few minutes of silence, Phil nudges me in the side. "Look who just walked in."

I glance toward the door and see Ranger Johanson standing at the doorway, scanning the room. He's wearing jeans and a T-shirt that hugs his torso, revealing a tight, lean body. Johanson's eyes turn toward us, and he nods his head in greeting. He walks over to the bar, orders a beer, and walks over to our table.

"You guys mind if I join you?" he asks.

I push a chair out with my foot. "Have a seat." I stick out my hand. "I'm Larry. My friend's name is Phil."

Johanson shakes our hands. "Mike," he says. His glance shifts from me to Phil and back to me again. "You find a good trail to hike?" he asks.

"We know the general direction," I say. "We're going to the top of the monument. We've just got to figure out what trails will get us there."

Patsy is off the jukebox, and now Merle Haggard is singing "Okie From Muskogee." A couple of relics are playing liar's dice at the bar, shaking the dice cup and slamming it against the counter. Mike gives a slight smile. "You guys are ambitious. That's a killer hike."

We work through the pitcher of beer, making small talk. The conversation is polite, remote. I catch Phil sneaking a glance at his watch. Halfway through the next pitcher, Mike asks us how we know each other.

"We met at school," I say. "We're both studying film."

"Oh, yeah?" Mike says. "You guys want to make movies?"

"Yeah," Phil says. "That's the general game plan." He's having a hard time keeping the boredom out of his voice.

Mike takes a long sip from his glass. "You guys ever see that Hitchcock movie *North by Northwest?*"

I freeze, my glass raised halfway, and stare at Mike. "Yeah," I say cautiously, "what about it?"

"I fuckin' love that movie," Mike says. "I've seen it at least half a dozen times. You may find this dumb, but that scene where Cary Grant and Eva Marie Saint are chased down the presidents' heads on Mount Rushmore was one of the reasons I took a job here."

The blood is singing in my ears, and the background noise fades to a dull buzz. "You like Hitchcock?" I ask, trying to keep my voice calm.

"Like him?" Mike says. "I fuckin' love the dude! Especially his American movies. Except for *Marnie*, which sucks."

I glance over toward Phil. He returns my look, his eyes bright. I feel my dick growing stiff. I lean forward, pushing my beer glass aside. "Listen, Mike," I say, my voice rising in excitement. "As far as Phil and I are concerned, Hitchcock is God."

Mike leans back in his chair and looks at me. "I really don't for a moment believe that you invited me to these gay surroundings to come to a business arrangement," he says in a clipped voice.

Phil stares at him blankly, but I laugh. "James Mason's line to Cary Grant in the Mount Rushmore cafeteria."

"You got it," Mike says, grinning. He drains his glass empty and refills it from the pitcher. He shoots us a shrewd look. "Why are you guys hiking up to the monument?" Phil and I don't say anything. His eyes shift from Phil and back to me. "Come on," he says. "You can tell me. What are you two up to?"

Another silence. Phil clears his throat. "We just have a little ritual we perform," he says.

"Oh, yeah?" Mike's eyes are curious. His lips curve in a faint smile. "Tell me about it."

Phil and I exchange glances. Phil nods slightly. "We're spending the summer having sex at as many sites from Hitchcock's movies as possible," I say.

Mike laughs. "No shit!"

"Yeah," I say, warming up. "We've fucked late at night on the steps of the Bodega Bay schoolhouse, where Suzanne Pleshette gets pecked to death in *The Birds*. And on top of the San Juan Bautista Mission bell tower, where Kim Novak falls to her death in *Vertigo*.

We've squirted our loads on the railway ties in the Santa Rosa train yard where Teresa Wright shoves Joseph Cotten in front of a locomotive in *Shadow of a Doubt*. Yesterday we sucked dick on the Statue of Liberty's torch, from *Saboteur*." I take a sip of beer. "And now we're going to do Mount Rushmore, in honor of *North By Northwest*. Our homage to Hitchcock."

Mike's gaze flicks back and forth to Phil's face and mine. For the moment the jukebox is quiet, and the only sounds are the click of the pool balls and the slap of the liar's dice cups on the bar. "Let me tag along," he says. "Tomorrow's my day off. I can show you guys where the trails are."

Phil and I hem and haw, but after the fourth pitcher of beer we agree. We spend the rest of the evening quoting lines from scenes from various movies. The drunker we get, the funnier this seems. When we get to the part where I play Judith Anderson to Mike's Joan Fontaine in the scene from *Rebecca* where Judith tries to convince poor Joan to jump out of a window, I'm laughing so hard beer is coming out of my nose.

The three of us stand on top of the bluff, looking down at the view. Washington's nose is at quarter profile, but Lincoln's face is angled so that we can see it completely. We can just make out the tops of Jefferson's and Roosevelt's heads. My shirt is plastered to my back, and I'm caked with South Dakota grit. "Hell," I say, "Cary Grant had it easy. He got to take a fuckin' *taxi* to the top."

We scramble down the steep slope between Jefferson and Roosevelt, granite scree slipping out from beneath our feet and pitching off into the distant drop below. I'm beginning to wonder just how good an idea this is. Lincoln looms on our left, like a Macy's Thanksgiving Day balloon float, while Roosevelt is right before us, in profile, staring off into the distance. Phil points toward Roosevelt's eyes. "Check out his glasses."

Roosevelt's spectacles are connected by a broad band of rock, a couple of feet wide, running across the bridge of his nose. Without stopping to discuss it, Phil starts inching across the tiny crevices in Roosevelt's face, finding footholds and handholds in small cracks and ledges. In a couple of minutes he's standing on the spectacle band. He waves at us. "Come on over," he shouts. "It's easy."

Mike seems to have no problem with this. He follows Phil's route, scrambling over the rock, and soon joins him. There's no way I'm going to chicken out now. I crawl across Teddy's face like a human fly, my heart beating like a piston. I look down briefly and see several hundred feet of cliff beneath me. I don't look down again. A couple of feet above my head, Teddy's giant eyeball stares down at me.

Mike reaches over and pulls me onto the spectacle band. I stand there for a minute, catching my breath. Lincoln's face on my left now looks like the face of God, filling the sky. Jefferson and Washington hang over empty air on my right. Roosevelt's giant nose sweeps out beneath me like a ski slope. Beyond it is nothing but empty air.

Phil's already pulling his shirt over his head. Mike's face is flushed and his eyes dart between us. He reaches over and slides his hand under my shirt, tentatively at first. I can see his hard dick pushing against his shorts, and I give it a squeeze. I lean over and kiss Phil, sliding my hand over his sweat-slicked torso. As Phil and I tongue each other, Mike unzips my shorts and yanks them down. My half-hard dick flops against my thigh, and Mike wraps his hand around it. He turns and does the same to Phil. Phil and I keep on kissing as Mike squats between us, playing with our dicks, stroking them, squeezing them, tugging on our balls. A moment later Mike takes my dick in his mouth and slides his lips down the shaft. I give a small groan of appreciation. Mike turns his head and starts tonguing Phil's balls, burrowing his face into them as he strokes Phil's dick. I reach over and tweak Phil's nipple and his eyes flash.

Phil and I each grasp Mike by the arms and raise him. We carefully strip him, first pulling his shirt off, then tugging down his shorts and briefs. His dick springs straight up, hard and juiced, ready for action, already leaking jizz. I reach down and squeeze it, milking another clear drop of precome out. I slick my palm with it and slide my hand up and down the thick shaft as Phil tugs and strokes at the muscles of Mike's torso. Mike has a beautiful body: cut, lean, the chest furred with dark blond hair. His nipples are wide and dark pink, their nubs standing out like chewed erasers. I bend over and suck on them, first the left, then the right, gently biting on the rubbery tips. Mike groans. I reach down and cup his balls in my hand; they're covered with a light down and hang low, filling my palm in a meaty pile.

We stand on the ledge, jerking each other off. It is such a hot sight to have these two naked men on either side of me, stroking my dick, bringing me to the brink. Mike has the dick of a Midwestern Swede: uncut, pink, and fat, with a red, flaring head, not as big as Phil's monster schlong, but still a respectable handful. I press my back against the granite cliff of Roosevelt's forehead, a dick in each hand, and stroke them both lovingly.

I glance over toward Mike. He stares back at me, his forehead beaded with sweat, his mouth open, his eyebrows pulled down in concentration. "Mike," I say, "how would you like to fuck my ass?"

Mike's blue eyes gleam. "What Hitchcock movie is that line from?" he asks.

"I don't think Hollywood released it," I grin. "He was ahead of his time."

I pull out a condom package and a small container of lube from my shorts pocket and hand them to Mike. He laughs. "You guys have got this down to a science, don't you?"

"We like to be prepared," Phil says.

Mike squeezes a dollop of lube into his hands and slides his fingers between the crack of my ass. I lick Phil's nipples as Mike slides a greased finger into my chute and starts working it in and out. Tingling sensations radiate from my asshole through the rest of my body. I bury my face in Phil's sweaty armpit and nuzzle it greedily as Mike removes his finger and replaces it with his sheathed dick. Mike grasps my hips and thrusts forward, his cock sliding in inch by slow inch. I groan loudly, and Phil pulls back my head, thrusting his tongue into my mouth. Mike grinds his pelvis against me, rotating his hips, and it feels as if I have two feet of cock inside of me. As he starts pumping his hips, I slide my tongue down Phil's smooth torso, past the hard, cut belly, the black, crinkly pubes, and take Phil's cock in my mouth, sucking greedily, rolling my tongue over the thick shaft.

It doesn't take us long to settle into our rhythm, Mike skewering my ass as Phil pumps his dick in and out of my mouth. The sun has cleared the mountain behind us, and I feel its heat pour down on us. Sweat trickles down my torso and back, dripping onto the rock ledge below. The wind whips around the corner of Jefferson's face, pushing us against the granite wall of Roosevelt's forehead. I close my eyes and feel the two cocks of these hot men plunge into me from both ends. I fantasize them meeting deep inside me, spitting me on a skewer of cock. Mike is breathing hard now, each thrust of his hips punctuated by a low grunt. My hands wander up Phil's sweat-slicked body, feeling the muscles of his torso, sliding down his back, squeezing the fleshy mounds of his ass as it clenches and unclenches with each thrust of his dick down my throat. I wrap my hand around my own dick and start stroking, matching my rhythm to that of the two men thrusting in and out of me. I manage a glance beyond Phil's pumping body and see Lincoln watching us benignly, his gigantic face serene. One wrong twist of my body would send the three of us plunging down Teddy's face onto the rocks below. I lean back harder against the granite cliff.

Mike's thrusts are coming harder and faster now, punctuated by grunts that are getting increasingly louder. He pulls his dick out just to the inner pucker of my asshole and slams it full in. I feel his legs tremble against me, and he cries out in a long, trailing groan. He pulls his dick out and whips off the condom. Jizz squirts out, some of it raining down on Roosevelt's nose, the rest carried off by the wind. Phil's dick is as hard as the granite we're leaning against, and his balls are pulled up tight against his body; I can tell it won't take much to make him shoot as well. I replace my mouth with my hand and give his cock a series of slippery, deep strokes. Phil suddenly cries out, his body shudders, and his jizz splatters against my face in thick, ropy wads, one pulse after another.

I stand up and beat off faster now, Phil licking his spunk off my face as Mike tongues my balls. As my orgasm sweeps over me, I arch my back and let 'er rip. My jizz spurts out into the air and joins Mike's upon the massive bridge of Teddy Roosevelt's nose. My body spasms, and Mike and Phil have to press me against the granite cliff to keep me from falling off.

We stand together above Roosevelt's nose, our shorts around our ankles, our dicks slowly losing their hardness. The afternoon sun is beating full on us, and our bodies are drenched in sweat. We look at each other and burst out laughing.

"Damn!" Phil says. "That's going to be a hard act to follow!"

We pull our clothes back on and carefully climb back to the top of the monument. Mike leads us down the trail toward the visitor center. Night overtakes us before we're done, and we have to hike the last couple of miles by moonlight. By the time Mike drops us off at our motel, it's almost midnight. He looks up at us from his car, grinning.

"Thanks, guys," he says. "It's been an experience."

In spite of the long day, I'm stilling feeling revved. And horny. Mike reaches over to start his engine, and I put my hand on his arm. "Don't go just yet," I say. "I just thought of one last scene. Why couldn't we pretend that this is the Bates motel in *Psycho?*"

Mike grins widely. "Sounds good to me." He climbs out of the car. "OK, guys. Let's hit the shower."

CHIMERAS

"A BIOLOGIST SAID YESTERDAY THAT HE HAS PATENTED AN APPLICATION FOR CREATING A BEING THAT WOULD BE PART HUMAN AND PART ANIMAL. THE PATENT HE HAS APPLIED FOR DESCRIBES A TECHNIQUE FOR MIXING HUMAN CELLS WITH THE CELLS OF AN ANIMAL. SUCH ANIMALS IN MYTHOLOGY ARE KNOWN AS 'CHIMERAS.'"

—*San Francisco Chronicle*

I encountered my first chimera two weeks after I'd moved to San Francisco. I was on the 31 Clement bus, making my way downtown to another job interview. The bus pulled over; passengers boarded. It was only after the bus pulled away from the curb that I turned my gaze to the crowd of people jostling for a position in the aisle. And saw him.

It was one of those surreal moments, like those dreams where you think you're spending a normal-enough evening with friends in a crowded bar, talking and laughing, and then you suddenly look down and see that you're naked. He was over by the bus's door, the other passengers crowding around him, and all I could see was that huge head of his, the broad shoulders, and one hand (paw?) clutching the rail overhead as the bus lurched down the street. He had the most amazing face: a mouth that was not quite a muzzle, whiskers, and eyes that were pale gold, with narrow black slits for pupils. He was wearing a suit and tie, and his mane of dun-colored hair was pulled back into something resembling dreadlocks. I couldn't take my eyes off him, but the other passengers took no notice of him, their eyes locked onto their newspapers or paperbacks, wearing their commuter faces.

After a while he must have felt my eyes on him. (I learned later that chimeras can sense such things.) He lifted his head, and those pale yellow eyes turned their gaze full on me. The muscles in his face twitched, and I could see his body tense almost imperceptibly. I quickly averted my gaze. When I worked up enough nerve to look at him again, his eyes were still trained on me, his body still tensed and unmoving. A memory flashed in my mind of the family cat sitting poised on the windowsill, staring at the birds on the lawn outside, its body quivering. I got off at the next stop, found a neighborhood bar and ordered a Scotch, keeping my back to the wall and my eyes trained on the door as I quickly drained it. I forgot all about job hunting that morning and took a cab home shortly afterward. It was an expense I could ill afford, but it was better than being out on the streets exposed.

After the incident with the lion-man, I began noticing things that I had missed before, like the gill-slits under my landlady's jawline, and the way the greengrocer's eyes moved independent of each other, like a chameleon's. I learned that San Francisco was ground zero for the chimera "movement," that local bio labs had been conducting animal-human fusion experiments with the same abandon that the trendier restaurants had been experimenting with combining different improbable cuisines. I found the situation perpetually unsettling: to walk into a fast-food restaurant and order a Big Mac from a counterperson with the face of a large-mouth bass, or to go clubbing and be asked to dance by some guy with spiral horns and the gentle, brown eyes of a gazelle. I thought of leaving the city. I didn't.

My first sex with a chimera was completely inadvertent. Not the sex, but the fact that it was with a chimera. It was in a backroom bar on Folsom Street, a little after two on some Sunday morning. I was drunk and lonely and very horny. I wound up going to the darkened rear of the bar, threading my way through the crush of bodies and leaning against the wall, waiting. It wasn't long before invisible hands tugged my pants down around my knees, and in a matter of seconds my hardened dick was in a warm, moist mouth, being expertly sucked on. I closed my eyes and let the sensations sweep over me, the tongue dragging up the length of my shaft, bathing my balls with it, flicking across the cock head in a way that made my knees tremble. I groaned, and my cocksucker gave a low, whinnying laugh. I reached down and stroked the top of his head. And felt the two short stubby horns, at the same moment that the door to the men's room opened and a shaft of light fell upon his bearded, goat's face. It took me no more than 30 seconds to pull my pants up and bolt from the bar, the goat-man's bleating, outraged protest ringing in my ears. In a way, it was a rite of passage. As I rode home on the bus, beneath all my confusion was the hard little kernel of memory of just how good that blow job had felt, how expertly that snaking billy-goat tongue had worked my dick.

I returned to the bar a week later, unclear as to why I had returned. I spent the entire evening in the front of the bar, sucking on my Pilsners and getting quietly drunk, resisting the temptation to go to the bar's back room. A little after 1 A.M. I looked around, distracted by the sound of urgent voices to my left. Two young men, each supporting a rack of antlers, stood next to me, whispering nervously and glancing beyond me. I turned and glanced too, and saw a lion-man, not unlike the first one I'd seen on that Clement Street bus, wearing a black leather jacket and staring at them intently, pale eyes lidded, lithe body tensed. I moved away to the other side of the room. The last thing I needed was to sit between predator and prey chimeras in a gay leather bar. I left a couple of minutes later.

As I waited for my bus outside the bar, I could feel myself sliding down into depression. *I don't have the instincts to survive in this town,* I thought. *I'm too human.*

"Hi," a low voice growled next to me.

I turned and saw the lion-man standing next to me, his golden eyes trained on my face. "Hello," I said. I could feel my throat tighten, and I took a deep breath. *Don't show your fear,* I thought. *They can smell it in a person's sweat.* I forced myself to meet his level stare.

"I saw you in the bar," he said. "You looked lonely. And kind of cute. I was about to offer to buy you a drink when you left."

"And you followed me out here?" I asked. I glanced around. We were alone on a deserted street.

"Kind of," he said. "It was time to go home anyway. After you left, I wasn't interested in anyone else in the bar." He pulled his lips back, showing teeth. *Does he mean that as a smile?* I wondered. I had found it impossible to read the expressions of chimeras and rarely even attempted to anymore.

"What about the guys with the antlers?" I asked. "I thought they'd be more your type."

The lion-man gave a low, throaty growl, and it took a few seconds before I realized he was laughing. "You've watched too many reruns of *Wild Kingdom*," he finally said. "I'm looking for sex, not to feed at the watering hole." There was a brief pause. "I'm Jack," he finally added. He must have detected something in my eyes. He laughed again. "What were you expecting? Leo?"

I blinked and shook my head. "I'm sorry, no." I laughed. "Well, maybe." I absently ran my fingers through my hair. "My name's Daniel," I said. I laughed again, nervously. "You gotta cut me a little slack. I haven't had much experience with chimeras."

"We can take care of that," Jack said, his eyes still trained on me. "Do you want to fuck?"

I stared at him. "You get right to the point, don't you?"

Jack bared his teeth again. "It's my nature," he said.

I didn't know what I was expecting with Jack's place, but certainly not something so spacious. Rooms seemed to radiate off from the central hallway in all directions. The furnishings were simple, but even I could tell that they were expensive. Jack saw me looking around. "You like it?" he asked.

"Yeah," I said, my eyes still scanning around. "Very nice." I looked back at him. "What do you do for a living?"

"I'm an attorney for a software corporation down in Silicon Valley," Jack said. He took off his leather jacket and threw it on a nearby chair. He was wearing a Hard Rock Cafe T-shirt. His arms were powerful and muscular and downed with a light, tawny fuzz. "Patents and copyrights." He smiled. "It pays well." I didn't say anything. Jack gestured to a nearby room. "Let's make ourselves comfortable." I followed him through the door. The room was small and softly lit, dominated by a giant leather couch that faced a fireplace in which a fire was crackling brightly.

"Very nice," I said again.

"It's my den," Jack said. He bared his teeth again. "And here you are: Daniel in the lion's den." He reached down and peeled off his T-shirt. His chest was tightly muscled and covered with the same tawny fuzz that coated his arms. He stood in front of the fireplace, and the light from the flames flickered behind him, giving his body a soft, ruddy glow. "Come here," he growled. I didn't move. "Please," he said.

I slowly walked over to him. He pulled my T-shirt off, and the heat from the fire played on my naked skin. He ran his paws gently over my torso. I could feel the soft leather pads and the small, sharp prick of the claws retracted beneath them. "Nice," he murmured. "So smooth." He gave his teeth-baring grin again. "Jesus, I love the bodies of humans." He looked at me, and I could see the amusement in his eyes. "I could just eat you up."

"Very funny," I said.

We fucked on the small, heavily napped Turkish carpet in front of the fireplace, without benefit of foreplay. We did it doggy-style, my teeth sunk into the wool as Jack plowed my ass, his thrusts quick and short, his furry arms and paws tightly wrapped around my torso, pinning me down. *So I can't escape back to the herd,* I thought. He growled in my ear with each thrust, his breath hot on my neck. I fucked his soft, soft rug as he fucked my ass, and we came at the same time, his load squirting in the condom up my ass as my load anointed the rug. He lay there on top of me for what seemed like a very long time, and I felt wrapped in fur: the carpet against my belly, his softly downed belly pressing against my back. Just when I'd thought he'd fallen asleep, he wrapped his arms around me and fucked me a second time with the same brutal efficiency. This time I came almost immediately, and then a second (or rather third) time as he continued to skewer me.

We fell asleep, curled in front of the fire. Once, in the middle of the night, I got up to pee. Returning to the lion's den, I stood for a moment over Jack, looking down on him. His muzzle was buried in his paws, and his legs kicked frantically as he dreamed of some bloody chase across a wide savannah. I curled inside the inner curve of his furry body on that wonderfully soft rug and pressed my body against the equally soft fur of Jack's tender belly. Jack stirred, whimpered, and growled, drowsily wrapping his arms around me, and then drifted down into sleep again. After a while I fell asleep too, embraced in the arms of my chimera lover, dreaming of jungles and green leaves and the hot breath of wild animals on my neck.

KNOWING JOHNNY

The single bulb that lights up the hallway is busted, and I have to negotiate my way to Rico's apartment by trailing my fingers against the wall, counting the doors. In the dark, the smells of the place seem a lot stronger: boiled cabbage, mildew, old piss. Heavy metal music blasts out from one of the doors I pass, and I get a sickly-sweet whiff of crack. Fucking junkies. I can hear loud voices arguing in the apartment across the hallway, then the sound of furniture breaking. Rico's apartment is the next one down. I grope my way to it and knock on the door.

I stand there for a minute, waiting. "Who's there?" a voice finally asks from inside.

"Open up, Rico," I say. "It's me, Al."

I hear the sounds of bolts being drawn back. The door opens an inch, still chained, and Rico's eye peers at me through the crack. He closes the door, undoes the chain, and opens it wide this time. "Get in," he growls. I slip in, and Rico bolts the door behind me. The room is small: an unmade bed, a beat-up dresser, a table by the window. The kid Rico told me about on the phone is sitting at the table, looking scared and trying not to show it. It's quieter in here than in the hall, even with the sounds of traffic coming in from the window. I can faintly hear above our heads the clicking of Writergod's keyboard.

I keep my eyes trained on the kid. He's sitting in a shaft of light pouring in from the street, and I take in the shaggy blond hair, the strong jaw, the firm, lean body. "Where'd you find him?" I ask Rico, without turning my head.

"Out on the street, hustling," Rico says. "I convinced him he could do better with a little management." Rico walks into my line of sight. "He tells me he's 18." Of course, Writergod has Rico say that to keep the censors happy.

"What's your name?" I ask the kid.

"Johnny," he says. There's a slight quaver in his voice.

"Did Rico rough you up?" Rico stirs, but I silence him with a gesture. "Did he force you up here?" And again, Writergod is having me ask this for the sake of the fucking censors. If there's coercion, the story won't sell.

Johnny shakes his head. "No," he says. "I wanted to go with him. Rico told me about you. I thought maybe you could help me." His voice is steadier now, firmer. But the wideness of his dark eyes still gives away his fear.

I look at him for a long moment, gauging him. "How good are you at taking orders?"

Johnny licks his lips and swallows. "Real good," he says.

This is the first sex scene of the story. Writergod usually limits it to oral only, saving butt fucking for the end-of-story finale. "Stand up," I say. Johnny climbs to his feet. "I always sample my merchandise first, Johnny," I say. "I want you to come over here and suck my dick. Suck it until I shoot my load."

Johnny's eyes flicker toward Rico and then back at me again. He shifts his weight to his other foot but doesn't move. He seems to be weighing his options. "OK," he finally says. He walks over to me and drops to his knees. His hands are all business as they unbuckle my belt, pull my zipper down, and tug my jeans and boxers down below my knees. I keep my face stony, but my dick gives away my excitement. It springs up and swings heavily in front of Johnny's face. Johnny drinks it in with his eyes. "You got a beautiful dick," he says.

"Just skip the commentary," I reply.

Johnny leans forward and nuzzles his face into my balls. I feel his tongue licking them, rolling them around in his mouth, sucking on them. He slides his tongue up the shaft of my dick like it's some kind of Popsicle and then circles the cock head with it. I stand there with my hands on my hips, looking down at the top of his head. Rico stands behind the boy, watching. His dick juts out of his open fly, and he's stroking it slowly.

Johnny's lips nibble their way down my meaty shaft (all our shafts are "meaty"; Writergod won't let us in the story without a crank at least eight inches long, and thick, always thick, topped with "flared heads" or "fleshy knobs" or "heads the size and color of small plums"). When Johnny's mouth finally makes it to the base of my stiff cock, he starts bobbing his head, sucking me off with a measured, easy tempo. The boy knows how to suck cock—I give him that. He wraps one hand around my balls and tugs them gently, as his other hand squeezes my left nipple. I close my eyes and let the sensations he's drawing from my body ripple over me.

Rico comes up next to me and yanks his jeans down. He strokes his dick with one hand, while his other hand slides under my shirt and tugs at the flesh of my torso. I reach over and cup his balls, feeling their heft, how they spill out onto my palm so nicely. I lean over and we kiss, Rico slipping his tongue deep into my mouth. Rico lets go of his dick, and Johnny wraps his hand around it, skinning the foreskin back, revealing the fleshy little fist of Rico's cock head (another favorite phrase of Writergod). He takes my dick out of his mouth, sucks on Rico's for a while, then comes back to me. I spit in my hand and wrap it around Rico's thick, hard cock, sliding it up and down the shaft. Rico lets out a long sigh. He starts pumping his hips, fucking my fist in quick staccato thrusts. Johnny pries apart my ass cheeks and worms a finger up my bunghole, knuckle by knuckle, never breaking his cocksucking stride. I lose my cool, giving off a long, trailing groan. Johnny pushes against my prostate, and my groan increases in volume. I whip my dick out of his mouth just as the first stream of spunk squirts out, arcing into the air, slamming against Johnny's face. My body spasms as my load continues to pump out, splattering against his cheeks, his closed eyes, his mouth. Rico groans, and I feel his dick pulse in my hand. Johnny turns his face to receive this second spermy shower, and soon Rico's jizz is mingling with mine in sluggish drops that hang from Johnny's chin. Rico bends down and licks Johnny's face clean, dragging his tongue along the contours of the boy's face. The clicking sound of Writergod's keyboard rises in volume and then suddenly stops.

We all look up. "Do you think he's done?" Rico finally asks.

I shrug. "With the scene, maybe," I say. "He still has to finish the story."

Johnny climbs to his feet and looks around the room. "Christ, what a dump. I hope we don't have to stay here long."

Rico laughs. "Hell, this is fuckin' *swank* compared to where I was before." He starts pulling on his clothes. "Writergod had me lying on some teahouse floor with a bunch of guys shooting their loads on me. Then he just left me there, stuck in that stinking piss hole." He looks around. "I just wish there was a TV here."

I offer a handkerchief to Johnny. "Here," I say. "Rico missed a few drops." Johnny takes it and wipes the last of my load off his face. I pull a deck of cards from my jacket pocket and sit at the table. "Poker, anyone?"

There are only two chairs, so Rico has to sit on the edge of the bed. We start with five-card stud. "It's no fun unless you play for money," Johnny grouses.

I shrug. "I don't have any money. Do you?"

Rico grins. "We could always play for sex." We all laugh. As if we don't already get nothing but that from each other. Johnny finds matchsticks in the drawer of the dresser, and we divvy them out.

I deal the first hand. "So what have you been up to, Johnny?" I ask, glancing at him. "Any interesting locales?" Johnny and I have worked together more times than I can remember. I've fucked him in locker rooms, in the backseats of cars, in alleys, on secluded beaches, once on the torch of the Statue of Liberty. Johnny is always "the kid" in Writergod's stories, sometimes going by the name of Billy, sometimes Eddy or Andy, always a name that ends in *y*. I look at him across the table, feeling the old frustration. For all the hot sex we've had together, I hardly know the guy. No conversation, no snuggling together under the sheets, just fade to black and then the cycle starts all over again.

"Oh, I was in a great place last story," Johnny said, laughing. "I was a street hustler in Cozumel who hooks up with an American tourist. You know him: It was Cutter."

"Shit," Rico mutters. I glance at him, but he keeps his eyes focused on his cards. Cutter's a stock character Writergod uses for his more upscale stories, usually about some married man straying to the other side, or a well-heeled gay yuppie partying in the Keys or P-town. I've only worked with him a couple of times, last time when I was rough trade he picked up in a leather bar on a slumming expedition. Rico and I both think he's got his head up his ass.

"Did you have a good time?" I ask.

"Oh, yeah, it was great fun," Johnny says. I look for sarcasm, but his smile seems sincere. "After Writergod wrapped up the fuck scene on the beach, we just hung out there, sunbathing, snorkeling, shell-collecting, the whole tourist thing." Johnny nods at the room around us. "Until I wound up here."

"I'm sorry you're disappointed," I say. I'm aware of how pissy my tone sounds.

Johnny grins. "Who said anything about being disappointed?" He looks across the table at me and winks. My throat tightens.

"Hey, are you guys going to flap your jaws or play cards?" Rico asks. He throws three cards down on the table, and I deal him three more. But the wheels are turning in my head. Writergod usually writes several stories at the same time. I glance at Rico sorting through his cards. Rico's all right, but I wouldn't mind it if Writergod suddenly pulled him for another story and left Johnny and me alone.

Johnny drops two cards on the table, and I deal him two more. I keep what I have. Rico starts off the betting with five matchsticks. Johnny throws in his five matchsticks and raises five more. Outside the window, a police siren wails and then trails off into silence. "Which one of your past scenes would you most like to go back to," I ask Johnny, "if you had a choice."

Johnny grins and shakes his head. "You'll just laugh."

"No, I won't, I promise." I throw in the 10 matchsticks and raise another 10.

"It was a college story," Johnny says. "Writergod had me gang-fucked in the U.C. Berkeley library by the football team. After he wrapped up the story, he didn't use me for weeks. I got to hang out there all that time, doing nothing but reading." He glances at me. "Have you ever read *Leaves Of Grass,* Al? Or any of Robert Frost's poems?"

I don't laugh, like I promised, but I do smile. "When would I read poetry?" I say. "Between blow jobs in a back alley?"

Johnny gives a rueful smile and shrugs. "That's my point. I hardly ever get to spend time in places where I can improve my fuckin' mind."

Rico sees my 10 matchsticks and calls. We show our hands. Johnny's got a pair of eights, Rico two pairs, aces and fives. I win with a straight, jack high. I gather up my winnings and deal us all new hands. Rico leans back on the bed and stretches. "I wouldn't mind going back to the story where I was a ranger in Yosemite," he says, picking up his cards and sorting them. "I ended up fucking these backpackers on top of Half Dome." He shakes his head and gives a wistful smile. "It was my one time out in nature. I loved it— all that bitching scenery!" He nods toward Johnny. "I know what you mean, kid. That was an exception. Writergod usually sticks us in some pretty crummy places."

I open my mouth to comment, when I feel my feet begin to tingle. The tingling moves up my legs, my torso. I know only too well what that means. "So long, guys," I barely have time to say. "I'm off to another story."

There's a knock on the door, and then Old Bert sticks his head in. "I got the lad here for you, Captain," he says. "Just like you told me to." He knows better than to give me a wink, the last time he tried such impudence I had him flogged, but his mouth curves up into a randy leer. I can hear the rest of the crew off in the distance fighting over the *Magdalena*'s spoils.

"Bring him in," I say gruffly. I'm lying on the bed that belonged to the *Magdalena*'s former captain. Since we've tossed him overboard with a slit throat, I don't think he'll be needing it anymore.

Old Bert opens the door wider, pushes the *Magdalena*'s cabin boy in, and closes the door behind him. The lad stumbles forward and then straightens up to face me. His dark eyes glare at me for an instant, but I can see the fear in them as well. He quickly lowers them. *So Johnny's in this story too,* I think. *Poor Rico, stuck in that room by himself.* The boy stands in the middle of the cabin, his hands at his side, head lowered, waiting.

"¿*Habla inglés?*" I ask.

He nods, his eyes still trained to the floor.

"Look at me, lad," I say. He raises his eyes, eyes that are as black and liquid as the sea on a moonless night. My gaze sweeps down his wiry, muscular body and then back to his face again. "What's your name?" I ask.

"Juan Francisco Tomás Santiago, sir," he says. His voice is barely audible.

I laugh. "That's quite a mouthful for such a young lad," I say. "I shall call you Johnny."

There's a moment of silence. I can faintly hear the clicking of Writergod's keyboard. I've never been in a period story before; Writergod usually confines me to slums and back alleys.

The heat of the tropical sun pours in, as thick as Jamaican molasses, and I feel my head grow light from it. I lie back indolently in the captain's bed, my eyes traveling up Johnny's body: There's a coltish quality to his muscular young body that makes my dick swell and lengthen. Johnny watches silently, his eyes now never leaving my face.

"Get naked," I say.

The blood rushes to Johnny's face, and he shifts his weight to his other foot. *Writergod should watch that little bit of business he always has Johnny do,* I think. *It's getting repetitious.* Slowly, hesitantly, he unbuttons his shirt and lets it fall to the floor. His torso is as smooth and dark as polished driftwood, the muscles beautifully chiseled. Johnny slips off his shoes, pulls his breeches down, and steps out of them, kicking them aside. He stands naked at the foot of the bed, his hands at his sides, his cock lying heavily against his thigh. His face is as pure as any angel's, but he's got a devil's dick: red, fleshy, roped with blue veins. In the stifling heat his balls lie as low and heavy as tree-ripened fruit. My throat tightens with excitement. "Turn around," I say.

Johnny slowly turns around. His ass is a very pretty thing, high and firm, the cheeks pale cream against the darkness of his tanned back. My dick stirs in my breeches, swelling to full hardness. Johnny completes his rotation and faces me again, his mouth set in a grim line.

"Well, come over here, lad," I say, giving an exaggerated sigh as I slip off my breeches. "And give me a reason why I shouldn't just slit your throat and toss you overboard."

Johnny stands where he is, head bowed but with his hands curled into fists. The silence in the room is as oppressive as the heat. "Aye, Johnny," I say softly. "Is it coaxing you want instead of threats?" I sit up in the bed. "Please do an old sea dog a favor, lad," I say in exaggerated politeness, "and come join me in my bed."

Johnny looks me in the eye, still saying nothing. His mouth curls up into the faintest smile. He crosses the small room and climbs into bed with me. I wrap my arms around him and kiss him, and he kisses back, lightly at first, then with greater force, slipping his tongue into my mouth. I pull him tightly against me, feeling his hard, young cock thrust up against my belly. I wrap my hand around both our dicks and start stroking them slowly within the circle of my fingers. Johnny reaches down and cups my balls in his hand, squeezing them gently, rolling them around in his palm. I nuzzle my face against the curve of his neck. "Tell me, lad," I whisper in his ear. "Have you ever been buggered before?"

"Yes, sir," Johnny whispers back. "Many times."

I don't doubt it. A young lad as handsome as Johnny would be fair game on any ship.

There's a jar of pomade on the table next to the bed. I reach over and scoop out a heavy dollop from it. "Well, maybe I can still teach you a few new tricks," I say as I work my hand into his ass crack and begin greasing up his bunghole. I slip a finger in, and the muscles of Johnny's ass clamp around it tightly, like a baby sucking on his mother's tit. I push deeper in, and Johnny's body stirs under me. "Do you want more, lad?" I growl.

Johnny nods his head. "If you please, sir," he says.

"Well, since you asked so politely..." I laugh. I grease up my dick with the pomade and hoist Johnny's legs over my shoulders. Johnny takes my dick in his hand and guides it to the pucker of his asshole. I push with my hips, and my dick slides inside him, Johnny thrusting his hips up to meet me. As I start pumping his ass, Johnny meets me stroke for stroke, moving his body in rhythm with mine, squeezing his ass muscles tight with every thrust of my cock.

I laugh from surprise and pleasure. "Aye, Johnny." I say. "Ye're a lusty young buck. I can see that clearly enough. And ye've learned your buggery lessons well." *This is the first story I've fucked without condoms,* I think. *Sweet Jesus, it feels good!*

I continue plowing Johnny's ass with long, slow strokes. A groan escapes from his lips, and I grin fiercely. "That's right, Johnny," I say. "Sing for me. I want to play you like a mandolin." *Where is Writergod coming up with this fucking dialogue?* I wonder. I thrust savagely until my dick is full inside him and then churn my hips. Johnny groans, louder. I bend down and kiss him, and he returns my kiss passionately, thrusting his tongue into my mouth. As I skewer Johnny, he reaches up and runs his hands across my body, twisting my nipples hard. He wraps his legs around me and rolls over on top. We're drenched with sweat, and our bodies thrust together and separate with wet slapping noises. I wrap Johnny in my arms and we roll again, falling off the bed onto the deck below.

I pin Johnny's arms down and plunge my cock deep inside him. Johnny cries out. "Do you want me to stop, lad?" I ask.

"No, sir," Johnny groans.

I thrust again, and again Johnny cries out. I can hear the pirates brawling outside. They're probably drunk by now on the *Magdalena*'s cargo of spirits. "Louder, Johnny," I snarl.

"Don't stop, sir!" he cries out.

"That's better," I grunt. I wrap my arms around him and press him tight. My sweaty torso slides and squirms against him as I pump my dick in and out of his ass. A groan escapes from Johnny's lips. I thrust again, and he groans again, louder. Johnny reaches down and squeezes my balls with his hand. They're pulled up tight, ready to shoot. He presses down hard between them, and my body shudders violently as the first of the orgasm is released. I throw back my head and bellow as my dick gushes jism deep into his ass. Load after load of it pulses out, and I thrash against Johnny like a man whose throat has just been cut. After what seems like a small eternity, the last of the spasms end, and I collapse on top of him.

I push myself up again. "Climb up on my chest, Johnny," I say, "and splatter my face with your load."

Johnny seems only too happy to oblige. He swings his leg over and straddles me. I look up at him, at the tight muscular body, at Johnny's handsome face, at the hand sliding up and down the thick shaft of his dick. "Aye, there you go, lad," I mutter. "Make your dick squirt for me." I reach up and twist Johnny's left nipple.

I feel Johnny's body shudder, and he raises his face to the ceiling and cries out. A load of jism gushes out from his dick and splatters against my face. Another load follows, and then another. By the time Johnny's done, my face is festooned with the ropy strands of his wad. He bends down and licks it off tenderly, and I kiss him, pulling my body tight against his.

Writergod's keyboard is suddenly silent. We wait expectantly for it to start up again, finish the story, but nothing happens. I look up at Johnny and we both burst out laughing. "Do you believe that fucking dialogue?" I say. I twist my face into comic fierceness. "Aye, Johnny," I growl. "You're a lusty young buck. How 'bout letting me bugger your ass?"

Johnny laughs again. He climbs off me and helps me to my feet. We hunt for our clothes strewn all around and pull them back on. I feel like I'm dressing for a costume ball. I look at Johnny appraisingly as he tucks his shirt into his breeches. "You look really good as a Spanish cabin boy," I say. "It suits you."

Johnny raises his eyebrows. "You're not putting the make on me, are you, Al?"

I have to laugh at that. "Right. Like I don't get enough sex from you as it is." Still, I'm feeling light and playful now that I'm alone with Johnny, between stories. I look around. The cabin is cramped, and a glance out the porthole shows nothing but sea and sky. The deck beneath our feet gently rolls with the movement of the waves. The tropical heat makes the small room feel like a sauna. I jump onto the bed and pat the empty side next to me. "Hop back in," I say to Johnny. "Let's just relax for a while. Maybe talk."

Johnny joins me on the bed, stretching his legs and placing his hands behind his head. My heart is beating hard, and when I notice this I almost laugh. I've forgotten how many times I've fucked Johnny in how many countless stories, and yet I'm actually feeling nervous. I cautiously wrap my arm around Johnny's shoulders, and he snuggles against me. "This is nice," he says.

"I've been wanting to do this for a long time," I say. "All we do is fuck. We never talk."

Johnny looks up at my face, his eyes amused. "What do you want to talk about, Al?"

I think for a long time. The only subjects I can come up with are back alleys, docks, and quarter booths in the back of porno bookstores. I'm struck by a sudden thought. "Tell me about the poems you read," I say.

"Do you want to hear one?" Johnny asks, grinning.

"Sure." I nestle back against the pillows, my eyes trained on him.

Johnny pulls himself up to a sitting position and turns to face me. He clears his throat.

In Xanadu did Kubla Khan
A stately pleasure dome decree:
Where Alph, the sacred river, ran
Through caverns measureless to man
Down to a sunless sea.

Johnny squeezes his eyes in concentration for a second and then looks at me apologetically. "I don't remember much more. Just the last few lines:

His flashing eyes, his floating hair!
Weave a circle round him thrice,
And close your eyes in holy dread,
For he on honeydew has fed,
And drunk the milk of Paradise.

He looks down at me. "Sorry, that's all I know."

I shake my head. "I don't get it." Johnny shrugs but doesn't say anything. "I mean, who would name a river Alph? And who ever heard of hair floating?"

"I don't know," Johnny says, laughing. "I didn't write the damn poem." He lies back down in the bed, burrowing back into my arms. "Just let the words create the pictures."

We lie in the bed together, Johnny's body pressed against mine. My arm lightly strokes his shoulder. I can smell the fresh sweat of his body, feel the heat of his skin flow into me. The rocking of the ship lulls me into half-sleep. "This is so nice," I say, half to Johnny, half to myself. Johnny says nothing but just lays his hand on my thigh and squeezes it. I close my eyes.

My feet start to tingle. "Fuck!" I cry out. I look up at the ceiling. "Writergod, you bastard! Can't you give me a just few fucking minutes of peace!" The tingling spreads up my body, and the ship's cabin fades out along with Johnny.

I've got Nash taking point 20 meters in front of the squad, and Myers and Benchly behind us working the radio, keeping the com line open with the base. The others are in different positions waiting for orders. That leaves me alone, with the kid, Jamison. Earlier reconnaissance reports indicated enemy movement about five clicks north of the base, working its way toward us, but fuck, that was hours ago and Charley could be anywhere. I look around. We're on elevated ground with good cover, and I don't anticipate any action for hours; our best bet is to lie low and hope Charley walks into our ambush.

I crawl over toward Jamison. "How you doing, son?" I whisper.

Jamison looks back at me, his eyes wide, his mouth set in a tight line. He's a green recruit, just assigned to the squad last week, and this is his first combat action. He still wears the look of someone trying to wake up from a bad dream. "All right, I guess," he says.

I put my gun down and sit down beside him. "It's a hell of a business, ain't it?"

Jamison grins, and I feel my throat tighten. I've been sporting a hard-on for the kid since he was first assigned to the squad. "What's your name? " I ask. "I mean, what do you go by?"

Jamison looks at me, and a little crackle of energy shoots between us. "Johnny," he says.

I put my hand on his thigh and squeeze. I'm risking court martial, but I'm sick and tired of this fucking war, I may be dogmeat tomorrow. I bend down and plant my mouth over Johnny's. He doesn't hesitate for a moment; it's like he's been waiting for me to get the ball rolling. He kisses me back, pushing his tongue down toward my throat.

Johnny, I think. *One of these days, between stories, we'll get that chance just to hang out, to talk, to get to know each other a little. I've got to believe it'll happen.* I look into Johnny's eyes, and for a moment I think he can read my thoughts. He gives a tiny smile and nods, a gesture out of character for the story.

As Writergod's keyboard clicks away, I reach down, unzip Johnny's fly, and pull out his thick, hard cock...